CW00704473

THE JOKER

RAKE FORGE UNIVERSITY BOOK 3

ASHLEY MUNOZ

The Joker
Copyright © 2022 by Ashley Munoz &
ZetaLife LLC
ISBN: 9781733791960
ALL RIGHTS RESERVED

No part of this book whether in electronic form or physical book form, may be reproduced, copied, or sold or distributed in any way. That includes electronic, mechanical, photocopying, recording, or any other form of information sharing, storage or retrieval system without the clear, lawful permission of the author. Except for limited, sharable quotes on social media, or for the sake of a review. There is absolutely no lawful permission permitted to upload a purchased electronic copy of this book to any free book sites. Screen shots of book text or kindle passages are not allowed to be shared on any public social media site without written permission from the author.

This book is a work of total and complete fiction. The story was thought up from the authors curious and thoughtful brain. Any names, places, characters, businesses, events, brands, media, situations or incidents are all made up. Anything resemblances to a real, similar, or duplicated persons or situations is purely coincidental.

The author acknowledges the trademarked status and trademark owners of various products referenced in this work of fiction, which have been used without permission. The publication or use of these trademarks is not authorized, associated with, or sponsored by the trademark owners.

Cover Design: Amanda Simpson from Pixel Mischief Designs

Editing: C. Marie

Proofing: Tiffany Hernandez

❀ Created with Vellum

To my mother-in-law, Marlene.
You were fire and light on this earth. It's dark and cold without you, and I'll never forget swiping at my face while pulling this book together.
My heart was aptly broken to match the brokenness found between these pages.
I'll love you forever.

To Amy, thank you for telling me to add more to Kyle's character in Wild Card.
Then telling me to add even more until you knew more about him. It's your fault he eventually got his own book.

the JOKER

PROLOGUE

November

"KNOW WHERE YOUR LINE IS." MY UNCLE'S VOICE BOOMED ACROSS the space as I walked away from him. One of his older cars was sitting as a storage piece in the far part of the garage, the hood open and the engine gutted. It was a project I was hoping to get to, maybe with Rylie…see if I could coax her into spending time with me.

I blinked, pushing the pain attached to my best friend away. I couldn't think of her face, or her tears…or how disappointed she was in me. After this, she'd probably never want to speak to me again.

I ducked my chin to my chest, muttering, "This isn't even a line. It's a life…two if you count the baby."

Scotty strode toward me and his arm flew, throwing one of Decker's baseballs against the drywall as he yelled, "It's not your fucking problem."

I shook my head, moving away from the man who'd practically raised me. I didn't want to let him down or make him regret all the time he'd sunk into me. He was important to me…and if I were being honest, he was the reason I was in this mess to begin with; I wanted to be like him. That, and I wanted to be useful for one goddamn second of my life. Dad always drilled into me that I was in the way, causing my mother stress.

Help your mother, Kyler. Can you find something productive to do with your time, Kyler? Did you do anything to help around the house today, Kyler?

He was always fuckin' disappointed in me. Maybe that was why he invested so much time into Decker with baseball. Maybe because Decker was the golden child and never did anything but help. If we were in the Bible, he'd be Jesus and I'd be the asshole who was always trying to convince him to jump off a building, just to see if he'd do it…that or to win a bet. Our roles were crystal fuckin' clear, and I'd made my peace with it.

People always seem so averse to the devil buying their soul and all that shit, but everyone has a price tag. Every-fuckin'-one. By standing on some moral high ground, it only delays the inevitable because every piece of ground will eventually crumble.

That's a fact.

So I gave in a little earlier than most, a little younger. It was my soul…who the fuck cared? I thought of Rylie and how she'd get teary-eyed if she knew what I was thinking.

She cared.

She always had, even before I even knew it was worth anything.

My uncle let out a sigh. "Kyle, you can't do this. You don't know this world like I do."

I laughed, unable to withhold the 'What the fuck' tone in my sarcastic scoff. Was he serious? "Is that why I was in the car with you at the age of eleven for drop-offs, or why my ass was in the passenger seat that time you completed a hit on our way to see the Hornets when I was fourteen? You don't think I know this world?" I shook my head. "It's the only world I've ever known. Decker had sports…I had a V8 engine and a loaded Glock."

"Jesus," Scotty snapped, running his hands through his hair.

I made him do that a lot…but at least he didn't give up on me, not like Dad had. In life and in death, he'd quit on me before he even gave our relationship a real try. So had Decker, but I wasn't about to sit there and cry about it.

"Come with me, or don't…but I owe her this."

"Juan has it handled." Scotty let out another exasperated sound, which was like a bullet to my chest.

I hated how that sound made me feel, how it transported me back to school nights at the kitchen table, my father reading a note from my teacher. My mother opening my bedroom door, seeing that I hadn't done what she'd asked me to do. Decker seeing me on his weekends home from college…like it was more work to have me at home with Mom than it would be to have her all alone. *Fucking worthless.*

I spun around as rage sparked and caught fire inside my chest, forcing every word out in an angry scream. "If all of Ivan's men go, he won't stand a chance. The only thing that can turn the tide is if an unexpected player shows up!"

The door to the house suddenly opened, and Decker shoved through the arch, hands in his pockets and a reserved look on his face. "I agree."

I scoffed, tossing a wrench to the side. "Don't tell me you're actually siding with me on something." I continued tossing the box of random shit off the camo green storage tote I needed to get into.

Decker thought I was a fuck-up, and even when I was getting my ass beat with a pair of brass knuckles courtesy of Juan Hernandez, my brother didn't do jack shit. Now he was chiming in on our little field trip?

Not fucking likely.

I decided I'd ignore him just like he'd ignored me the night before, and I focused on checking my inventory. Pulling back the plastic lid, I hauled the canvas bag free and unzipped it. I had knives, guns…a fuckin' grenade somewhere…I'd stolen it from Ivan's stock, and the fucker didn't even know.

"I'm going with you," Decker said, walking over to my bag of weapons and pulling out a 9mm handgun.

Scotty and I both turned toward him, asking in unison, "What?"

Decker released the clip, checking the ammo, and slid it back into place.

"We're family, and Taylor's family. It's what we do."

His eyes locked on our uncle's, probably reminding him that he was the only one who'd ever taught us that code.

Assuming Scotty would whine about this new development, I ignored him and asked my brother, "You sure?"

Decker nodded. "Mallory needs this too…she'd go if I let her. We need to protect them—they need our help."

"We might die," I said, zipping up the bag.

"If we do it right, we won't."

We started toward my car, which ironically was owned by Ivan. I had been racing it for him, winning several races to help add to his illegal gambling. Not anymore. We got in, and right before we took off, I had to be sure of something. I turned to look at them both, Decker in the back, Scotty next to me.

"Ivan is my kill."

They were quiet as I drove toward New York, until Scotty piped up.

"Just remember, the second you sink in that blade, you'll have a thousand eyes on your back. It won't go unnoticed."

"I'm aware."

I wasn't lying; I *was* aware—just like I was aware that I had sold pieces of my soul to the devil in order to help my mom save her house and keep my older brother in college. Just like I was aware that I'd slowly been losing my best friend each time I turned down time with her to spend with Scotty.

I was aware of everything…the question they should have asked was if I was ready.

CHAPTER ONE

Rylie

December

Snow was falling and sticking to the roads, defying every law of nature in this part of North Carolina. We were going to be snowed in within hours, and we were still weeks away from Christmas, so we couldn't even enjoy it.

"We're literally only going to get maybe three inches."

I rolled my eyes at my best friend's rebuttal, mostly because he knew me well enough to know I was thinking about snowmageddon, but also because everyone kept acting like it was not a big deal that we would be buried under the arctic blast battering our coast. Okay, so maybe that comparison wasn't exactly accurate, but I was known to make pragmatic comparisons. Or, as my mother—and everyone else I had ever met—called them, "worst-case conclusions in any given scenario."

Rylie the Reaper is what a few of my friends called me because I was always bringing news...and yeah it did always happen to be something sad or negative, but shouldn't people know what's happening out there? Shouldn't they know they have a better chance at living if they apply sunscreen and avoid eating genetically modified foods?

That's why documentaries exist…am I right?

The brake lights of the car in front of us lit up for the thousandth time, the car in front of it swerving toward the middle of the road.

I let out a hiss, moving my head to the side and screwing my eyes shut.

"Relax, Ry." Kyle reached over, gripping my knee. That did make it better, but then again, I was irrational when it came to Kyle James.

I was fully self-aware of this fact.

I could put Bella Swan to shame with how frequently I fawned over, obsessed about, and even secretly smelled my best friend. I was completely obsessed with him. However, he was wholly and distractingly unaware…oblivious and one thousand percent *just* my friend.

Did he ask why I suddenly agreed to go with him to this random party?

Nope.

We had gone two weeks without speaking, then he showed up on my doorstep in a tux with that infamous Kyle James grin, and I was warm, melted snow. You know, the kind that shouldn't be sticking.

It wasn't reasonable for me to be going. In fact, I should have stood my ground with him, taught him a lesson…but that just wasn't me when it came to Kyle. It didn't help that he had used that smile, because somewhere over the past four years, he'd grown up, and his smile extended into a devastating thing that made my heart race like one of his modified muscle cars. He'd never had braces, and yet his teeth were straight, save for the canine on the far right…it was just a millimeter off center, but it only added character to his smile.

I marveled at how he'd gone from gangly and disproportionate to a defined jaw, sharp cheekbones, and, again…that smile.

I never stood a chance.

I, being the expert on all things Kyle, knew this because I was already head over heels when we were merely cootie-carrying youths, bogged down with backpacks and lunch pails, waiting for the bus at the same stop since kindergarten.

Our mothers were to blame for our friendship, and ultimately my demise and constant broken heart. I'd hold a grudge, but the two of them were truly exceptional women and do-gooders, his mom a nurse, my mom an elderly caregiver. There was never a chance to hold a grudge.

Dad built us a treehouse, back when he liked the boy across the field. Kyle was very much the Diana Barry to my Anne of Green Gables. An acre full of dead, yellow grass separated our properties, and we absolutely tried using flag signals at one point, but just like for Anne and Diana, they didn't work for us. Then Kyle thought up walkie-talkies, and those helped to keep us both aware of the werewolf likely to be creeping around our properties back in the fourth grade. That was our heavy Harry Potter phase, so there were spells, wizards, and all sorts of things we were on alert for.

If I had a glass bottle that carried all my memories with Kyle James, it would be stuffed to the brim with pink paper hearts. Beyond anything we had ever done together, any grand adventure or outstanding scheme we'd created, it was always my undying obsession and love that would stand out.

And the fact that he didn't suspect a thing.

Of course he didn't because I had never told him. I'd die first—let that go on the record. I knew without a shadow of doubt that the second I revealed to my best friend that I had dreamt of nothing else but shattering our friend zone into a billion pieces and him being my imaginary husband and us having three imaginary kids, he'd ghost me.

He'd leave; I knew this because Kyle didn't like emotions or anything that made him feel. It was why he played everything off as a joke, because then it wasn't going to hurt him. I had designs on how I would tame him into hearing me and succumbing to my love one day…but it likely involved tying him to a chair like Rapunzel did with Flynn Rider in *Tangled*.

"I'm fine." I cleared my throat, watching the snow cling to the road. People were driving like maniacs, and of course Kyle wasn't fazed whatsoever. "Can I ask why you even want to go to this?" My eyes swung over to the driver side of the car; my arms crossed in defensiveness. Why had he needed to show up at my house, begging for forgiveness? And why had I forgiven him?

Because you always forgive him.

Kyle's gaze darted toward me before returning to the road. That infamous smile hitched his lips up in that expression that made me both dazed and entirely dumb.

My best friend shrugged as a goofy smile stretched along his face. "I guess I feel like it would be nice to see everyone. Mal and Decker will be there."

But that was literally it. Everyone else were practically strangers to us. He knew Taylor, obviously; otherwise she wouldn't have shown up at his house in the middle of the night, carrying a baby and asking to talk to him.

To that end, Juan, her crazy boyfriend, wouldn't have shown up an hour later, nearly beating my best friend to death. But you know, I guess water under the bridge and all that.

Who was I to judge?

My mood soured further as we crested the private drive up to a mini mansion, decorated so perfectly it looked staged.

"Should we try to steal some shit?" Kyle asked, leaning closer to my side, getting his fill of the sight before us.

I laughed because the image of him pocketing silverware or a coaster from this house was comical. What made it worse was that I had no doubt whatsoever my best friend would do it in a heartbeat, regardless of how ruthless and terrifying the man who lived here was.

"I made you laugh—mission accomplished." He smirked, pulling up behind a dark truck that looked an awful lot like Decker's.

I bent my head toward the window to take in the entire mansion in front of me. It was stunning, with arched windows and twinkle lights strung up along the roof line, framing the doorways, and dangling along bushes. It looked like a Christmas wonderland.

"This is where the party is being held?" I asked in a soft tone, suddenly feeling shy and a little out of my league.

I was a small-town girl who had lived in the same house my entire life. Both my parents worked, and we still clipped coupons, shopped at thrift stores, and only upgraded our furniture if we found a good deal on some swap site.

The mansion in front of me was out of my entire universe.

"Come on, Rylie Jean. It'll be fun."

I blushed at his use of my nickname. No one else ever called me that. I was Rylie Roo to my parents, Rylie the Reaper to half the student body, and Rylie that-girl-who-always-scowls to the other half of the student body...but to Kyle, I was just Rylie Jean.

He exited the car and headed over to my side to let me out. I could exit just fine on my own, but he liked to open it for me when I rode with him. While he skirted the hood of the car, I took a deep breath and held it. I imagined we were married and he was rushing over to help me exit our family vehicle.

The realization of how pathetic I was drowned me as the door swung open and the cold December air hit my face.

Stop fantasizing.

We walked up three wide steps, each one decorated with beautiful poinsettias, and on the door was a wreath so big I wouldn't have even been able to hold it.

"Seems like a lot of work for a simple Christmas party," I mused to myself...but again, my parties were always dollar-store variations with a little Hobby Lobby discount code thrown in. Not to mention, if I were to ever be fancy enough to host a holiday party, it wouldn't be three weeks before the actual date...but again, not judging here.

"Yeah, my guess is they're turning it into a big-ass birthday party too."

My head swung to the left where my best friend stood wearing an outrageously expensive overcoat and tux.

"What?"

He paused, assessing me with dipped brows and a confused look on his handsome face. "Didn't I tell you that?"

For the love. Why did I have to fall for an idiot?

"No, Kyle, you never mentioned that..." I leaned closer to him, hissing, "We didn't bring a gift."

Kyle rang the doorbell, ignoring me with a smirk. "It'll be fine—our presence is a present." He shrugged his shoulders and shifted on his feet.

He's nervous too.

Which only made my anxiety spike to unhealthy levels.

The heavy door swung open, letting out a gust of warm air.

"You guys made it! I'm so happy," Mallory, Kyle's sister-in-law, said excitedly.

She had red lips and wore a black dress that looked like it was glued onto her body in all the right places while loose and flaring perfectly around her hips and thighs. She looked like something I'd pin to my "How I want to dress when I grow up" board on Pinterest.

I stepped inside, suddenly insecure about taking off my jacket. I felt like a middle schooler being invited to a high school party.

"Rylie, I'm so glad you made it…we didn't get to really talk at my wedding, and I was dying to chat." Mallory shut the door and gently took my coat from me, but Kyle was right there taking it off her hands. Suddenly he froze in my peripheral, taking a sudden quick breath in. I spun around to see if he was okay.

"Did you swallow your gum again?"

I watched his face, realizing his eyes were glued to my chest, slowly moving down to my stomach and all the way to my toes. This was a rather low-cut dress; maybe I had embarrassed him by wearing it. Oh well, it was the only fancy dress I owned, and my boobs had finally grown enough to fit the bust. He'd have to get over it. I shrugged and moved inside with Mallory.

"So you guys came as friends?" Mallory asked innocently.

I had heard she was a reporter; her easygoing tone must have been what relaxed her victims before she tugged all their secrets out. Her inquiry was obvious though; everyone always assumed Kyle and I were more than friends.

I didn't respond because I couldn't stop staring at the house. Every way I turned there seemed to be more of something—more lights, more garland, more space. I thought of my own house and how there was an artificial tree barely five feet tall with a few missing branches because we'd had it so long. Ugly garland wrapped around our banister because my mother loved the way it looked, and a cheap twelve-dollar wreath adorned our front door. That was the extent of our Christmas décor. This place was like something out of a movie.

"What else would we be?" Kyle finally responded.

Hurt barreled into me like a punch to the face, his words echoing loudly around the grandiose space, rolling through me like a tsunami. Each syllable took out the structures I'd built for us in my mind. All the images of our lives intertwined, the hope that we'd one day be more—all smashed within seconds.

I sucked in a sharp breath with them at my back and no one to see my face.

Mallory turned, maybe to say something to him... Quickly averting my mind and clearing my throat, I was suddenly stuck like glue to the sight of what looked like a fifteen-foot-tall Christmas tree.

"Holy shit," I whispered, slowly dragging my gaze up each branch.

Kyle stopped beside me, his warm shoulder bumping against mine. "Looks like the one we saw in—"

"New York," I finished for him.

We'd gone together when we were sixteen. His Uncle Scotty took us both, even after my father refused my request. Scotty swore my dad would never know, and he never did. That was one of my best memories to date. The snow that had fallen in Rockefeller Center was like a dream, coating my lashes and dusting my friend's nose. We had taken a million pictures together, being goofy all while his uncle left us alone in the city. Of course, I had put my share of the photos in a secret scrapbook with about a million pink hearts around each page.

Kyle's hand went to my hip, pulling me against him as if he was remembering too. Usually, I didn't mind his touch—in fact I welcomed it with a loud chorus of hope bursting from my chest—but after his comment, something in me bristled at the contact.

What else would we be?

"Kyle." A deep voice pulled my friend's face away from the tree and toward the massive staircase behind us.

I turned with him in time to see the man from that night at Kyle's house, Juan, the one who had kept hitting and kicking my friend. I stiffened as he drew closer. His hair was mostly styled so that the longer strands would stay out of his face, but a few pieces still hit his brow. Those dark brows encased amber eyes that looked like maybe the devil was hiding behind them. I watched my best friend freeze up, his knuckles going white as his skin stretched along the bone as he clenched them.

My hand went to Kyle's back to offer support, not that I would be much help, but it was my silent offering that we were a team.

"You came." Juan smirked, sticking his hands into his pockets. He wore a black suit, not an inch of white, red, or any other color on him. Against his mocha skin, it was attractive…really attractive, but I still turned my nose up in solidarity with my friend.

"I was invited," Kyle quipped.

No one else was near us, no one to witness if this guy did something deplorable or underhanded. He looked like he was two seconds away from slamming a knife into my best friend's chest.

"Babe, stop it." A soft voice carried down the stairs, followed by the woman I'd seen show up at midnight that night at Kyle's, the one who'd caused all of this. I was still unsure how I felt about her…I knew she was Mallory's sister, but she was also the daughter of the most dangerous man on this side of the country.

She was flawless tonight with her long blonde locks tied back in a classy way, leaving curled strands around her face. Her lips were red like Mallory's, her eyelashes dark and long…she descended the stairs like a Disney princess in a floor-length black dress. It hugged her tightly, and if not for the baby cradled in her arms, you'd never even know she'd just given birth a few weeks prior.

Lucky bitch.

"Rylie, right?" She looked right at me as she cleared the last step, and the man next to her pulled her into his side, staring down at the sleeping baby in her arms.

I nodded, unsure of what else to do.

"I'm Taylor. Nice to officially meet you."

They looked so beautiful together, and the way the man's features softened the second she came into his orbit was like watching the sun rise.

She turned her face, lowering her lashes as she pecked the man on the lips. "Juan is just being intimidating—you both are more than welcome. We're glad you came." She smiled at us then moved toward the living room.

"Happy birthday," I suddenly yelled at her back as she walked into the living room.

I was such a dork. These people seemed so grown up and cool, and I still had chemistry homework at home.

She turned and smiled at me. "Thank you."

Kyle shoved his elbow into my side, holding back a laugh.

I elbowed him back. "And I'm sorry for being rude that time you were at the house." I followed after her, still talking to her back as she proceeded into the living room, where a swarm of other people waited. "I was just so nervous about everything, and your dad and just…my dad talks a lot about everything, and I was worried about Kyle." I rambled, knotting my fingers together.

I must have been projecting much louder than I thought because all eyes were on me as we stumbled into the center of the room. Taylor turned toward me with a broad smile on her face, her baby lifted to her shoulder. Mallory was on one of the wide leather chairs smiling too, and Decker, perched on the arm, was laughing into his fist.

"I like her. Can we keep her?" Mallory asked as everyone burst into laughter.

My face burned bright red. At least they laughed and weren't awkwardly quiet; it was really bad when people got quiet after my weird ramblings.

Kyle sat down and tugged me into his lap. It was a normal position for us, but rejection screamed at me to push away from him. I considered shimmying out of his hold, which would land me next to a woman I had seen at the wedding that summer. She was next to the guy who'd walked Mallory down the aisle, so I assumed they were the parents of the two. It was difficult keeping everyone straight, but I didn't want to be sandwiched between a stranger and Kyle. So, instead of moving, I just sat frozen like Pinocchio, awkward and terrified that my lie would begin to show.

Kyle's fingers dug into my hip, holding me in place, while his other hand toyed with my hair. These were the moments I usually savored, the ones where if I didn't look directly at him, I could pretend we were a couple. Me on his lap, him playing with my hair…like this, I could pretend all day that he was mine in a completely different capacity.

We listened as Taylor talked about her baby girl. Everyone had questions for her, and little Alex was such a trooper as she was passed around from person to person. Watching Juan hold her nearly made my ovaries explode. I didn't like the guy, but my gosh, him with a baby was pornographic.

The time passed as we played Christmas games for a while, until I moved from Kyle's lap to wander and grab a cup of cocoa. People had dispersed, doing the same as Mallory regaled a few with a story she was working on.

The house really was magnificent. Even the back patio was lit up with lights and set up for the party. Under the stairs was a cute hutch with a writing desk inside, and they'd set up a mannequin Santa as though he was writing a letter. Soft music played as I wandered down the hall, closer to an alcove of books, which sat across from something that looked like the library.

"You snooping?" someone asked from behind me.

I spun, already knowing it was Kyle but still rattled that someone might think I was prying.

"Are we not allowed to look around?"

He laughed, his lips curving into a genuine smile. Those were rare these days. I couldn't help but remember how they used to be, before the year when Kyle really started going off the grid. More time in New York with his uncle, less time at school. I was truly freaked out when he even started racing less. It was like chasing a man dancing along the edge of a knife, knowing he could die at any second but didn't care enough to change course.

I blinked, pushing my growing list of grievances away.

"Of course we are, but you're looking in the boring places. Come see outside."

He whirled us around, grabbing my hand and tugging me toward a separate exit. It was off the side of the house, through the laundry room, taking us out to the side closer to the orchard. I thought the patio space was something, but the trees were all lit up, making every single one like being in a fairy tale.

"This is…"

Kyle smiled again, pulling off his jacket and placing it around my bare shoulders. We walked through the low-hanging trees, slowly and at an unhurried pace while the world was still and quiet around us. I began to shuck the weight of his earlier words, realizing I wanted to talk about everything that had happened that night when I came flying into his house, throwing myself over him like Pocahontas did with John Smith in the poorly adapted but still-one-of-my-favorite Disney movies. I thought surely he'd see in my actions what was always pounding under my skin.

I thought we'd finally begin to move past this flirtatious existence where my best friend held my heart hostage, unwilling to ever nurture it the way it deserved and denying it to anyone else who'd ever try. I was both thriving and withering in his hold.

That was why it hurt so badly when I realized he hadn't stopped his involvement with his uncle. It hurt as a friend, but it landed ten times harder in that soft space that I reserved for loving him.

"So, you want to tell me what happened?" I finally braved asking.

His hands were tucked into his slacks, and the muscle in his jaw worked a few times while he trailed our feet with his eyes.

"Ry, I told you it wasn't what it seemed. Taylor thought I had access to someone she needed to see, and Juan assumed I'd given her the info. It was all a big misunderstanding."

There went a pinprick into my heart. It felt like a pincushion, each needle slowly being reinserted for storage and safekeeping.

"But Decker said…" I watched the lights intertwine with the branches like extended vines, remembering that night in their living room. Decker's dark gaze, his unwillingness to step in and help…

Kyle shook his head back and forth. "Decker didn't have all the information either."

"So nothing happened? Nothing at all?" My heart thrashed around in my chest, reminding me it wasn't safe in the hands of Kyle James. It never had been, and it never would be. I kept ignoring it, though, determined to force this into existence.

His gentle expression stopped me, followed by a light tug on the ends of my curls. We turned toward one another, one of his massive palms coming out to land over my heart as if he could read my thoughts. We'd done this gesture since we were kids, placing our hands on each other's chests; it was our own version of a pinky promise or cross my heart, hope to die. Our palms bore scars that made us blood brother and sister—or in my case, just connected. Bonded. So when we placed those scarred palms over the other's heart, it was serious business.

"I promise you, Ry. Nothing happened."

I searched his eyes for the lie, but under the lights in the orchard, I fell. I tumbled into his oblivion, his mass of stars and midnight promises. He was mine in thought, in a place that didn't exist, and yet I silently tugged and pulled at that invisible thread tying our hearts together, hoping he'd realize what made him exist ached for me.

I chose to believe him, and because I was feeling the rush of love and pride in the fact that nothing had happened with him, I did something reckless and stupid.

"We talked about this already, but we never set a date."

His eyebrows flirted with his hairline, showing how surprised he was. I stepped closer to take advantage.

"We swore we'd be each other's first, and I want to make it happen before college. Preferably this summer."

Why hadn't I asked for it tonight? I silently screamed at myself for not making him vow to do it tonight, but I wasn't ready, not really. When he took my virginity, I wanted him to be as in love with me as I was with him. I wanted our hearts to connect as significantly as our bodies. That would take some time, but by summer, I could make it happen.

He nodded, ducking his head as if he wasn't sure what else to say.

My head roared at me to fix this; I didn't want him to not want me.

I wet my lips, searching for words. "I mean, if you still want to… we don't have to if you've changed your mind."

"Rylie…" He put his hand up, covering my mouth as he often did to stop my ramblings. "I want to…" Was it in my head that there was heat behind his stare? "You're sure you want to wait and everything? I figured you'd want to when you turned eighteen."

I'd be turning eighteen in a matter of weeks—not enough time.

I shook my head. "Summer…before college starts."

He locked eyes with me and nodded his agreement. "Summer it is."

Kyle's phone went off a second later. He pulled it up and let out a sigh.

"It's my brother, we need to head back."

THE PARTY WAS STILL IN FULL EFFECT ONCE WE RETURNED, BUT THERE seemed to be a cold current running through the room. Taylor's friend Fatima had left, along with her kids and husband. Jackie and Charlie were saying their goodbyes to Taylor and Mallory, all while flicking their cold gazes back toward us as if we'd done something wrong.

"We didn't mean to offend anyone by walking around outside, we were just trying to—"

Juan stood from his spot in the living room where he was sipping whiskey, or something close to it. "Rylie, you didn't offend anyone."

His eyes remained locked on Kyle.

I looked up and over, trying to piece together what had happened while we were gone.

"What's wrong—" I started, but movement by the kitchen caught my eye. There in a long overcoat, dressed in all black with his hair slicked back, was Kyle's Uncle Scotty. He carried two guns on the inside vest of his jacket, and hanging from his hand was a shotgun.

"Wha—"

"What happened?" Kyle interrupted me, and instead of being

outraged that he was carrying so many weapons, he just seemed concerned.

I looked between them, trying to find what I was obviously missing.

"What happened is you brought your piece-of-shit uncle into my home, where my daughter sleeps, and into my territory. This is a complication, Kyle," Juan said, walking between the men. His tone was as sharp as a blade, and his eyes carried a type of crazy that usually ended in poor decisions and violent delights.

"If he's here, there's a reason," Kyle said in defense.

Juan slowly took off his jacket, which made me incredibly uncomfortable because he seemed like the type of guy to dirty his hands the second his jacket came off.

"There is never a reason to bring someone who worked for that sick fuck into my home—someone who, for years, delivered messages, roped his underage nephew into the mess, and then suddenly tried to play savior." Juan turned toward Kyle, raising his voice, pointing a finger at the floor. "Someone who stood there and watched while my pregnant fiancée was grabbed by the hair and slapped."

You could have heard a pin drop. Kyle's face was red, his jaw clenched tight along with his fists. There was the white of his bones straining against the skin. I wanted to caress him there, but I was so confused about what was happening. Where was Decker?

I didn't dare take my eyes off the two men in front of me, or the one beside me.

"Can we talk about this privately?" Kyle asked softly.

My head swung toward him, unsure if I'd heard him correctly. He'd hide this from me? It hurt…it slid in between my ribs, mocking me with each crack of my bones as it went, whispering that I knew better than to trust him. Maybe he just wanted to protect me; I knew Kyle had mentioned that a long time ago, that there was power in being completely oblivious to something dangerous. Not knowing a name or a face—it could save your life. I couldn't muster the hope that his intentions were to protect me; it felt like he just wanted to protect himself.

Juan's gaze swung to me, and a sick smile erupted across his face. "You know what, no…I think Rylie should hear this."

"Juan." Taylor cut in, her arms folded across her chest, her lips curved down.

He held up a finger, still looking at me. "Wouldn't you want to know, babe?" His gaze rose briefly, swinging over to Taylor.

She moved her jaw back and forth and gave me a pitying look, but in the end, she nodded and turned away.

I felt like I'd just been handed my death certificate. Stamped, filled in, official and undisputable.

"Scotty is here because he's worried about you being on my turf." Juan tilted his head, staring at Kyle as if he were inspecting something odd or complex. "Surely you understand the gravity of what you've done…that there will be repercussions for it."

"Fuck you, man." Kyle seethed angrily.

A laugh erupted from Juan's chest. "Fuck me? How about this— your uncle doesn't know this yet, but you're being watched by the heads of at least five families. Sweet Uncle Scotty doesn't want you left undefended in case you're hunted. Either way, it's because of you that shitty piece of human trash has come into my home…it's practically considered an act of war."

Kyle shook his head, looking down.

My breathing had gone so shallow I wasn't sure I was doing it right. I remembered hearing my father talk about when rival gangs or mafia families went to war over turf or negotiations gone wrong. It was a bloodbath, generally done to wipe out an entire family line so there would be no one else in the future to pop up and get retribution.

"We helped you…we ki—" Suddenly Kyle looked over at me, hesitating.

Juan caught the movement. "You killed him. Yes, you killed Ivan, Kyle. You did, and you've painted a target on your back by doing so."

"So why are you so angry with us then? We helped you."

Juan laughed again, but all I could think of was that my best friend had killed someone. It was as if the sounds of the room stopped completely, leaving only a loud ringing in its place. I couldn't seem to connect to what was going on around me.

He'd killed someone.

Supposedly the most dangerous man on the east coast. He'd killed a man in cold blood and told me nothing had happened. He'd sworn with his palm on my chest.

I tried to breathe, but my rib cage constricted so tightly only a shudder released, and with it came a burning behind my eyelids.

There was a roaring in my head now, repeating the same thing over and over again.

He lied.

He lied.

He swore to you and then lied.

A shattering sound snapped me out of my thoughts. Juan had kicked a small end table into a wall. His eyes were wild as he looked between Scotty and Kyle.

"You think in any life I'd forgive the fact that you both stood there and did fucking nothing while Taylor was nearly kidnapped from my home? While she was held by her hair, slapped around? I'll never get that image out of my head. Fucking never. I don't care what you did in the end—my vengeance doesn't understand grace or second chances. It wants the head of every man who stood by while she was harmed."

I looked back toward the living room and saw that Taylor was crying silent tears while watching Juan. She wasn't angry; it was more like she was just emotional, reflecting on what had happened to her.

"She is my entire life, and you threatened her existence, which means you are at war with me, forever. I'll make allowances for you Kyle because of Mallory, but not that piece of shit." He pointed at Scotty. "Not ever for him."

Scotty stood there as if he were bored: inspecting his nails, armed to the teeth.

"Why allow him in with all his weapons?" I quietly asked, unable to stop the question from escaping my lips.

Juan scoffed, running a hand through his hair. "He's no threat to me. Let him have his guns—he knows who watches him right now, and he knows what weapons I carry. He'd be dead before his arm rose to shoot."

Well, that was terrifying. I was suddenly very done with being in this room, with these people and all this fucking drama.

I was over my best friend lying to me, and he was obviously caught up in some dangerous shit—things I wanted nothing to do with.

I backed away, shaking my head, and turned around.

"Rylie," Kyle called after me, but I couldn't. He'd killed someone and he hadn't told me.

He had lied, and what the hell did it say about our friendship if he couldn't even tell me the truth?

I grabbed my coat and swung the door open. I didn't have a car, but I'd walk at this rate. It wasn't that far to the end of the drive; I could order an Uber on the way down.

"Rylie, stop," Kyle yelled after me, but I knew Scotty would be on his heels, and I knew that wasn't something I wanted to see. I was starting to hate his uncle. I was nearly there with the stupid racing and shit he'd gotten Kyle into, but I had a soft spot because Scotty had been like a father to Kyle when his own dad wouldn't spend time with him. Racing was their thing, but so was killing people apparently.

I began walking down the driveway, aware of every step and every slick spot making my heels wobble and shake.

"Rylie, let me drive you at least." I heard commotion and some scuffling, as if Kyle was pushing someone or being pushed; I wouldn't look back. I just wouldn't, but I knew Scotty was there, talking to him or explaining himself.

The start of the engine roared behind me. I prepared my heart to see Kyle, to hear his excuses and more lies, but it was a dark truck that pulled up next to me.

The window rolled down and Decker's tight jaw greeted me. Mallory leaned over the console, a look of worry and concern filling her eyes and marring her red lips.

"Rylie, let us give you a ride back."

No complaints here. I opened the door behind Decker and crawled inside, buckling in. I let my stare settle on the frozen world around us while Kyle's brother pulled away. The car was silent until Mallory found a Christmas station, and then Decker's eyes met mine in the rear-view mirror; it was the same look he'd given me the night I pathetically threw myself over Kyle's body.

It was an expression that said he was sorry, but his brother wasn't going to be the man I needed him to be. It was a look that told me to wake up and get the fuck on with my life.

I let out a heavy sigh and looked away while giving the smallest nod of agreement.

Kyle: Ry, it's been three days...are you going to talk to me?

Kyle: Haha very funny, you're giving me the silent treatment, I get it...I fucked up, but if you let me explain myself...

Kyle: Our moms talked...apparently they're worried about us because we've never gone this long without communicating. It's been two weeks...we should talk...

Kyle: You want to know what sucks? Window locks and the fact that you have a dad who's in the FBI...that shit sucks because it means I can't sneak in through your window and force you to talk to me.

Kyle: It's Christmas, Ry...you really not going to see me? This is our holiday, we were supposed to watch Christmas movies and bake weed into our families' Christmas treats...remember how my mom can never tell?

Kyle: I miss you.

. . .

KYLE: IT'S ALMOST YOUR BIRTHDAY…I SWEAR I THINK MY HEART HAS shrunk to the size of a goddamn pea. I hate myself, Ry. I can't lose you. Please…

KYLE: HAPPY BIRTHDAY, RY. I …NEVER MIND…JUST BE HAPPY TODAY whatever you decide to do.

CHAPTER TWO

Rylie

January

I HAD BEEN PLANNING MY EIGHTEENTH BIRTHDAY SINCE I WAS IN THE sixth grade. I used to think it would be the night my best friend finally confessed his love for me, or the night I received my first real kiss right as the ball dropped and we welcomed a new year. Whatever I had conjured up, absolutely zero of the scenarios looked like snow falling and disappearing onto cracked asphalt, red taillights illuminating the midnight air, and flickering bonfires dotting the ground below my lonely perch atop a hill littered with dead grass.

Below me, there were people everywhere, waiting for the next set of cars to fly down the road, competing for the next street racing championship. Kyle held first place; that hadn't changed in the past four years since he started racing. Every now and then people liked to speculate on why they thought he was so good, if it was raw talent or if there was something else there. I was never asked my opinion, not that I'd have shared it, but the answer they were looking for was that Kyle wasn't afraid of death. It wasn't that he had nothing to live for, but he didn't exactly care if he was lost to this life. He could go out in a blaze of glory and be perfectly content that he'd somehow touched this world in some capacity, even if it was miniscule.

The idea made me wince. Even if I was angry with my best friend, the idea of him not knowing the value of his life made my heart heavy.

Case in point, I was still watching his races even though I had cut off all communication with him weeks ago. I was addicted to watching him race, seeing that glow overcome his features when he won. I still remembered the first time I had seen him sitting in the front seat, prepping to race. I was terrified…it was the summer after his Uncle Scotty came to stay with his family. Eleven years old, opening the passenger door and telling me to get in and be his good luck charm.

I smiled, breathing into my frozen hands as I considered that crazy night. I had jumped in, buckled up, and watched as the car took off, peeling away from the pavement. Kyle was in control, perfectly…it was like the car was a part of him.

Which was why I knew, for my birthday, I wanted to be here watching him, wishing he'd pull me into that passenger side and take us away from here. Drive until we found a new life, one away from his ties to his uncle, one where my father didn't hate my best friend, away from the ghost of the man he had killed. The memory surfaced, and with it the entire replay of how stupid I had felt.

He'd played me.

Then he'd tried to fix it, like he always did, and he knew our bond was strong enough that there was no way I could stay angry with him forever. Even now, I felt my resolve crumbling into pieces as I considered how badly I wanted to see his face tonight.

My phone dinged inside my pocket.

Pulling it out, I fought a smile.

Hazel: The best way to celebrate this birthday of yours is to make the best friend you're still pissed at but are secretly in love with realize he doesn't get to spend it with you. Get down here and pretend he doesn't exist.

Me: I don't want to…I have a great view from here.

Hazel: But he doesn't know you're watching him, and I really want him to know you don't give a shit that he's racing tonight...even if you do. Take the power back.

I laughed, realizing she was right. I didn't want to be alone for my birthday. Somehow, I felt like I was punishing my best friend by being up here, unreachable and absent from the one place he wanted me the most, but really it was me who was suffering.

Me: Okay...I'm coming down, standby.

I got up, packed up my blanket, got into my car, and began driving down the grade to the abandoned freeway that acted as the racing strip. Once I parked, I began wandering toward the little bonfires, keeping my eyes open for Hazel and a few girls from school. My hood was up, but Hazel would be able to spot me. Being the daughter of the local sheriff who'd turned FBI didn't make me very popular at illegal street races. Two years back there had been a few girls who'd tried to beat me up, but Kyle had stepped in.

He always stepped in. It was because of him that no one dared to mess with me now or touch me, but with us on the outs...I had no idea what would happen.

People held the necks of dark beer bottles, tipped back champagne, and wore glittery party hats as music blared from one Bluetooth speaker to another. Kissing, fucking, hitting...all sorts of debauchery was happening around the fires, and the cars were preparing to race by warming up their tires.

I stayed away from them because I knew it was the only place Kyle would be. He didn't come here for the parties, only for the feel of getting lost behind that wheel and making money to help his mom out...or at least that was why he used to come. Since working for Ivan and Scotty, I had no idea why he did it. He'd more than paid off his mom's house, and Decker was taking that over now anyway.

Music blared, thrumming through my body as I wove through groups of people. I skirted as many clusters as I could, keeping to the shadows. I could hear the start of one of the races behind me, but I kept my eyes on the blazing fires, searching for my friend.

Turning my head, I tried to examine where I'd come from and if I had passed her, then a second later someone grabbed my hand and began pulling me away from the flames.

"Hey!" I nearly tripped trying to keep my balance while the person who held me powered on, moving swiftly through couples and groups toward the cars lined up to race.

I tugged at the hand holding me even as a strange sense of peace filled me up. Deep down I knew it was him. I knew it because if anyone else had touched me like that, Kyle would have been there a second later with his hands wrapped around the assailant's neck.

Still, I wasn't going to make this easy on him. "Let me go."

Before I could make another argument about releasing me, his car door was being opened. My head was pushed down and my body shoved inside, my ass landing on leather.

"Scoot," his familiar voice commanded before his body folded in after mine, and I shifted to the right along the bench to make room for him.

"Seriously, Kyle?"

My hand went to the door, but a second later the rumble of the engine started, making my butt vibrate.

"Kyle."

I looked at his profile. His firm chin was dipped, his eyes trained forward on the clock…shit, it was counting down.

"No." I tried the handle once more, but it wouldn't budge. "Did you child-lock me?" I knew that wasn't possible on this old of a rig, but he'd done something…this wasn't even supposed to have automatic locks.

"It's your birthday, Ry—this is where you belong, and you know it." He didn't take his eyes off the road, and I knew this was something he and Hazel had planned together. Even if Hazel hated him, she knew I didn't. Even if I wished for it, it wasn't there. I wanted to be here, and they both somehow knew it.

Still, I wasn't admitting defeat.

"Kyle," I warned.

Right as the clock ran down to zero, the starting gun went off, and I knew when Kyle looked over at me, he'd have the biggest smile on his face. I couldn't help it; I smiled back. Then my back slammed against the seat as we took off.

A small squeal slipped past my lips as the lights outside blurred past the windows. My heart thrashed, loving the feeling of being by his side again, the way he maneuvered along the roads as if it was as simple as breathing. That was how it had always been. His playlist started, and a new level of calm overtook his features as he crept up to the midway point. Except he didn't turn the steering wheel to drift around it...he kept going straight.

"What are you doing?" I looked over my shoulder.

He gassed it, pushing us further, even faster, and with his music playing and his face so serene, I couldn't bring myself to care that he'd just abandoned the race.

"Since when do you drive American muscle?" I asked after a few minutes, running my fingers over the leather seats. This specific model was a Dodge Challenger; that much I knew because they were Kyle's favorite, however the year had changed drastically. He usually drove newer models, right off the show floor. This one we were in was from the 1970s era.

"Since I don't have to push shit for Scotty or anyone else anymore." He downshifted, and we smoothly came up to the edge of the abandoned freeway, aptly named Hoopers Cliff. It was dark, a massive drop on the other side of the concrete dividers and strangely not a place any of our classmates ever ventured. The road was cracked and in disrepair so there was a big chance of popping a tire or messing with the alignment if you didn't know what you were doing. So, we had the stretch of asphalt to ourselves, along with the perfect view of the clear, white moon hanging over the gorge.

The music minimized to a low thrum as he turned the car off and shifted toward me.

"We need to get past this. You belong in my life, nowhere else. But right now, it's your birthday, and a brand new fuckin' year...so we're going to celebrate."

I looked at the clock, and sure enough, it was midnight.

I smiled right as the clock moved over by a minute, and then my best friend was pulling up a bottle of hard cider and popping it open.

I laughed, smothering my smile because he knew I hated champagne, and even though he didn't mind it, he'd purchased something I'd enjoy on my birthday. The gesture was sweet and hit my chest in a way I knew I wouldn't recover from. I took the bottle, downing a long swig before offering it over to him. He only watched me with those dazzling green eyes before setting the bottle down in the console near the gear box.

"It's the new year, Rylie Jean…do you think we should bring it in with a kiss?"

My heart stopped. Was he serious?

"I mean it's good luck to kiss someone when the ball drops, and just because we can't see the ball doesn't mean we should miss out on the luck. Besides, it's just symbolic."

He seemed so sure of himself but entirely bored by the prospect of pressing his lips to mine, like kissing me would be as memorable as going to the dentist. Still, if I turned him down, it would seem suspicious, and I didn't want him knowing why this kiss would mean more to me.

I nodded while my tongue stuck to the roof of my mouth, acting like it was nothing, like it didn't mean anything.

He smiled then began to scoot closer to me along the bench, and his Irish Spring scent was overwhelming. I would die before I admitted to going to the grocery store and hunting down the kind he used then buying it in bulk. I loved smelling it when I missed him, or when I realized we were cursed to the friend zone for all eternity.

His warm hands cupped my face, and then his breath was washing over my lips. He was all minty apples from the cider, and I almost groaned into him.

My eyes fluttered shut as I tried to control my breathing. My only other kiss had been with him when we were eleven and experimenting. I hadn't kissed or dated anyone else since then.

"Relax, RJ. We have to get used to this, right? I mean if we're going to take each other's V cards this summer." He laughed but my eyes flew open, remembering what I had asked him in that orchard, under those Christmas lights.

We swore we'd be each other's first, and I want to make it happen before college. Preferably this summer.

Before I could remind him that I had set that date before learning he'd lied to me, his lips descended on mine in a slow and steady motion.

Darkness clung to him as he moved into my space, as his head slanted to the side, forcing his lips to mold perfectly to mine. Heat erupted along my neck and face as he moved, hunching his shoulders while he pressed me into my door, my body trembling at how good it felt to be touched by him. He was taking too much; did he even know he was claiming pieces of me I had always reserved for him but never in a thousand years thought he'd want?

I opened my mouth for him, my fingers going to his wrists, silently begging him to deepen the kiss. A groan slipped between our lips as his warm tongue swept into my mouth, teasing as if he thought I'd retreat or back off...instead I pushed mine into his mouth, tangling them. It was his turn to groan as our lips began a frantic pace, moving so desperately his hand was moving down my body, his fingers pressing into my hip, pulling me against him.

"You taste fucking perfect." His voice was raspy as he broke our kiss but kept his forehead pressed against mine.

I didn't dare move an inch. We just breathed in the same air as we both seemed to wait for what was coming next. If he leaned in for more, it would mean more than just a New Year's kiss. If he pressed his lips to mine again, it would send a message, one I had been waiting to receive for years.

Just when I thought his silky lips would caress mine again, he pulled back with a pained groan.

"Guess that went a little far...sorry."

His body retreated, the cold air filling the space, invading my lungs as reality barreled into me.

I sat up, pushing my hair back, trying not to let him see how embarrassed I was.

"Yeah guess so."

I looked out the window, watching as more stars popped free along the expanse of the sky.

"Wanna drive?" He looked over, smiling at me.

It was the way his lips spread over his white teeth, the way his eyes lit up with excitement that had me remembering our places.

He was my best friend. He was also an idiot, but he was my idiot.

I smiled back, nodding my head. Even if he didn't want to make out with me, he had still kissed me, and it was my birthday…he'd given me a gift with the feel of his velvet lips, with his taste that I'd remember forever. Getting some air would feel good and help to cool down my overheated face.

Before I could move, his hands grabbed for me. Gripping my waist, he pulled me over his lap.

"You should race tonight—a win would feel good on your birthday," he suggested, flicking the top of his Zippo lighter back and forth. The clicking sound was familiar; it was a tic of his. He'd started doing it more and more after his father passed away and Scotty took up more of his time, his heart, and his soul. He started smoking when we turned sixteen, and I hated that I loved the smell of cigarette smoke when it mixed with his aroma. He was the only exception I made for the scent.

I laughed, turning the key over. I loved the feel of the engine rumbling under my legs and through my fingertips. "I've never competed against anyone but you. They'd smoke me."

"Ry, you're one of the best drivers I've ever seen because I trained you…go show 'em up."

I put the car into first gear and slowly turned the wheel until we were flipped around, heading back toward the races. I didn't want to race, not ever. Racing would always be Kyle's thing, not mine, and I was perfectly fine with that.

"Put on my playlist please." I smiled, switching to second, gassing it until we were flying down the road.

Kyle shook his head, putting on my list and blasting it. I rolled down my window, and my best friend hit the ceiling with his fist.

"Fucking crazy girl, it's January."

I shook my head, a fat grin on my face as the cold wind wrapped around me, whipping my hair against my cheeks. This was what I needed tonight.

Bypassing third gear and switching into fourth, I sailed down the freeway, leaning into the curve that suggested a speed of twenty-five miles per hour.

"You don't know how to drift muscle—don't even try, baby girl." Kyle laughed from beside me.

I licked my lips, moving the wheel to the left while I downshifted and breezed into the curve, completing a perfect drift.

"Fucking hell, Rylie Jean, what can't you do?" He tugged on a few flying pieces of my hair as he laughed. "You just drifted better than me in this fucking car!"

I smiled, pushing the car back up to top speed as we came into a straightaway.

I looked over at my best friend and smiled. "Thanks for this."

He gazed back at me then squeezed my thigh. "Any time, Ry... happy birthday."

As we slowed, getting closer to the bonfires and the massive group of people, our reality surfaced, reminding me why I had pushed my best friend out of my life for the last few weeks.

I put the car in park and let out a heavy sigh. A few girls were at the door, confused to see me driving but quickly swarming Kyle's side, tugging on his door only to find it still locked. I stared over at my friend knowing he already knew what was coming next. No matter how badly I craved his presence or how intensely I missed him...the truth was, he'd lied to me, blatantly, and there was just no way of getting around that fact. He had lied in such a way that I couldn't overlook it, not without him making a pretty big gesture of some kind.

"Ry..." he started, reaching over to grab my wrist.

I shook my head. "What's the point when all you do is lie to me?"

His eyes searched my face as little panic lines settled around his eyes.

"You don't mean that."

A tear slipped free. "I do. You're my person, Kyle...if you can't be honest with me then we don't have anything. I'll never be a casual acquaintance of yours, and you know that." I watched as more people gathered around the car, more girls from school pressing kisses against Kyle's window, red lipstick residue peppering the glass.

He shook his head, his nostrils flaring.

"You're my person, too—is it too much for you to believe I didn't want you to see me that way? I'm scared, Ry, okay? That shit from last month, about Scotty being worried about retribution…well it fucking scares me, okay? Some of the guys from different families pop up down here on the race scene, tempted to just beat my ass on the pavement instead of delivering a bullet to the head. I play a game of Russian roulette every goddamn day."

He shook his head back and forth, his jaw clenching. My heart softened as I watched him struggle with his emotions.

"I'm not perfect, Ry. You know why I got started with Scotty…you know more about me than anyone else on this entire fucking planet. You're my person too, so stop leaving me," he yelled, the veins in his neck bulging with desperation.

I pulled his hand into mine, my resolve crumbling.

Tears strangled my words as I realized this was more complicated than I understood.

Kyle's eyes watered as he pulled me against his chest and tucked me under his chin. I breathed in his scent and let my heart shatter so it could be made new. I needed him. I missed him.

"Just don't lie anymore."

I felt him nod, pressing a kiss to the top of my head. "Promise."

I wished that word still held weight with me, but sadly it didn't.

CHAPTER THREE

Rylie

August

THE STARS SPEARED THE VAST MIDNIGHT SKY, MAKING IT LOOK LIKE A snow globe made of starlight. A warm breeze cocooned my body as I sat with my knees to my chest, surveying the shadowed landscape below. The entire summer had passed, with just a few weeks left before I was off to college. I had already started packing, which was depressing. Mom had burst into tears about a thousand different times, even as we shopped for the things I needed. I tried to limit how often we talked about it at dinner so she didn't melt down. Besides, it was getting more and more difficult to discuss.

I had always known I was going to leave for college someday. I knew where I wanted to go from the time I saw my first Devils game and had walked around campus with my older cousin, Denise. When I saw that library, I was a goner. It was the most beautiful thing I had ever laid eyes on. At the age of ten, that wasn't saying much…but it stuck. It wouldn't unstick. Even as my dad asked me to apply to other places, better places, Rake Forge stood out like a beacon, calling me to its canopy-covered campus, sprawling with red brick buildings and moon-white sidewalks.

I was excited to start my freshman year, but there was still apprehension itching under my skin, and it all revolved around my elusive best friend.

For months we seemed to drift further and further apart. As much as I wanted to place the blame on him…it was really me. After what had happened at Christmas, there was just too much pain surrounding the way he'd placed his hand over my heart and vowed something untrue. Still, he was always around, as though he woke each morning craving my presence.

He'd shown up a few nights over the past few months, but I'd pretended to be asleep.

Other times he'd beg me to drive with him, and every now and then, I'd go—but my heart wasn't in it. Despite the magic that had crackled between us on my birthday, I could feel the loss of having him, and it made my heart pitch in a thousand different ways. His green eyes begged for forgiveness, but his lips had stopped requesting it. So, we existed in the awkward moments, the stifled laughter, and the missed phone calls and unanswered texts.

Not once had I mentioned our agreement. He hadn't either, and a part of me assumed we'd just let it fade, like so much of our friendship had.

Gravel crunched below my window, forcing my heart to lodge in my throat. I knew it was him. Even if he had given up hope that I'd ever be awake, he still came every so often. I thought back to when I had seen him the day before, when something had seemed off with him. His eyes were constantly flitting to the window, to the back of my house…where his was just beyond the empty field. Something was bothering him. I wouldn't really have known though; our talks and discussions had essentially stopped after my birthday.

I had no idea if he was planning on going to college. I assumed he was, especially since Decker had, but Kyle never talked about it, and his time with Scotty seemed to be increasing more and more. We were both eighteen; I knew he had plans to leave, to spread his wings and do whatever it was he wanted to do, even if that meant following Scotty wherever the hell he decided to go.

The sound of the lattice moving below was the only indication I had that he was nearly up. I had mere seconds to decide to pretend to be asleep or face him for once. I toyed with the leather band around my neck. He'd made it for me, tied it off with a silver ring he'd made in metal shop. I brought it to my mouth, bit down, and considered what to do.

I'd acted asleep the past five times he came, but truthfully, I was way too curious to see what he'd do if I were awake. He might just want a round of Mario Kart, but something told me it wasn't about that. Something told me he might just bring up the deal and fulfill it.

I'd wanted him to love me the way I loved him, but it hit me that we might be on more equal footing than I originally thought. I was still angry with him, hurt, punishing him, and he was still pushing and keeping us safely in the friend zone. It was nice and chilly between us...perfect for our first time.

I decided to keep my lamp on and settle on the bed sitting up while toying with the edge of my sleep shorts.

Kyle was as silent as always as he made his way up. His posture was rigid as he crawled inside, his knee pressing into my cushioned window seat. His chestnut hair was recently cut short, though the strands on top remained the longer length, making him look much older than his eighteen years. He set something down then he was peeling his sweatshirt off, slowly raising his hands then tugging that gray material over his head.

I loved that sweatshirt. It had his last name on the back with a sketch of his favorite car on the front. It looked gritty, and I knew from how many times he'd washed it that the inside was insanely soft.

"Hey." He hesitated like he wasn't sure if I'd bolt. I hated that things weren't how they used to be between us. I hated this vast void that was eating up every single inch of our pasts, barreling into our future. If I didn't do something, we'd never be the same. I could feel it deep in my bones.

So, I gave him a smile. A real one.

It momentarily stalled him, stopping him in his tracks. That devastating smile he'd grown into hitched up his lips, a light pink color tinging the tips of his cheeks.

"I made you smile," he murmured, still grinning...still blushing.

"Mission accomplished." I finished his familiar saying for him.

He walked to the edge of my bed and stopped. His tanned arms hung lifeless at his sides as if he wasn't sure what to do with them. His green eyes were on me as he slowly lifted his fingers and gripped the edge of my comforter.

"Is it okay that I'm here?" he implored, concern lining his voice.

My heart wilted that he even had to ask, but that was where we were now. I moved, shifting closer to him, to put him at ease.

"Of course it's okay."

"You've just been distant with me…I wasn't sure."

I shrugged, trying to play off the past six months even though we both knew exactly what I had been doing.

"You live in here." I tapped my chest, smirking to lighten it up. "Even when we're distant, you still have a place in there. You can always come back."

That seemed to break something open in him. His lips parted, but halfway through his smile, he faltered, his lips thinning into a firm line.

"Where are your parents? I saw the SUV was gone." His thumb jutted over his shoulder, indicating the patch of gravel below us.

"Away for the weekend…something to do with my mom's sister up north."

He nodded, bumping his knuckle against his leg. I wanted him to tell me if it mattered that we were alone tonight, I wanted to know what he was thinking, but I stayed frozen on the bed, just waiting.

"That's good then…that is…" He cleared his throat. "I was wondering if you were still up for our deal." He turned his gaze on me. It was more of a glare than anything else, but I still took it with a greedy anticipation that had been hiding in my belly for too long.

I nodded, swallowing my nerves. "Yeah, I'm good with it."

I nearly winced, hating myself for making it seem like he'd just asked if I wanted the other half of a cookie or something. I was a total moron.

Surely there was something sexier than *Yeah, I'm good with it.*

He seemed to move past it, not focusing on my blunder and

instead plowing on. My stomach knotted tight as I waited for him to explain.

"Before we do this, you need to know a few things." He leaned forward, staring down at me so hard I thought he knew his imprint was on my soul, knew he'd been devastating me since I was old enough to love. But his stare wasn't full of love and affection...it was full of hunger.

Raw and animalistic.

My heart burst at the implication.

"Number one: You're so fucking beautiful it hurts. I haven't ever told you that, but I've thought it a million different times, and I thought you should know it before we do this."

I didn't dare let a single breath escape from my lungs, too afraid that I was dreaming.

He thinks I'm beautiful?

"Number two: I'm taking your virginity, you're taking mine...but if you think it will be a sweet affair of awkward bumbling and goofy shit, you're wrong. I plan to fuck you thoroughly, Rylie." He leaned closer, making my lips part and in between my thighs slick. "I'm going to fill you, and after you're past the pain, we're going to fuck so deep neither of us will ever forget our first time."

He straightened, pulling away from me once more. With the movement, he lifted his shirt over his head and tossed it into the corner.

I eyed the shadowed spot, curious if I should be shedding clothes while he spoke, to save time.

"Number three: The most important thing...we go back to how things are after this. No strings, no expectations. Nothing..."

A hole the size of his fist seemed to expand in my chest. I was positive that if I looked down, I'd see blood gushing from where my heart used to be. There seemed to be more to what he was saying, like he was warning me that something was changing or shifting...but he wouldn't tell me what. I understood what he was getting at, trying to lay it out for me so I could refuse him.

"You deserve to give this night to someone else, someone who will give you more than what I can…it won't hurt my feelings if you tell me to get out."

My gaze flicked up to his, realizing I had been staring at his chest. His muscles were defined, nothing grotesque, but lean and mild. *Perfect.*

I considered what would happen the next day but slammed my eyes shut, hating that I was jumping ahead. This was here and now. He was in front of me, offering me the one thing I had always wanted from him, to give him this, to feel protected with this piece of me. If he wouldn't take my heart, I'd settle for him taking my virginity and being the owner of that for the rest of our lives.

To answer him, I leaned forward, sitting taller on my knees. He still towered over me, but I pressed my palm to his chest, staring up into his eyes.

"I agree to it, all of it." I wanted to say more, wanted to tell him I loved him, had always loved him, but I didn't want to ruin the tentative truce we seemed to be existing in.

His gaze turned dark as he searched my features…likely for the lie, but after a few seconds, his hands came up, cupping my face, and then he nodded.

My heart raced, matching the rhythm behind my palm. We were doing this. It was finally happening, and all I could think of was that I'd live for tonight, cling to every second of it until morning came, and then I'd release him back into whatever he wanted after this. It clearly wasn't me, but I refused to consider what else it could be.

This night was ours, and I planned on taking whatever he offered.

CHAPTER FOUR

THERE WAS SO MUCH SHE WASN'T SAYING. I COULD ALWAYS TELL WITH her. I knew her better than I knew myself, better than I knew the feel of the engine before I needed to shift or the way the road curved along Hoopers Cliff. She had her very own tempo, beating in my chest...something she probably didn't know. Yet, this...I needed this from her tonight, and while I knew I didn't deserve it, I planned on taking it.

The past six months had been shit between us. I knew I'd ruined us, and I hated myself for it. She hadn't been the same after the Christmas party, after I had fucked up and lied. I had known what I was doing in that moment, and I deserved the fallout from it...I just hadn't realized the pain from losing her would be so severe.

She was like a ghost, here but not, around but elusive...like she couldn't have cared less about my future or if hers was connected to mine in any way. I had tried a few different tactics to get a response from her, but the only thing that awarded me time with her was just acting like the goofy friend she had always known me as.

Now I was demanding things from her, telling her my intentions, and she had agreed. She'd fucking agreed to them.

My heart was still battering against my chest as if it was a massive piece of chopped pine barreling into a thick castle door. I wanted in, into places she had kicked me out of, her head, her heart...even her soul. I wanted access, but if this was all she'd give me, I'd fucking take it.

Her warm palm came up, cupping my jaw. Hesitant, insecure. Unsure.

I gripped her neck, wrapping my fingers around the base of her slender spine and relishing how good it felt to touch her skin, feeling the smooth surface brush against my fingers. Knowing she was giving herself to me for tonight, knowing I'd own this part of her forever... even when she married someday, started having kids. This part, this thing would be ours.

"Perfect," I whispered in her ear, pressing a kiss to the space below it. My lips moved down the column of her throat, consuming her as I went. Tasting, biting. Owning.

I moved my fingers up to the bottom of her cropped shirt and pulled it over her head, revealing her full breasts. The cool air fluttered in from her window, shifting a few strands of her dark hair over her shoulder. The dull light from the small lamp illuminated her taut stomach, her pale skin that ended at her dusky nipples, practically throbbing against the night air.

I sucked in a breath, latching onto the image, locking it away for the rest of my fucked life.

I trailed my fingers up along her ribs, seeing her skin pebble as I skimmed. Giving her my eyes, I needed her to see how badly I wanted her. I needed her. Then I lowered my head, wrapping my lips around her supple flesh.

Her breast fit perfectly in my palm; her nipple hardened under each stroke of my tongue. I groaned as she released her posture, curving into me.

My right hand went around her, drifting down her back and under her shorts. I gripped her ass and relished the slight moan that left her as she brought those dainty fingers to my hair and gripped the strands roughly.

That spurred me on, needing more from her.

I pushed at her chest, helping her down to the mattress where she lay looking up at me as though I were the stars she loved so much.

It made the rope around my heart twist and burn.

Fuck.

I moved down her body, tugging her shorts off and tossing them over my shoulder.

"No panties?" I quirked my brow in question.

I expected her to blush or get embarrassed, but instead she opened her legs for me and let out a sigh. "I've been waiting for this."

"Shit." I groaned. I had all these plans on lasting all goddamn night with her, but I was already hard and leaking, two seconds from blowing my load.

Having her bare in front of me and seeing she'd waxed recently was another knife in the gut. She'd prepared herself for me, unsure of when I'd come...or when I'd fulfill our deal. It wasn't as if I hadn't tried over the summer, but she had kept acting like she was asleep, giving me her answer without having to say a word.

"Fucking hell, you're so perfect. I bet you taste delicious."

I didn't wait to see if she'd protest. I spread her and licked through her folds, pressing my palms to her stomach to keep her in place. A growl reverberated from my throat as her taste burst with hints of rosebud and lust along my tongue, like she was mine...waiting for me to come and claim her.

My mouth assaulted her, sucking her lips into my mouth. My tongue delved into her center with such force that she began recklessly rocking her hips to match the pattern of my mouth working her.

My hand drifted to her ass, squeezing and forcing her thigh back, exposing her crack to me.

I let up, letting my eyes fixate on her green ones. They were little flames of heat, licking at my spine, silently begging me to do what was in my filthy mind.

Keeping my gaze on hers, I lowered my head and licked slowly around the tight bundle of nerves in her ass.

Her guttural moan was loud and echoed off the walls. It also was hot as fucking hell.

"Oh my god, Kyle." She breathed heavily, her head falling back while her hips thrust forward.

I repeated my ministrations, pressing my tongue into her while my fingers began stroking her clit. Rubbing, fucking, and making more of those moans leave her while she bucked ruthlessly to catch the friction of my touch.

"Yes. Oh god. Yes."

"Come for me, Rylie," I demanded, rubbing furiously at her clit while I moved her leg so she was in front of me. "I want to taste you coming apart on my tongue."

"Yes. Fuck, Kyle…" She cried out, and a second later her orgasm was on my tongue. I lapped up every fucking drop, savoring the fact that I'd made her come so undone her breathing was ragged, filthy curses falling from her lips while her hips continued to rock.

She was so responsive that I wanted to repeat what we'd just done over and over again, seeing how long I could make her last, how much dirtier we could make it.

But I needed to sink into her before I came in my jeans.

I'd done that once after hanging out with her. I had never told her, but…fuck it.

"You don't know how many times I've jerked off thinking of you." I moved, pulling my jeans and boxers free. Gripping my erection, I rubbed it up and down, coating it with the liquid that had begun beading at the crown. "One time, I actually creamed my jeans because of you."

She gasped, giving me that smile that made the small dimple in her left cheek pop. "What? When?"

"We were fifteen…we were at my house, watching a movie. You had your feet in my lap while you ate a popsicle. You licked it, moaning and pressing your toes right into my jeans where my poor unsuspecting cock rested."

She laughed, tossing her hand over her face. "Oh my god."

"Your shirt was riding up too, and I wanted to touch you so bad. Instead of moving or adjusting myself, I just let you do it. I kept thinking you'd freak or realize you were touching something that wasn't my leg."

She burst out laughing, likely remembering that day. It was pure hell, but the best kind that I kept dreaming about after that night.

"I finally couldn't help myself…after a few times of you pushing your toes against it, I came in my boxers. I had to leave."

"I remember that. You didn't come back downstairs forever. I thought I heard the shower start…"

"You did." I laughed, moving over her body, going for the foil of the condom.

"Can I ask you something?" She licked her pink lips.

I nodded, trailing a finger over her stomach, up over her breasts, and then back down to her core.

"Tell me what you imagined happening. What would you have done if we were older and had nothing stopping us?"

My eyes snapped up to hers, heating. Big green eyes, lustful and waiting. Those pink lips parted. I remembered exactly what I had thought after I got up from that couch and awkwardly made my way upstairs. I remembered exactly what filthy thoughts I conjured up while gripping my cock in the shower. With a shuddering breath, I closed my eyes and answered her.

"First, I'd grab your ankle and pull you closer to me, until you were sitting right next to me, practically in my lap."

Her hooded eyes shifted down to my mouth, her lip suddenly trapped between her teeth.

"Then?"

Slowly, I moved my fingers, sliding along the slick space between her legs. My dick throbbed with the need to sink into her, but I wanted to wait. I needed to.

My voice was pure gravel as I continued. "Then I'd unzip my jeans and show you the mess you'd made, and then…"

Fuck. I didn't want to admit how filthy my mind had been back then…

"Don't stop." She exhaled, pushing into my fingers, but I knew she meant my story.

"I'd grab your chin, kiss you, and then shove your head into my lap and force you to lick up every last drop of the mess you'd created. I'd fuck your mouth and then come again down your throat."

Her hips bucked against my hand in wild, hungry moves. She continued to bite down on her lip, watching me until she rasped.

"I want to…" She trailed off, her face flushing a beautiful pink as if she was embarrassed by being turned on by my story.

"You want to…"

She moved, sitting up. "I want to do that, exactly what you just described. I want to taste you, see you…all of it."

My gut clenched tight at the vision of her taking me in that way.

I moved, sitting back. "Rylie, you own me. Just take what you want."

Her hair cascaded to the side as she shifted to her knees and began crawling toward me. I would never get the image of her tits swaying or the hungry look in her eyes out of my head.

She lifted her left leg, getting off the bed, but she twisted and was on her knees within seconds, placing her hands on my thighs.

My hardened cock sat erect, hitting my stomach as she watched in fascination. Then she was wrapping her soft hand around the base, heaving in a shuddered breath.

"It's big…" She stared at the precum leaking like a sieve. "It felt big…I remember feeling you so hard and thick through your jeans that day. You think I didn't know it was your cock?" She licked up the length of my shaft, and with her eyes on me, she whispered, "I knew."

I swallowed the anxiety building in my chest. I'd never had my cock sucked, but I'd fantasized about it too many times to count. She never looked this good in my head though, never this hungry or sexy. The lamplight only highlighted certain features of hers, like her eyes and her lips. The rest of her, like her hair and body, seemed to be swallowed by the shadows.

"Put your mouth over me, Ry. Let me feel those big fucking lips wrap around the head of my cock. I've wanted this for so long, baby." I whispered my confession, too much of a coward to let her see my eyes when I said it.

Seconds later, her warm, hot mouth was taking me down her throat.

"Shit." I hissed as she barely licked the tip and then slowly went deeper until she was practically choking. "Fuck that feels good," I muttered, playing with her hair as she bobbed her head up and down on my length.

A moan came from her chest as she moved her thighs, rubbing them together.

"Does this make you wet, Ry?"

Her eyes tipped up to meet mine, and she whimpered as a response, taking me deeper. I wasn't going to last.

"You ready for this cock to fill you?"

She sucked harder then let me go with a pop. I yanked her up by her arms, setting her on my lap.

Her cunt pressed against the base of my dick, proving how wet she was.

"Rub against me," I instructed, and she did as I said, rocking her hips to rub her pussy against my shaft.

"Feel good?"

She threw her head back, bracing herself by putting her hands on my shoulders, increasing her speed.

"I want more...I need it, Kyle. God, I need it." She moaned.

"I'm going to fuck you like this another time, where I can watch your tits bounce and see your mouth gape as I fill you so intensely you can barely breathe. But for now, I need you on the bed."

She got up, staring down at me, breathless, her chest heaving, pussy dripping, and crawled onto the bed.

I stopped her before she could flip onto her back, pressing my fingers into her cunt.

"You're so wet, Ry. You're dripping...is that how bad you want me?"

She turned her head to look back at me and pushed her ass back into my hand.

I added two more fingers and began applying pressure.

Without thinking too much about it, I smacked her ass, watching to see what she thought of that.

"Do that again." She sighed and rocked into me.

So I did, seeing two pink handprints on her ass cheeks and groaning into her skin as I moved my lips there, caressing the two spots. Grabbing for the condom again, I began tearing at the top, but then she gently stopped me.

"It's our first time...we haven't been with anyone else...I've been on birth control for over three years…it's regulated and all that. Can we, um…" She paused, red flushing her neck. "Can we go bare?"

Fire raced along my veins. I nearly growled my response before thinking it through. Of course I wanted to go bareback…I'd never fucked before and I didn't want my first time with a condom, but there were still risks with that…then again, if she was asking for it, what could I say?

"You sure?"

She nodded. "Positive."

Well fuck. "Okay, but I'll pull out at the end, okay?"

I gripped my cock, letting out a grunt as I gripped her hips, and, without letting another thought into my head, I slipped the tip of my dick into her cunt.

Then, slowly, I began pushing through her folds until I was sinking into her. Her thighs spread apart for me, making more room.

"This okay?" I asked, feeling my brows pinch together.

Her tongue darted out, wetting her lips as her hands clutched the sheets. "Yeah, keep going."

I watched, looking down as my length slowly disappeared inside her. There was pressure and resistance, and I knew this was when she'd hurt.

"Shit, I mean it makes sense that you're tight, but I never imagined it would feel like this." I breathed out, realizing she still wasn't through the worst of it yet, but fuck it felt good.

I watched her expression pinch with discomfort and froze.

"Just do it." She breathed out, her chest heaving.

I rocked gently, trying to make it as painless as possible even as my own need thrummed through me, urging me to release.

Suddenly she made a little sound of pain, and instead of freezing this time, I pushed harder until I was completely seated inside her. We stayed still for a few seconds, our heavy breaths mingling. I lowered my face, my forehead pressing against hers.

"You feel so good, better than I ever imagined," I whispered, and then she kissed me, licking my bottom lip.

"Move, Kyle."

Her words shot straight to my cock, making me groan as I moved my hips in a slow rhythm.

"Yes, that's it…it feels so much better now, keep going," she begged, wrapping her legs around my hips. My hand went to her ass, pulling her to me as my hips moved faster, pumping into her, rotating and fucking her. Our bodies were so tightly connected I didn't know where she ended and I began. The low light of the room cast her in a dreamy glow as her dark hair fanned out against the white pillow. My heart nearly burst as I realized how badly I had wanted this, craved it, and didn't want to let it go.

"Oh my god. Yesssssssss, Kyle," Rylie yelled, clinging to my arms, her nails imprinting on my skin as I continued pumping and moving until I couldn't hold back anymore. Her eyes shut tight again as her mouth gaped and a pained sound fell from her lips, slowly transforming into a cry of pleasure. I groaned in cadence with her as I realized there was no way I would have been able to pull out even if I wanted to. She was too fucking tight, and it felt too good. She came with a scream as I groaned my release into her, spilling my seed, filling her like I'd said I would.

But it wasn't enough. I slowly pulled out and looked down, seeing a red tint to the cum spilling from her pussy. Bringing my fingers to the folds, I began spreading it around, rubbing all over her cunt, branding her with it and needing it on more of her. I wanted to see it on her tits, on her stomach, on her ass, and even on her face if she'd let me. I wanted to take her as many times as she'd let me tonight.

We lay there for untold minutes, our bodies slick with sweat, my heart full, and my stomach pitched with worry.

She moved her fingers, tracing words into my skin. Her nails gently tugged at my hair as time ticked by, and I didn't want to leave. She would have to be the one to make the call. If she wanted me gone, I'd go, but if not…I'd give her the entire night.

Sometime later, Rylie wanted a shower and grabbed my hand, silently asking if I'd join her. We fucked again, and this time I sucked her cunt with her leg thrown over my shoulder. Then I lifted her and fucked her against the wall. Once we returned to bed, she wanted to sit on my lap and fuck. We used a condom so she'd know how to properly roll it on; after all, this whole deal was supposed to be for our education, for future partners, but fuck if I could think of that.

I knew Rylie was ignoring her soreness, knew she was pushing her own pain aside to enjoy the one night we'd have together. I knew this, and I still fucked her. I entered her from behind, leaving more handprints on her ass. I fucked her enough times to see white ribbons of my seed spread on her tits, on her ass, and on her stomach. There were a thousand moments I committed to memory, and I was half tempted to actually take photographic evidence but was too afraid of creeping her out to ask if she'd let me capture her naked, or mid fuck, or with my seed rubbed all over her pussy.

There were quiet moments between us too, darkness spreading over us like a blanket, harboring our secrets.

I had my eyes closed and was relishing the feel of her skin against mine when I heard her confession.

"I love you. I have my whole life."

I didn't say anything because I was afraid, terrified she wasn't lying, scared this was her deepest truth.

"It's not love like it should be, Kyle. I'm *in* love with you."

At that I opened my eyes, watched her lips continue to move with more truths, but I couldn't take them…so I pressed my mouth to hers to silence her. I couldn't hear her pour out her heart when I knew I'd be breaking it within a few hours. I kissed her then rocked my hips, sinking so deep into her that her mouth gaped and she didn't have any more words.

I was still wrapped in the sheets with my best friend when the sun rose, and I heard gravel crunching outside her window. Her parents were home, and my time was up.

I kissed her bare shoulder, moving her chocolate hair out of her face, mesmerized by how her dark lashes looked so long and delicate against her freckled skin. My heart throbbed; my eyes watered as a shuddering breath rattled my lungs. She'd never understand; I knew she wouldn't, and if I had been a better man, I wouldn't have done this to us.

"I'm sorry," I whispered into her mouth before I kissed her.

Then I left.

CHAPTER FIVE

Scotty

I WATCHED THE CLOCK, GRIPPING MY GUN TIGHTER AGAINST MY THIGH.

Kyle had exactly two fucking minutes to walk through the door before I drove over to his little friend's house and set it on fire. Did he think this was a joke?

His life was on the fucking line, and hers too because of her connection to him. Yet he needed one last night. He'd taken the entire goddamn summer but begged for one last fucking night. Probably to get his dick wet. I didn't blame the kid, but now he was pressing against my timeline, and if we went over, even by a few minutes, the entire plan would be fucked.

The door opened, and my nephew sauntered in.

I set the gun down on the table next to me and crossed my leg over my knee. "Hope she was worth it. I almost killed you myself for being late."

His angry glare cut through me as his broody teenage jaw clenched tight. His steps echoed along the floor as he headed for the bathroom, then his bedroom.

"You didn't pack?" I asked even though I already knew the answer. I watched as he walked to the kitchen pantry.

Pressing his hand along the false wall, he began loading his weapons into his duffle. "You didn't check?"

"Why would I? It's your shit."

He grunted while emptying his small collection of guns, knives, and ammo.

"How long?" he asked, moving to the back of the couch. He flipped it over and used a knife to cut the back open.

"Two minutes."

He grabbed his assault rifle, AK-47, shotgun, and a few piles of cash.

I watched, seeing his jerky movements betray his emotions.

"You know it's the right thing to do…either way, she's dead if you stay."

He nodded without looking at me.

"You go with Gino, he'll know about her…you don't go, he'll kill her to hurt you or use her as leverage."

"I know." He stood, carrying his two black bags toward the front door, then pulled on a leather jacket.

"Get it out of your head…you can't kill him."

Green eyes the color of my sister's flicked up to mine. "Who says?"

"Me, motherfucker. You already started one war—we need to put that fire out before you burn down another family."

"See, Scotty…that's where you're wrong. I think we should set it all on fire, let the whole goddamn thing burn then take it for ourselves."

I considered what he'd said, thinking it over. The thought had crossed my mind a few times, but we had no one in our corner or on our team at the moment. Ivan's men were loyal to him and would be loyal to his brother. They wanted retribution and would come for it. Kyle was young and eager, had an inflated ego over handling Ivan himself, but one day…

"Give me time, Kyle. I'll make you into the person who knows how to light the match."

He laughed, shaking his head. "Isn't that what we've been doing?"

The timer went off.

"Our time is up."

He shook his head, smashing his back teeth together. "It's been up…we're just too dead to notice."

CHAPTER SIX

Rylie

I DIDN'T LIKE FEELING THIS WAY.

Like I was a pathetic stalker, watching for just one sign that I wasn't crazy, that I hadn't made the entire thing up in my head. My best friend had come, taken my virginity, and then made love to me until the early rays of sunlight hit my floor. I could still feel his arms around me, holding me to his chest. I could still feel the way he buried himself inside me so deep he groaned and whispered things about my body and what it did to him. We'd crossed a line.

He'd confessed things to me and whispered them into my skin with every kiss and lick of his tongue, with every thrust of his cock… but then he was gone.

Completely gone.

As if he'd never even existed. I swung by his house, and his mom gave me a sweet smile. Too busy to talk, she said Kyle was on a trip with his friends…*hiking*. I laughed because Kyle didn't hike.

He didn't.

She was wrong.

I came back, thinking I could catch sight of him sneaking in after a race or after seeing someone else. Surely that was what had happened here…he'd gone too far and now he was feeling awkward about it and ghosting me.

A dark truck pulled up, and Decker hopped out, grabbing a bag before heading to the porch. I exited my car and briskly covered the space between us so I didn't miss him.

"Decker!"

He turned, a quizzical look in his eye. "Rylie?"

I crossed my arms, feeling cold even though the summer air was thick. Never in my life had I felt so out of place in the gravel driveway of Kyle's house. I'd run up the steps more times than I could count. I knew the dirty words we'd etched with knives in the wooden posts near the bottom of the deck. I knew there was weed stashed under one of the flowerpots because Kyle liked to sneak it when he thought his mom wasn't looking. His dad always knew, but my best friend took advantage once he'd passed. Not that I blamed him.

"Where is he?"

Decker's face fell just the slightest bit…but it was enough to tell me that he was about to lie to me, and that something was wrong.

"He's gone, Ry…you're headed to college, he's not."

I already knew I didn't want the answer, but I asked anyway. "Where is he?"

Decker hesitated, letting out a sigh then running his hand through his hair. He looked down at me and said, "Hiking in Europe."

"Bullshit!" I snapped, stalking up the steps. "He wouldn't go without me—or at all. Kyle hates Europe, hates hiking and back-packing and anything at all that would take him away from me or from racing."

Decker's green eyes sized me up, his jaw twitching while his chest expanded. I looked down at the titanium wedding ring on his finger and internally wanted to cry. I remembered sitting there next to Kyle, feeling his knee press into mine as his brother looked into Mallory's eyes as if the whole world could burn away and he'd be perfectly happy as long as she stood by his side. It was the most beautiful moment I had ever witnessed… and I had stupidly wondered if Kyle would ever look at me like that, if I could ever make him feel for me the way Decker felt for Mallory.

"Rylie, I don't know what to say…he knew if he told you, you'd talk him out of it. He went…" Decker trailed off, the muscle in his jaw jumping.

"He went…?" I restated, encouraging him to continue even though my heart smashed against my ribs, screaming at me not to hear him explain. What I didn't know couldn't hurt me.

"He went with a girl he met at one of the races…she had a free ticket, he took it. There's a group of them…he's going to be gone for a few months. He didn't take his cell. He's off the grid."

I tried to swallow, but my throat wouldn't work. I ended up falling to the first step of the porch instead. I was practically hyperventilating.

"I'm sorry, Rylie…" Decker whispered, crouching to look me in the eye.

Tears sprang to my eyes, falling free as I processed the reality of what had happened. He had used me. He'd fulfilled our agreement, had gotten his experience so he wasn't embarrassed…shit, this was because I'd told him I loved him.

Humiliation swarmed my chest like a hive of angry bees. How could I have been so stupid? He had essentially been shutting me up as I poured my bleeding heart out to him. He hadn't said a single thing in response, just kissed me and then…we fell asleep after that.

This was exactly why I had waited so long to tell him how I felt, because I'd known it would be too much for him. Then again…one of his rules was that nothing changed between us after that night. Maybe he'd known he was going to leave me.

Either way, it didn't change the fact that he was gone.

"So there's no way to contact him?" My voice was paper thin… much like my heart.

Decker was quiet, so I looked up. His dark brows caved in, the denim of his jeans stretching over his knees as they jutted out near my face, and those green eyes stared at me, begging me to not make this harder for him than it was. He shook his head. Silence.

Quiet.

It was final…and over. Whatever I had assumed my best friend had started with me that night in my room…was a lie, and I was an idiot.

I let the truth fill up my heart like a tank of wet cement, fortifying all the tiny cracks and holes, smothering all the places that thrived with love for Kyle James. It would die with time, with no more soil or water…no more sunlight. This love would end, and I would be fine.

I would be…with time.

FRESHMAN YEAR OF COLLEGE

August

Dear Kyle,

School started…you aren't here. I guess we never really knew if you'd come anyway, right? I think I always assumed you would just to hang out with me.

It's logic like that that got me into this mess. My heart aches, my stomach feels empty…this wasn't how it was meant to be. I keep expecting you to call me. I keep hoping you'll text me. Every single day I watch my phone for some sign of life.

In the end, deep down, I know you'll come back to me. In your own time, you will.

I love you. Even if you don't love me back…that's how this works. Sorry but it's true.

Ry

DECEMBER

Dear Kyle,

It's Christmas day. I'm at my house with Dad and Mom…there's no snow, but we frosted the glass so it would be like there is. Your mom invited us over to bake pies and sugar cookies. I cried when I went. Only Decker and Mallory were there with us, and it felt empty. Is this punishment for something? Whatever it is, we can move past it.
Please come back to me.
Love, Rylie

JANUARY

Dear Kyle,

I turned nineteen...you will next month, makes me wonder where you are, if you're having fun with someone, if you've fallen in love. I drove to Hoopers Cliff tonight, where we made up last year...I watched the stars, drank some cider, and cried for two hours. Then I drove home and tried to make better resolutions for the next year. Mainly, I want to stop missing you.
Love, Rylie

MAY

Kyle,

School is over…I'm headed back home for the summer. I have stupid hope that you'll show up. My window will be open for you.
Love, Rylie

SOPHOMORE YEAR

September

Dear Kyle,
My mom is sick…you aren't here. I really need you.
Love, Rylie

DECEMBER

Kyle,

I got an invitation to Taylor's birthday party. It's going to be a Christmas party too…just like old times. For a few seconds, I actually wanted to say yes, just in hopes that you'd be there. I let the entire thing play out in my head. You would show up with a date, obviously having no idea I was coming…the look on your face would be priceless.

Still, I turned her down because I'd die if I saw you like that. I'm already empty inside. Somehow my heart began rotting out like an old pumpkin the second you ditched. I gave it to you completely, you asshole, so there's nothing left.

I still miss you,

Rylie

FEBRUARY

Kyle,

Hazel found your Instagram account today…you seem to suddenly love hiking, and not showing your face. Seems odd. Hope you're having fun.

MARCH

Kyle,

I thought I saw you today…it was the strangest thing. You were right there, smiling at me. Then you weren't.
I really can't wait for that shit to stop. I feel like I'm always seeing you in the shadows, in the reflection of shop windows, in clubs when Hazel drags me out… you're everywhere and nowhere and I'm so fucking tired of it.

MAY

Kyle,

Another school year is ending, I have no hope whatsoever that I'll see you this summer…in fact, I'm going on a trip to ensure I don't.

JULY

Kyle,

I had sex with someone. I threw up afterward…here's to moving on.

AUGUST

Kyle,

Mom died.
You missed her funeral. I needed you…

JUNIOR YEAR

September

Kyle,

I changed my number so you can't call me or text me anymore. Not that you would…but in case you suddenly decide to give a shit about our friendship again, you'll have to work a little harder to get in touch with me.

DECEMBER

Kyle,

I have a boyfriend. I'm thinking of taking him to meet Dad…what do you think? Think he'll like him? He's nice, a little clingy, but wouldn't it be crazy if I complained about that after everything you've put me through?

JANUARY

Kyle,

I turned twenty-one, broke up with my boyfriend, and drove out to our spot. Oh yeah, by the way, I dubbed it our spot. Someone wants to tear it down and build some family homes there...I think some things should just be left alone, even if they're rotting and empty. Some things need to stay exactly where they are... Anyway, I turned twenty-one in the lamest way possible, and I think I have finally hit rock bottom.

MAY

Kyle,

There goes another year…I think you would have dropped out by now and opened your own garage. Remember when we talked about that back in freshman year of high school? You were going to call it Kyle's Karts or something horrible like that. We laughed for a while, coming up with different names.
I wish you'd do it…no matter how corny the name, I wish you would open that garage and be happy…just anything to bring you back. Maybe you did though, maybe you're happy and married with kids running around your feet while you fix cars. I'm going to imagine that for you. This is the last letter I'll ever write you. I'm moving on.

CHAPTER SEVEN

SENIOR YEAR

Rylie

September

THERE WAS A LIMIT TO HOW MANY TIMES IN ONE NIGHT I COULD handle men hitting on me. I mean, the act of complimenting me in itself wasn't what made me want to crush glass with my teeth; it was just the way their egos transformed these men from dangerous MMA fighters dripping with secrecy and stealth to douchebag assholes with dirty mouths and cheesy pickup lines.

Especially the men who walked in through the metallic blue door of Deacon's, or as most everyone in Rake Forge called it, Mak's.

Case in point, the man who just walked in. Tall, wearing a tight camo tank that displayed most of his chest and arms, a matching beanie on his bald head, tattoos for days, but they were all wrong. The man had cartoon characters…legit Disney and Looney Tunes cartoons littered all over his bulky muscled arms. His semi-decent face was stern and stoic until he caught sight of me, and I just wanted to scrunch my face up like I was about to witness a car wreck, because it was that bad when they let their eyes wander over my body like I was an exhibit in a petting zoo.

Don't do it.

Don't do it.

His eyes narrowed.

Don't do it, I repeated in my head, wiping down the bar to try to seem busy and very unavailable. *Maybe I should get myself a wedding ring…*

His left eye dipped. *No.*

The wink commenced, initiating the same song and dance these guys performed every time they wanted to try their hand at asking me out. His was completed with a quick flex of his overly venous arms.

I wanted to puke.

Instead, I remembered that I was representing Mak and his bar, something he'd worked damn hard to open. So, I gave this guy a warm smile and turned away to check the glasses. They were still clean and dry…just like they'd been for the last hour.

"Hey."

Oh no. He wasn't just looking or biting his lip today…he was actually going to give it a go.

I slowly spun in my discount Doc Martens and gave the guy a smile.

"What can I get for you?"

He knocked his knuckle against the bar top, his eyes moving from my head to my chest in a slow perusal. If I could put texture to the way his gaze made me feel, it would be one of those big-ass dogs with dangling spit hanging from the edges of its mouth licking you in the face.

Disgusting.

"How about ten minutes alone in the back?" He flexed again as if I'd just suddenly give him a lap dance purely based on the number of muscles protruding from his neck. Spoiler alert, I wasn't into guys with massive neck muscles. It was a major turn-off for me.

I slapped the white rag to my left down on the bar with a little more force than necessary then explained, "This isn't that kind of joint. Go talk to Mak if you want to get some info on one of his clubs. I'm here to serve drinks, that's it."

He seemed to mull that over with a twist of his lips as his large fingers drummed the counter. "What about your name—can I at least get that?"

I withheld the urge to sigh.

"Murphy." A stage name of sorts. The less people knew about me, the better.

"Okay, Murphy…I'll be back later tonight when I'm about to fight. I'll win thinking of you. Maybe then you'll give up more than your name." He winked, leaning closer for the briefest of seconds before shifting away from the counter.

I felt my lips twitch with the need to tell him he was fighting Vega tonight, and I knew for a fact no one beat Vega…especially a guy built like him. He had too much bulk; it would prevent him from moving as swiftly as his opponent. I probably shouldn't mention that I'd give Vega a lap dance for free any day of the week if the man would just ask me.

Tonight, I might actually enjoy watching the cage as the fighters went at it. Usually, since my shift officially ended at nine, I would put in a pair of headphones and watch a show or read a book instead of heading home, just to help keep my eyes open for Mak.

When had this gig gotten so boring? Once upon a time I was enthralled by the gleaming black floors and neon lights that turned an underground fight club into something from an acid trip. It was classy, but dark and gritty. You knew as soon as you walked through the doors that you might have to leave a part of your soul on the stoop.

It was a place where blood was shed and bets were made. I was merely a puppet in the grand scheme of things, a tiny valve in a well-oiled machine, but after years of playing this part…the shine began to dull, and everything that made this place special wasn't anymore.

I'd seen behind the curtain, and now I just wanted to move on with my life and get it started. Being a bartender in a seedy fight club wasn't the epitome of my aspirations; no…in fact, I, Rylie Jackson, was about to graduate with my bachelor's degree in criminology.

That's right. I studied how to put people behind bars, and I had every intention of one day putting that shit to use.

"Is Hazel coming in later?" Mak yelled at me from across the room.

He turned a barstool right side up, setting it on the floor before looking back at me. I knew Mak had a thing for my best friend but was too complicated in his own head to do anything about it.

"She is." I pulled out a few limes to cut up. Really there wasn't a reason for me to come in as early as I did, but Mak needed someone to man the counter during his hours of operation, regardless of how busy or—in most cases when I came into work—not busy the place became. My bar top acted more like a secretary's desk from the hours of four to seven. The real action began around seven thirty and stayed crazy until half past midnight.

Mak grunted, returning to his task of settling all the barstools around the room. It was so quiet, and sometimes I would take the peace and analyze tiny pieces of my life with it, like why I worked here, in one of the most dangerous clubs in North Carolina. Mak provided the means for his sensitive clientele to have privacy while they watched amateur UFC matches and stayed out of the spotlight.

I wasn't an idiot. We might not have been living in a massive city, but that didn't mean we didn't get our share of big-city action. If the east coast was a drug lord, New York would be its heart and North Carolina the inner lining to its trench coat. North Carolina was where secrets piled up and things that needed to remain in the shadows stayed hidden, which was why a local gang had thrived here for so long.

El Peligro was the gang Taylor's husband ran, and from what I understood, things had changed over the years. There were rules, but the fist that used to crush now tossed seeds in the community and planted hope for people living below poverty. He'd altered things, the entire gameboard had shifted, and while he seemed to soften over time, other players thought that meant he had weakened too.

Now, there was a war brewing on the streets. More players had begun surfacing than had ever before…more product was being moved, more bosses were being killed. Things felt unsettled.

"Murph, you going home this weekend?" Mak suddenly asked, his hips kissing the counter that separated us. He was a bulky dude in his own way, thick like a tree. Corded muscles ran around his lean arms, but his face was too long and his chin too dominant for me to find him attractive. Didn't mean he wasn't; he just wasn't my type. That and I was pretty sure Hazel secretly liked him.

I kept my eyes focused on the clear bucket of fresh limes and nodded. "Yep, gotta check up on Pops." I went home every weekend, much to Hazel's chagrin, but I enjoyed seeing my father and catching up on what had taken place during our week apart.

Mak nodded, his hands coming up to the bar top, drumming out a random beat. "I got something for him…somethin' big, and I don't think it can wait until our usual meetup. You think you can take it?"

My stomach flipped. Big as in a big player or big information? What did that mean? I adjusted my expression so it didn't look like I was freaked out.

"Of course."

Mak and I both worked as informants for the FBI, and while my role was more lax in the sense that I just shared things I saw or heard around the bar with my dad, Mak's role was much different.

He was supposed to be serving fifteen to life in prison, but they'd cut him a deal knowing he already had a thriving business established where illegal activities went down. They'd offered to let him keep running it as long as he reported everything back to the feds.

Only Mak and I knew of this arrangement; not even Hazel knew of any of the roles we played here. My best friend just thought I enjoyed the underbelly of the city because of my roots that had started in the same garden bed as Kyle's. She couldn't have been more wrong. I took pleasure in turning players in because I hoped one day the man I'd be turning in was Scotty. I wanted him to burn for what he'd done to my best friend, what he'd put him through and exposed him to.

"Head to my office after the fight, and I'll get you the info."

I silently nodded as my boss walked off, knowing we couldn't really discuss these things while his business was open.

THE NIGHT PASSED LIKE ANY OTHER NIGHT. PEOPLE SWARMED INSIDE, desperate for a front-row seat to the fight. I made drinks while keeping my eyes on the door and the people who came through it.

I was in the middle of making a Long Island iced tea when I noticed two men dressed in all black casually walk in. Their long strides took them past the commotion of the fight, skirting the fringes of the crowd. Their eyes focused on the chaos, ignoring the person making drinks behind the bar. Neon LED lights lit up the space behind me where shelves of liquor perched, and mixed with the myriad of other glowing lights around the bar, it was enough illumination to make out the two men as Dietrick and Damon Finelli.

I ducked my head, trying to become less noticeable while the men made their way to the back, but just as they passed the edge of the bar, Damon flashed me a blinding smile and…dear God…

He *winked* at me.

My wince was automatic, which made the jilted brother stop in place.

Fuck.

"What's wrong, doll…you don't like my face?"

No, I did not like his face. It had pockmarks all over it, along with a gnarly scar that ran through his eye, down to his chin, and his lips were too wide.

I shook my head, leaning over the bar top with a smile. "Oh no, I just had a tiny paper cut that got lime juice in it."

His brother smirked, pulling his cell phone from his pocket, his thumb swiping along the screen.

"If I wanted to have you in the back room, I could, little Murphy. Don't think we don't know who you are." He flipped a playing card between his fingers. It wasn't from a standard deck of cards from what I could tell; instead it was solid black on one side, and on the other…

I watched as it rotated between his knuckles once more…and saw the outline of a joker's face.

Odd.

When informing for the feds, every interaction with a player became a poker game. You learned to watch for tics, signs of weakness, anything that might give away their motives. The card meant something; I just had to figure out what.

Drawing my eyes up away from his hand so they didn't think about my focus, I blew the man a kiss and then gave him a flirty smile before spinning on my heel.

I gave both men my back, toying with tickets stacking up on the back counter, and willed my heart to calm down. The Finelli family was powerful. I remembered my father explaining the different roles each one played and what territory they each held. Their family held one of the largest chunks of the east coast, running all the way up through Canada. Their boss was someone I never wanted to meet. The things he was rumored to do to his women, the way he diced up his victims…they were psychopaths, and yet they were here in my little college town, making deals.

Maybe this had to do with Mak's big news to break to my father. Suddenly I was eager to get out of the bar and head back home, but I still had at least two hours before I could.

The night moved along at a snail's pace. I perched on a stool at the end of the bar, a glass of club soda in front of me while I watched the fight. Vega knocked camo guy out. It took him twenty-three seconds. It happened so fast I barely had time to cheer for my favorite fighter. Instead, I ended up scrambling off the stool so I would be ready to take his drink order, regardless of the fact that my shift had ended over an hour earlier.

"Congrats, big man." I began gathering ingredients. "You want the usual?"

He nodded, tugging on the butterfly stitch near his eyebrow.

"He got ya?" I lifted my hand toward his face, holding up his drink.

Why are you pointing out the obvious, Rylie?

I flushed red, embarrassed that I was being so awkward.

His smile widened on me as he humbly ducked his head. "Yeah, guess so." He accepted the drink then said, "Thanks, beautiful."

My ovaries exploded into a joyous song begging me to marry him and make a million babies with him.

I liked Vega, as in kind of had a big fat crush on him. He was kind and always respectful to me, and he was also insanely humble. He won every fight he entered and never bragged, never got a big head about it. He was a good guy, and it didn't hurt that he was six foot three with lean muscle and caramel skin that made his dark tattoos stand out, or that he had blue-gray eyes that made him look like a wolf shifter.

I read too much paranormal romance, but that was neither here nor there.

Unlike his opponent, Vega's tattoos all meant something to him. Words in Spanish, the Puerto Rican flag, names of people he loved, sayings—there was even a quote on his skin from *The Iliad*.

But he'd never asked me out.

Not once, and I was too awkward to ever be brave enough to do it first.

"Well, I better head home." Vega sipped his drink and gave me a half-smile.

Dammit. I wanted him to make some kind of move, anything to shove us out of the friend zone, but he never did.

"Okay, enjoy your night." I grabbed a white rag and began wiping down the counter. He gave me a heated look then shook his head and walked off.

What in the heck did that mean?

I watched his back disappear through the door on the opposite side of the bar and deflated.

"Are you seriously never going to make a move?" my best friend said beside me.

"How long have you been standing there?"

She smiled, brazenly breaking the rules. I automatically searched for my boss so I could rat her out.

His eyes met mine from across the room and then he flicked his smile to the woman next to me.

Shit. Of course Mak had given her permission to be behind the bar.

I rolled my eyes, feeling juvenile. "Shut up." I moved, loading the dishwasher with dirty glasses.

Hazel began helping me. "I'm just saying…" Her sugar brown eyes looked more like honey under these lights. "You always look like a lost puppy when he comes to get a drink after one of his fights. You need to just make a move already."

"And what about you and Mak?" I volleyed back.

Her lips spread into a smile, revealing her white teeth. My best friend was the kind of beautiful that made you stop and look, the kind that made you wonder if you'd mistaken her for a movie star or a model. With dark mocha skin and wavy black hair, her being mixed race of Hispanic and Black gave her distinct features that blended better than a makeup contouring YouTube tutorial.

She waved her hand off. "You know that shit is complicated."

I smirked, about to say something snarky back when Mak appeared.

"Ready to chat, Murph?"

I liked that he never broke character while we were here. He obviously knew my real name, but he always called me Murphy when we were in his bar.

"Yep." I wiped my hands on my apron then untied it and handed it to Hazel.

Mak's office sat in the back of the bar, and a slim door made of metal greeted us as we both squeezed into the space. With one lamp on inside, Mak took a seat in front of his desk and handed me a card.

"Give that to your dad."

I carefully inspected the small card, bringing it closer to my face.

"What is…" It was the same card I'd seen the Finelli brothers carrying, with the joker face on one side.

"There's a new player…he's got people freaked out. His stamp is on everything that comes in…he's either stealing or owns more H than any other player to date. Either scenario is dangerous for Rake Forge. I think the feds need to get ahead of it."

I nodded as my brows crumpled in confusion.

"How many carried this tonight? I saw the Finellis with one."

Mak leaned back in his chair, running his palm down his face.

"Three families…they're carrying it as a token of sorts. As far as I can tell, if you have one, it means you're off the market for shop talk, that you've essentially already agreed to have one provider…if something were to happen to that family from retribution, the card is supposed to be shown. If they move regardless of the card, it's supposedly fair game for this guy to go after whoever ordered or completed the hit. From what I've heard, you don't want this guy after you."

That didn't make any sense.

"So, there's one major player now, and who is this guy? What does the card mean?"

Mak's eyes lit up as he leaned forward and smiled. "The Joker of course."

CHAPTER EIGHT

Rylie

My knees bunched up against my chest as I brought the hot cup of coffee to my lips and sipped. I was in my favorite chair, back home just waiting for my dad to wake up and join me. This was our weekend routine, and while I knew I should have more of a life back at school on the weekends, this place reset me in a way that other places couldn't.

I didn't get energized by going out with Hazel or the girls. I certainly didn't like waking up in the middle of the night hearing Hazel have an orgasm from some guy she'd snuck into the room. I just liked going home, seeing the sun rise over the field in front of my parents' house.

"Rylie-Roo," my dad said cheerily, stepping into the living room and planting a kiss on the top of my head. I spun in the chair, watching as he made himself coffee in the small alcove near the kitchen.

"You slept in."

He stirred in his cream and sugar then headed toward the chair opposite mine. He wore blue striped pajamas, the same ones he'd had most of my life. There was a coffee stain near the middle of his shirt and a red mark on the collar from one Christmas when my mother had kissed his neck after she'd put on her red lip stain. The strings of my heart seemed to pluck along to the same tune every time I saw him wear those pajamas, a melody of happiness now tarnished by grief. It pinched, but I'd have been completely devastated if my dad stopped wearing them too.

"I'm on a tough case that has kept me up."

I didn't like the stress lines around his eyes, or the new gray hairs that now invaded his scalp. I worried about him, worried he was too involved with his work and was getting lost without my mother here to keep him grounded.

"Speaking of work…" I let my feet drop to the floor then pulled out the card I had kept in my purse. "Mak wanted me to give you this."

I handed the card over to him and watched carefully as his brows shot to his forehead.

"How did he get this?"

My father's tone was sharp and lethal. I sipped my coffee to settle my stomach. I knew this meant there was something big going on. So, I explained the Finelli brothers and what Mak had mentioned.

"That means he's got his hand in more things than we realized." My dad let out a heavy sigh and rested his fingers on the bridge of his nose.

"He?" I asked, knowing already he was probably talking about the Joker person.

"A new player…we aren't sure yet, but we think he may have started his own family, or it might be a gang. It almost feels like the cartel though with how frequently his symbol pops up on products."

That wasn't good. That meant more danger…more product and more potential for war.

"Do you think there's going to be a war between the families?"

His gray eyes met mine, the graying scruff along his cheek more prominent this morning than his usual clean-shaven look.

"I don't know…there's enough evidence to prove that if there is a war then it will be against this guy, the families pulling together to go against him. My informants tell me he's pissing on everyone's turf."

The talk of turf reminded me of that night in Juan's house when Scotty showed up with guns.

I took another sip of my coffee, watching the sun soak the world with warm rays. Summer clung to the grass and trees as the wind and weather agreed not to move on to fall. My throat felt too tight as I watched the swing shift outside the window, near the large tree. I remembered when both my parents were alive, when my dad was just a small-town cop and she was his supportive wife. I missed when life was easier, when my best friend was still here.

"I miss when you were just a cop." I ducked my head, shocked I'd let that confession slip free. I had worked diligently to keep that under wraps for years, ever since he'd been approached by the bureau.

"This was always my dream, Ry." He ruffled my hair, getting up to head toward the kitchen. "You want eggs?"

I spun in my chair and eyed his position in our small kitchen. It was still difficult not to see my mom standing there in her pink fluffy robe and her hair thrown up in a messy bun. She had loved making breakfast while sipping coffee and listening to the latest news headlines.

"Yeah, I'll take some."

I felt like he was hiding something. He was usually more forthcoming about work stuff; this was the first time he'd shut it down rather quickly and changed the topic.

I set my coffee down and walked in to help with the food.

"So, this Joker player…is it as serious as it was when Heath Ledger played the role in that one Batman movie, or…" I joked as I washed my hands, but Dad didn't laugh with me.

"It's nothing like that, sweetie. This is pretty serious stuff…he uses the moniker and we see it everywhere, but we can't pinpoint a physical face or location for him." Dad's face screwed up with more worry, and I didn't like the feeling it left me with.

"What have you gathered so far?"

His shoulders shifted under his pajamas as he stirred the eggs, but he didn't respond.

"Dad?"

He finally let out a sigh and faced me. "It's nothing personal, sweetie…but I can't talk about this stuff with you."

I was actually pretty shocked…he'd never hidden things from me before.

My brows crumpled while my shoulder rested against his, standing side by side while we cooked.

"Since when?"

Another long sigh exited his lungs while he served the scramble onto two plates.

"Is it because I'm only graduating with a criminology degree? Is this bias against the fact that I didn't go for my criminal justice accreditation?"

My father laughed like I knew he would. My degree was a constant point of jokes for us. Criminology would potentially land me a position as a local cop, but getting into the FBI academy, something my father had hoped I'd want to do, wasn't as likely.

"I still think you're wasting your time. It's not too late to change your major and go for your criminal justice degree."

I knew it.

He sipped more coffee while his eyes flicked toward the Joker card he'd set on the table. A pensive look crossed his features, as though it troubled him…but more than if he were just trying to catch a bad guy. There was something else going on in my father's head, something he didn't want to share with me, and I had a feeling deep down it had nothing to do with my major or where I'd end up after graduation.

We'd joked about me applying at the local Pinehurst police department, but it wasn't serious. Truthfully, I had no idea what I wanted out of life…sure, bitter parts of my heart wanted to one day be the agent who put Scotty behind bars, but then what?

Everyone knows vendettas only last so long, and once you fulfill them, they make you feel like crap. I needed something more meaningful to cling to, something that was just mine. Unfortunately for me, I had no idea who I was or what I wanted out of life. So, I was just floating until something tugged me down to reality to keep me here.

"Are we going to watch the Hornets play today?" I asked, trying to get my dad out of his head. It seemed to work; he shook it briefly and smiled.

"Maybe next weekend, honey. I really need to get back to the office."

He was keeping something from me; I could feel it. We'd been inseparable after my mom passed, and of course Kyle had left. I didn't have anyone but him and Hazel…she was there, but my dad was my rock. We knew each other's quirks and I knew he was stressed now, but there was something strange about how he'd transitioned topics from the Joker card, and now he was basically ending our weekend early. Something was off with him.

"Okay, no problem. I have a lot of homework to catch up on anyway, so I will head back to school."

Please tell me to stay. Please remind me that I just got here. Please want me.

"Sounds good. I'll catch up with you later this week." He walked over, kissed the top of my head, and then ran upstairs. Once I stood up, I realized he'd taken the card with him.

CHAPTER NINE

THERE WEREN'T ENOUGH WORDS IN ANY LANGUAGE TO DESCRIBE HOW much I currently hated my uncle. I had already cursed at him in Russian, then Italian, then Spanish…and now…fuck, I didn't actually know any other languages, but if I had, I'd have told him to go fuck himself in those too.

"You can do better," Scotty mused, peering at his watch, unfazed as usual.

I stretched my arm in front of me as sweat dripped from my face, scaling the ink on my arms. Three years and I had quite the collection now…I hadn't really noticed until this moment that they covered both my arms from my shoulders down to my fingertips. I was running out of room…guess we'd have to start working on my chest next.

"Hold," Scotty said, his voice echoing through the cold garage.

My breath came out in little puffs in front of my face. It was cold enough to freeze a fucking Klondike Bar in here, but you wouldn't know it based on the lack of clothes I wore, or Scotty's damn suit. The space was set up to essentially work like a meat locker, keeping large cuts cold and providing me with a space to train in. Why did we need large slabs of butchered meat? Scotty knew since he handled all the minuscule details of our business ventures. It had to do with moving product, but I didn't know how. I just showed up and did whatever he told me to in order to get my workout in.

I held the position, my body folded in the most uncomfortable of positions, my muscles straining, my limbs trembling to hold myself in place. My time to beat was five minutes. It felt like I had surpassed that, but who the fuck knew. Scotty liked to torture me.

"Enough." Scotty got up, walked toward the wall, and threw a towel at my face.

I collapsed in a heap on the dirty floor. We'd removed the mats after I had managed to stay in that position for one full minute. Scotty told me to learn how to avoid the mold, otherwise my face would be landing in it.

Fucker.

"Time?" I wiped at my forehead and cheek, clearing it of sweat and grime. I'd have to run back to the manor to grab a shower before I left.

My uncle crossed his arms, watching me as though he expected me to answer my own question.

I eyed him, giving him a glare. "Time?"

"How long is this going to go on for?" he said in response, which did nothing at all for my actual question.

I let out a heavy sigh and got to my feet. I didn't want to have this conversation again. "I just wanted to know what time it was, not that fucking difficult."

"No, you wanted to know how much time you had before her class got out…you think I don't know you've been stalking her since we moved back?"

I clenched my back molars together—not because he was right, but because he acted like I was still a kid, a teenager making reckless decisions and choices. I wasn't. I was a monster now, one of his own design…but even monsters occasionally like looking at flowers.

"I don't need to explain myself to you."

Scotty laughed, moving away from the door. I tugged it open and immediately regretted it. The sun blinded me, and although September was half over, there was still a warm thickness to the air. My body wasn't ready for it. After living in Russia, Hungary, and

London over the past few years, it felt odd to settle back into North Carolina. We hadn't been planning on it, but it made the most sense for our operation to be here.

I wanted to jog back to the house, but Scotty wouldn't run with me, and I knew he had something to get off his chest…even if I didn't want to hear it.

"You're supposed to be traveling, Kyle, living an elusive life and keeping the people who want you dead busy."

I listened to the sound of our feet crunching the gravel as we made our way back to the house. My eyes stayed transfixed on the ground while Scotty's head was up, probably looking around.

"You *do* have to explain yourself when you're putting yourself in harm's way."

"I don't have to fucking explain myself to you," I restated, clenching my jaw a little too tight.

My uncle suddenly stopped and turned toward me. "I've watched you for three years…every time a piece of ass comes your way, you turn it down. Every time a stripper or one of the girls in the outfit wants to fuck…you turn them down. You had the guys thinking you were gay, so they started asking for guys instead."

I burst out laughing. "Is that why there were two guys in my room that one night? We ended up playing video games for three hours, and we exchanged numbers—they're my go-to teammates on Fortnite now."

My uncle rolled his eyes. "You can't have her! Not ever…get it out of your fucking head!" He pushed at my temple.

"I know I can't!" I yelled back, stalking off toward the house.

I had fucking known for three long-ass years I couldn't have her. I'd lost my best friend and the only girl I ever loved in one night.

Scotty was suddenly next to me, his eyes forward on the looming house.

"Her dad is an FBI agent, Kyle…you can't go near her. Tell me you understand."

"I understand…but if she shows up in my life, comes back into my orbit on her own, then don't fucking intervene." I kept my eyes frontward so he wouldn't keep pushing the topic.

I didn't get many things that were just mine in this life, things my uncle didn't have a say in, and while I knew everything he had done was for my safety, I also knew he would toss Rylie in a fucking second if he thought she was a threat to what we'd built these past few years.

Scotty was right...I knew he was. There wasn't a chance she'd ever forgive me anyway...not that I needed it. I'd done what I had to to keep her safe. I had no regrets, but I did have a shit ton to lose if I were caught.

Looking down at my hands, seeing the tattoos of my new moniker peek back at me, I let out a sigh.

"You're right."

Scotty smiled, opening the back door. "I know I am."

I shook my head at his arrogance while we ventured further into the house.

Garrison and Holt worked as head of our security, and they made it a little easier to let our guard down if we wanted a breather. They'd both been on with us since the beginning and went way back with my uncle from when they were kids.

Garrison lowered his glasses and assessed us, his eyes narrowing on me. "You have a visitor."

I grunted, taking a swig of the water Holt handed me.

"They pay?"

Holt's silence had me turning toward him.

"Well, did they?"

"Boss, it's just that there's been a wrinkle, and he said he has information you're going to want. He's calling it a fair trade."

Fuck.

My nostrils flared as I stared at the ground, sweat from my hair falling in fat drops to the wood floor.

"I charge one hundred grand for these fuckers to meet with me, and you're saying it's a fair trade?"

Holt raised his hands. "It's a reliable source."

I shook my head. "There's a reason you're not in charge, Holt. Did you even run him by Scotty?"

My uncle's frozen posture told me he hadn't, but the fact that he hadn't already shut Holt down told me there was a significant wrinkle my men hadn't told me about.

"The fuck is going on, Scotty?"

My uncle ignored me, nodding at Holt. "Tell him we'll meet him."

Well shit, this wasn't good. Garrison and Holt moved down the hall, ready to execute the order, while I hung back and waited for my uncle to explain it to me.

"There was a drop-off last week, but the merch wasn't picked up. Our guys disappeared, not a single trace left behind."

I crossed my arms, a sinking feeling filling my gut. "Who?"

Scotty shook his head. "I was waiting until I had more info before I told you."

"Meanwhile you, Holt, and Garrison all knew?"

"There wasn't enough intel."

I shook my head and tugged my shirt free, tossing it into the laundry room before running upstairs. I knew my uncle would follow, but I was curious now who the fuck was sitting in my living room.

Padding into my bedroom, I veered for the shower and gripped the chrome knob, turning it to the right. Steam instantly began filling the space as I stripped out of my clothes.

My uncle, having followed me in, leaned against the door frame, inspecting his nails. "Garrison thinks the feds are involved."

I opened the glass door, stepped inside, and yelled back, "Based on what?"

Running my hands through my hair, I scrubbed my bar of soap over my scalp, thinking over why the feds would be involved in a simple merch trade. There wasn't even anything wrong with that drop; in fact it was actually about as legal as a Facebook Marketplace meetup.

"An old informant. Said they're plugging more and more under-covers, trying to infiltrate our ranks. They're targeting you as the king-pin." My uncle's voice echoed through the spacious bathroom, booming over the shower head.

I scrubbed harder, letting out a scoff. They weren't wrong, but did they even know who *I* was? No one knew who I was; it was the reason I hid behind the new name and identity.

"So we hear this guy out then?"

Scotty grunted in response.

I chose not to respond, knowing we'd said as much as we needed to. We'd hear this guy out, make a plan, and do what we needed to. I ran the bar of Irish Spring over my skin, eyeing the tattoos on my arms, only this time I wished I could watch the ink swirl around the drain. I wished for the millionth time that this wasn't the life I had been thrust into, that maybe I had just accepted a fucking hole in the head instead of letting this hole inside my chest fester and grow. I felt like the darkness of this new life had begun to gather and spread throughout my system.

"We'll make a plan, kid. The feds have come before, shoving their noses up our ass. It's not new."

I slapped the knob to turn off the shower and wiped the water away from my face. I knew once I opened the door, Scotty would be gone and my bedroom door would be secured. I didn't have a lot of privacy in this life, but the few moments I did get, I treasured. I chose to take a few minutes to myself.

Wrapping a white towel around my waist, I leaned over the sink, watching my reflection in the mirror. My eyes, free of the blue contacts I usually wore, had circles under them. My jaw was sharper than it had been back when she'd last seen me, my hair was longer, and my dark tattoos made me look different. She wouldn't even recognize me now. Three years of killing and becoming a different man made it that much harder to come to terms with the fact that I wasn't the same guy she knew.

I'd given up racing and my best friend in one quick decision. Occasionally I drove on back roads, but there was something exhilarating about crossing that finishing line. I missed my old life. I missed her.

I let out a sigh and turned to get dressed, preparing for the nightmare waiting downstairs.

CHAPTER TEN

Rylie

THE NEXT WEEK CRAWLED ALONG. HAZEL HAD BEEN BUSY WITH parties, it was our senior year, and there was so much going on, keeping her away from our little dorm more than usual. Football was in full swing, so the fraternities were throwing ragers left and right. There were a thousand different events around town ushering in the beginning of fall.

It was thankfully starting to cool down more and more, but the itch under my skin couldn't be soothed by the world changing around me. I had worked so hard to get to the end of my school career; I wanted to be like Hazel and enjoy my time, go to random parties, hook up, laugh, joke, stay up all night.

I just didn't have it in me, and I didn't even know why. I just felt like something was missing…something I had no recollection of losing.

"Girl, it's your breakup-anniversary…your break-iversary." Hazel cut into my thoughts, crunching on a chip, her eyes on the bag her hand was inside. It was early afternoon, so she was home for once, not that she'd stay.

I laughed, moving around our dorm to collect my books and laptop. "What?"

"With you and Kyle…it's why you're always so mopey this time of year."

I stood, mouth gaping, watching my best friend stuff her face. "What are you talking about? I'm never mopey."

I wasn't. Was I?

Hazel held her thumb out as if to make a point. "Freshman year, you stayed in the dorm all of September and half of October. I had to bribe you to come to a party with me. I was literally dragging you out of the room to converse with guys."

"Pshhh." I rolled my eyes, crossing my arms. "Not even close."

Her next finger jutted out. "Sophomore year, you…" Her eyes went soft, her nose twitching before her fingers fell away.

"What?"

"Nothing, it's just…I realized it's not just him…you were dealing with your mom's sickness over the summer."

Oh yeah. Fuck it hurt that I had forgotten how painful that summer was. I had set up a shit ton of trips to distract me from the fact that Kyle was gone and wasn't coming back. I still went on most of them at my mother's request because she would say she was fine. *Feeling better. The treatments must be working because I feel good.*

She had lied.

She'd lied to make me feel better.

"Then junior year…" Hazel trailed off again.

My chest constricted as the painful memory surfaced. In August, we buried her. By all accounts, I should have taken a gap year…but I just wanted to keep my mind off the pain, so I came back to school.

"Sorry, I'm a shitty friend for trying to pin it all on Kyle."

I waved her off, turning my head to hide the way my eyes were now watering. I missed my mom. I missed her hugs, and the way she knew me better than I knew myself. I missed how she would encourage me whenever I felt upset or down about life. She was always encouraging me, telling me I could do anything I wanted to. Even if I wasn't great at something, she would pretend I was.

Suddenly there was a hand on my shoulder, spinning my chair.

"Want to come grab some greasy carbs with me?" Hazel popped a crumb in her mouth then wiped her fingers on her jeans.

I laughed, swiping at my face. "Where do you put it all?"

"Girl, I burn these calories in the most orgasmic of ways." She shimmied her shoulders, and I laughed again.

Standing, I pulled her into a hug.

Her arms went around me, holding me tight against her.

"I just want you to be okay, Ry. You know that."

I let out a shuddering breath. "I'm getting there, I promise."

But it was a lie. I wasn't getting anywhere but more disconnected. The piece of me that was missing wasn't my mom. I had come to terms with her death, believed with all my heart and what was left of my soul that she was in a better place. It was something else that tugged on my heartstrings, reminding me there was a tangled mess beneath my breastbone.

It was something I hadn't worked out…heartache I left unattended that had become infected and diseased. Now it was all rotted out, a constant reminder that I was missing a piece of myself.

Deep down, I knew it was him.

It was always him, and I feared it always would be.

FRESH OFF MY INNER REFLECTION REGARDING MY STILL-BROKEN HEART and Kyle, I decided to change things up with Vega.

I needed to do something to get over my best friend, and the two guys I had dated over the past three years hadn't cut it. This was different because Vega truly acted like he didn't see me as a female, so the challenge was real with this one. I'd need to get him to see me as a viable option for a date…or if I was being really honest, a one-night stand.

I was prepared to risk my body to find out. Besides, hooking up with Vega wouldn't be anything but a wet dream come true; from there maybe we could find out if we had any actual feelings for each other. Yeah, maybe that was it. I needed to work backward with this entire thing, with my libido at the forefront, calling the shots, and my feelings and emotions at the very end.

Desperate times called for desperate measures, or in my case…just looking the part. Instead of my normal crew collar crop top and ripped jeans paired with my Doc Martens, I wore a plunging tank, allowing easy viewing of my lifted breasts, paired with skintight black jeans and my usual shoes...because, well, I was a girl of habit and I liked my shoes.

Sure, this wasn't the brightest idea or the best use of my time, but this was new for me, something I didn't usually do, and sometimes you have to do something so vastly different from your norm to find out who you really are, like shocking the system or something. I knew it would be a hellish night given my fashion choice, but if it got me anywhere with Vega then it would make dealing with all the idiots worth it.

"What the fuck are you wearing?" Mak asked from behind me, and I nearly dropped a glass. Okay, I hadn't actually thought through what my boss might think.

I shrugged, fighting a blush. "What?"

"Jesus." He groaned, bringing his hand to his nose, then he moved his finger back and forth in the air with his lip curled in disgust. "You have these criss-crossy things in the back tied off with a ribbon...it makes you look like a present to be unwrapped, and your tits are practically hanging out."

So, this was what rock bottom felt like. It was hotter than I expected.

"I..."

My hands were sweaty. Why did I feel like my big brother had just caught me having sex?

"Mak, what's the big deal? I dress in ripped jeans and a crop top every shift...does it really matter if—"

"If you look like one of my girls from Juicy's? Fuck yeah it does."

Juicy's was a strip club on the other end of town that Mak owned. It was the reason Hazel would never actually commit to him; she couldn't get past him running it. I didn't know why. Mak was a good guy and treated his employees well. He also provided excellent security for the girls over there, something I needed to bring up regarding my spot behind his bar. It would be nice to have someone to keep away all the men who constantly hit on me.

I let out a dramatic sigh. "You're being ridiculous."

"And you're being super slutty. What the fuck gives?"

"Hey." *Ouch.* "You can't call me a slut, dude."

"I didn't call you one, I said you're being slutty…and you never ever are, so what gives, Murph?"

This was so ridiculous. "You know most bar owners want their female employees to dress skimpy to increase traffic and the purchase of beverages."

He crossed his arms over his chest. "I'm not most guys, and I can't have you lookin' like that tonight."

My brows caved as I thought through why that might be. "Why, what's going on?"

Leaning against the bar top, he looked left and right briefly before leaning closer and whispering, "Someone is coming in tonight…I want everyone to keep a low profile. I don't need any fighting outside of the cage, and you have the ability to turn my fighters crazy. Imagine the shit show when they see you dressed like that."

Well then. Dammit, that was cryptic and kind of freaking me out, but I wouldn't let it show.

"Now it's your turn to tell me what gives." He lifted his hand, shoving it through his hair.

I blushed deeply, completely mortified that I was about to admit this…but it was Mak. I trusted him with my life.

"Vega…he doesn't even know I'm alive. I was trying to get his attention."

A burst of laughter exploded from Mak's chest, forcing his head to tip back.

"You don't have to be so rude about it…" I crossed my arms defensively.

Mak finally slowed, wiping tears from his eyes.

"Really? You laughed so hard you started crying?"

His bright eyes settled on me. "Sorry, Murph. Aw, baby girl…Vega is gay."

Dammit, that hadn't been rock bottom…this was.

I deflated instantly, feeling like a total and complete moron. I hadn't had the slightest hint at all that he was gay. I tried to replay our conversations, our interactions…he was always nice to me. He seemed to give me heated looks…was all that in my head?

I laid my forehead on the bar top, directly in front of where he stood. "Are you serious?"

"Yeah, honey. I'm sorry. He's bi, but he has a pretty serious boyfriend from what I remember…I've seen him look at you and I know he's interested, he's just off the market."

"Shit."

"Now that we cleared all that up, will you pretty please"—he put his hands together like he was praying—"put something over your shirt, because the morons who come in here are going to rip each other to shreds for a second of your time. It confuses them that I own two spots. They assume any female in my employment is from the strip joint and open for business, catch my drift?"

I groaned, standing up and spinning toward the little shelf that held my stuff. I opened my messenger bag and dug through it.

"About that—can I have some security like they get?"

Mak laughed again, shaking his head. "They need it because they get naked on stage. You don't. Just don't dress like you're offering lap dances and you'll be fine."

It was on the tip of my tongue to argue that I didn't dress like this ever and still got harassed all the damn time, but he'd already walked away, having been called over by Jarred, his fight coordinator.

There was a sweatshirt at the bottom of my bag. It was the one I lugged everywhere with me because it was like a good luck charm or security blanket…something I knew I shouldn't have on me, or even among my possessions. I tugged it over my head, brought the soft material to my nose, and inhaled.

It didn't really smell like him anymore, but Kyle's sweatshirt would always make me feel like he was still here. The front of the hoodie had a muscle car outlined in black with ink leaking from the frame, dripping into letters below that spelled out Rake Forge Racing. It was the one he'd worn that night…and left behind.

The night progressed, and my shame over the Vega incident began to wear off, especially as less and less guys looked my direction.

The sweatshirt was key; it hid my boobs, and if I pulled the hood up it would hide my long, dark hair too.

"Murphy, get a round of drinks set up in the back room, will ya?" Mak asked around ten at night. My shift was supposed to be over once Trixie started. She was a single mom who needed the tips way worse than me, so I always took on the early shifts and gave her the later ones so she'd get more money, but as I looked at the floor, I realized Trixie wasn't coming in. She would have been in by nine.

"Where's Trix?" I yelled toward my boss over the noise.

He stood there for a few minutes, watching his cell as he yelled back. "Out sick, her kid has somethin'."

I started prepping the shots for his meeting, setting them up on a black tray, then moved around the counter toward the back.

The room narrowed into a dark hallway, illuminated by more neon LED lights hung near the crown molding of the room and the trim at the bottom. A few dark doors littered the hall before it widened in the back, and there was just a velvet curtain that separated the room from the hall.

A massive circular couch sat against the far wall, its soft leather like butter, and when Mak's was closed, I would sometimes do my homework on it, or even take a nap. During business hours, it was used to host some of the most wanted criminals in the country.

In the middle of the room was a circular table where I set down the shots and began arranging napkins. Knowing they wouldn't have a server available to come back here, I moved to the wet bar to ensure it was fully stocked with all of Mak's go-to picks.

I was arranging the bourbon when I heard the door to the back parking lot open and close, which meant one of Mak's employees had arrived since we were the only ones who used the back entrance. Everyone else had to use the front, even his distinguished guests.

"Trix, that you?" I called out, my back still to the room while I adjusted the bottles.

"Who the fuck is Trix?" The male voice echoed in the room like a thunderclap.

My hands froze on the bottle, my heart slamming into my ribs. No one was supposed to use the back entrance, and because they had, I was completely alone with a potential criminal.

"How did you get in here?" My voice was raspy, and I was terrified to turn around.

In fact, my eyes nearly screwed shut to hold off the tears welling in my eyes. This was bad. Very, very bad.

"An old trick," the guy said, sounding like he was moving around the room. Something about his voice was familiar, like closing my eyes and hearing an old song I knew as a kid, but I couldn't quite place where it was from.

"You weren't supposed to do that."

Shit, that made me sound like a second grader tattling on the kid who was trying to eat glue.

His snicker told me he thought the same. I needed to turn around, but I feared the second I did, he'd pull a gun or end me for being able to identify him. In this messy world of the underground, there was power in not seeing who your monster was...it made the monster less concerned with you turning his ass in to the feds.

"I'm just going to go grab Mak." I kept my eyes down, my voice low as I slowly made my way to the door. The sleeves of my hoodie were too long and covered my hands, I was sure he felt like I was out of place, swallowed by the hoodie, looking too young to be in an underground fight club.

"Wait," he suddenly yelled from his spot on the couch. He sounded urgent. Curious.

I didn't want to have someone like him curious about me.

"What's your name?"

I felt like I was in a Rumpelstiltskin fairy tale. Even my fake name felt unsafe in his hands...whoever this guy was. I waited...desperate to get out of the question. Perhaps if I waited long enough, Mak would show up and save me.

"Name?" It sounded like he shifted on the leather.

Keeping my eyes on the open velvet curtain, knowing Mak was somewhere out there and at the ready to keep me safe, I muttered, "Murphy."

The guy behind me let out a resigned sigh. "You remind me of someone…that sweatshirt…"

My throat squeezed tight. It felt as though I had swallowed dirt. How did he know this sweatshirt? The only identifiable piece he could have seen was the name on the back…right? No, the logo for Rake Forge Racing was on the back, and his name had mostly peeled off. I exhaled a relieved, silent breath realizing he must have been referring to the location.

"It's a common place here in Rake Forge."

"Right…well if you see Mak, tell him his appointment is here."

I nodded, even if the guy couldn't really see, and then exited the space. As soon as I was clear of him, my lungs seemed to expand. I rushed back to my place behind the bar and grabbed Mak's wrist.

"Someone is back in that room, Mak. I didn't see him, but he said to tell you your appointment is here, what does that—"

Just as I was about to finish my thought, a barrage of men wearing long coats sauntered in. A few had on tuxes, but most just wore black jeans, black combat boots, and dark jackets. It didn't take a genius to know what lay beneath their coats. Most families that walked in through those doors wore leather jackets that didn't go past their waist. Every single man in this outfit wore a long black overcoat.

Which meant they had heavy artillery underneath.

At least ten of them walked in together, and there at the front of the pack was someone I'd have recognized anywhere. In my sleep. In my nightmares. In a crowded room.

I'd have known Scotty anywhere.

With the way his eyes narrowed on me and he changed trajectory, it seemed he recognized me too.

CHAPTER ELEVEN

Rylie

I watched in horror as Scotty's feet carried him closer and closer to me. I wanted to close my eyes again, like I had in the room with that man, but instead I planted my feet and decided to weather this interaction like I would a rogue wave trying to uproot me from my toes up.

He pointed a finger at me while half of his men moved to the back and the other half waited for him. "Stay away from the back—it's the only warning you'll get. If I see you snooping or trying to make your way back there, I'll put a bullet in your brain."

I didn't say a single word, even as tears threatened to fall, even as my chest was screaming at me to release the breath I was holding. His eyes held a warning I didn't understand but wouldn't argue with. He saw me for the first time after three some odd years and immediately threatened my life…what the fuck did that mean?

After they'd gone back, Mak came up to me with a worried expression.

My hands shook as I grabbed for two shot glasses, seeing there were orders that were in and hadn't been filled.

"What the fuck was that about, Murph?" Mak asked, standing close to me.

I wished we could go back in his office, just so I could calm down or melt down in private. As it was, there were patrons everywhere, the bar packed full of people waiting on drinks and watching the fight on the big screen above me.

"Just forget about it, Mak."

I moved around him, grabbing the vodka.

He grabbed my wrist and pulled me off to the side. "That is one of the most dangerous men I've ever known in my life. How does Scotty Ventrelle know who you are?"

Ventrelle…how strange that I had never once asked what Kyle's mother's maiden name was, or just in general known Scotty's. The man had constantly been around while Kyle and I grew up.

"I used to know his nephew…a long time ago. He must think I'm the reason the guy took off, I don't know." I shrugged.

That theory had some merit. If Kyle had abandoned everyone including his uncle, maybe Scotty thought I was the cause.

"Well maybe you should get out of here." His hold lessened as his face turned contemplative.

"We both know that's not possible. Trixie is a no-show, and Raven wouldn't come in to cover even if you offered her double the wage. I can stay. I'll just be sure to stay up front."

Mak let out a sigh, running his hand through his hair. "Okay, just be aware of what's going on, yeah?"

I nodded; we both knew that was code for *Be on the lookout for shit to report back to your dad.* I continued working on drink orders as another massive group of men made their way through the edges of the club. These men wore suits, no coats, and they all looked like they'd just stepped out of *GQ* magazine.

I watched, flicking my gaze to the man in front then to the man in the very back, and I realized the man who'd just entered was Markos Mariano, the head of the Mariano family…a huge player my father constantly had his eyes on.

The men moved like water, all in unison as they ventured toward the back. Not one of them looked at me, and I couldn't have been more grateful. I just wanted to disappear, maybe slip through the cracks in the floor until I was back in my bed, watching Netflix.

The night moved on. Vega fought and won. He came for his drink, but this time I wasn't flirting or doing anything at all to encourage him, and it was obvious that he noticed.

"You seem down." He sipped his vodka cranberry.

The neon lights glowed against the darkness of the upper section of the bar, as opposed to closer to the cage where the lights were on and the crowd was thick.

"Just a hard night." I loaded the massive pile of dirty glasses into the small dishwasher and pressed start.

"Want to talk about it?"

Obviously not if I'd told him the bare minimum of details, but what the heck? Why not.

"I had a crush on you. Dressed all cute to try to finally get you to ask me out."

His wince was confirmation enough that Mak had been telling the truth. It wasn't that I thought he'd lied or anything, but I was still holding out hope that maybe he'd been mistaken.

"Murphy...I'm so sorry, I never meant to..." His light eyes widened with concern, his hand going to mine on the bar top.

"It's Rylie."

His eyes narrowed. "What?"

"My name...it's Rylie. Figured you should know since I daydreamed about boning you."

His laugh rolled through me like a summer wave.

There was movement in my peripheral, another customer trying to flag me down for a drink. I let out a sigh and smiled at the man in front of me. "For what it's worth, I'm really honored to be your friend, even if we never do anything more than talk."

His smile was generous and broad. "Well, for what it's worth, Rylie, if I weren't in a relationship, I would have asked you out months ago, and I wouldn't have stopped until you said yes."

I laughed right as the person trying to flag me down slammed something hard against the counter.

Fuck. I hated when customers got all bitchy about me noticing them. I was on my fucking way. I spun on my heels, a smile already in place to help calm down whoever the tool was.

"How can I help y——" My light tone tapered off as my eyes took in who stood in front of me.

Dark, brooding features peered up at me from a pair of blue eyes encased in dark lashes. My mind tugged, and pulled at the vision, practically forcing my feet to move on their own.

"Do I…" I stammered, feeling a blush creep up my face as the question burned in my mouth like acid. I knew him. I'd know him in the dark, without a single trace of light to see by…and yet I felt like I didn't know who this person was at all.

The man was hunched over the counter, hiding his true height, but something sparked under my skin, making my heart pound in an angry rhythm against my chest. My senses screamed at me to go to him…plunging into my soul that the universe had finally brought my best friend back to me. Deeper down, self-doubt warned me not to hope. It harassed my heart at the prospect of taking this and actually believing that it could be him.

If it were Kyle, he'd be smiling at me, jumping over the counter to sweep me into a hug. If it were him, he'd have already wrapped me in his arms and stuck his nose into my neck, asking me how I've been. A lump the size of a golf ball wedged itself into my throat as I realized I was still chasing a ghost.

The man at the bar tilted his head like he was expecting me to do a dance or say something cute.

"I was hoping to get a round of shots, for the back."

His request was a loud clanging chorus of mockery, proving it wasn't him. He didn't recognize me.

Realization dawned, forcing my eyebrows up in surprise as I released the notion that this man was my friend. Instead, I wrapped my mind around the fact that this was the guy who'd snuck in through the back. My palms instantly began to sweat, along with my heart trying to escape my throat. He emanated danger, but my body seemed to react in the opposite way. Instead of hiding, I wanted to push the longer strands away from his eyes and see him under a bright light. Did Scotty have another nephew stashed away? This guy…*it was Kyle. My Kyle.*

But it couldn't be. He was so different.

My feet moved. "Yeah, sure, no problem." I grabbed glasses and accidentally dropped one.

He let out a small, mirthless laugh. "Did you just start or something?"

His voice slithered down my back like a warm caress, screaming at me to remember. It was there in my mind, in the back, digging and digging…something was burrowing out of the deep recesses, telling me I knew him.

Not him. It's not him. I tried to remind my heart in a soothing way so that it wouldn't break again.

"Sorry, I'm a little off my game. Your boss threatened me and told me to stay out of the back. I assumed he didn't want me to see your face." My eyes flicked his way briefly.

My stomach muscles relaxed as I watched him. Something about him made me feel at home, comfortable…with him looking off to the side, it allowed me a moment to fully take in what he wore. A tight black dress shirt covered his lean chest, the sleeves rolled up and revealing dark tattoos that marred every inch of skin, down to the length of each finger. His hair threatened to cover his eyes but wasn't so long it went past his ears. It was inky black, which looked amazing against his olive brown skin, and under the neon lights, it made his blue eyes pop, especially against the dark eyeliner he wore.

The person I had still been subconsciously hoping for, drowned in ash, reminding me once again that I was wrong. This man had the wrong eye color, the wrong hair color…everything was wrong, and yet his presence was as familiar as my own shadow.

This man had a defined jaw that was as menacing as his aura. All in all he was hot, broody, and dangerous—exactly the person my mother had warned me not to fall for when I was young.

"Those kinds of men break hearts, usually bank accounts, and, if you're not careful, your very soul. Stick to the man who makes you feel like you have the sun under your skin. Trust me…when you get older, it's nothing but rain clouds…you're going to need someone to be your sun."

"He threatened you how?" the guy asked, his eyes swinging back to me. The way he watched the room wasn't out of curiosity; he seemed to be looking for a threat.

His posture hadn't changed; his elbows rested on the bar top, his body leaning forward while people seemed to make their way around him.

I shrugged, my face on fire. I felt like a preschooler tattling on my bully. "It was nothing bad, just warned me not to go in the back for any reason."

The man let out a sound, something so dark it was like it had been pulled by a rusty chain that was locked somewhere inside him, like the sound had been waiting forever to break free and now it was all worn and rusted. It was about as terrifying as hearing the rumbling of a volcano about to erupt, a wave crashing into the sand. I set a tray of shots in front of him and hoped he wouldn't mind that I was forcing him to take them back.

He laughed. "I'm not carrying these." Then he stalked off, and I was left standing there, gaping.

I had just told him what his boss said—I wasn't going to follow him.

He must have noticed, because a few feet away he stopped and turned toward me.

"Come along."

Fuck this guy. I wasn't a puppy.

I shook my head and turned away.

If it were quieter in the club, I probably would have heard him scoff or his boot scuff the floor as he returned to the counter. "Wow, figured you'd have to have a spine to work in a spot like this."

His mirthless laugh skittered down my back again.

The shadows in the room played against the planes of his face, morphing him into a sinister-looking thing. His dark hair against his tanned skin, the dark swirls of ink that clung to his arms…I suddenly felt very cold.

"Your boss seemed really serious."

Blue eyes of pure destruction flashed in anger. "Spoiler alert, princess—I'm the boss, not him. Now let's go, and lose the fucking hoodie. It makes you look like you're thirteen."

My face was going to melt. I was demanding a security guard for my post; I didn't care what Mak said. I needed one too. One second, this man made me shake, made me feel completely unsettled and a little bit like I was about to die, like the Grim Reaper had suddenly taken interest in me and wanted to see if I was dumb enough to follow him back to hell. The next moment his expressions were softer, as if he were coaxing me to relax...and it worked. I felt at peace, comfortable, ready to step in between the teeth of the wolf.

It was on the tip of my tongue to tell him to fuck off, to stand my ground as I had with Scotty when he walked up to my face and threatened me, but just as I gathered the breath to deny him, I saw the token he'd left behind on the bar where he'd been standing moments ago.

There outlined in all black, which stood out so strongly against the white background, was the emblem of a joker.

It was the card I'd handed to my dad...

I sucked in a sharp breath as a new kind of fear gripped me and forced my body into compliant movements. I pulled at the hem of my sweatshirt with shaky hands, fumbling with it as it went up over my head. Mak would be pissed when he saw me walk in, but that failed to compare with what Scotty would do. This guy was signing my death certificate.

I had no idea how to get out of it, or what I could do to get this man's attention off of me. If there were another server available or someone who could take the tray back...something told me even if there were, he wasn't letting me out of this. It was a power play.

I turned my back on him, about to toss the sweatshirt under the counter, into my work cubby, when I heard the man mutter a few curse words from his spot above me. I stood, trying to fix my hair, feeling like a complete idiot that this entire outfit had been worn just to impress some guy with whom nothing would ever happen.

I gripped the tray, made my way around the bar, and followed after the man in front of me. The dark room swallowed him, a few neon lights bouncing off his face here and there, his defined cheekbones and jaw glinting in the light. He was tall, too...over six feet easily. He never looked back once, as though he knew I would follow simply because people didn't ignore his instructions.

My breathing seemed too loud, especially as my ears thrummed with my erratic pulse. My hand was sweaty, so I gripped the tray with more force, which caused one of the shots to tip over. I sucked in a breath when the man didn't stop to look back or berate me.

I wanted to cry. I wanted to run, but none of that would happen as he held back the black velvet curtain.

CHAPTER TWELVE

"Come on in, don't be shy." I taunted this fumbling, terrified girl who didn't recognize me. It made sense now, why my uncle had put up such a fight about me going to grab the tray of shots. I was curious about the girl in a hoodie I'd last worn in my best friend's bedroom, the night we fucked each other into oblivion.

She reminded me of my Rylie, so I wanted to see her again. Scotty threw a fit, a fucking tantrum fit for a toddler wearing a goddamn tiara.

It only intrigued me more, and now I knew why.

She was *my* Rylie, and she had no fucking clue who I was.

Of course, that made my jaded heart flip me the middle finger with a big, fat *Serves you right*.

How could she not recognize me? I thought for a second that she had… but no, she treated me like a customer. A stranger. Sure, I might look a little different now…my hair was longer, darker…my skin had more color because we'd just spent the weekend in Florida… and yeah, I guess I was wearing colored contacts and eyeliner, but I was the same guy she'd known since she was seven years old. It was me, standing right in front of her, and she had no fucking clue.

So, of course I wanted to show her off to Scotty. Let him see that she didn't know me, but also, I wanted to see his face when he realized I knew he'd threatened her.

I watched her as she moved in front of me with the tray. Her back was on display with measly black scraps holding up the fabric she called a shirt. Her tits were pushed together, and the deep cut in the front left nothing to the imagination. It made me wonder if she'd gotten cold feet about wearing it since she was in that hoodie.

My hoodie.

But then I remembered overhearing her little conversation with that guy…she'd dressed cute for *him*, wanted to fuck *him*.

Rylie made her way in, setting the tray on the table, forcing her to dip down in front of her boss, Mak. His eyes widened when he saw her, which made me curious about their relationship. I noticed a few shots had toppled over, which meant she was nervous.

I looked over at Scotty, who looked like he'd just found out I murdered his dog.

He fucking knew about her.

He fucking knew, and he might die for it.

"What was your name again, miss?" I asked, taking a seat next to Scotty. This was funny, a big-ass practical joke that she didn't recognize me.

She wet her lips, darted her eyes once to Scotty. There was the lie.

"Murphy."

I snapped my fingers. "Such an interesting name."

I wanted to jump up and yell in her face that I knew why she had picked that name. Her childhood dog was named Murphy, and after he died, Rylie had carried his name around her neck in the form of a dog tag, something I then turned into a project in metal shop, attaching it to a leather band so she could properly wear it around her neck.

Scotty narrowed his eyes on her, more than likely silently warning her about not coming back here.

"Pretty name for a pretty girl," I quipped, leaning forward to grab a shot. "You have a boyfriend?"

I was being shitty and reckless, but Scotty had tried to keep her away from me, and she didn't recognize me…so it felt like two bullet holes were lodged in my heart at the moment, and I wanted everyone to feel the pain.

"I…" She darted her eyes to Mak, who cleared his throat then shook his head.

He stood a second later, putting his hand on Rylie's elbow. "Sorry gentlemen, I realize there might have been a mix-up, but Murphy doesn't do anything here but serve drinks. She doesn't dance, strip, or tell anyone about her personal life. I'm going to have her head back to the bar." He gently nudged her toward the curtain.

I held up my finger. "Actually…I think I will have her answer the question first. Then she's free to walk back."

I already knew she didn't have one, but I liked seeing her squirm. I wanted her to remember me. I wanted her eyes to widen, wanted her to reach out and grasp my face, tug me to her, and demand to know where I'd been. I wanted her to cry, tell me she missed me. I wanted her to be mine again.

Rylie's eyes watered as she looked around the room, wringing her hands nervously. Mak clenched his jaw and seemed to silently communicate with her, nodding his head.

Suddenly Rylie took a step forward, clearing her throat.

"I don't disclose personal information to guests. Ever. I don't care who you are." She narrowed her eyes on me in a vicious manner, and it did deliciously painful things to my dick.

That right there, that sharp tongue, that bravery…that was my Rylie Jean.

I waved my hand, done toying with her, and watched as she scuttled back to the main room.

"Well, gentlemen…I think I've had enough talk for one evening." I stood, buttoning my jacket.

"But we haven't even talked terms yet," Markos whined, the fucking cunt.

I tugged a blade free, a gift from Juan Hernandez, then I took one of my calling cards and, with one swift movement, buried the blade, sinking it into my uncle's thigh. I tossed the card toward Markos, dismissing him.

I leaned over toward my uncle and whispered in his ear. "Did you honestly think you could keep me from her?" I twisted the blade as a few guys started gasping and murmuring behind us. "The blade is for threatening her. Be thankful it wasn't in your heart."

I stood and moved away from the man who'd essentially raised me, pushing through the back door and inhaling the scent of rain.

"WANT TO WRAP YOUR HANDS?" GARRISON ASKED FROM THE doorway, a worried expression on his face.

I shook my head. "Fuck off for a bit."

I never had any privacy in this house, in my life…for anything. We'd returned to the house about an hour ago after a silent car ride. Scotty had tried to pull me aside to discuss what happened, but all I could see was red. One blade to the thigh wasn't enough. I wanted him to hurt in the way I hurt, to feel how painful it was to see the person who meant the entire fucking world to you, only to have her threatened by the one man who'd vowed to protect you.

I slammed my fist into the bag, over and over, trying to push away the image of when she saw me and how there was absolutely nothing whatsoever in her gaze. Vacant…empty. I was no one to her.

It didn't help matters that she was somehow more stunning than she'd been three years ago. I had seen her from afar in between classes, but it didn't compare to seeing her eyes or the fresh freckles she had from the summer. She looked different now, so good it made it difficult to breathe. But that wasn't it…I knew what was inside of her, down deep under the fissures in her heart, and the blood in her veins. I knew this girl—her scar tissue had my name on it. She was mine; she always would be. No matter where she went or what she did, she belonged to me.

"Boss!" someone screamed for me, breaking my focus.

I turned to look, and Garrison stood there, holding a rag and a pained expression on his face.

"Your knuckles are torn the fuck up—take a break."

I looked down at my hands and realized he was right, but I couldn't find it in me to care.

"Just give it a rest for a bit. Gretta's going to cry again if she sees blood all over that bag." Gretta was our maid who'd followed us after Hungary. She was very tenderhearted, hated the sight of blood, and liked to give me lectures on being a good man every chance she got.

I nodded my head. I'd take a break for a bit; I probably needed it.

Instead, I hit the shower and thought over what the fuck had happened to garner that meeting.

We'd had a disagreement regarding distribution of product with one of our customers, meaning someone had tried to steal from me. The details had led me to Markos, which had resulted in me agreeing to a meeting with him.

The shit bag I'd nearly had to kill that day we broke into his compound to save Taylor. He was still thriving in Ivan's stead, gathering what crumbs he could with his easy smile and jawline. He was the darling favorite of the families, that was for sure, and I wanted him to die. Scotty said we couldn't just kill people because we wanted to, but again...I didn't see the harm in one measly bullet to the head.

It would resolve a complication.

So, we had ourselves a little meeting, in which nothing actually happened. Markos swore he knew nothing of the theft, and I swore I didn't trust him. Then he wanted to talk about a new opportunity and discuss terms. Fucking as if.

Flipping the knob on the shower, I got out and dried off and dressed. Once I exited my bathroom, I jogged back downstairs, having finally worked up an appetite. I was about to open the fridge but stalled when I spotted my uncle sitting in the dark, running his hand over his German Shepherd Bronson's head, pushing his ears back.

"I break it?" I turned away from his bruised face and the white tape across the bridge of his nose. I wouldn't ask about the leg. I knew he'd limp for a while, but he was fine.

His silence was louder than Bronson's panting.

I grabbed a bottle of water and slammed the fridge shut, eyeing the man who'd given up his life for me and protected me from the men who wanted my head on a platter. The man who spent time with me when my own father wouldn't. The one man who invested knowledge, skill, and confidence into my life. He was good to me, and with one wrong move, I'd stuck a blade through his leg and possibly broken his nose.

Shame threatened to drown me.

"You threatened her," I stated firmly, as if to reduce my actions down to something easily defendable.

"I wouldn't have hurt her…you know I wouldn't have." His quiet confession only made me angrier. I clenched my teeth and grabbed a bagel from the counter, content to eat it dry.

Shaking my head, I kept my eyes on the counter while Bronson whined, lowering himself to the floor.

"I haven't seen her in three years…not in any real capacity, and the first time, she's too fucking scared to even step foot back there because of something you said. How was I supposed to know you wouldn't hurt her, Scotty?" I shifted on my feet, stretching my fingers as rage coiled inside my chest. I had little tolerance for when people justified a fucking stupid decision with a presumption.

Stalking closer, I spoke in a voice I knew would set him on edge, but I didn't care. "This life we lead…this darkness and the shit we sort through every fucking day—a bullet in the head is just another Tuesday in our world. Why wouldn't I assume you'd do it?"

My uncle raised his gaze, allowing his dark eyes to clash with mine. His jaw was set, a familiar muscle jumping along the edge.

"Because she matters to you. She has always mattered to you, Kyle. I wouldn't have hurt her."

I stood, throwing the bottle of water against the wall. "Then don't ever stand in the way of me getting to her again. Don't try to cover it up by threatening her and then trying to make excuses for why I can't go grab a fucking drink."

Bronson lifted his ears but looked to my uncle for direction. He slowly stood, taking two steps closer to me.

"You're not just Kyle James anymore…you aren't her best friend. You've become an entire fucking empire. You can't throw away what you've built, what you've sacrificed for someone you knew a long time ago."

His voice began to rise as more emotion and conviction bled into his words. With each one, I began to feel my stomach tilt and my heart sink.

"The very fact that I had to get involved at all tells me how fucking wrong I was about you being ready for this. You saw her—she wore that goddamn sweatshirt like a day hadn't passed since you left!"

My heart thundered, remembering how she looked in her bed the last time I was with her.

"I stabbed you because you acted on your own orders today, and you know the score, Scotty. I'm the one who makes the calls. I'm the one who should have made that decision, not you."

He smirked, his lips twitching with the movement. "You stabbed me because she looked like one of Mak's Juicy girls, and then her pouting doe eyes looked to him for protection, not you. Fuck, she didn't even recognize you. And you know why, Kyle?" He stepped closer to me, and my chest was heaving so hard I let him cow me. "She's moved on with her life and hasn't passed up the chance to fuck other people while you were away. Unlike you, the pussy-whipped asshole who deserted her!"

My fist flew into his jaw, forcing his head to turn. My body trembled with rage. My raw knuckles radiated pain, but I pushed it aside. My uncle straightened, spitting blood on the floor but smirking at me again.

"You haven't kept tabs on her, but I *have*. Which is how I knew she'd be there, and how I knew to scare her off. I knew who in the club she's wet for on a regular basis."

I blinked, my heart thrashing in my chest as the image came and tore me in two. "Stop."

He only wiped at the corner of his mouth and drew closer. "I know how many men she's fucked over the past three years."

I sputtered, grasping the edge of the counter to avoid losing my footing. "Stop!"

"I know which dark corner of the bar she sucked her boyfriend's dick in. I know where she let him fuck her in public. Fuck, I even know how she sounds when she comes…why? Because she's your greatest fucking weakness!" He pushed me, and I had no fight in me to stop him.

I couldn't breathe. I was going to pass out.

He just kept going, tearing at my heart, removing it from my chest and squeezing all the hope out of it. He kneeled down, which meant I must have somehow fallen or moved. I wasn't standing anymore.

Scotty whispered, "Most of all, I know she isn't worth the fucking waiting and pining you keep doing. Let. Her. The. Fuck. Go!"

Shit, my face was wet. Were those tears? I shoved the palm of my hand into my eye socket and pressed until the moisture stopped and Scotty's fucked face stopped being the only thing I saw.

I had no idea how long I lay on that floor, ironically next to Bronson, Scotty's best friend. He lay his head down next to mine while I watched the room spin. I stayed there until the dark hue of the room transitioned to a bleak gray. He'd ruined me.

He knew it.

He knew exactly where to hit, what to say…and it was effective.

She'd moved on. She hadn't waited for me, and why should she have? The story I sold to her, the way I left…fuck, she'd have been crazy to wait around. Besides, we'd only taken each other's virginity so we could be with other people. I was the only one who'd caught feelings and decided I didn't want my dick in any other person again. I was the one who'd deemed her the only person to ever get to touch me in that way.

I was an idiot, and Scotty had just rubbed that shit in my face until I suffocated on it.

I blinked, hating how the reality of what he'd said needed to soak into my head. I needed to grasp it. She was gone…and no matter what happened, that version I had of her in my mind would never return.

CHAPTER THIRTEEN

ONE MONTH LATER

Scotty

"YOU CAN'T JUST MESS WITH THE ORDER OF THINGS—WE HAVE rules!" Delgado screamed in my nephew's vicinity. Spit coated his bottom lip, rolling down his chin.

I leaned against the wall, favoring my good leg, and counted. I calculated the number of breaths Holt took, I tallied how many times Delgado said 'Fuck,' and I counted how many times my nephew laughed.

Kyle was unnerving when he laughed, like this was all truly funny to him—the blood leaking from Delgado's fingers, the hole in his knee. Kyle wanted to appear unhinged; it helped build the character he played in front of the families...but sometimes it was difficult to piece together what was real and what wasn't.

And after what I had said to him last month...I had no idea how broken he was now. Our relationship had been tense and quiet for a few days. Kid made me feel like shit for hurting him so bad, but I had to remind myself that I was breaking his heart so he didn't ruin his future.

Kyle's long fingers wrapped around Delgado's face, forcing his eyes up.

"Which rules are you worried about specifically?"

"There are guidelines within these families, and we live by them. It keeps order within the chaos…you're shitting all over it," Delgado said through gritted teeth.

What a fucking moron. Did he honestly think the man in front of him didn't understand the intricacies of how a crime family worked? Kyle had been living and breathing this shit while he was on the streets of New York with me, every time his old man told me to take him with me.

Say what you will about my sister's dead husband, but he was a shitty man for allowing his son to be around me as much as he did, especially knowing what I was into. What did he think I'd do with my nephew? Go to the movies?

"See, that's just it, Don."

"My name is Lui."

Kyle shrugged, walking toward a table that held a few choice instruments used to extract information.

"You're all Don to me."

Delgado rattled his thumb up and down while Kyle ran his fingers over each tool. *Ten times. Eleven…twelve.*

Finally, Kyle turned. "I don't give a fuck about your rules. I report to no one, and I have no issues burning your entire family to the ground."

Delgado spit again, his eyes wild. "You'd go to war with that many families at once?"

My nephew smirked. Prideful—he was too fucking prideful.

"Sounds like a good time to me."

"You think you're so untouchable? You think there aren't men sicker in the head than you? We have feds in our pockets—you touch us, and you'll be burned."

Fuck.

"Which one, Don? Which little bird do you have singing for you?" Kyle grabbed a chair and spun it until he was straddling it.

I let out a sigh.

He shouldn't have mentioned the feds. It would only make Kyle think of his little friend who was now tied to them because of her father…which only reminded me that I should have stopped Kyle and

Rylie's interactions years ago; it would have saved me a goddamn headache.

Delgado spit again. This time it didn't even reach my nephew's feet.

Kyle shot him through the kneecap, forcing the man's face to twist in agony.

"Which one do you have on your payroll?" Kyle yelled, pointing the gun at Delgado's forehead.

The man bleeding to death fought against his restraints, turning his head from side to side. Kyle shot through the man's left hand; bits of blood splattered the front of Kyle's shirt.

"Tell me."

"Jackson..." Delgado breathed through the pain, barely able to get the words out. "Paul...has a daughter who works as a bartender at Deacon's. We're going to leverage her."

"What did you just say?" Kyle's voice quieted, dripping with rage.

Yeah, the fact that he knew about Rylie was fucking bad. My stomach suddenly tipped, like the floor was shifting...we'd worked so hard to keep her safe, to keep her away from all this. Kyle wanted her safe; I merely wanted her not to be a complication for him.

Delgado shook his head, fighting to breathe.

He'd thought he had gained the upper hand here...Kyle's reddening face only proved he had.

"He's desperate to prove himself as the rookie agent on the team, wants to crack a case with big players...it's too fuckin' easy. We're watching her...plan on bringing her in just so he keeps singing."

That was enough. I pulled my gun, the silencer barrel jutting out toward the man, and pulled the trigger.

The slug landed between his ear and the crown of his skull. His large body slumped forward while Kyle stepped back toward the table, shaking his head.

"He might have had more for us."

I repocketed my gun. "That was plenty."

"So they're watching Rylie?" Kyle threw a drill bit across the room.

I shrugged like I couldn't care less.

My nephew's jaw tensed, and he had that look on his face like he wanted to kill me. "Don't fucking act like that."

He was right, but he was also panicked, and I had taught him better.

"Get control of your emotions, Kyle. Delgado saw you crumble when he mentioned her. You do that shit in front of anyone else, they might start looking into her background, and you know they'll ultimately find you."

"No, they'll find Kyle…"

We moved out of the garage, through the doors, until we were heading toward the exit.

"Someone will connect the dots."

I pulled on the door, my eyes quickly assessing our property. We needed more men.

"Well shit, what do we do?"

I spun to face my nephew. "That wasn't the point of his little diatribe. The point was that they're trying to turn Rylie's dad…if he can be pocketed by one of the families, we're fucked. We need to find a way to stop it or turn him to our side."

Kyle looked down, tugging his Zippo lighter from his pocket. He opened and closed it. One. Two. Three. Four.

"He'll never come over to us if he knows I'm at the helm. Even if we can manage to convince him I'm not Kyle, he'll be turned off just knowing you're a part of it."

I grunted, knowing he was right. Paul Jackson was just as likely to shoot me as Juan was when I walked into his house.

"But…" Kyle clicked the lid open and shut another four times. "I might have an idea…and you're probably gonna freak."

Five. Six. Seven.

Click. Click. Click.

"I hate when you draw it out. Just say what you're thinking."

We walked shoulder to shoulder to the house, both of us watching the property. My left leg still had a slight limp from where he stabbed me, forcing my stride to falter just the slightest.

"If they're trying to pocket him, maybe we should try to get someone too."

My nephew tucked away his lighter once again and nervously ran his hand through his messy hair.

Pride surged in my chest as I realized he was starting to think like the head of a family. As much shit as he talked about burning down the rules and starting over, he was essentially sliding into the role of a mafia boss.

Problem was, we had no territory save for what we stole and no legacy to speak of. If he had an idea I wouldn't like, I had a feeling I knew who it would involve. There was only one place my nephew's armor was rusted over and cracked.

Rylie.

CHAPTER FOURTEEN

Rylie

"JUST COME OUT WITH US." HAZEL LEANED FORWARD TOWARD HER mirror, applying her mascara.

She had asked me for the past several Fridays to go out with her and a few other girls, but I had turned down each request. That wouldn't be changing tonight. As if I needed to show her my rejection rather than tell her, I rummaged through my dresser and pulled on my period sweats.

My best friend eyed me from her side of the room, raising her dark brow.

"So…that's a no then?"

Crawling into bed, I pulled my comforter over my legs and adjusted my laptop.

Her heavy sigh made part of my gut sink, but she didn't understand why I had to do this.

"Ry, it's been three weeks since you've gone anywhere besides class…you haven't even gone to the grocery store, much less work. You just keep eating microwavable food, and that shit is super bad for you."

"Hey, I eat food from the cafeteria." I snuggled more into my pillows and added, "Fresh food!"

She spun around in her small desk chair. "Why though? What the hell happened at Mak's?"

She knew bits and pieces of what had happened, but not the whole thing. Truth is, as soon as I left the room that night at Deacon's, I ran. I grabbed my things and ran home, getting a text from Mak hours later telling me not to come back—not because he was mad, but because he was worried about me. I knew it. He knew. He even confirmed it when he met me for coffee two towns over.

"Somethin' was off with that guy…he's the most dangerous guy out of all the families I deal with. He has more money, power, and leverage than anyone else. Strangest thing? He doesn't belong to a family name…not a single one. People pay outrageous amounts of money just to have an audience with him, and for whatever fucked-up reason, he took an interest in toying with you, like a goddamn cat and mouse game. Keep your eyes open, and don't come back for any reason."

I'd told Hazel that Mak wanted to hire one of his girls from Juicy to be stationed there, said it would be better for money to have someone who would be a little more willing there at the helm. Mak told me to tell Hazel this lie so she would stay away too. He knew she'd go and talk sense into him about hiring me back unless it was something that would keep her away forever, and Juicy's was the only unredeemable thing about Mak in her eyes.

I knew Mak wanted Hazel, but he knew the life he led wasn't good for her, and he was always in danger with the connections he made at his clubs. I couldn't stop thinking about Scotty, or how he was out there, watching for me to mess up or turn him in. The second I left my room, he was probably going to kill me.

"Nothing, I'm just trying to stay focused." I moved my finger over the mousepad on my laptop and made a selection on Netflix.

Hazel was suddenly there, peering over my shoulder, scoffing. "Yeah, real focused, Ry."

I let out a little laugh and shrugged. "I just don't want to go out, okay?"

"But why?!" Hazel threw her hands in the air and practically stomped to her side of the room, digging in her purse for her lipstick. "You were my wingwoman, my ride or die, and suddenly you're Miss Recluse…what gives?"

I felt guilt threaten to smother me as she continued her rant. If our roles were reversed, I'd be just as angry…we'd known each other too long not to tell each other the truth, but saying it out loud made it real.

"Is it about that guy, Vega?"

My eyebrows rose at her conclusion; I'd nearly forgotten I had been trying to impress him. "No…he's actually gay, and I think he might even be in a relationship right now. He was super sweet about letting me down easy. It helped that Mak gave me a heads-up."

"Then I don't get it—what changed?" She threw her hands up in frustration.

I didn't want to argue, but I also didn't want to sit here and discuss this because if I did come clean, Hazel would force me to talk to my dad and tell him about Scotty, and I wasn't ready to do that.

"Leave it, Haze, please?"

I returned my gaze to my computer screen, ignoring the vibes she was giving off.

"I can't. I'm calling your dad if you don't come out for at least an hour."

My gaze collided with hers, my mouth gaping. "You wouldn't!"

Narrowing her focus on me, she pulled her cell phone up as if to demonstrate that she very much would call my dad. "I'm worried, Ry…you know how I am when I worry."

Fuck, that was exactly what I would have done if she was pulling this and her dad was an FBI agent.

Swinging the blankets off, I sputtered a few cuss words as I began to pull off my oversized sweater and period sweats.

"I'm not putting any makeup on or doing my hair!"

Hazel laughed, slow-clapping my tantrum. "Fine by me."

I pulled on a tight black sweater that ended right above my belly button then ducked under my twin bed and tugged out the pair of jeans I'd kicked off earlier.

"And don't expect me to pay for a single fucking thing either." I pointed my finger at her with one leg shoved into my jeans. "*And* you'll buy me the fattest steak fries."

"Yes, Rylie, you can eat your weight in fries. Now let's go. Stace texted me that there are some hot-as-fuck guys at the pub tonight." Hazel pushed me toward the door even as I hopped, shoving my left foot into my Doc Martens.

Everything was a blur as Hazel rushed us down to our waiting Uber. I continued complaining the entire way so she knew how put out I was by this entire situation.

"I was looking forward to that TV show too. It's been on my watchlist for like a month."

I could practically hear my friend roll her eyes as she texted the other girls about where they were inside the pub.

The weather seemed to finally be cooling, so I tugged my leather jacket around me, crossing my arms over my chest.

"Don't even get me started on how cold it is outside. I was so warm under my covers."

Hazel let out an irritated groan followed by a sigh. "Ry, at least let me get drunk if you're going to keep going."

We pushed inside the packed bar, and the warmth slammed into my face and enveloped me, made worse by the packed bodies inside. It was difficult to maneuver around the tall guys all huddled around the massive flat screen watching a college football game.

"Stace is in the back, Ava and Kass are in the bathroom, I guess. Stace says she's got some sexy company though."

I rolled my eyes but followed after her, setting my mind on the fries and cider I was going to be ordering. A circular pine booth sat near the back of the bar. A petite blonde with long hair and big blue eyes was already on one side, staring down at her phone. Stacey had a fruity margarita in front of her, as per usual, and absolutely no food. Hazel slid in first, letting me have the open space on the end.

"Oh my god, you got her out of the house?" Stacey's berry-colored lips formed an annoying O shape. I was tempted to tell her to go fuck herself with that energy but settled for a fake smile instead.

"Don't be a salty bitch, Ry," Hazel said, reading my expression too easily.

Stacey let out a fake laugh then emptied her drink by tilting her head back, her mouth gaping around the glass. Moments later, she pursed her lips while waving her hands furiously at us. "Oh my god, he's coming back—holy shit, he's the hottest guy I have ever seen with my real eyes, so don't fuck this up for me." She pointed her manicured finger at me. "I'm talking about you, Rylie."

I waved her off, tugging my cell free, content to check out with my AirPods and the Netflix show I had planned on watching. My eyes were on my phone, my brows crinkled as I scrolled through title after title, when suddenly there was a shadow looming above me. Out of the corner of my eye I saw a tattooed knuckle dragging a chair, untucking it from the lip of our table.

My thumb hovered over a title. I held off pressing down, considering the show compared to another I was wanting to see.

"Baby, you don't need a chair—just squeeze in next to me," Stacey whined.

I didn't look up for fear they'd pull me into their conversation. I wanted to give the illusion that I wasn't available in any capacity this evening.

The man sank into the chair next to me like a midnight shadow, emanating fear and power.

"I'm good." His voice was familiar but muffled with me having one earbud in.

I wanted to look up, but Stacey got possessive of her dates, especially if there weren't any other guys present to offset our wandering eyes. I thought back to when we were in the room and Hazel mentioned that Stacey was with a few hot guys tonight.

Eyes still on my phone, one AirPod tucked into my ear, I asked, "Where are all these hot guys Hazel promised would be here?" I wasn't really interested in the answer, but it would give me a timetable to work with for how much longer I'd have to shut out the people at the table.

"They're waiting for the other—" Stacey started but was cut off by her date.

"What's the matter, Rylie Jean? You worried about having someone to fuck this fine evening? Need someone to warm that rancid bed of yours?"

That voice.

That nickname.

My heart slammed into my chest as I processed hearing my name spoken in that timbre again…it was deeper now, darker. Like sitting in the dark, all alone, only to have someone suddenly speak your greatest fears to you. *Startling…unsettling.*

My eyes slowly traveled up to the man who'd pulled up the chair…Stacey's date, presumably.

Hazel's sharp intake of breath from my right told me she either had just realized who was sitting with us or was about to stab him for being so goddamn rude.

Stacey stared at him adoringly, completely oblivious to what had just transpired, and his eyes…those blue eyes that were once green, ones I had loved my whole life…they were trained on me, devouring the sight of me as though I were an apparition about to disappear into thin air any second.

My stare stayed on his familiar face…not the face of the boy I grew up with or the one who took my virginity…but the man from several weeks ago in the bar.

The Joker.

Fuck, I knew it was him, deep down I knew…but how could he pretend that he didn't know me? He'd been standing there in front of me, talking to me, toying with me. He'd known it was me, and he had thought it was funny to play with me like I was a field mouse and he was a spoiled house cat. Being ghosted for three years was a special kind of pain, but then being found and released just as easily hurt on a level I hadn't realized was possible.

He'd known, and he'd waited a month to come and see me.

Fuck, he wasn't even seeing me now…he was just…

A tight knot wound its way into my throat as I realized he was here with Stacey, on a date. He'd merely stumbled upon me like you would a lost hair tie or a sock you lost months ago and finally found under the dryer.

Heat infused my cheeks and neck as I began to process how badly Kyle had hurt me all those years ago, and seeing him now was like ripping the stitches open with a butterfly knife. *Careless.* He'd left me, and he's seen me a month ago and left me again.

Clenching my teeth tightly together, keeping my rage locked up tight, I briskly exited the booth, bypassing his tall form folded into the wooden chair. My previous best friend snickered, tipping his tall glass of beer back as though I didn't matter...as though he was completely unaffected by this reunion.

Tears welled in my eyes before I could even fathom shutting them down. Stacey began murmuring something about me, asking Hazel what was wrong as I walked away. I was free of the table without extending so much as a backward glance, then I was off, shoving my way out of the bar.

Once outside, I inhaled a sharp breath, but it wasn't enough. I needed another and another, until my hands were on my knees and I was hunched over, straining to get air into my chest.

Minutes later—I had no idea how many—a hand was on my back, soothing me as I hyperventilated on the sidewalk. There were people everywhere, which was why I hadn't wanted to come out tonight. It was a Friday night in Rake Forge, and the college town went crazy during football season.

"Calm down, Ry. Just breathe," Hazel encouraged softly in my ear, but all I could hear was the pounding of my blood.

Coughing, I straightened, swiping at my eyes.

"It's him, Haze. It's Kyle."

Hazel looked at me like I was crazy, shaking her head. "Honey, that's not Kyle...that's Tom or something. Kyle had brown hair, and it was always cropped short, and he had green eyes. Have you seen that guy? His was dark, almost midnight black, and it was longer. He has blue eyes, and the tattoos on his hands...besides, Kyle has social media, and he posted something yesterday from London or somewhere."

I shook my head frantically and pointed back toward the bar. "That's him, Haze. I swear it."

"Sweetie," she murmured placatingly, bringing her arms around me. "I know you miss him. I know this is a hard time of year for you."

I pushed her off. She didn't know about the bar. She didn't know how dangerous he'd become, or how he'd left me and, upon finding me, walked away again.

Ducking my face, I pushed the hair off my forehead with shaky hands and gave Hazel a watery smile.

"You're right. I think I'm just going to grab an Uber back to the dorm."

Her brows dipped with concern. "You sure?"

I hooked my thumb over my shoulder. "Yeah. Text you when I get there."

"Okay, be careful."

I was already turned around, walking away. I wouldn't be grabbing a ride though. I needed to walk and clear my head. For the past three years, I'd mourned my best friend as though he'd died because he had left my life so completely it felt like he had. Hell, for all I knew, he *had* died and no one had ever told me.

Regardless of how often I had shown up at Kyle's house, seeing Decker and Mallory live their lives there, I never got any information out of them. I did hear that Decker's mother decided to move to Arizona to be with her two sisters, so it was just the married couple living there now. When I'd ask about Kyle on Christmas or on his birthday, the answer was always the same. *He's in Europe, no plans to return.*

I crossed my arms over my chest tightly as the wind picked up, brushing against my skin. I crossed the street, heading toward the dorms. They were just a few blocks from the pub, and I didn't mind the walk. I was still trying to process what had happened, still struggling to keep the sob creeping up my throat at bay.

I was halfway across campus when I heard a clicking sound from up ahead. The orange cherry of a cigarette lit up the dark, someone perched against the tall statue, all shadowed and protected from the safety lights.

I knew it was him, and I hated that I suddenly felt like I could relax…only because deep down in places I would never be able to look at or access with clarity, I knew Kyle James would never physically hurt me.

"You ran off, Rylie Jean…something spook you?" he asked, still leaning against the statue, clinging to the shadows. My throat itched to scream that he wasn't allowed to use my nickname anymore, wasn't allowed to act like he knew me at all anymore.

I kept my arms crossed, but my boots carried me forward...closer to him. One step.

Two.

Three.

"I really hope you don't walk across campus by yourself often, because that would be stupid and really dangerous." He blew out a plume of smoke. "Then again, a girl like you who works in an underground fight club probably isn't afraid of getting kidnapped or raped."

His boots scuffed the cement as he kicked his foot backward, pressing the tip of his toe into the ground, his heel at the base of the statue.

I took another step closer, completely entranced by the look of him. He'd changed so much in the past three years, I should have went with my gut that night in the club. Even if all his features had been lost to the shadows in that place, I should have known. He wore a jacket tonight, but I could see the tattoos along his hands and fingers, which made me think of the ones that covered the expanse of his arms. He had that longer dark hair that fell to his eyes, and his clothes seemed to fit him perfectly while remaining slightly loose. Tonight, he had on black jeans, ripped at both knees, and a black scoop-necked t-shirt, snug under a light leather jacket.

He took another hit of his cigarette before sweeping his eyes up and down my frame. "Or maybe you always have one of those big-ass fighters on call to keep you nice and safe?"

My breathing bunched up, like a broken accordion unable to stretch to produce the intended note. His eyes burned with just as much rage and anger toward me, but I couldn't figure out why. He had left me. He'd abandoned our friendship the second I made him feel something. Just like I'd known he would.

"Nothing to say?" He mocked me, that devastating smile curving his mouth. It was broader now, fit to match his wider jaw. He looked like a full-grown man...that couldn't be right though; he was still just a boy.

I wondered what he thought when he looked at me. Did he see the pessimistic girl who used to text him at all hours of the night, asking if he thought aliens were invading? Did he see our childhood or how I looked into his eyes when he took my virginity? Maybe he just saw a stranger now.

I wanted to speak. I wanted to scream at him, force him to tell me where he'd been all these years, but I knew no matter what he said, it would never satisfy the flames burning in my chest and the anger gripping my soul at being forgotten. If he explained that he'd been in Europe or just needed to find himself, I'd likely push a pencil into his chest, or something equally as deranged.

Because he'd completely killed me when he left. I hadn't survived it. I was a shell, a ghost, and whoever he thought stood before him right now…it wasn't the girl he once knew.

His eyes narrowed and his nose flared as he watched me stand there in silence. He seemed to realize I wasn't going to say anything, especially when another mocking laugh left his chest. I didn't want to be dismissed by him again, didn't want to be left, so I turned on my heel and continued walking toward my dorm room.

I counted each step, breathing through my nose. I had no idea if he'd come after me or if he'd just leave, but I knew I absolutely could not talk to him without breaking down, which meant I just wouldn't speak to him at all. He likely wouldn't be around for long anyway, which would be fine. He'd leave again and forget me, and I could go back to living my life.

Just like before.

CHAPTER FIFTEEN

Rylie

I WAS RUSHING THROUGH THE HALLS, MY LEATHER MESSENGER BAG holding on for its life as it barely stayed in place on my shoulder. I hated being late and had made a point not to be these previous three years of school, especially to Dr. Carr's class. He was a criminal mastermind, specializing in things we shouldn't even have had access to until we decided to attend one of the academies. Seats were always difficult to find in his lectures, especially if you ended up being late. One time a student came three minutes after the lecture started, and there weren't any chairs left, so he had to sit on the ground.

As far as I knew, it was a major fire hazard and a school violation. Still, it happened more often than you'd think, and of course I had overslept, which caused the rest of my day to collapse like a stack of dominos.

Late. Late. Late.

Huffing out an exasperated breath from running at a breakneck speed, I swung the wooden door open and found an entire room of eyes turned, staring back at me. Dr. Carr, bless his soul, didn't even stop or waver from his flow of conversation. People began taking notes, and a slideshow popped on at the front of the room.

Scanning the room, it was easy to see that I'd be left without a seat, forcing me to sit on the steps, clogging the main artery of the room, or stand near the back wall and try to use the shelving as a table. Just when I was about to head toward the rear wall, a splotch of white caught my eye three rows down, four desks in.

An empty desk. A lone little unicorn amongst the mass of backpacks and laptops, and all I had to do was discreetly make my way past the students who were already sitting and ready to learn without making a huge scene or alerting Dr. Carr that I was seven minutes late to his class. He currently had his back turned to us while he wrote something on the board.

Decision made. I descended the stairs, careful not to stomp my discount Doc Martens as I went. There were a few grumbles as I stepped over open bags littering the space in front of each desk, but I ignored them. Finally, in front of the open seat, I was about to spin and plant my ass in the burgundy chair, but I stopped at the sight of a pair of unlaced combat boots crossed at the ankle, perched dead center in my spot.

My gaze drifted up the dark jeans, the rips in the knees, and the loose white shirt that clung to a lean, muscled form. Tattoos wrapped around his arms, spiraling all the way down each finger and across every knuckle.

My gut sank while my heart slammed into my throat, desperate for air to show the proof of all the scars littering the organ from the boy I once loved. They were like two magnets trying to disconnect from one another.

Green eyes on faux blue ones danced while we assessed one another. He had a row of beautiful girls surrounding him. One of them had her hand on his shoulder, while the one on the other side had her desk scooted so close to his it might as well have been in his lap. Her glossy, injected lips spread wide as everyone in the room slowly became aware of what was happening.

Kyle smirked while he chewed on the toothpick perched in the corner of his mouth. This was amusing to him, and the two girls clinging to him like plastic wrap giggled, one of them pushing her face into his arm.

I was going to be sick.

"What's wrong, Rylie Jean?"

He wanted me to speak to him, wanted to rattle me, but I still didn't know why. He had made his choice, and now he was back in my world, smashing it to pieces like he was some unearthed Titan.

I just stood there, staring at him...willing him to move so I could sit.

"Just ask it, Rylie. Open those pretty lips and ask me to move." His eyes danced with delight as he rocked his feet back and forth in the seat.

Why was he doing this? My face heated as I continued to stare and stare, wishing this wasn't real. As many times as I had hoped my best friend would come back to me, there was no way to accurately describe how painful it was to currently wish he'd just disappear.

"Miss Jackson, is there a problem?" Dr. Carr asked from his spot on the floor below. He did not tolerate disruptions, and I was about to be kicked out of my favorite class if I didn't do something. The problem was I knew if I asked Kyle to move, I'd just get rejected, and then I'd be embarrassed.

"No, sir...just trying to secure a seat," I replied, turning toward my teacher. His eyes were narrowed under a pair of thin glasses, his hand going to his hip as confusion swept over his features.

"You know my rules, Ms. Jackson."

I turned back toward Kyle; he'd opened his feet, bracketing the seat, indicating I should sit in between them. I didn't know if he thought my ass was miniscule or was still mocking me, but there was no way I'd fit in between them.

I rolled my eyes, irritated all over again because I wouldn't be asking him to move. I'd rather miss this class, which was like taking a tiny paper cut right across the heart.

I shifted back toward the aisle and moved up toward the back. The extra lurkers who'd come in after me took up any and all available space, so to avoid any more interruptions, I pushed the door open and exited the lecture.

I was sitting on one of the benches that faced the library. I liked it because the view was exceptional. The library was all gray stone and brass and gold windows, up three stories and surrounded by lush, green trees.

I felt like I was in a different world when I sat on this bench and stared at the old building. It held pieces of life from long ago within its walls, and each person who walked through its doors somehow left a piece of themselves inside too. It gathered memories, holding them and providing them for others to check out and thumb through. A gift and a curse, depending on which chapter of history you're poring through.

"Why this spot?" a raspy tone asked from somewhere behind me.

I recognized it now...I'd gotten used to the fluctuating timbre in his voice, the inflection he used when he was trying to hide his real emotions. That night in the bar he was a different person, hiding in plain sight. This version of Kyle was the one I remembered.

It was on the tip of my tongue to repeat back what I'd just been thinking, to bring him into my world, get him up to speed on what he'd missed. Then reality hit, and my heart tanked down into deep, dark waters.

He soundlessly shifted, only made known by the way his presence suddenly shifted...his body was beside me within the blink of an eye. "I would watch you sometimes...once I moved back, I knew you were still attending here, so I would watch you in between classes, but I could never understand why you chose this bench. What makes it so special? The other ones over there face the fountain." His finger darted past my face, but he might as well have shoved it into my chest with enough force to stop my heart. He'd not only returned, but he'd watched me. He had seen me at school, had been close enough to call my name or run up and hug me.

Yet, he'd stayed away.

"Those over there are closer to the beverage carts." This time his finger darted in the opposite direction. "This one is directly in the sun, no shade, and narrow as fuck."

I continued staring at the library wishing I could disappear and be set free of this pain he'd stirred up. Seemed he was always kicking up dust and ash, forcing it down my lungs and into my eyes. Anger fought for dominance in my mind as I tried to process the elation of knowing he hadn't died. Revenge was right there on the cusp of my movements and actions as I worked through what he'd done since we'd been back in each other's orbit. Why come to me now?

What was he gaining from this?

"You can't hold out forever, Ry. I know you want to know about the past few years…I know you're curious about the club incident. I'm here…I'm back. Just ask."

Was he beginning to crack?

He had been all venom and ice since the pub, and now he wanted to talk about park benches?

No. I wouldn't do that.

I stood, gathering my notes and books. Dr. Carr had been sweet enough to do a live recording of his class, shooting me an alert to sign into the link just minutes after I had left.

"Rylie…" Kyle tried for my attention.

I ignored him, zipping my bag and tossing the leather strap over my shoulder. As soon as I took a step away from the bench, I felt hands on my hips. I was being lifted off the ground and tugged into a firm chest.

"I know what you're doing." He breathed against my ear.

I closed my eyes tight, though not tight enough to hold off the sudden tears clambering to be set free. His touch was fire against my skin, a stark reminder not to trust people because they would always let you down.

"You think you can be here and be apart from me? We share the same shadow, the same soul…you're in me, and I'm in you. That's how we haven't lost each other all these years…you're still mine."

Still mine. Not his best friend, not his person. Just his.

He spun me, forcing my eyes to shoot open. Our noses kissed, our eyes wide, watching each other. I inhaled a shuddering breath, my lungs burning right along with my eyes. He wanted me to speak, wanted to hear my thoughts…but I wouldn't give him the satisfaction. I slowly slid down his body until he towered over me, our bodies still flush, his hands a steel plate around my back.

He waited.

I breathed.

Then he moved, his lips crashing into mine in an angry panic. His tongue delved toward mine, swiping and claiming me in a way that transcended what we had that night we took each other's virginity. We'd kissed, but it was nothing like this. There were old places, flaring with need, begging me to accept the crumpled, broken, ruined dream he was offering.

But I couldn't.

I pushed at his chest, turning my head.

His breathing was erratic, eyes wild like he was watching someone steal from him. I pushed away the sensation to cup his jaw, to reassure him. He wouldn't have access just because I felt weak, just because I had loved him for most of my life. He was a calculating man now; he knew how to sniff out a weakness and exploit it. He was mine, still... and unfortunately probably always would be.

He stepped back then smirked. I knew he was going to hurt me the second he recovered, and instead of running so I wouldn't bear the blow, I stood there waiting for him to deliver it.

"You taste like my childhood...now I remember why I left it as soon as I had the chance."

I knew his words were blades now; it was the only way he had such power to wield over people. Still, I felt it cut deeply into an entirely new wound, one made of fresh hope that I was incapable of being hurt any more, especially by him.

Without responding, I turned away, pressing my lips together to keep in the sob creeping along my throat.

Then, once I found my car, I drove to the only place I felt I could be myself and free of him.

CHAPTER SIXTEEN

I DIDN'T HAVE TIME FOR THIS STUDENT BULLSHIT, SO THIS WHOLE meeting with my counselor thing wasn't going to happen, and neither was any class that didn't have Rylie in it. This entire plan was fucked, and I should have known better than to assume I could show up after three years and be able to talk casually with her

Fucking nonsense.

Of course I couldn't just act casual with her, not after what Scotty had pounded into my conscience about her...then seeing her up close. Fucking hell, I couldn't shake the visuals lacing my mind, all chock-full of Rylie fucking other men in illicit positions. Threaded in between every good memory of the girl I loved was the knowledge that I had pathetically waited for her but she hadn't done the same. Hell, the very night I saw her she was trying to get some fighter to fuck her. My jealousy was petty and entirely unwarranted, but I didn't give a single fuck. I was pissed, and now Rylie wouldn't talk to me. That just pissed me off further, making me desperate to get some kind of reaction out of her.

I'd settle for anything.

But I also wanted her to hurt.

I wanted her to burn the way I burned, to regret moving on with other men. I wanted her to feel my presence so strongly it threatened to bury her. I knew it affected her; words or not, that girl was all actions.

Shaky, shuddering, wide green eyes—action.

My phone buzzed in my pocket. Without taking my eyes off the baseball field where a bunch of players tossed the ball back and forth, I answered.

"Yeah."

"Do you have eyes on your little project?" Scotty asked, sounding perfectly calm.

Scotty would sound calm if he was held at gunpoint, so it was no indication of what was going on around him.

"Not anymore." The players' jerseys looked just like Decker's used to when he played for the Devils. In fact, they'd readopted the name after my sister-in-law broke open their secret society bullshit. Looking at them tossing that leather ball around just made me remember how many times my father didn't toss it around with me, only Decker.

Then he died before he could make that shit up to me.

Was I bitter?

No, I was *better*.

"She's back at the club, working."

I spun on my heel, my eyes narrowing on the dead grass at my feet. "The fuck?"

We'd kept an eye on Rylie's behaviors since we saw her that night, and we knew she'd either quit or been fired from the fight club. Which was good—I didn't want her ass there, not with the sort of men Mak catered to. Everyone knew his location at Deacon's was a neutral meeting place. It was preferable to his other joint Juicy's because easy pussy had the tendency to make men stupid and distracted.

Scotty didn't let out any sound to indicate he was alive. Meanwhile I was breathing like a sixty-five-year-old smoker into the receiver while I briskly made my way to the parking lot.

"I'm looking at her right now. I can solve this pretty easily…" He let his words trail off because he knew I knew what he was talking about.

"I told you we weren't doing that."

"No need to yell, Kyler. I was merely offering to simplify the situation."

I jumped down from a retaining wall, skipping several sets of stairs, and headed toward my car. "Nothing to simplify...I'll go get her, and I didn't yell."

"Yelling is a natural state of being for you. Does this mean your reunion went well?"

Fuck. I let out a frustrated sigh and tugged my car door open.

"Guess that means no. Do I need to remind you how important it is that we—"

"Scotty, you don't have to fucking remind me, and just one month ago you were telling me to stay the fuck away from her, so don't pretend you're exasperated by my inability to get her to *want* to be near me for more than two seconds."

He chuckled, the fucker.

I started the engine and pulled out of the lot, the phone still pressed to my ear.

"Are you laughing?"

"I just find it funny."

Funny that I was forced to shed the lining of my heart, losing her in the process? Yeah, fucking hilarious.

"I'll be in touch." I hung up, tossed my cell into the leather seat next to me, and gunned it to the other side of town. The sky was pink and orange, signaling the end of another pointless day. For the past three years, the days all seemed to join together like a comic strip, broken up by solid black lines and gaudy ink. A story could probably be found if anyone took the time to fill in the thought bubbles...but no one in my life would. It was all just bullshit.

Loud, annoying bullshit.

Mak's bar was in the abandoned warehouse district. An old lumber mill and two empty factories sat idle and in disrepair, stretching down the block. The sidewalks were just broken chunks of concrete, as were the parking lots. Deacon's was mostly just dirt, gravel, and some dead grass.

Yet it was packed full of cars, overflowing to the street. I found Rylie's little Toyota Camry in the employee parking area, which was on the opposite side of the building. I parked in the loading zone near the back and used the same entry point I had the night I had visited, using a Capener Chisel to prop open the locked door and slip inside. There was a security guard waiting for me, which was new. Rylie must have let it slip that I had let myself in through this entrance.

I looked at the burly man; he looked at me. He made a slight move forward but then glanced down at my fingers and stopped mid-step.

A red flush came over his sharp features before he swallowed. "Sorry, sir. You need anything?"

I smiled and dug out a few bills, handing them to him. "Just your discretion. Does Mak have any appointments scheduled this evening?"

The man shook his head. "Not tonight, just the fight."

Good, then there might not be blood shed tonight.

"But…" the guard continued, shifting on his feet, "there are supposed to be a few families attending the fight. He's a favorite of theirs."

Fuck.

"Who?"

"DeMarco."

Tonight wasn't my fucking night. "Little DeMarco, the baby of the outfit?"

He nodded. That meant the Rossi family would be here, and likely the Brambillas.

"He's fighting the Irish tonight."

"Shit."

This was going to be a bloodbath, especially if I showed up. I was the bastard usurper to every throne in the underground. At this point, nearly every family collectively wanted to kill me while courting my inventory behind each other's backs. The dirty mistress of each outfit, denied by all while each one slipped their business cards, phone numbers, and meeting requests into my uncle's waiting palm.

I needed to get Rylie out before any of them realized she was here, especially after what Delgado had said.

I stormed past the guard and headed for the bar.

Music thrummed overhead, indicating the start of one of the

fights. There were cheers echoing around the space, even from as far back as the far wall, where I was hiding in the shadows. Rylie was manning the bar, expertly pouring drink after drink. Another girl was with her, tag-teaming the massive crowd. There was a VIP section for the fights, even in a dilapidated shithole like this, which would undoubtedly be occupied by the families that had already arrived.

More security than normal seemed to guard the edges of the crowd, which wouldn't do shit for anyone that actually needed protection. Speaking of which, I wondered where my overprotective uncle was watching from. I doubted he'd leave Rylie to me. If he already had eyes on her, he had eyes on them as well.

I pulled my phone out and shot off a text to him, just so we were on the same page.

Don't know if you noticed, but DeMarco is fighting the Irish tonight, probably Quinn. It's a full-on fucking family reunion here…I'm trying to extract without notice.

I pocketed my phone, watching the bar. Rylie's movements were as fluid as water as she flipped, poured, and smiled. She acted completely unaffected by what had happened between us at the bench. I flicked my eyes to the crowd at her back, realizing she was also acting wildly calm for how many dangerous men currently filled the space. Something prowled behind my rib cage at the idea of her here, something dangerous with teeth and an appetite for blood.

I didn't want her here.

She laughed, tossing her head back. Her dark hair was a glossy wall as she moved, and men's eyes darted to where the long strands bounced against her back, nearly touching her ass. She placed a glass of whiskey in front of a guy our age. His eyes were mesmerized, especially when she leaned closer and whispered something in his ear. She spoke to everyone so freely…yet wouldn't utter a goddamn word to me.

I was desperate for those glossy, pink lips to open and her laugh to pour out of her, or to hear her thoughts on something random and depressing, like I used to. I wanted to hear her yell at me for the stupid cars I kept driving and tell me how bad the exhaust was. Fuck, I just wanted her voice to carry one word my way, just one.

I'd yet to hear her say my name, and it was killing me that she hadn't. Mostly because I didn't even know if I was still that guy anymore, but I felt like if she called me by it, I'd somehow come back to her...and to me. I'd discover where I'd gone for the last three years, because fuck if I recognized myself when I looked in the mirror. I almost laughed to myself as I realized not even Rylie had recognized me. I mean fuck if that wasn't the truth staring me in the goddamn face.

My phone buzzed with Scotty's response. I pulled it free and smirked.

Noted. Thank you for not trying to kill yourself. I'm assuming the best way to get her is through someone she trusts. That would be Mak in this scenario.

He hadn't said anything to hurt me like he had when he had rubbed in my face that Rylie had moved on, but his text felt like he'd twisted the proverbial blade still stuck inside my chest with that comment. She trusted Mak. Not me.

I hated admitting he was right, but if I approached her, she'd run.

The problem was Mak's current position was in the VIP section, talking up his clients.

So...that was a fucking problem, and I didn't have time for this shit.

I moved my neck from side to side, cracking it, and then decided I'd do what I did best.

Create a little chaos and piss everyone off.

CHAPTER SEVENTEEN

Rylie

I WAS ON PROBATION WITH MAK. IT WASN'T THAT I WAS IN TROUBLE or had done anything wrong, but he was worried about me. Upon arriving, I noticed right away that there were three new security guards roaming the space and one specifically placed by the back door. It made me feel marginally better, and it was nice that Mak was taking this, and me, seriously.

He hadn't spoken to my dad about anything yet and wasn't sure what he was going to say. If Dad became emotional about it, worrying and afraid for my safety, he might put me in more danger just by reacting wrong. It would mess things up with Mak too, and he knew as well as I did that the feds wouldn't be able to protect him against a downfall that big.

It was a busy night. Two fighters I didn't actually know much about were about to go head to head in the cage. They must have been popular because they were drawing in a crowd like I'd never seen. The VIP section was maxed out, Mak had his hands full with pacifying them, and Trixie and I were swamped with drink orders. Most of the regulars were forced to sit further back, the nosebleed section if you will, closer to the bar, which was great for tips but made us insanely busy.

"Ladies and gentlemen…" Mak's friend Trav began announcing the start of the fight with the microphone, the sound traveling into every nook and cranny in the bar. Finally, people began to disperse away from the bar top, drawing closer to the edge of seats that faced the cage. "Tonight, we have the privilege of seeing two fierce opponents battle it out in an extraordinary fight," Trav continued, and I took the opportunity to slip out and take a quick break.

His voice trailed me, talking about each fighter's attributes and home turf as I moved swiftly down the hallway, toward the back. Neon lights led the way to the private, employee bathroom that required a key. Just as I pulled mine out, someone's hand was over my mouth, pulling me backward, toward the rear exit.

I tried to scream and began kicking against my captor, but it was no use. They weren't hurting me, just scaring the shit out of me. The guard who was supposed to be on duty watching the door was gone, and no one would hear any commotion back here with the start of the fight and everyone cheering.

Just as we were about to head down the stairs leading to the back door, the lights went out.

It stalled my attacker long enough that I elbowed him in the ribs, and for one glorious moment, he let me go.

"Fuck."

I was already moving away, but he grabbed me again, this time by the hair.

I screamed, and then there was just so much fucking chaos. Someone yelled, but it was muffled by the bicep of the man who held me in a head lock. My boots scraped along the floor as he pulled my dead weight through the door until we were completely outside. It was a reprieve from the pitch-black, but I still couldn't breathe. My lungs had constricted so tight it felt like a tattered rope had been tied around them.

Suddenly our trajectory stopped. There was more yelling, and then my abductor let me go.

My elbow was snatched in a firm but not painful grip, and I was suddenly being pulled next to someone, into strong arms, all firm and lean muscle. The smell of Irish Spring soap invaded my senses.

It all rushed in at once—the sounds, the conversation, the parking lights, the scent of cigarette smoke and soap. I blinked, trying to catch up.

"You had no right. What the fuck are you doing?" Kyle thundered angrily. Something like fear and worry charged his tone, and it was like the past three years suddenly vanished. It was just the two of us standing shoulder to shoulder—against everyone.

"Calm the fuck down and get in the car," his uncle demanded, snapping me out of my nostalgia.

Wait a second…was it Scotty who'd kidnapped me? My eyes bugged out as I took in his dark overcoat, his black Henley, and denim trousers. My heart lurched…he'd warned me to stay away, threatened me. Movement from Kyle forced my eyes off his uncle.

He shook his head angrily, his firm jaw clenched tight. "I had it under control."

Did that mean Kyle had been planning to grab me? His anger toward his uncle was contrary to that line of thinking, but still, something was off with this entire scenario.

Scotty laughed, shaking his head, his graying dark hair shifting with the movement. "Taking out the lights…that was your big plan?"

Kyle lifted his free hand. "It would have worked…"

Scotty let out a sigh and briefly looked behind us. "We need to move."

I tugged my elbow, trying to free it from Kyle's hold. "I'm not going anywhere."

Kyle gaped, tilting on his heel to stare at me.

"She speaks."

Not to him. I kept my eyes on Scotty.

"Why were you kidnapping me?"

Kyle answered. "One of our…" He paused as if he were searching for the right word. "Clients happened to target you by name in one of our conversations. Seeing as at least three rival families are going to be here tonight, we wanted to be sure you were kept safe."

I laughed bitterly. "Bullshit."

There were gunshots echoing from inside, making my heart race indecently fast.

"What did you do?" I swung my gaze to Kyle. "Mak is in there, Trixie—people I care about!"

Kyle's eyes flickered with something as he narrowed his focus on my mouth. It only angered me more, but before I could say anything else, he pushed me toward a nondescript black car. Carefully pushing my head down, he encouraged me to get in the back. My hands weren't bound, and yet I knew if I tried fighting, it might just delay us...not stop us. Deep down I didn't believe Kyle would hurt me, and he seemed surprised that Scotty had tried to.

So, I slid into the car, and Kyle slid in next to me.

The car moved, the tinted windows protecting us from anyone seeing inside, and Kyle's arm brushed against mine from sitting too close. I tried to move away, to cling to the door, but his hand shot out, gripping my knee to pin me in place.

"Someone will need to come get both cars," Kyle explained easily, his uncle grunting his acknowledgment. It made me curious which of them was really in charge. I'd observed men coming in, how foot soldiers interacted with other made men. I knew about their hierarchy and who they reported to, and yet Kyle's relationship with Scotty didn't seem to make much sense.

I kept my face firmly toward the window as we passed by the front of the bar. People were running, trying to get to their cars. Some of them had bloody noses and scratches of various kinds, Mak was on the phone as he paced on the side of the building, and Trixie was huddled on the curb, her big lashes fanning her face as fat tears slipped free.

My heart wilted with the realization that I should have never gone back. Kyle had taken out the lights to get to me, and with so many volatile people in one space, he must have known what a blackout would do. Yet, even as I was angry with him, I knew the blame landed squarely on my shoulders.

I ducked my head, wanting to rest it on the glass so I could pass the time avoiding everyone in the car, but Kyle just held me in place, making it impossible to shy away.

So, I decided to close my eyes and allow the sway of the car to lull me to sleep. I woke up some time later, tucked under Kyle's chin and halfway sitting in his lap.

I immediately tried to shift out of his hold, but the way his arms were wrapped around me was like a vise, like if he let go, he'd never get me back. His head hung limp next to mine, his eyes closed. He was asleep. My eyes flicked forward for a brief second and Scotty caught my gaze in the mirror. I glared. He smiled, but it was a *fuck you* smile if I had ever seen one.

I sat there immobile, cringing at how my body was responding to being near Kyle again. It was like every other time I had ever sat on his lap: comfortable and safe. Like this, I could appreciate how different he looked, how grown up and how handsome. Honestly, though I would never tell him, he was a thousand times more handsome now than he'd ever been in his teenage years.

After what felt like forever, Scotty pulled the car to a stop outside a dark farmhouse. It was nearly pitch-black outside with zero lights around, save for one on inside the house. The more I looked, the more I realized how familiar it was.

"Why are we here?" Panic seized my lungs.

I had class tomorrow, work…although at this rate, Mak was not going to ever let me come back.

Scotty ignored me, opening and slamming the car door shut.

The sound made Kyle jolt awake. His hands immediately went to my hips, and when I thought he'd move me to the side, he just steadied me as Scotty moved around the outside of the car.

Alone in the back seat with my childhood best friend, I suppressed all the questions I had, irritated that my pride was so insanely big that I refused to speak to him. He must have sensed it, because he scoffed, letting out a small laugh while rubbing my thigh. Why he was even touching me, I had no clue. The kiss had proved he hated me, proved I had scared him off, yet here he was touching, grabbing, keeping me as if I belonged to him.

Scotty opened the door, moving so we could exit, and that was when Kyle finally let me go. I darted out, and without a single second to think, I started running.

I knew this property like the back of my hand, unless of course someone had built another structure in between ours or something, but I wouldn't be staying at Kyle's mother's house. Or Decker's— whoever lived there now. There was a measly acre between this prison and my dad, so I put every ounce of energy and effort into pumping my legs, going high in the knees to avoid branches and rocks.

My breathing was loud in my ears as my blood rushed and adrenaline pummeled through me. I had no idea what their plans were for me, but Scotty had straight-up tried to kidnap me, so there was no chance I was risking staying with them. I had cleared enough ground that I could see the porch light glowing from our back door.

This was close enough. I started screaming.

"Dad!"

I was able to get one scream out before I was tackled to the ground and warm fingers pressed against my mouth.

"Fuck, can you chill out?" Kyle snapped close to my ear, wrestling with my octopus arms and legs kicking in anger and revulsion.

I shook my head, trying to scream behind his hand. Rocks and dead grass dug into my back, but I didn't care.

"Stop. Okay, stop…we just want to crash for the night and take you home in the morning, but you cannot, under any circumstances, see your dad tonight. Do you understand?"

No, I didn't.

I shook my head to indicate as much. Why did they care? I wouldn't even tell my dad anything, just that I borrowed a friend's car and needed to see him, or some other bullshit lie. If Kyle would remove his hand from my mouth, he'd know that.

Kyle shifted his weight, lying completely on top of me. It was hard not to notice how perfectly his hardened edges fit with my softer tones. The way my breasts heaved under his firm chest, the tender way he fit between my thighs…it was perfect because he was perfect for me.

"Look…there is a lot to unpack from tonight. I need to talk to Scotty about why the fuck he thought it was a good idea to kidnap you, then we can all sleep and have breakfast together, then we'll get you back home. But you look like you've been crying, and you're scared enough that you'll spill your little heart out to good ol' dad. We can't have that, okay?"

Dad was an FBI agent, and Kyle was involved with organized crime…in a very real capacity that now engulfed his entire life. Of course he didn't want me going home tonight; my dad would put him behind bars for a very long time.

Letting go of my fight and believing they'd return me to school… my arms sagged to the ground, my legs stopped trying to kick him, and I nodded my agreement.

Kyle narrowed his eyes. "If I let go, are you going to fight me?"

Always.

I shook my head no.

"Okay, then let's go back to my house, and we'll see if Mal and Decker have anything to eat for dinner."

My eyes lit up at the prospect of seeing them. I knew bits and pieces of their lives thanks to Mallory keeping me updated via her Instagram messages and stories.

Kyle's hand shifted but stayed in place on top of mine, pinning us to the cold ground. The night was so dark it was hard to make out his expression. There were a few stars weaving throughout the inky sky, but otherwise the moon was a slice of white in the vast darkness.

Our breathing intermixed, and as he hovered above me, I realized I felt safe like this. It made no sense; it was the opposite of smart, but my body reacted like Kyle was my own personal safe room, designed to protect me from any harm. I knew it was a stupid thought, yet when it came to him, I never had any trouble thinking foolish things. He was an unattainable dream; nothing had changed on that front.

"You look so grown up now…it's fucking with me…you're beautiful. I mean, you were always beautiful…but now? Now I feel like I can't stop looking at you."

I wanted to laugh, ask if he was serious. He had left after fucking me, and the story in my head that looped on repeat was that I wasn't enough for him. Not in looks, and certainly not in bed. That was why he'd left me…why pretend now?

"Still that same Rylie the Reaper spirit though…stone cold, reserved, and distinguished. I'm glad I left you so you could become this."

Again I wanted to scream at him, ask what the fuck that was supposed to mean, but I stayed silent.

"You're back to not talking again?"

His left arm moved, but then so did his leg, and I could feel his erection pressing into my core. It was the choice of a lifetime not to rock into him.

He, however, did not make the same decision.

He shamelessly thrust into me, and even through our jeans, he hit at some place inside me that I needed from him again and again, but instead of opening my legs wider or rocking back, I clenched my thighs.

He laughed, obviously catching on to what I was doing, and shook his head. "Alright, I'll stop, but damn I miss this."

He escaped the confines of our little cocoon a second later. The cool air rushed in and reminded me why we were in a field in the first place. On our way back to the house, I wrapped my arms around myself, and within seconds, Kyle's jacket hung over me.

I didn't refuse it, because I was cold. We walked in silence as I tried and failed not to think over what he'd said about missing me. Or rather, not me...but...my body?

I wanted to ask him. I wanted to fill the silence with inquiring where he'd gone, why he had left...but I knew I'd never be okay when he finally told me. I'd rehearsed his potential answer a thousand times, and in each scenario, he'd moved on, healthy and thriving, and I was left with an ugly truth I had thought I wanted and no way to undo how badly it hurt. Because what it boiled down to, regardless of any excuse he could provide, was that I wasn't enough to keep him here.

He had every right to leave, to travel...anything he wanted to do, but why not tell me? Why not sit me down and explain that he needed wings, and while he knew it would hurt, he felt he needed to go alone? I would have understood. I would have encouraged him, written him letters, even met his future girlfriends—hell, attended his wedding if he wanted me to, because I loved Kyle James in a way that made room for him not to love me back.

I just couldn't withstand him leaving me with no explanation, no opportunity to prove my love to him. Even if it looked like me supporting him in something I didn't support or want…I still wanted the choice. So as much as I wanted to know, I would never ask him, because this silence I clung to was my own way of leaving *him*. It was my way of dealing and not allowing him to get too close, because if he was capable of leaving me once, he was capable of doing it again.

The front porch light was on as we crested the steps to his house. I heard people talking behind the screen door; they had left the front door ajar for us from the looks of it. My heart thudded in an erratic rhythm, begging me to turn around and try to run again.

I didn't want to see them. I didn't want to hear that they had known this entire time where Kyle was…I couldn't.

Kyle opened the screen, letting it snap shut behind us. The entry was darker but warm as lighting from the living room barely kissed the hardwood floors…I looked around and realized the entire space was different.

"Last I heard, Mal redesigned a few things…" Kyle said, apparently reading my expression.

I grunted but didn't respond.

Kyle took off his boots, leaving him in white socks with a red line along his toes. It was the strangest thing in the world to see him standing there in socks…it transported me back to seventh grade for some reason, when I came over during Christmas and realized I wanted him to like the gift I got him more than the one Jazzy Cartwright had gotten him. I had dealt with crushing on him off and on again since kindergarten, but seventh grade was when I realized the way my heart shredded in half when he opened my gift, tossed it aside, and then bragged about what Jazzy had made meant I was in love with my best friend. I understood then the pain of loving someone who wouldn't love you back the same way. It was like extending a lung to them and explaining that you realized it would likely be difficult to breathe or even survive without it…but you'd make do.

"You can leave your boots here." Kyle broke me out of treading down memory lane. I blinked and did as he suggested, standing in ankle socks, a pair of ripped skinny jeans, and a cropped t-shirt.

I followed Kyle into the belly of the house, picking out Decker's voice instantly, and then Mallory's gentle laugh…but then there was something new that made me pause.

A soft, gentle cry…a…

"Holy shit, you had a baby?" I balked as I came into view, seeing Mallory cradle a tiny bundle in her arms.

A beaming smile crested her lips as the tiny baby girl bundled in white sucked on her pacifier. "Rylie! Oh my gosh, it's been so long."

"Hey, Rylie," Decker added, sounding a little surprised from his spot on the chair behind me.

I walked forward a few steps, smiled at Decker, ignored my kidnappers, and hugged Mallory. Over the years, she had been the best person who helped keep me posted about Kyle. As few and far between as the updates were, she took over for Decker after a few pathetic texts from me. I followed her on social media though…and had never once seen a post about her being pregnant.

"Did you guys adopt?" I gently touched the baby's foot, peering down at a pair of deep green eyes and a nose that looked awfully familiar.

Decker laughed, bringing his hand to his jaw. "No, why would you assume that?"

I turned toward him, furrowing my brow. "I follow her on Facebook and Insta…she never once posted about being pregnant, much less having a baby."

"Does that mean you follow Taylor too?" Mallory asked, pushing her back into the plush rocker so she and the tiny babe swayed in a gentle rhythm.

I turned back toward her and nodded. "She's doing nonprofit work, right? She seems busy but happy. Alex looks like she's getting big, at least I think it's her—I only ever see the back of her head."

Mallory looked down at her baby, smiling. "Taylor just gave birth to twin boys two months ago."

"What the actual…?" I asked, totally confused. What was going on here?

Suddenly I turned toward Kyle, wanting to ask about his account…about the hiking and Europe.

"Is it all fake?" I was careful not to look at my ex best friend when I said it.

Mallory's dark brows dipped as the baby began to wiggle in her arms. "Not at all. We're just really careful what we share because of the—"

"Nature of Juan's business." Kyle gave Mallory a look that essentially told her to shut up.

I wasn't stupid. I knew whatever she had been about to say had to do with him.

Pieces of his life were starting to fall into place, what he made it look like, what his family had made it look like—as if they were living a carefree life, but it lacked any real details in case their enemies came looking.

Was Kyle running?

I must have looked introspective because Kyle tugged on my shoulder a second later, herding me toward the stairs. I wanted to pry more information out of them...especially seeing as they likely had known where Kyle was for the past three years. They'd lied to me, and I supposed I couldn't be entirely angry with them about it. Kyle was their family, theirs to protect, and I was just...

Nobody.

I allowed Kyle to lead me to a bedroom, grateful it wasn't his old one. This room was an elegant guest suite with a queen-sized bed, beautifully arranged with white linen and soft yellow throw pillows. A warm braided rug rested under the bed, and a refurbished dresser hugged the space under the window.

"You can sleep here. I have your phone...it's turned off at the moment, but you'll get it back when we drop you off tomorrow."

Fuck, I hated this. I wanted to argue with him and say he needed to talk to Mak, tell him I was okay, but that meant he'd win this little war of words.

Instead, I nodded and turned toward the bed.

"Are you hungry? Can I get you anything?"

I allowed my body to sink into the mattress and then stared at the wall, ignoring him. Was I hungry? There was a searing pain in my gut, but it had nothing to do with hunger pangs or food. It revolved solely around memories and how on earth I'd gotten caught up in this nightmare.

He lingered near the entry for what felt like forever, until he finally let out a heavy sigh, holding back his words just like me, and opened the door to leave.

Just as he was about to shut it, he said quietly, "I already let him know you're safe."

The door shut tightly, and a huge sigh escaped my chest. A tear threatened to fall at how well he still knew me. Once my head hit the pillow, I let the tears fall, hoping by tomorrow my life could just go back to normal.

CHAPTER EIGHTEEN

CARTER MARIE JAMES LOOKED LIKE MY BROTHER. OR MAYBE IT WAS my father, but I wasn't giving him any credit. She had a little bit of Mal in there too, her dark hair thick and already curling at the ends just like her mother's. She had Mal's lips too.

I smirked, peering down into the tiny crib that sat next to the rocker Mal had been perched in since we walked in. She got up to get some water and use the bathroom, asking me to watch over my niece, someone I didn't even know existed, thanks to this fucking life I led.

There was an odd feeling shifting around in my chest, as if all the weight that usually sat there was suddenly being manhandled and moved. Fuck it hurt. Missing my brother's life, missing my mother… hearing she'd moved to Arizona as my uncle took a bite of a hot dog while we walked down a New York street corner wasn't what I'd had in mind when I took on this fucking gig.

I knew I didn't exactly have a choice, but this feeling I had…it was right up there with being locked behind bars.

"She's somethin', isn't she?" Decker appeared at my shoulder, watching his daughter sleep while sipping on a beer.

My throat squeezed tight, but I wrangled the emotion, pushing it away. "Yeah."

We stood there silent for a few seconds until Decker nudged me with his arm.

"Where the fuck have you been? Last I heard you were in New York, lying low…then you show up in the middle of the night with Scotty and fucking Rylie of all people."

I heard his accusation. I heard what he wasn't saying, and what I wasn't telling him. I had been hiding my entire life from him since that day three years ago and only sent him updates that looked more like telegrams from a million fucking years ago.

They usually went like this, sent from my burner phone.

D.,I'm safe. New York. Tell you more when I can.

I just never did.

As time went on, the location would change, but that was it. No wonder he never told me he had a kid, or even that he was going to have one. I knew him and Scotty spoke more than ten words to each other every three months, but for whatever reason, I just couldn't.

"It's a long story." I wasn't about to bring him up to speed, not when it would get him all worked up right before he was about to go to sleep.

"God it feels good to pee." Mallory let out a sigh as she walked back into the room. She had on a silk robe that ended high on her tan legs. It was obvious they hadn't been expecting company, but Mal didn't seem to give a shit.

"I mean I know that sounds weird, but I'm not even joking. I feel like baby girl is plastered to some part of my body twenty-four seven. So, peeing in peace is as magical as taking a vacation."

Decker smirked, laughing to himself while he shook his head.

It made me want to say something snide or rude to piss him off. Only because he seemed to have everything, and I was jealous as fuck of it. Girl of his dreams, big-ass house fucking handed to them, a company that made a sick amount of money, and now a baby.

"You guys probably think I'm crazy." Mal kept going, pushing her curls out of her face.

I finally cracked a smile, laughing too. "Nah, I just think you're a mom now, and things like grocery shopping alone will now be fun to you. Decker's probably one birthday party away from having other dad friends who stand around drinking beers while the moms talk about their kids shitting their pants and the dads not coming home from work."

They both stared at me.

"Seriously, where the fuck have you been?" Decker inquired again.

"And why do you look like you started a punk rock band?" Mal narrowed her dark eyebrows, yawning while pulling her robe tight.

I looked down at my clothes then back at them. "What the hell are you talking about?"

They both snorted. Fucking snorted.

"Are you wearing eyeliner—not that we care!" Mallory swung her gaze to Decker, biting back a laugh. "But are you?"

"And look at all these tattoos, and your hair…fuck, dude, you look like a different person."

I rolled my eyes.

"Haha, very funny. Now can you just tell me if you have some food or…?"

"We're just kidding, Kyle…we missed you," Mal said sincerely, and from the way her eyes glossed over, it felt like maybe she really had missed me. I had this idea lodged in the back of my mind that she didn't really like me after what went down with Taylor and my previous employer.

Mallory had slapped me pretty hard when she learned I had been involved with Taylor's dad's efforts to kidnap his daughter. I was just a foot soldier then, barely getting my feet wet in the Varga family business. Scotty was a made man, saying it was better to stay under the radar, not move up too high or too soon, not until you were sure of the person you worked for, and he wasn't sure about Ivan. In fact, he'd mentioned about a thousand times not to trust the fucker, which was why it had been an easy kill for me.

Taylor herself had told me to sink a knife or bullet into the guy if the opportunity ever presented itself. She was right—I didn't regret it at all.

"I missed you guys too," I finally admitted, ducking my head.

I wasn't used to all this.

I jutted my thumb over my shoulder. "I saw turkey and bread… can I make a sandwich?"

"You don't have to ask…you're family, make yourself at home," Decker replied, sounding a little mopey.

Did he think I was just going to kick back in the house we grew up in, knowing he'd inherited it and not me? Forget the fact that I'd paid off all the debt that was left of our mother's bills, including the house…but yeah, fuck it.

I walked into the kitchen and found Scotty already there, stuffing his face with a handful of Doritos. I paused momentarily at the sight because it was so domesticated that I nearly burst out laughing. We'd lived together for three years and I had never caught him eating like a teenager.

"Is that a Mountain Dew?"

Scotty finished chewing, throwing me a glare. "I plan on staying up…"

Pulling on the handle of the updated fridge, I scowled at all the healthy food. "Where did you find that shit?"

Scotty wiped the edge of his mouth with a paper towel. "The garage. Decker is hiding it all out there."

Of course he was. My uncle followed me out then leaned against the wall while I dug around for snacks. I knew he wanted to say something, but he was also acting as my bodyguard. Adorable given how much shit he'd put me through during training so I wouldn't need one. I knew how to kill a man in three moves, was a crack shot with any gun put in my hand, and let's just say I knew my way around a tire iron. Don't get me started on the other skills thrust upon me by my *other* teacher.

"You gonna stab me again?" Scotty drawled, folding his arms across his chest.

He was referring to his little kidnapping stint with Rylie. Yeah, I kind of did want to stab him for that shit, but I knew he had only been keeping her safe and wouldn't actually hurt her. Besides, he was annoying as fuck with his limp.

"Nah…but you scared her. You need to apologize tomorrow…and make her breakfast. She likes lemon poppyseed pancakes."

He scoffed. "I'm not a fucking butler. Let's get that clear right the fuck now."

"Say that to the folded pair of flannel pajamas I found on my bed this morning. Gretta didn't do that shit—you're the only one who has a weird kink with folded pajamas."

If his eyes could have turned black, they would have.

I lifted my hands. "Just joking. Look…it's about showing her you're not a monster. She thinks we both are—how are we supposed to get her to trust us if we keep scaring the shit out of her?"

Scotty seemed to consider my point, searching the ground for his next argument or whatever the fuck.

I searched for a Mountain Dew but decided against it at the last second. Somewhere under my skin, something ached to go curl up behind Rylie and sleep for a week. I was exhausted…not just from tonight or the past week, but from this life. I considered the look Decker and Mal had joked about and wanted to wash it all away, but I couldn't.

This was who I was now.

A fake, a fraud…a joke. A motherfucking *nightmare*.

I couldn't be the same person they'd known. As far as the families went, Scotty's nephew was in Europe, hiking away his worries. I was the Joker now. No real name. No family association and absolutely no fucks given about their hierarchy or way of doing things. I wanted what they had, and for the past three years, I had been slowly taking it.

"Fine. But just this once," Scotty warned before turning and stalking off.

I ended up grabbing a Clif Bar and jogging upstairs. My old room sat untouched, exactly how I had left it three years ago. Posters of cars and half-dressed models adorned my walls, sketches I had made, a few Rylie created for me over the years. My twin bed was stripped, no sheets on it, but the mattress was still there, same with my small desk and shitty dresser.

My eyes narrowed on my closed closet door.

Taking a few strides to clear the room, I tugged on the knob and pulled on the string to illuminate the small space.

There on the back of the wall were four homemade maps taped in place. Smiling, I carefully pulled each one free and examined them.

The first was a map to Rylie's tree house. An X was on my poorly drawn house, and there was another on the tree that housed our little fort. There were dashes between the spots and a few warning remarks jotted to the side.

Saw a snake that one time

Definitely saw a werewolf once here, be careful

An entire valley of spiders lives under that big rock

I laughed to myself, wishing I could go show them to her. She'd laugh too…we were so sure Hogwarts was real and we were secretly half Muggle, like Hermione. Our real parents were wizards, and we were just lost to the Muggle world, like Harry.

The second map was of a poorly drawn lake, a trail leading up to an odd shape with the words *Road Island* on it and a note that said: *Not an island made of roads, deeply disappointed.*

I burst out laughing.

The map was from Rylie's trip to Rhode Island in the fourth grade. She drew me a map and sent it to me in the mail while she was there. It was a part of our promise to one another to always recreate our trips to show each other once we got back from wherever it was we went.

I glanced at my tattoos and smirked. Would she ever inspect them close enough to see what they were, to see I'd continued this little game of ours for the past three years?

Would she even care?

Shaking my head, I crumpled the maps in my fist and grabbed the string to turn off the light.

I had to stop assuming I could pick up where I'd left off with her. She wouldn't even talk to me. If that wasn't a big fat sign that we were unrepairable, I didn't know what was.

CHAPTER NINETEEN

Rylie

THE GRAYING CLOUDS CLUNG IN LITTLE WISPS AROUND THE HOUSE, blocking out the sun and tarnishing any hope that today would be a good one. My natural pessimistic self soaked up the bad vibes, and internally I was making bets that something terrible would happen. Sunshine meant happiness; the gray, watery mess outside was a blaring warning for people to stay inside and curl up around the fire.

Instead, I made the bed I'd slept like a baby in and barged downstairs like a Nordic queen on a warpath. I would verbally tear my kidnappers apart, warning them that this was all bullshit and I was headed to my father's no matter what they said.

"Rylie, good, you're up," Scotty said, smiling warmly at me.

The pink apron tied around his waist, muting his dark trousers and Henley, made my feet freeze in place. He stood at the oven flipping pancakes, and there were thin strips of bacon on a griddle. I slowed my steps as I descended the rest of the steps and cautiously padded to the table.

There was a white plate already there with a glass of orange juice, a cup of coffee, and silverware.

Scotty walked over a second later, dishing up two pancakes for me with two strips of bacon.

"Lemon poppyseed?" My head snapped back, taking in the man who'd abducted me the night prior.

He was already walking away, so I couldn't read his face.

Over his shoulder, he answered, "Kyle said it was your favorite."

It still was…but no one had made me this dish since…Mom had died.

Feeling my throat squeeze tight, I started cutting into the soft dough and shoveling it in my mouth so I didn't have to thank him or sob about losing people I loved only to have pieces of them come back to me.

"I wanted to apologize to you for how I behaved last night," Scotty started, his eyes looking soft, his expression relaxed. "We were trying to keep you safe and extract you without tipping off any of the other families that we were there. Kyle had the idea to create the blackout then find you and grab your hand so you followed him out. I should have let him do that. Instead, I scared you, and that was never my intention."

His dark brows sank as though this was a confession truly pulled from his heart.

I knew better.

I quirked a brow, arching it in question. "And how about when you threatened me that first day at Mak's? Did you mean to scare me then?"

He stared at me. I stared back. His softer features suddenly turned dark as if I were watching a dragon wake from a deep slumber with an appetite for blood. Before he could answer, Kyle ran down the stairs, interrupting us.

When he pulled a chair free and slid into it next to me, I nearly turned my head and buried my nose in his neck to breathe in the familiar scent.

Instead, I kept my head down and watched my food, but after a few seconds, I couldn't take it. I turned and looked.

Freshly showered, his hair was swept off his face, revealing his eyes without any dark smudges added to create a duskier expression. He wasn't wearing any of his menacing clothing for once, and he didn't have his lip ring in. Instead, he looked like the boy I used to love…or at least the closest version of him. I could see his defined jaw and high cheekbones, but it was the smile in his eyes that struck me.

His tattoos were still visible with the t-shirt he wore, and that was when I realized what he had inked into his skin.

My lips burned with the need to ask, the desperation to have him fill me in on the story he had clearly spun along the expanse of his skin. The darker colors and swirls danced upward, disappearing under the sleeves of his shirt. I wanted to rip it from his body so I had every line, every stroke…every story.

"See somethin' you like, Ry?" His right eyebrow quirked up, his lips were slung to the side, and that happy expression was replaced with mischief.

I quickly looked away.

Scotty was back in the kitchen, flipping burners off while Kyle ate next to me in silence. I wanted to ask about Mallory and Decker, but I feared Kyle would be the only person to answer me.

Instead, I ate and waited for what was to come next. Mostly, I ignored how surreal it felt to be in the presence of the one man who'd left me so empty and so confused for the past three years.

TRUE TO HIS WORD, KYLE DROPPED ME BACK AT SCHOOL, RIGHT outside my dorm. My car was parked in the exact spot I always put it, and my keys were handed over to me, along with my cell. Kyle gave me no indication that he'd see me again, or that he'd stay in touch. He didn't offer a hug or an awkward conversation. Scotty had driven, and this time, Kyle sat up front with him in the passenger seat.

I felt the sting of it numbing my heart, reminding me that I'd allowed it to soften toward him—something I needed to be careful not to do again. I wasn't willing to even speak to him, yet knowing he'd chosen to sit apart from me made me feel angry and jealous. I didn't even have anyone to be petty over…it was just this life he led, this new thing that held him captive and directed him into whatever it was that he did.

I shrugged it off, heading up to my dorm.

Everything was how I'd left it. A prim note from Hazel said she was seeing her brother a few hours away and would be back in a few days. So, she hadn't even noticed that I was gone, or that I had essentially been abducted?

"Nice…really nice." I crumpled her note, feeling irritated all over again.

No reason why. Just angry. Just irritable.

The day was essentially a complete waste as I tried and failed to catch up on the classes I had missed earlier in the day. I had called and texted Mak, but he wasn't responding to me. Neither was Trixie…she at least finally broke down after a few hours and a fake sob story from me about being abducted and freaked out that I didn't know what was going on.

Trixie: I think you need to stay away for a bit…Mak knows you know the guy who did it, and he's in some trouble because of it. You know he thinks of you as a little sister, just give him some time to sort it all out.

That made me feel like shit. It wasn't my fault, and I knew deep down that Mak knew that, but I also understood wanting to get some distance from me because of my association with Kyle. Or, as Mak knew him, the Joker.

Apparently, the loss of Kyle's presence was already messing with me, because I kept checking my phone…for what, I had no idea. It wasn't like he was about to text me or FaceTime me to ask what flavor of slushie I wanted from 7-11. Things weren't back to normal for us, and just because he was reacting to me physically didn't mean he cared about me.

I had to shake it. Like water off my raincoat on a miserable day, I wanted him gone.

Thankfully around six, Hazel came back. Hearing her talk about her trip and all the drama in her family filled all the empty space that had lingered in my dorm and in my head. I was fully invested in her saga, glad it could distract me from what was going through my skull and what was on the tip of my tongue.

I wanted to tell her about all of it, about the club and Mak. I wanted to cry on my best friend's shoulder and ask what I should do, but she already thought I was crazy for thinking Kyle was back. It was certainly hard to recognize him these days, but if he confessed to her who he was, maybe it would help. Who was I kidding? After what happened to Mak, there was no way I would drag Hazel into that mess.

The next day, there was a seat saved for me in Dr. Carr's class. The placeholder was a playing card with the Joker imprinted on the front, nothing on the back.

Kyle had saved it for me.

I picked up the card, held it in between my fingers, and looked up. The back row was full of his admirers while he sat like a king in the center. He caught my eye, winked, and then stuck his tongue into the mouth of the girl to his right.

I quickly turned my head, looking away, all while my face burned.

It shouldn't have mattered that he was making out with someone in front of me. It shouldn't have. We weren't anything but friends, and now merely ashes just swaying toward each other every time the wind picked up. Once the sun came out, we'd settle and go back to the way things had been—dead to one another.

I made it a point to ignore him, more so than usual, but it didn't stop how often I had to hear about him or see him around campus.

Kissing girls, their arms wrapped around his neck as I passed by… Kyle's eyes searching for mine while his lips marked someone's neck.

It made my skin crawl, so I would just push away and walk faster.

He acted like the previous weekend hadn't happened, when he'd held my hips in place on his lap, when he'd almost kissed me in the field. It wasn't that I needed him to start acting like that meant anything, because if he did, I'd tell him to go fuck himself. So, maybe it wasn't the worst thing to have him acting like it hadn't happened.

His dark tattoos and dark eyes gave him an edge that girls on campus were salivating over and gossiped about loudly every single place I went. He was referred to as 'Holy Hotness' by everyone who mentioned him. Girls in class talked about how sexily he walked in those big combat boots, how dangerous he seemed with his lip ring, and the way his clothes clung perfectly to his sculpted muscles. Hannah Mason from my lit class gushed about how she'd traced his tattoos with her fingernails and seen how hard it had made him. She had wanted to suck him off, but he'd gotten a phone call.

My damn chest felt like a damn hole had been punched through it, merely because I had noticed his ink and wanted the story behind it. The idea that he was getting touched and inspected by all of Rake Forge made me want to puke or smash something...preferably Scotty's face.

I tried my best to clear out of any space that had girls talking about him, and instead, I would drift to my bench, watching the sun rays as they tangled with the branches hanging over the library. Occasionally, I'd feel someone watching me, but I'd shake it off. Other times, I'd take refuge in the building, especially on nights when Hazel wanted to go out. I knew I'd see him if I dared to go somewhere, and I just couldn't bring myself to play the silent game he'd begun to participate in.

He had stopped trying to communicate with me. Now he just watched...raising a brow or staring so hard I thought his eyes would combust.

By Friday, I couldn't take any more.

After classes, I packed a small bag, got in my car, and headed back home. Away from the gossip about a man who smashed my heart into a billion pieces then came back to make finger art out of the blood left behind.

CHAPTER TWENTY

THE GOLDEN CURL BOUNCED AS I TUGGED IT AND LET IT GO.

A pair of pale blue eyes stared back at me, the girl glaring with such force I thought she might kill me. She pursed her little lips and crossed her arms.

I burst out laughing, covering my face. "Sorrrrryyyyy."

"I'm telling my daddy on you." She pouted, speaking in the cutest little voice; it nearly made my heart crack.

"Alex, I thought we were friends!" I held my heart as though she'd smashed it.

She rose from her tiny chair, and I swear to Christ, she looked down her nose at me, just like her mother did. "Daddy says I no have to worry about boys' hearts because he will break dem' for me."

I laughed again, this one full-bellied, and Juan came into view, grinning from ear to ear.

"That's right, baby girl." He swung down and picked her up, kissing her head while he sank into the couch cushions.

The house was cozy, smaller than their last one, but nice. The interior was completely them, every small touch and piece something they'd picked or designed together, and that was something I greatly admired.

"So, you gonna tell me why you're here, sulking like a dog who's been kicked?"

I looked up from my spot on the floor where I'd been trying to sneak up on Alex while she hosted a tea party for three massive teddy bears.

"I'm being forced to go to college, and it feels like I'm pretending to be a fuck boy in high school…how would you react?"

Juan laughed, not bothering to cover his daughter's ears. She'd likely seen and heard much worse. Although, if Taylor were down, she might have an issue with her being in the same room as the two of us. She usually did, but only because we had the tendency to bring out the worst in each other.

"I'd probably stop." Juan typed in the passcode for the tablet Alex held up to him.

I smirked, eyeing his three-year-old in her little white dress and zebra print tights. Girl was crazy funny, and a miniature version of Taylor, super cute.

"Last week, she knew the code…what happened?"

Juan cut a glare toward me and shook his head. "Did you fucking teach her?"

I shook my head, stifling a laugh.

"Well, someone did. She keeps learning whatever code we pick, and then I have to change it."

"She's smart—that's not a bad trait to have for a daughter who's going to inherit all this shit."

Alex crawled off her father's lap, and her tiny feet carried her to the massive corner decked out in princess décor, complete with a castle and a hammock stuffed with pillows.

"You honestly think Taylor would ever allow that?"

"She'd prefer the twins take it?" That didn't seem right either.

My friend ran his hand through his hair, his gold wedding band gleaming under the lights as he let out a sigh and checked the monitor that showed his wife rocking one of the twins in the nursery. I knew better than to show I was looking for too long. He was protective as fuck of his wife and the kids…it was another level of insane that I had seen in the man who once wanted to kill me.

"Any chance you change your mind about things?" His brown-gold eyes searched mine, his fingers running over his wedding band now.

"Nah…but there's time, Juan…they're young still. In another twenty years, they might want to take over merely because it's tied to you. By then it won't look like something you don't want to hand to them."

He seemed to consider this, the sun breaking up the dark clouds in the glass behind him.

"As long as we keep things going according to plan, I wouldn't mind handing it over. Speaking of which, any news?"

Pulling myself off the floor, I took the lounge chair across from him and checked my watch. I had ten more minutes before Scotty started getting antsy.

"Ivan's brothers have been traveling back and forth between Hungary and New York for the past nine months. Istvan just purchased a penthouse on the Upper East Side, and there's talk that he's trying to get back the territory Ivan lost."

"Why the fuck would they wait so long?"

I shook my head, toying with a plastic figurine on the side table. "Rumor has it things were too unstable over there for them to leave, and they had no one ready to come take over something as large as what Ivan had."

"So, we've taken his territory, his pickups, and his inventory…is there anything left?"

"Not a fuckin' thing."

"It's owed to Taylor anyway since it was all her father's, so if they really want to split hairs, I'm fine with that."

A sinister smile curved along my lips.

Juan laughed, peering back at the small screen.

"They'll come for us, but I'm not worried. They're new players and no one wants them here. The Italians are trying to ensure there isn't another slow take over like Ivan did throughout the past fifteen years. They're embarrassed they allowed him to take as much as he did. They won't be giving them a single inch."

"The Russians won't either, but the sooner we start their war, the better."

A door suddenly opened upstairs, and the sound of someone walking echoed above our heads. I watched Juan's gaze as he stared at the stairs, waiting for his wife to come down.

Taylor materialized a second later, her hair up in a messy bun and a pair of what looked like Juan's sweats rolled down on her hips. A pair of tall white socks went up over the cuff of the baggy pajama bottoms, and her white tank top barely concealed her freakin' huge breasts. She didn't look great, but she'd also just had twins, so who was I to judge?

"Kyle, it's nice to see you." She smiled wide, brushing part of her hair back, giving no fucks that I was seeing her like this. It made me feel like I was a part of the family. Truthfully, I felt more relaxed in front of Juan and Taylor than I did with Mal and Decker. Probably because for the past three years, Juan had been my friend and teacher. When Scotty didn't train me, Juan did.

After our little shitshow Christmas party three and a half years ago, Juan and I had encountered each other on a job, on opposite sides of a bad deal being set up by the DeMarco family. They'd planned to double-cross Juan and assumed the Joker would just go with it, assuming I wanted the territory.

They were wrong.

I ended up killing the fuckers before they had a chance to take aim at the man who'd wanted me to leave his house that night all those years ago.

My debt with him was cleared, he invited me home for dinner, and since that night, he was my friend and I considered him family. It went deeper than that though; Scotty didn't even know what I was planning with Juan.

My uncle assumed I just wanted a seat at the table...he didn't truly understand that I planned to burn the fucking thing, the chairs, and everything else they had too.

I wanted it all.

So did Juan, and we were going to take it.

I stood to hug Taylor. "You look beautiful—can't even tell you just pushed two watermelons out of your vagina." I pecked her cheek while she pushed at my chest.

"God, don't remind me. Things are not the same, Kyle."

She walked over to her daughter's play corner and smoothed the loose curls around Alex's face behind her ear, smiling at her daughter while her little girl beamed back up at her. I felt a sensation begin to burn in my lungs. It always burned when I was here, seeing what they'd built for each other, what they'd done to get here. Now that Rylie was back in my life, it seemed to burn a little extra hot, whispering thoughts and ideas of what I could have if I wanted it.

Especially given my fuck boy role at Rake Forge…shit, I didn't want to play that part anymore. Girls pawing at me every goddamn second, making up rumors that they'd fucked me or touched me in some capacity. The only people I had touched were the ones Rylie had seen, and that was merely because I wanted to get a reaction from her, because I was petty as fuck and hurt that I'd waited for her.

"Mal says you were over there last weekend." Taylor walked back over, sipping from a large clear jug of water.

I nodded. "Saw little Carter Marie, she's beautiful."

Taylor smiled. "Right? I'm headed back over there tomorrow, but we're both just so exhausted…it's hard to see each other, and it's not like we can help each other since we both just had babies. They're all only a week apart, can you believe that?"

"How are little Kingston and Giovanni?"

Juan grabbed Taylor's baggy sweats and tugged her until she was landing in his lap. His arms went around her while her arm draped around his neck. It was seamless, like breathing for them to touch, to be near each other.

"They're so perfect, but they're going to be handfuls. I can already tell."

"They'll have Alex to watch out for them, so they'll be alright," I said, pulling my phone free to check the time.

Taylor looked longingly over at her daughter. "She's the best big sister ever."

I stood, walked over, and placed a kiss on Taylor's head then ruffled Juan's hair, just to piss him off. Alex was waiting for me with her arms stretched out for a hug. I bent down to grab her and tugged her to my chest.

"One," she whispered.

"You're my favorite."

"Two." Her cute nose had something green in it, but she rubbed it against mine anyway.

"You're the most beautiful princess in all the world."

"Three." She stretched her arms out like she was flying.

I tossed her in the air, caught her, and held her up like she was a rocket shooting through the living room. "You burn brighter than any star."

"Love you, Uncle Kyle."

"Love you too, baby girl." I set her down and darted out the front door, where I found an irritated looking Scotty leaned against his car, outside the iron gate that protected Juan's house.

Hector, Juan's cousin, watched him while patrolling the property. I gave him a high five, which only made my uncle roll his eyes before getting into the car.

Once I exited the gate and ducked into the vehicle, Scotty was starting it up and putting his sunglasses on.

"You don't have to wait for me anymore, you know."

We had this talk way too often, yet he wouldn't leave me here alone.

"Juan's as volatile as a teenage girl—I'm not risking you pissing him off and suddenly he wants to kill you. You annoy people far too easily to risk it."

I laughed, shaking my head as he pulled away and started down the drive. My gut always felt full of unicorns and fluffy heart shit when I left Juan's house. Usually I went and trained to get the extra energy out of my system; this time I planned to surprise my once best friend and see if she was ready to verbally spar with me yet.

CHAPTER TWENTY-ONE

Rylie

DAD WAS DRINKING WHEN I WALKED THROUGH THE FRONT DOOR. IT was such an odd sight to see that I tripped over the coffee table. A fifth of whiskey sat in front of him, and his nice work shirt looked soiled and crumpled while it hung in two limp pieces split open over his chest. His white tank underneath looked just as bad.

Even when Mom had died, he'd never looked this bad…and as far as I knew he hadn't taken to drinking back then, but perhaps I was lost in my own grief and never noticed.

"Dad, what's going on?"

His glassy eyes searched my face, a red flush overwhelming the tops of his cheeks as he seemed to finally register my presence.

"Honey…what are you doing here?"

I made my way over to where he sat, deflated in his chair, and pushed his greasy hair off his forehead. He looked so different…so pathetic and tired. It scared me. "Dad, I'm here for the weekend."

I left it at that. I wanted to open up to him, but a part of me wanted him to open up more.

My father's head rested on the back of his chair. "You shouldn't have come."

That was like a sledgehammer to whatever was left dangling in my chest, my heart in lacerated pieces, destroyed by the men who were supposed to love me.

I stood, walking away from him while tears began to burn my eyes.

My father groaned, slowly getting to his feet, swaying as he tried. "I'm sorry, I'm just…" He let out a heavy sigh, pushing back the loose strands of his hair.

I sank into one of the dining room chairs and tugged at the bracelet on my hand. It had previously been the leather band around my neck, but after giving up on Kyle, I'd transitioned it to my wrist, minimizing it. At the time it felt very metaphorical.

"You gotta tell me what's wrong—you're freaking me out."

Dad stood and began pacing the floor, tossing his hands out.

"I'm in trouble, sweetie…" His wild eyes swung toward me, panic flaring bright and uncontrolled in his terrified expression. "I messed up."

His words made my stomach knot with worry, especially as suspicion began to scratch at the back of my mind. Too much had happened over the past week for me not to assume there was some connection to Kyle.

Dad's pacing continued while his hands carved a path through his hair. "I was approached by someone…a new source, other than Mak, to provide details on the inner workings of the new players on the scene. My boss has been hounding me for more from Mak…telling me to pull the plug on him and throw him in prison because he lost his usefulness."

Oh shit. No, he couldn't do that. Worry gnawed at my gut as I waited for him to finish, but he just shook his head, thinning his lips… shutting down once more.

"But Mak has helped you for over two years, and so have I…we risked a ton to get you all that intel."

"I agree, honey, but the people in charge are saying it's not enough."

I crossed my arms, searching the room for some sort of answer, something to give me some hope that Mak would be safe.

"Why all of a sudden is it not enough, and what do you mean you were approached by someone?"

Dad finally took a seat, stopping the frantic pacing, and stared at me with hopeless eyes. Dark circles marred the space under his lashes, and his skin looked pasty and gaunt. I understood it now; he was desperate.

"There was an incident where someone my boss has been after was in Mak's club. You remember giving me that playing card?"

I wanted to scream at him that I remembered trying to get him to talk to me about that card, but he'd shut me out. Instead, I merely nodded, biting my tongue as unease slid along my insides.

"Mak was supposed to inform us when he arrived that night, to confirm the visual we needed in order to move. We waited and tried to get a follow-up, but Mak fell off the grid for three days. When he finally surfaced, he gave us some bullshit story about how only Markos showed, but there was a mix-up that prevented him from contacting us. We had a strike team ready to go, but he never gave us the green light that the Joker was there."

The silence in the room was overwhelming, just my heart rattling behind my lungs and pounding in my ears. Mak had risked himself for me; I knew it deep in my bones. That entire encounter had freaked Mak out because of how Kyle had responded to me...so instead of turning him in, he shut out the feds to protect me.

My eyes burned, my throat tight as I processed the gravity of the situation. Mak might actually go to prison because of me. He had been good to me, gave me a spot in his bar and worked with my school schedule, protected me and made sure I was always safe in his bar. He was my friend, and after being abandoned by one, I was insanely protective of the connections left in my life.

"The Delgado family approached me a few months ago, about working with them. A trade of sorts, help me get promoted while I cut them in on the intel I grabbed from Mak and made sure they were always protected from the raids."

My eyes bounced from the floor to his crumpled form in the chair. I thought back to what Kyle had said about one of his clients knowing about me at the bar…Dad was the source…that was how they knew about me. They were probably watching us right now.

I moved until I was kneeling in front of my dad.

"What do you need…what can I do?"

He shook his head, his lips turned down in a frown as he gave up hope.

I grabbed my father's hands and pulled them into my own, forcing his eyes to meet mine. "Dad, what do you need?"

"I need the Joker…I need intel…" His explanation burst from him like he'd been holding it in.

I couldn't give him Kyle. As pained as I was that he'd left me, he hadn't betrayed me, just broken my heart…and that wasn't enough to ruin his life, even if he was into illegal and shady shit.

"What if I can get you intel on all the other players? The families?"

He shook his head. "I have that…I need *him*, or I'll need to see if I can work with the Delgado family. Otherwise I'll lose my job."

I scoffed, shaking my head. "But working with Delgado could make you lose your life…it's not worth it."

He pushed to his feet again, letting out a patronizing sound while he shook his head. "What exactly do I have left to live for? Building this career has been my goal, my focus for the past five years…I'm so close to promoting if I could just catch this break."

Fuck that hurt. It hurt so insanely bad that it momentarily removed the air from my lungs. It felt like a punch to my stomach, making it squeeze tight, forcing a burning sensation up my chest. A sob scraped at my throat.

I wouldn't fall apart; I couldn't. Mak needed me. I would focus on him—he deserved my help.

"If you get the Joker, Mak will be safe?"

His watery eyes rose, meeting mine, curious…suspicious.

"Yes…I'll be sure of it."

"In writing, a pardon…I want it in writing that he'll be let out of his deal."

He shook his head. "I can't promise that…but I'll do what I can to move him so he's safe and not behind bars."

That would have to be enough. At least it would give me time to tip him off so he could run if he wanted.

"Okay…I'll get you information on the Joker. I can't get you him exactly, but I have the next best thing."

My dad stood, practically salivating over the words that had left my mouth.

"What are you talking about? Who do you have?"

"I have access to his crew."

I wouldn't deliver Kyle on a platter, but I'd certainly give away a few crumbs.

My dad's eyes widened, his brows shooting to his hairline. I wanted to snap my eyes closed and take it all back, but I didn't. I just met my dad's eyeline and nodded my head, confirming that I'd just saved his ass and delivered him a golden ticket.

Part of me wanted him to change his mind, wanted him to tell me not to endanger myself, to protect me in the way Mak had…but he didn't. My chest hollowed out as I waited and waited for him to say something to stop me, to turn this around, but the protest never came.

Instead, I grabbed my bag and left without another word, feeling pieces of my heart shatter one step at a time.

CHAPTER TWENTY-TWO

"WHERE IS SHE?" I WAS LOSING MY GRASP ON REALITY, IF I'D EVER even had it to begin with. We had returned to Rake Forge, only to find that Rylie wasn't in her dorm—or anywhere else for that matter. Scotty was busy babysitting me at Juan's, leaving her to the whims of some new muscle he had hired.

I trusted him with that shit, but he knew damn well if he wasn't on Rylie then I wanted Holt or Garrison. Instead, he put some dipshit who looked like he'd just graduated high school and another fucker who looked like one strong wind would blow him into the grave.

My uncle's gaze never left the asphalt as he pulled his smoke from his lips and exhaled. My rage began to simmer, tearing at the same cords that snapped when he had tried to keep me from her in the bar that first night. They had pulled again when he came out of that club with his hand around her mouth like she was some fucking human trafficking victim, and now it was sweeping through my chest, about to explode.

"Where the fuck is she?" I roared again, ripping the cigarette from his lips and tossing it behind my back.

His eyes finally rose with that dead stare he always gave, like nothing on this planet fazed him.

"They lost her."

Jesus, I was about to burn the fucking school down just because I could, and I didn't give a single fuck that it would stress my uncle out. That seemed to be the only thing that caught his attention—if I caused a scene or got showy with my tantrums.

I spun on my boot, running my hand through my hair.

"They saw her leaving her father's house about an hour ago, but she took some sharp turn somewhere and they lost her trail."

Rylie wasn't stupid. If she'd gone and talked to her dad, he had likely told her she was being followed. She had probably spilled the whole goddamn story to her old man.

"Thought we were working interference to keep her from the feds…meaning her dad."

Scotty dipped his head again, nodding.

"She had class this afternoon…I assumed we'd catch her before she tried to leave."

Well, that was fucking great.

"The roommate likely knows or has a way to contact her."

The roommate being Hazel Ward, someone Rylie and I both grew up with. She hadn't recognized me that night in the pub, but if I went in there demanding to know where Rylie was, she'd freak the fuck out.

"Head back, I'll wait for her. She's obviously going to return at some point. If we talk to the roommate, she'll tip Rylie off. If we even knock on the door, we will, so I'll wait."

"You aren't waiting alone," Scotty warned, shooting off the brick wall he was leaning against.

The darkening sky toyed with shades of gray and purple while the wind picked up. The brush of cool air against my skin helped me calm down and not be an ass to the man who practically raised me.

"I have this. I'll be in touch." I gave him a pointed look and stalked off toward the heart of the campus, wishing for once that he'd just listen and let me be. Lately I had been feeling more and more of this need to separate from him, to get some room to breathe. I knew he worried about me, knew he had designs on how we could essentially take over, have our own family. He wanted me to be the head of it, but only because he knew he could pull my strings any time he wanted.

I'd essentially be his puppet, his hand up my ass for any deal or whatever the fuck he wanted to score. I had gone along with it for so long that I was just used to it. The only time I had really deviated from his course was when I demanded that we go help Taylor by shoving a blade into Ivan's back. It was shitty that I had to plan to murder some fucker when I was supposed to be in high school, dealing with parties and watching fuckers flirt with Rylie.

I was meant to be slowly making my move, proving how much I was in love with my best friend, and then by graduation we'd start dating and whatever the fuck else. I had it all planned. Then Scotty started taking me to New York with him, plugging me in with Ivan's crew, and it was exciting. I liked feeling powerful, liked not living in my big brother's shadow. The ability to finally cast my own was too damn tempting, as was having the means to help pay off the debt my brother felt was his to sort out.

Now, I was paying for it with my soul. I didn't care if I died. Honestly, I really just didn't give a single fuck because everything was ash and heat. I'd taken a bite of forbidden fruit, costing me the one girl I had envisioned a life with, and I'd lost her.

Now, I walked the earth an empty vessel of vanity and violence. Everything I did was a joke, fake...a lie to keep me safe.

I wanted to come out of the shadows and burn to dust, once and for all, which was why I had been working with Juan to take it all down.

I'd go with it...just as long as Rylie was safe, and my life finally held meaning.

THE DOORKNOB RATTLED AS A KEY WAS SHOVED INTO THE LOCK AND turned. I sat up, wiping the sleep out of my eyes, and tried to process what was happening. The clock on Hazel's side of the room showed that it was close to one in the morning, and since I knew for a fact she was spending the night with someone, I knew it had to be Rylie.

Unless Hazel had had a change of heart or a fight…but when she'd slipped out earlier, taking a call from some guy, and left, I'd slipped in and made myself comfortable in Rylie's bed. Her scent had lulled me to sleep, and I'd even wrapped my arms around her pillow like I was fifteen again.

The door swung open, revealing Rylie's form, shadowed by the lights in the hall. She shut it and clicked something that lit up a string of LED lights around the room. My planned reveal of being all dark and mysterious was interrupted by rainbow colors blinking across my face.

Rylie caught sight of me perched on the edge of her bed, my sock-covered toes resting on the rug in front of it, and my head swung in her direction. I expected her to freak out—I knew she would as soon as she registered that I had access to where she slept at night—but instead of panic in her eyes…I saw relief.

That made me feel wildly unprepared.

She took a step toward me, slipped her boots off, and then set her purse down.

I inhaled a silent breath, terrified I might scare her off by making a sound.

Her eyes stayed on me as she tugged an oversized sweater up past her head, leaving her in just a fitted tank that hugged the swells of her breasts so perfectly it showed off the top of her cleavage. That was one thing I'd yet to get used to—Rylie had grown up over the past three years: more curves, a more round and deliciously plump ass, and bigger tits. Her waist remained small and her stomach flat, but every place that held any sort of softness or curve was accentuated to the point that she was a walking wet dream.

She dressed nearly every day in big, loose-fitting boots with tight, ripped jeans and loose shirts that cut off at her midriff, but tonight she was in that tight tank and a pair of light blue leggings that looked like they were a second skin. Fuckable—she was utterly and perfectly fuckable.

I didn't say anything because I knew she wouldn't respond, but I watched her.

I watched as her eyes betrayed how curious she was about me, how they drifted to my arms and the ink spanning my skin. I watched as she glanced down at my feet, saw how she watched the space behind me on the bed. I wondered if she ever thought about our night together like I did.

Scotty made a big deal about me being celibate for three years, but honestly, what I'd had with Rylie that night filled me in a way that meant I couldn't ever touch another, not when I'd started out so strong. I knew I'd never have what I had that night with anyone else. She obviously felt differently, but I had a theory that she had forced those relationships just to get over what we had. She had been in love with me...and I'd broken her heart.

"How long before you started dating?" My voice came out as a whisper as my eyes slammed shut. I didn't know why I asked it; must have just slipped right off my tongue since my heart turned to mush around her.

She stepped closer, grabbing the bulk of her hair and tugging it over her shoulder. Slowly, she sank down onto the edge of Hazel's bed, facing me. There was a good-sized gap between us, but we still sat close enough that I could hear her intake of breath and see the way she bit her lip.

I tilted my head, feeling frustration burn in my chest. "That's right, you aren't talking to me."

I waited, watching her feet and mine, the way the rainbow lights from the LED strips bounced along the wood floor and off the planes of her face. Her lips rolled, her fingers knitting together in her lap as if she was considering an answer.

"I'm only curious because you mentioned loving me...and after what we shared, I was just wondering how long it took you to start fucking other guys."

She made a sound of disbelief, shaking her head, bringing her fingers to her nose, exhaling a breath.

"How long did *I* wait, you ask?" I pretended to incline my ear as if she'd asked a question. "Funny thing about that...I never stopped. You were my first and my last."

"Bullshit." The words burst out, her expression accusing me with narrowed eyes and thin lips.

I was almost too shocked to respond. I had finally gotten her to talk to me…granted, we were off to a rocky start, but it was something.

I tucked my hands into my crossed arms, leaning forward and smirking at her. "Excuse me, did you say something?"

She stood, towering over me. "I said bullshit, because there's no way you went three years without having sex. Hell, half the girls on campus say you've fucked them. You make out with them in front of me every chance you get."

I jumped to my feet, our noses nearly touching with our proximity. "So, you've noticed me then? Because from the way you've looked through me, ignored me, and generally acted as if I don't exist, I was beginning to think I was invisible or something."

"Don't play stupid or act like the victim, Kyle. It's so pretentious." She rolled her eyes, shifting her head in disbelief.

"Does hearing the truth really bother you that much?"

She made an irritated sound, pushing her hands into her hair. "Fuck, you annoy me."

I stepped closer, our chests heaving. "You don't even know what you do to me, baby."

She didn't step back, just lowered her head, still shaking it in frustration.

"At least I got you talking to me…my new mission." I smirked while silently inhaling her jasmine scent. It was like going back in time…to our tree house, to my back yard, to playing video games and creating new maps. Like a burst of thunder in my ears, pounding vigorously to go back, to fix it, to change course.

Quietly, as if she was remembering something, her brows crinkled while her ass sank into Hazel's bed. "I was going to start talking to you tonight, regardless of what you said."

I decided not to ask or clarify, hoping she'd keep going. I mirrored her movements, slowly sinking back into her bed. My silence seemed to encourage her.

"I need a favor from you…" Her green eyes flared, slowly traveling up, tracing my face.

I smiled in response, excited by what she might ask. Tipping my head, I encouraged her to continue.

Her tongue darted out, wetting her bottom lip. "I need information."

Adorable...she was so fucking adorable. I'd known it would only be a matter of time before she couldn't resist knowing what had happened during our lost years. I nodded, watching our feet before glancing back up and smirking.

"About where I've been...the past three years?"

She leaned forward, pressing her elbows into the tops of her thighs. The lights reflected off her eyes, shimmering flecks of gold like the sun breaking through an evergreen.

"No, Kyle. As far as I'm concerned, the past three years didn't happen. I don't ever want to talk about it. What I need from you is information on the Joker."

CHAPTER TWENTY-THREE

Rylie

I KNEW MY RESPONSE WOULD SURPRISE HIM. HE SEEMED SO SURE OF himself, sitting there so cocky and certain I'd be groveling for crumbs about his life. His eyes narrowed shrewdly, quickly becoming the man I had met in the bar that night. He wanted to toy with me, but I wouldn't let him.

"I see," he replied evenly.

I wasn't sure what to expect…I guess a small part of me wanted him to hold me or tell me he'd do anything for me. As far as scenarios went, the one where I had the opportunity to rebuff him would obviously suit me best.

The silence ticked by, sounds from the hall clamoring to get through our door, same with the walls and the girls surrounding us in either direction. This specific dorm was co-ed, but there were only girls along this block of rooms.

Kyle let out a heavy sigh, getting to his feet.

My stomach dipped.

It took me back to the hours I had lost after leaving my father's house, when I had driven out to Mak's strip club on the other side of the city, desperate to see him, to warn him. All I received was an early show of the girls dancing and a few leering guys. No one would tell me anything, which in the grand scheme of things was good. It was good to have loyalty.

But it did jack shit for me and what I was after. I had tried his cell, I'd gone and waited outside his apartment...then I had tried to find Kyle or Scotty.

I had no idea where they lived, so I drove all the way back to Pinehurst, seeing if they were at Decker's. They weren't, and neither were the two new parents. The house was empty, and from what it looked like, Decker and Mallory had left a few days prior and didn't plan to come back any time soon.

It was made obvious by the way Decker had packed up his tool shed and how the back yard was prepped for winter.

Worried that Kyle had disappeared on me again, I drove back to Rake Forge with a heavy heart and an exhausted soul. I had already told my dad I had access to Kyle, so this had to work. Mak's freedom depended on it.

Kyle made no indication that he'd speak again, merely pacing to where he'd dropped his boots.

I didn't want to chase him. I desperately didn't want to be the one to have to beg him to do this, but at the same time...my friend was worth it.

"Where are you going?" I stood, gripping Kyle's elbow, trying to halt him.

He watched the point of contact, turning his head and staring...as if a ghost had just reached out and grabbed hold of him. I dropped my hand under the scrutiny.

"You think I'm about to just give information about my life, about what I've worked for years to attain, to you of all people?"

His words cut and bruised...but the places they hit were already scar tissue. So, I squared my shoulders and pressed on.

"Yes, I do."

"And why is that, Rylie?"

I swallowed my nerves, reprimanding myself for letting this man make me feel insignificant. I hated how easily I felt useless when he suddenly wasn't interested in talking to me again.

"Because you owe me...you abandoned me. After fucking me

senseless for hours, you left me without so much as a goodbye or an explanation. I thought I was going crazy for a while, Kyle. Decker was probably about to get a restraining order against me. I was pathetic and weak, and it was all because of you."

"Why, because you finally experienced dick for the first time?" His crass words were tiny paper cuts along my heart.

My voice was barely a tremble as I tipped my head back to meet his gaze. "No, because I was with the boy I loved for my first time. Because what we did that night marked me forever...because you broke me so entirely I was forced to forge my broken heart into some-thing new, hoping someone else might accept the sharp shards and mismatched pieces...but no one ever did."

His jaw was set so firmly it looked like it might snap in half. His eyes burrowed into mine, daring me to keep going. I wouldn't. He'd heard what he needed to; I had no other cards to play.

"I need to think about it."

With that, he took three big steps forward and slammed the door shut behind him.

I sank back into the bed, placing my face in my hands, hoping for a miracle.

KYLE DIDN'T TALK TO ME FOR THREE DAYS. HE WASN'T AT SCHOOL; NO girls were sticking their tongues down his throat on the quad, and no one was lurking near my bench. It seemed peaceful, almost like he'd left again, or had never come back in the first place.

Unfortunately for me it made my nerves spark, nearly catching fire every five seconds. I kept constant watch over my cell, waiting to see if Mak or my dad reached out. Neither did. I had no idea if Kyle had my new number, but I wasn't expecting him to reach out via phone. He was a power player, revealing his true strength in how he could make his opponent fear him.

Meanwhile, I felt like I'd been swimming in murky water, just waiting for the big bad shark to get me. I knew he was waiting, out there, circling...eventually he'd come in for the kill.

I just didn't know how exactly he would take me. Either he'd deny me and Mak would go back to jail—or worse, die—or Kyle would give in, but with some bullshit ultimatums and rules. Neither outcome would benefit me; this much I knew.

Finally, at the tail end of the fourth day, his answer arrived.

He sat on my bed again, this time with his arms behind his head, making his biceps bulge, and his face look soft. His dark hair was swept away from his face, revealing his natural eye color and zero signs of the dark liner that usually sat under his eyes. He was my Kyle. For one brief moment, as the sun warmed the floorboards of my room and softened the colors of my walls, he was the boy I remembered.

I moved in, shut the door, and made myself comfortable on Hazel's bed, just like before.

I'd never tell him what it did to me to see him lay on my sheets, filling up every fiber with his scent, conquering something that wasn't offered, not that he'd ask regardless. Kyle consumed and filled every single space he came within contact of.

"I have a few conditions," he said lazily, his eyes trained on my ceiling.

There was nothing special up there except the galaxy when I remembered to turn on my little star projector.

"Okay." I swallowed thickly, desperate to hear him say yes.

"First, you will agree to come live with me."

My heart flipped upside down, emptying out. "Wha—"

He suddenly sat up and spun toward me. "No interruptions. I'll explain everything. Just hear the terms first."

Swallowing my objections, I silently nodded.

"You will come and stay with me. Do school online if you want, drop out—I don't care, but you can't live here. You have to be with me until our deal is fulfilled. This is for your safety, and mine...as things get leaked, there will be a trail leading back to you as the fed's daughter. It's important to have you somewhere safe, and in turn, it will help me know you're not sharing anything you aren't supposed to with unapproved contacts."

My stomach roiled and knotted as the memory of our night

together surfaced, when he had doled out rules regarding our first deal. We were making a new one now, and all I could wonder was if this deal would ruin us like the last one had.

"Next, you will only share what I tell you to, exactly and nothing more. You will get a burner phone to call your father with, and approved personnel from my team will be with you when you make these calls. You will not see your father in person until our deal is done."

I exhaled evenly, realizing there was a really big part of me that didn't mind that specific clause. I was angry with him. He'd hurt me by forcing me into this shadowy crevice.

Kyle watched me carefully as he continued. "Lastly…" He shifted closer, gripping the edge with both hands and leaning in. "We will talk about the past three years…you will spend time with me, you will ask about what I've done, and you will answer my questions. At no time are you to play the silent game with me or shut me out."

Butterflies took off inside my chest as I processed his words, as the realization dawned that he had missed me, that somewhere under his armor, he was weak and broken just like me and wanted to be whole.

I wet my dry lips, my stomach pulling at the mere notion that I'd be near him in such close proximity.

"How long is our deal for?"

He shrugged, watching me as the fading light from the day gathered in his green gaze. "That I will leave up to you. I assume you're giving this information to your father for a reason. At some point he'll have enough, at which point you're free to end the deal and go back to your life…as long as it's safe for you to do so."

That sounded like an odd caveat, but I was too far behind in days to argue it or ask any further questions.

I nodded, dipping my head. "I agree to all of it, but I can't just leave Hazel—she won't understand. Can you do something for me?"

He twisted his head to the side, inspecting me as his lips quirked. "Here I thought this deal was me doing quite a fucking lot for you."

Feeling my face heat, I pushed onward, not willing to let this go. "I need to convince her I have a good reason to just up and leave…

otherwise, she'll tear the world apart trying to find me, starting with my dad."

He raised an eyebrow. "Won't your dad know you're gone?"

"To a degree, but that's complicated...he can't be distracted by her right now, and it'll confuse her further when she realizes he doesn't give a shit that I'm gone."

Kyle's brows hit his hairline, his eyes going wide as they searched my face for the reason my beloved father wouldn't care that I was removed from his life.

"Okay...what did you have in mind?"

Hot flames of embarrassment danced under my skin as I stood up and walked closer to the boy who was once my best friend.

"I know you can't let people know who you are...but can you take a picture with me, maybe wearing a hat or closing your eyes, and..." I wet my lips, gathering courage. "Can we make it look like we're together?"

He tipped his head, his lips spreading wide over his white teeth. "So, Hazel would believe you'd just drop out of school and go off the grid if I showed up?" His legs pulled back, his arms shifting as he stood toe to toe with me, peering down. "And she'd be convinced if we were *together*?"

This was so fucking embarrassing. Why was he making me explain this?

I looked down at my hands, not wanting to give him my eyes. "Yes, okay...she knew I was madly in love with you, knew it broke my heart when you left. She knew I wai—" My breath caught, tears creeping up behind my eyelids as my heart caught up with the pace of my words. It hurt to say this out loud, to confess it to him knowing he would just harshly kick it to the side as if it meant nothing.

"You waited for me," he whispered, gently gripping my chin between his fingers.

"I did..."

I couldn't say any more. Thankfully he didn't force it. He tugged on his hood, adjusting his hair as I pulled my cell out, prepping for the photo. My chest ached, but I pushed it down into the same pile of ash that had been in Kyle's place for the past three years.

I wasn't ready for his touch, or the way he took the phone from my hand, holding it up in front of us. I smiled at the screen, seeing myself reflected back, and then his thumb pressed the button, forcing the timer into action. It counted down to one, and right as it was about to transition over, Kyle turned his head, pressing his lips to my skin as he pulled me closer to his chest.

It all happened fast, and when the image was finalized, I straightened, pulling at my phone. The picture was clear, my eyes tipping up to try to see him, a dreamy expression painfully obvious on my face. But I wasn't alone—his face reflected desire, his mouth firmly pressed to my skin in a desperate way, his eyes shut and a smile tugging at the side of his mouth. We looked like a real couple.

"Thank you." I pushed past him, heading for my closet, where a duffle bag waited to be filled.

"I'll let you pack. When you're ready, come downstairs—I'll be waiting with a car. I already have someone scheduled to come get yours tonight so there's no overlap."

I nodded with jerky movements, preparing to leave a massive chunk of my life and my heart behind.

CHAPTER TWENTY-FOUR

RYLIE WALKED BEHIND ME TOWARD THE CAR, AND MY EYES automatically scanned the area. Delgado's words had been a burning boil on my skin ever since he'd mentioned Paul and their knowledge of his daughter. Scotty said he hadn't caught on to anyone watching her, but that didn't mean jack shit.

My mind tugged out all the little things Rylie had mentioned and the things she kept quiet. Something was off with her dad…why go through such lengths to face me and this shitty mess we'd left ourselves in if not for him? Who else would she do this for?

"You can throw your shit in the back," I said, rounding the hood of my car.

I watched, clenching my back teeth as she tugged on the back door and tossed her duffle and backpack in the back seat. She'd left behind a ton of clothes and shoes in her dorm. I guess it was better this way, but there was already a part of me that was piecing together an image of her living with me for much longer than our deal would hint toward.

She settled into the passenger seat, slamming the door shut, and buckled her seat belt. One thing I liked about this arrangement was getting to have her in my world again. I felt like the devil being granted access to heaven through a back door. I knew I didn't deserve my end of this deal and I was an asshole for even asking for it, but I was far too zealous where she was concerned to do the right thing.

I started the car, the loud roar of the V8 engine coming to life under the hood, causing Rylie to glance over at me. I revved it three times to force a smile on her face…it had always worked with her, except this time she just turned her head, moving her focus to whatever was outside her window. I slammed my back molars together and punched the gear into first, taking off with my tires burning rubber.

We hit eighty miles per hour while in the city limits, blowing past stop signs and red lights. Nothing got her to look my way. Then again, even three years removed, she was used to this. She was used to me. We knew one another, even if we'd changed. Even if one of us was a monster now, she knew the rhythm of my heart, and I knew the feel of her chest rising and falling when she was scared and excited.

Right now, she was neither.

We continued past the city, toward Pinehurst, but turned on a small, unmarked road halfway there. The terrain was rocky for a quarter of a mile before it transitioned into asphalt, and we came upon a massive gate surrounded by ten-foot brick walls bordering the property, making it impossible to see anything inside.

Rylie sat up, looking around like she couldn't get enough details. "This is where you live?" After her silence for the past hour, it was nice to hear her talk again.

"Sometimes."

The gate moved while one of my men shifted to the side, packing his AK-47. Every guard on the grounds carried heavier artillery. Rylie watched the man move; he did well not to do anything more than briefly glance at her. Mostly because for any guy with functioning eyes, it would be impossible not to stare at her big, curious green eyes that held that innocent look every guy wanted right before he sank his dick into her. Her dark eyebrows were always moving, betraying her emotions, rising in surprise, narrowing and caving when she was concerned or confused, flat when she was pissed. Her dark lashes framed those emerald eyes, resting against her high porcelain cheeks.

She was a goddamn dream.

"You have a lot of men..." she mused quietly, almost like she didn't think I'd hear.

I nodded silently and parked in front of the house, next to Scotty's Duster.

She opened her door, not waiting for me. "Who all lives here?"

I grabbed her bags from the back and watched as her head tipped back, taking in the mansion. It was a monstrosity compared to the one Juan had all those years ago.

"Gretta, my housekeeper and cook...she does my laundry too. Scotty...Holt, Garrison...my men." I shrugged. I didn't know who the fuck was in the house on a regular basis. "You're safe here, that's all that matters." I pushed through the entry, hearing raised voices coming from the other half of the house, followed by the smack of skin against the mats. Rylie's face reflected the question, so I answered her, moving up the stairs. "The guys are training in the gym."

"Will I be able to use it?" She stepped behind me, keeping her eyes focused.

I laughed. "Yeah...you can use anything in the house. Make yourself at home."

"Not likely, but thanks," she muttered quietly, keeping up with me.

We bypassed multiple doors, her gaze bouncing from space to space, likely curious about where her room would be. I braced myself for her reaction as I powered on, going all the way down to the end of the hall.

She hesitated near the doorway, crossing her arms as I set her bags down in the walk-in closet and began explaining the space to her.

"Gretta already made room for your stuff in the closet. There are fresh towels in the bathroom, and a new robe for you. She put on fresh sheets too."

"I'm confused...this looks like your room." She took a step inside, swinging her gaze to the king-sized bed encased in dark mahogany and black sheets. An eighty-inch flat screen hung on the wall with a massive built-in below it, complete with sculptures, three game systems, DVDs, and games. Pictures of my family sat in a few scattered frames around the room, and if she inspected them carefully, she'd see she was in three of them.

"It is my room." I moved to the bathroom and kept the door open. "There's a huge soaking tub in here. Feel free to use it whenever you want…same with the shower."

"Wait…I'm lost…" She shook her head back and forth, her face reddening. "Where will you stay?"

I laughed, hoping to make her uncomfortable. "Here."

"No…we aren't staying in the same bed…or the same room." She faltered, her face getting to an angrier red color.

"We are."

She huffed, moving her gaze around. "There have got to be like sixty bedrooms in this place…there's no reason whatsoever for me to stay with you."

"There are fifteen, and they're all taken by my staff…sorry, no room. You'll stay in here with me. Not to mention, Rylie Jean, your privacy has been limited significantly due to our deal. I can't give you the private room you want and deserve because one of us needs to keep an eye on your activity."

She made a sound of annoyance. "Are you serious? This was not a part of our deal."

I already knew she was desperate enough to do it, but some stupid part of me wanted her to want to be in here with me.

"Did I not say you would stay with me?"

"You meant in your house…" she argued, tilting her head like I was an idiot.

"You sure?"

"Gah! You drive me insane, Kyle. Fine, I'll stay in here—but if you make a move on me, I will fucking break your nose."

I smirked, skirting around her. "Wouldn't expect any different from you."

REGARDLESS OF WHAT I HAD TOLD RYLIE, I WOULD OBVIOUSLY GIVE her the privacy she needed. As soon as she registered that she would in fact be staying with me in the room, I left her alone.

I'd let her settle, figure out what she wanted to do, and let her adjust to life inside the madhouse. I'd gone down to the gym to work in a few rounds with the guys. Holt was a monster and wasn't easy to take down. Garrison was even worse. The rest of the fuckers were a waste of my time and Scotty was still too injured to fight, so I worked with what I had.

I grunted, dodging a hit from Garrison.

"Fuck, you nearly took my head off." I danced around him on the balls of my feet. My shirt was off, sweat dripped from my hair and hit the mats, and my sweats sat low on my hips, apparently drawing the attention of my new little roommate.

"Move faster, boss." Garrison laughed, swinging at me again.

I dodged and homed in on his movements. He was fast but big. I was leaner and faster. I danced around him, kicking the back of his leg while pulling him back into a headlock. He tapped out immediately, knowing we didn't need to waste energy on a battle of grips.

"I'm done for the day. You've made me sweat like a pig and bleed like a stuck one. Gretta will kill you for what you've done to the mats."

I gulped down a bottle of water and smiled.

A few other guys milled around, working the punching bags and treadmills. I noticed too late that their heads were swung over toward the doorway where Rylie leaned her shoulder against the frame, wearing another pair of skintight leggings and a hoodie that ended right below her breasts, showing her toned stomach. She wore her hair in a high ponytail, and for whatever reason, her lips were recently glossed. Would it have killed her to come down wearing my sweats or a paper bag?

Fuck, I had to handle this now before it became a problem. Knowing she might knee me in the balls, I lazily walked over, still sipping my water bottle.

Once I was close enough, I gripped her chin with my fingers. Her green eyes locked on mine in confusion as I increased pressure.

I flicked my eyes down to her lips then back up to her eyes. Just to see if she'd understand, I glanced to the side, where the guys were still watching. She followed my focus, and after her nose flared, she gave me the smallest nod of understanding.

She knew I had to mark her, otherwise they'd trip over themselves to please her or try to get time with her and I'd end up killing them. That would just be a waste of Scotty's time and effort in interviewing men to replace these fuckers.

I leaned down, still holding her chin, and pressed my lips to hers. I stayed there, taking more than I needed to, but that was what I did…I was spoiled and, when it came to her, entirely too greedy. She kissed me back, but I knew it was for show…still, I was grateful.

We both had roles to play here, and she seemed to fall into hers seamlessly. She broke away first, ducking her head, hiding her face. I didn't move; instead I tugged on her hand and spun us toward the hallway, clearing the view of all the men inside the gym.

Rylie fell in step with me, crossing her arms. "Was that necessary?"

This was going to be a long week; I could already feel it under my skin. I let out a sigh, stretching my arm behind my head. "Rylie, you look like you should have your own OnlyFans account. Trust me, if you did, every fucking guy in there would be paying your bills for the foreseeable future just to see you strip. Yes, it was necessary, because if any of them touch you or even look at you like they want to fuck you, I'll kill them."

We stopped in the hall, facing each other. She didn't seem rattled by my confession—if anything, just bored.

"You've changed, Kyle…or am I supposed to call you Joker?" Her head tilted like she was trying to be cute…like she was honestly confused about my identity.

I gripped her elbow, pulling her closer to me. "Try to be cute with me, Rylie…it won't get you very far. You wanted this, you asked for this, so don't come into my house and start tearing shit up."

She swallowed, her eyes holding a glint of anger in them. I let her go, and as soon as I did, she pulled away from me and stormed up the stairs. I watched her, hating how good it felt to have her here with me, hating that I would rather have her captive like my own little bird in a cage than free and away from me. I knew it was sick. I knew it was wrong, but secretly it made my heart thunder and my pulse race. She was here with me after so many years apart, and she couldn't leave.

"Does she know the rules?" Scotty asked, hesitating with a neon yellow ball gripped between his fingers.

I pulled the smoke from between my lips and watched as the sun sank behind a pink and orange sky. Bronson's dark ears twitched as he waited for his owner to throw the ball. His brother Baretta finally ran back from the perimeter fence, and a small animal was bleeding between his teeth.

These dogs always found something out here and always brought back their spoils like they wanted to care for us. Made the fuckers endearing.

"What kind of question is that? Of course she knows."

Scotty threw the ball again, keeping his focus on his dogs. "Where she's concerned, you lose your goddamn head, so I like to be sure."

"Why do you think she's in my room? I plan on keeping a close eye on everything she does."

My uncle laughed and turned toward me. "You have her in your room so you can fuck her. Let's not play games here, Kyle. You aren't a kid anymore, neither is she, and I honestly don't give a single fuck about it. Just make sure she doesn't talk to anyone else. Kill her phone, give her the burner when it's time to talk to her old man. We're keeping an eye on him too, to see who tries to recruit him now that Delgado is gone."

I nodded, finishing my smoke and tossing it. "I want to be clear about something."

I waited to ensure my uncle's attention was on me.

"We both agreed to this...that's why I explained it to you, why I brought you into it."

"We agreed that having her here would be our own form of leverage, and we'd be able to doctor what's fed to the FBI...you essentially have her as an informant. The question is, did you explain to her that this deal benefits you more than it does her?"

A small flame flickered in my core, warning me that, if not handled properly, this situation could ruin anything I had with Rylie, but my thoughts were all tainted with lust and obsession. I wasn't thinking clearly where she was concerned, wasn't doing what was best for her. I just wanted her. I needed her to myself in whatever form that happened to come.

"All you need to worry about is that I won't hesitate to kill you if you hurt her or threaten her. I love you, but I'm telling you the score."

He dipped his head, nodding his understanding.

"Also…you encourage any of our men to talk to her or touch her, and I'll kill Bronson and Baretta."

His eyes widened; a red coloring began to show above his collar. I knew that was his true weakness. He didn't give two shits about himself, but threaten his dogs, and it was as effective as threatening his kids. Deep down, I didn't think I could ever hurt an animal…but I supposed it would depend on the circumstances.

If Rylie were hurt because of his actions, I just might take it out on whatever he loved most. That was the monster he was training me to be after all.

I didn't wait to hear my uncle respond. Instead I walked inside. Gretta had already gone upstairs to help Rylie get settled and decided on her own to take Rylie's dinner up to her so she didn't have to eat with us. That was something I'd rectify really fucking quick.

Right after I got to spend a little time with my old friend.

CHAPTER TWENTY-FIVE

Rylie

I held my breath as my body sank under the water. The bubbles had long since dissolved and the water was beginning to turn cold, but I couldn't bring myself to leave. I counted to sixty then felt my lungs constrict and began to surface again.

Except this time, my ex best friend leaned against the door frame, watching me with a heated glare. Maybe if I weren't in a stilted existence where I was going to be sharing a bed with the man who shattered my heart, I would try to hide myself. I would put up a big fat 'Fuck off' sign that I would keep pushing and pushing, much like with the customers at Mak's. But I was here in the palm of his hand, and I was so exhausted of fighting him. I was tired of not speaking with him, not asking him questions. I was so weary of pretending I didn't care about him.

When really, deep down, he filled up every empty space that echoed his memory back at me. Caverns of pain he'd dug deep inside my heart wanted to be filled, wanted him to fix everything he'd broken.

So, I rose from the bath. I watched his gaze heat, taking in my breasts and hips, lower until he was staring right at my sex. I held my hand out to him.

"Can you get me a towel please?"

He waited a brief second, his tongue sweeping across the metal ring in his bottom lip while he calculated something. I wasn't sure what. I knew he physically wanted me, but I had no idea if I was merely a few holes for him to sink into, or if he cared about the heart underneath.

A chill swept through the room. It was still warm enough outside during the day for the heat not to be set for the house, but the sun had set, so the rooms were cold now. My skin pebbled, my nipples hardening as he waited to move. Embarrassment unfurled in my stomach, a familiar feeling coiling deep where this man was concerned. I thought me standing here would move him, similar to a chess piece I could control with merely being naked in front of him. His frozen stature just proved me wrong.

I lifted a leg, pushing it over the lip of the tub as heat betrayed my face, warming it from underneath my skin. My feet hit the mat, soaking it with drops of water, dripping from my hair and wet skin. My other leg followed suit, and suddenly Kyle moved with jerky limbs to grab the white robe hanging off the door.

He walked toward me, his eyes still encased in the colored contacts he wore. I didn't like the Joker version of him; he was crass and mean. I knew it was a suit of armor he'd worn for so long he had likely rusted to his core now. My fingers itched to pull it apart and see where the real version of my friend was.

I turned my back to him as he steadily moved across the marbled floor and tugged my hair so that when the soft fabric hit my shoulders, it wouldn't get tangled underneath. I slid my hands in and tugged the panels closed, tying it off at the waist.

Kyle didn't move; if anything he shifted closer until the heat of his chest engulfed my back, his nose at my ear, inhaling. I closed my eyes, letting this happen, allowing it…wanting it.

His tongue darted out, licking along the seam of my ear, leaving it heated and wet. His teeth grazed the spot a second later, going lower until he gently bit down on the lobe. He buried his nose into the soaked strands of my hair as he continued to smell me. His hand was at my waist, tugging me into his chest.

I silently breathed through my nose, unsure what I wanted to do. I desired his touch, but I also wanted to punish him for hurting me. I didn't want to release any part of myself so easily to him. I wanted him to work for whatever crumbs I'd swipe off the table of our friendship, and it took me a few seconds to realize he wasn't going to give me a choice.

His teeth returned to my neck, skimming the space there until they were sinking more firmly into my shoulder. He groaned as his tongue lapped at the spot. My breaths came in heavy bursts, forcing my chest to heave in brittle spurts. My naked thighs under the robe were suddenly slick right where they linked together.

"Kyle." I breathed his name, a plea and a warning as I turned in his arms.

He seemed to understand, lifting his head, his eyes half closed with desire, watching my lips.

His hand squeezed my ass through the terrycloth. "You're a dream, Rylie Jean, the one I've had on repeat for three years. Now you're here in front of me, soaking wet, and you're telling me I can't have you?"

I opened my mouth to explain why, but his lips were there a second later, his tongue sweeping in, filling me with his own silent reasons for why he was taking this. I gripped his shirt between my fingers, and with a wave of desire sweeping through my chest, carving out a space for my need for him...I kissed him back.

I pressed my lips firmly against his and slanted my head to the side. Opening for him, tangling my tongue with his, ignoring how his hands went to my hips and lifted me against him, ignoring how he walked us to the counter and shoved his body between my legs, driving them wide.

His hands cupped my jaw, cradling my head as he tilted it back and his lips moved in a rhythm against mine, promising more. Begging, warning that he'd take what he wanted, with or without my consent. This was raw, the way he held me...it was power and possession.

In whatever version existed in his head, he owned me.

So, I owned him back, gripping his shirt, pulling him closer while my tongue melded with his. Warring, breaking, needing with every swipe and every pant between our breaths.

His hands moved, so quickly I couldn't process it fully. The tie for my robe was pulled completely free. I blinked at the hungry expression in his eyes, realizing I had never seen him look so crazed or desperate. The heady feeling I had knowing it was me doing that to him was too much to let me consider refusing wherever this was headed. I was sick in the head because I wanted to know. I craved it from him.

My hands were jerked away from my body and shoved up over my head, my figure pushed back toward the mirror, my ass half lifted onto the counter as my hands were joined and tied to the metal ring used to hang hand towels.

I inhaled a sharp breath as I realized what he'd just done. I tugged my wrists, trying to free them, but they wouldn't budge. He'd knotted the tie around my wrists in a firm and unyielding hold.

The robe covered my body, leaving a small slice of skin on show as the tie holding it together no longer kept it closed.

Kyle's eyes moved from the slice, unravelling the two panels, and traveled up to my eyes.

I didn't dare ask what he was doing, because I already knew.

He was claiming me, and while he might not completely conquer me tonight, he was going to have some part of me, whatever his appetite craved.

His hands slowly moved, pushing apart the fabric that kept me concealed. My arms were above my head so my breasts were pushed up, and my nipples pebbled.

His finger skimmed the dusky nub and hissed as he palmed my left breast.

"You're practically spilling out of my fingers now…you've grown into them, Ry…fuck they're perfect."

His hands moved until both breasts were being held, his thumbs rubbing over my sensitive nipples. His eyes bore into mine before he lowered his head, taking me between his teeth, tugging and lapping at my pebbled nerves.

I made a sound of surprise…something, I wasn't sure what, but I knew my hips bucked. Not being able to hold his face or touch him was the oddest feeling, like being presented for him to feast on, to pick and choose his favorite parts and do with them whatever he wanted.

The slickness between my thighs intensified as he worked both nipples, biting, licking, and sucking them. His head slowly traveled down my body, his tongue swiping over my belly button, going lower until he was breathing on the apex of my thighs.

I wouldn't spread them for him, no matter how badly I wanted to.

He got on his knees, and his blue gaze dared me not to, emphasized by a quirk of his brow. I smiled down at him, clenching them closed, daring him.

He smirked and pushed them apart with force, tugging a cry of pain from my chest. His tongue was pushing through my folds a second later, removing any sting that might have lingered. He lapped at my core, delving deep, sucking me into his mouth.

"So fucking delicious…" He groaned. "I've missed this."

Leaning back, watching me, he slowly pushed a finger inside me and began rubbing at my clit. He watched my face as he moved his finger around. "Does this feel good?"

I didn't answer. He added another digit, creating more friction.

"Our deal was that you wouldn't be silent anymore, Rylie…answer me."

Exhaling heavily, I responded. "Yes, it feels good…"

"Do you want me to fuck you with these fingers, Rylie, and make you scream?" He shifted until he was three fingers deep then his other hand came up, his thumb rubbing at my clit while his fingers stayed buried in my cunt.

"Answer me," he demanded, watching me, my eyes barely able to meet his because of my arms being above my head.

I swallowed thickly. "Yes…"

"Beg me, Rylie."

The feeling of him rubbing my clit, working my core…it was too much. I needed it.

"Please…Kyle," I muttered on a gasp.

He made a sound, something similar to a feral growl, and then my legs were being lifted over his shoulders, my cunt secured to his face as he fucked me with his tongue.

I rocked my hips, grinding them against his mouth as he sucked and lapped at my core. The most sensitive sensations swept through me as he perfectly devoured me. I wanted more, wanted to come completely undone, unravel to the very origin of our story, see where we started and where we were supposed to end.

His palms caressed my ass cheeks as his eyes focused on mine, his mouth still secured to me, licking my core so intensely a cry suddenly ripped through me, my orgasm shattering me so powerfully I screamed.

My eyes screwed shut as my chest heaved up and down. I felt the absence of him a moment later, the cool air hit my soaking sex, and I knew I should see what he had planned next, but I felt like a part of my soul had just exited my body. I needed a second to recover, to process what we'd done.

His hands were around my hips a second later, lifting me, and then the tip of his cock was gliding through my soaking folds.

My eyes flew open, my heart thrashing around in my chest. *Am I ready for this?*

"Kyle…" I warned, but his gaze was all heat and need.

He didn't penetrate but kept rubbing his cock through my wetness. "Just reminding you where you belong…" He exhaled, holding my waist while he lightly teased my core. "I want you to break for me," he confessed, increasing his speed, the feeling of his erection against my sensitive entrance so intoxicating.

I didn't even care that my hands burned or that my arms hurt. I just didn't want him to stop.

"I want to fuck you so hard you forget the other assholes you were with." He pushed in further, and I gasped.

I had forgotten how big he was. I'd forgotten how badly I'd burned and ached after that night together, how I had literally felt like I'd been ripped open and sewn shut. It had taken two weeks for me to not wince when I walked.

"I want you to remember only me." He thrust. I screamed as his length nearly tore me in half. "Only this." He pulled out and thrust again. "Forever me."

He pulled out again and lunged forward so hard the back of my head hit the mirror. His eyes fixated on me as he pulled completely out and repeated the movement, this time pushing in even harder, seeming to relish how much harder my head landed. The pain was a tiny burn against my heating, pulsating climax that kept climbing. I wanted him to do it again and again, until the glass shattered behind me.

Instead, he pulled out aggressively, leaving me to slump against the restraints of my hands. I hissed in pain.

He gripped his cock, still wet from my arousal and gliding inside of me, the tip weeping, the veins bulging as his thickness throbbed and twitched. He rubbed up and down, watching me, his movements fast and jerky, his guttural groans filling the room, making my hips buck with need.

"That's right, baby, we will be fucking and very soon, but when we do, I want you to take it. I want you to want it."

His wrist flicked in rigorous movements as he milked his length, roaring his release with ribbons of pleasure bursting all over my skin. He leaned closer and pressed the tip of his pulsating dick to my cunt, letting his seed spill all over my pussy.

He groaned, watching as he came against my skin. I felt his hot orgasm dripping between my legs, sliding down my ass, through my crack. I felt filthy but in the best way, and all I wanted was for him to flip me, use that lubrication, and fuck me in the ass.

Instead, his fingers touched the cum coating me, and he pushed his thick digits inside, pushing his pleasure in through my folds. His eyes darted up to mine as three of his fingers rocked inside me.

Then, he did something filthy and brazen. With his seed still coating his fingers, he brought his hand up to my mouth and wiped my bottom lip with his arousal.

"Open these fucking lips, beautiful."

I watched him, his lids weighty from his lust-filled gaze, and did as he said, opening my mouth for him to push his fingers inside. I sucked on them, lapping at the remains of what we'd done, swallowing it down my throat.

He gasped, watching my throat dip. "Shit, baby." He removed his fingers a second later, and then he began untying my hands.

My arms went limp; I couldn't even hold myself up on the counter. His body was there, taking my weight a second later and helping me to my feet. They were unsteady as well because of my orgasm. I was sore from how hard he'd thrust into me, and because it had been well over nine months since I'd had sex. I could feel him dripping down my thighs as I stood erect. He smirked at me, seeing the mess he'd created.

"I'm getting in the shower…I'd like you to stay exactly the way you are and get into bed. I want to know you're going to sleep with my cum between your legs."

I rolled my eyes, pushing past him. "This wasn't a part of the deal."

"Do you need a deal to enjoy a few filthy orgasms from me?" I didn't respond, and he spun me by my elbow. "Do you need my cock inside your cunt again, or did you forget that you're supposed to talk to me?"

I tugged at my arm. "Let's be clear about something: I allowed that to happen. You know as well as I do that if I had asked you to stop, you would have, and if I want a moment to myself to think, I'll fucking take it."

I stormed past him into the bedroom, knowing he'd throw a tantrum if I tried sleeping somewhere else. I tugged the blankets back, staying in my robe, and privately enjoyed the feeling of his seed between my thighs. I was so fucked, because I knew if he wanted to touch me, I'd let him. If he wanted to fuck me, I'd gladly open my legs. Because all this time, the pieces I was missing were him. He was in fragments now, but I didn't care.

I'd get out the Krazy Glue and start sorting that shit out, because I wanted my friend back, and I was damn sure I'd do whatever it took to get him.

CHAPTER TWENTY-SIX

THE SUN LIT UP THE KITCHEN, BRONSON AND BARETTA RESTED ON their beds by the back door, and the view outside the windows gave way to the pool and lush yard. The tree line was bursting with colors as the last few days of October dwindled. I sipped my coffee, watching like I did every morning, but this time my heart was pounding at a sickening pace.

I must have checked the fuck out the night before with a momentary lapse of insanity. Rylie had been naked, dripping wet in the tub, and the next thing I knew I'd been tying her up and nearly fucking her brains out. I had been so out of my mind with wanting her that I would have done anything to have her. After my shower, once I had cleared my head, I'd realized the gravity of what I had done.

I had walked into my bedroom and seen Rylie's dark hair fanned out along my pillow; she was already asleep. I'd hung my head, feeling like an asshole of the greatest measure for what I had taken from her and how I had lost myself to my lust. Three years of abstinence had all slammed into me at once when I saw her standing there naked, not that it was an excuse…it was just a fact. So, to punish myself, I'd left her there to sleep alone.

Bronson had woken me by licking my face, his owner standing

over me in a pair of joggers and a white tank. Scotty had eyed me with a raised brow but didn't ask. It wasn't that he hadn't likely heard what we'd done the previous night—the whole fucking house had probably heard—but it was my home and my life, so fuck them and their nosy-ass judgment.

"Good morning, sir," Gretta said warmly, bustling into the kitchen. "Can I get some eggs started for you?"

"Thank you, Gretta, that would be great…please make enough for two."

Gretta gave me a look, smiling coyly. "The house nearly shook off its foundation with what we heard from you and the new missus last night."

Right as she finished saying it, Rylie stopped short, clearing the arch leading into the heart of the room.

"Ah…sorry, I can come back later." She blushed as Gretta giggled, turning toward the fridge.

"Ry, it's fine. Gretta is going to make us some breakfast, take a seat."

She awkwardly walked forward but stopped short when she saw the dogs lift their heads toward her.

"Hi handsome, look at you." She bent at the knees to pet Bronson's ears, scratching under his chin. Baretta licked his lips and shoved his head into her chest, not wanting to miss out on the affection.

My uncle was ruthless as hell, but his dogs were gentle as bunnies, the complete opposite of what he likely should have roaming the grounds, but part of me thought maybe he needed that in his life. I'd never once seen him with anyone, not a man or woman. I'd never seen him soften or take time to relax, nothing that made him human —except those dogs.

"Such good boys." Rylie cooed, smiling at the dogs. Fuck, now they would be obsessed with her and Scotty would be pissed.

"You take your eggs with peppers and tomatoes?" Gretta asked Rylie.

Ry stood, spinning toward my chef and housekeeper. "Sure, whatever you have on hand…in fact, I can help you, or make my own. I don't mind."

Gretta waved her off. "No, you're the missus of the house, very important that you sit and drink café." Her accent rolled off her tongue in a heavy brogue.

Rylie gave her a polite smile and finally headed toward me. "Hi." She sat, her face flushing red. She was already showered and dressed, boots on her feet and hair braided into two symmetrical rows. I hadn't seen her wear it like that since we were in high school.

"Morning." I moved my cup of coffee in front of her.

She accepted it and started sipping. "Thanks."

Gretta walked over with our plates a moment later and then left us in peace.

"This view is incredible." Rylie sipped the coffee, her hand automatically going down to pat the top of Bronson's head. Both dogs had moved from their spots and now sat at attention, next to her chair. I was about as whipped as them, so I couldn't judge.

I nodded, cutting into my eggs. We ate in silence as the sun warmed the earth. Meanwhile a rogue dark cloud hung over the trees, promising rain.

"So, I was hoping we could start with intel this morning." Rylie jumped right to it.

I smiled, liking her ability to pretend the previous night hadn't happened, but we needed to talk about it, even if it killed me to apologize or confess that I'd been a dick for taking so much from her.

"We can…but first I need to talk to you about last night."

She shifted, ducking her chin to her chest, suddenly very focused on her eggs. "We don't have to talk about it."

"We do. I fu—"

"Ah, good, you're both here." Scotty walked in, interrupting me. He set a burner phone down in front of Rylie and pulled up a chair. "Say exactly what we tell you to."

"What the fuck?" I felt my brows arch as I watched my uncle. Why was he just jumping straight to being a complete asshole?

"You're needed in the gym." He pointed at me then turned his dead stare back toward Rylie. Had I not been fucking clear enough the night before?

"I'm not needed anywhere, and forgive me if I don't ask how fucking high when you say to jump."

"Fine, we need to—"

I grabbed the phone, flipped it open, and punched in her dad's number then held it out for her. "Tell him the Joker's base is in New York, but as far as you've heard he moves around often. We will be listening for any questions he gives you, to help as we can."

Rylie watched me, nodding her head. "I know he's curious about who the Joker reports to…he wants to know who the family is made up of."

Scotty looked over at me, his knee bouncing. I wasn't sure if he noticed or not, but Bronson's head was still resting on Rylie's lap. She pet his ears while she waited for us to reply.

Scotty piped up. "Tell him it's a proper family setup…the Joker is the head."

Incriminating as fuck if we were caught. I stared at him then nodded. "Don't offer it freely, only if he asks."

Rylie wet her lips and tugged the cell closer, pressing the green call button.

It rang a few times then her dad's nasally voice picked up.

"Hello?"

"Dad…it's me." Rylie closed her eyes, an odd expression flitting across her features.

"Rylie, where are you?"

"Doesn't matter. Listen…I have some info for you."

He hesitated, and my molars slammed together. Why the fuck would he hesitate over questioning where his daughter was? She seemed to wonder this too, her eyes watering the slightest bit. She looked away to hide it.

"You ready?" She cleared her throat.

"Yeah, let me get my tape recorder…" He shuffled a few things around on his end then came back on. "Go ahead."

"The Joker's base of operations is in New York…but he moves, shifting it every few weeks. He never stays in one place for very long."

"Okay. What family is he tied to?" Paul asked, moving along with each question.

Rylie's eyes flicked up, waiting for us. Scotty wrote down a response.

"None…they're scratching out their own place…"

He paused, moving a few papers around on his end of the line. "That can't be possible—your intel must be wrong, Rylie. With how much product they have, they'd need significant backing to start that, but whoever would offer it wouldn't do so without requiring loyalty."

Rylie watched the table, unsure of what to say.

I wrote something down.

"There was a backer, but he's dead now…"

"The only big player that has recently died…was Ivan," Paul rattled off.

I wrote down a name quickly.

"Did you know the head of the Delgado family is gone, same with the McMillians?"

"How long?" Paul asked, the greedy motherfucker.

Rylie shook her head. "That's your job, Dad…figured you would have already known."

"Rylie, this is about as good as Mak gave…which is why he's in the shit house. I'm trying to keep him safe, but you have to give me something more. Otherwise I won't have any other choice. Why don't you tell me about where you are, who you're with? You said you had access to his crew—what does that mean?"

My pulse beat against my throat and pounded in my ears. She'd risked all this, had started talking to me again and had given up school and classes for Mak? He meant that much to her? It fucking hurt. Even if they weren't fucking one another, she obviously cared a great deal for him…something she used to feel for me but didn't anymore, not if she'd already thrown my name in there to use as a ticket out.

Rylie put her hand to her forehead, thinning her lips.

"Dad…I—"

Scotty held up the notepad for her to read.

"I need to be sure I can share that stuff. I'm doing what I can, but I have to be careful."

"Tell me where you are, Rylie, and why your phone is going to voicemail," Paul pressed.

"I can't…but I'll be in touch soon."

"You have two days, then I have to make a decision about Mak."

She grit her teeth, red marring her face as her voice rose. "Then decide to be merciful…decide to keep him on as an informant. Decide to do the right thing."

Paul didn't say anything for a few seconds, then uttered, "You already know I can't. I really don't want to be forced to work for a family, Rylie…I need you to help me out."

What a fucking cunt. I stood so fast the chair shot out from under me and crashed against the wall. I couldn't hear any more.

The fact that he was so willing to risk his daughter, knowing she had some sort of connections to the most dangerous crew amongst the families, yet he didn't want to have to report to one of them so he'd risk her?

I threw a glass bottle of Jameson against the wall in the living room.

Seconds later, Rylie ran in. Her eyes were huge, her lips pressed together in worry.

"You…" I pointed at her, shaking my head. "You're fucking being used by him!"

I felt the irony burn in my chest. I was using her too, but it was complicated. I loved her, I needed her…it was different than what she was doing for Mak, or what she was offering her father.

"Kyle…" She looked down, looking deflated.

"Ry, he didn't even care that you might be with my crew right now. He didn't care that you're putting yourself in harm's way…and for what?" I threw another bottle against the wall. Amber liquid dripped down the pristine walls while glass chunks littered the ground. Gretta ran in, and her graying brows caved inward, replaced within seconds by an angry twitch and a sound of disapproval.

I turned away, feeling like shit about making a mess. "Gretta, I'll clean it."

"Nonsense, Mr. James. This why I'm here." She started in with her rag and small broom, brushing pieces into the pan.

I turned back toward Rylie. "Is he worth it?"

I meant Mak, but honestly, I was referring to all the shitty men in her life, me included.

Her expression softened, her arms crossing over her chest as if she wanted extra protection. "Yeah, Mak is like an older brother to me. I can't let him go back to jail, or worse…"

I understood loyalty, and I could even respect her for it…didn't change how much it fucking hurt how far she'd be willing to go for him. Even if she hadn't yet, I knew deep down she'd hand me over if it meant protecting him.

"I'm going out…I'll be back later." I turned away, grabbing my keys on the way, ignoring Rylie calling me back.

CHAPTER TWENTY-SEVEN

Rylie

I PULLED MY CELL UP, SEEING IT WAS PAST MIDNIGHT AND KYLE STILL hadn't come home.

I had no idea if this was his usual behavior, or if he even knew I had my cell, but I was tempted to text him. I'd found his cell number on the bulletin board hanging in the office, where Gretta pinned notes and messages.

Speaking of the housekeeper, I had spent my day helping her fold linens and hearing about her country and family back home. We'd talked about the house, what she liked about it, what she missed about the previous one, and how tired she was of Kyle moving. She had played cards with me and showed me how to work the television in Kyle's room, which was where I'd ended up after dinner.

I'd taken another luxurious bath, soaking away all the stress from the morning and reading one of Kyle's books. Then I had snuggled under the covers of his massive bed and hoped he'd return. I'd also tried to coax Bronson and Baretta into keeping me company, but Scotty had said something in German that forced them both downstairs. He was a killjoy, and honestly such a dick.

I avoided him every time he came remotely close to me, which was actually fairly easy since the house was so massive.

I read the text from Hazel where she freaked out about Kyle's return and our reunion. She asked where we were, and I lied, telling her we were slumming it in Arizona for a while. She seemed to buy it…at least for now.

I stared at the text thread with my friend, belatedly realizing the photo I'd taken with Kyle was gone. Sitting up, I moved my fingers at a breakneck pace, diving into my photo folder, but it was gone from there too.

"Motherfucker." I knew Scotty had done it. He hated me, and at any sign that Kyle and I were even remotely close, he seemed to want to stop it as soon as he could. I was somewhat surprised he hadn't bust in through Kyle's bedroom door the previous night, breaking up our little reunion.

Setting my phone back down on the side table, I sank into Kyle's mattress, staring up at the wide slats along the top of his bed frame. It looked like a custom build for the masculine four-poster frame. I blinked, toying with the covers, hating that I was feeling worried. But he'd shown so much of himself today, and I knew from when we were younger that he didn't do well when it came to emotions. He didn't do well at all when it came to being vulnerable, and somehow, I'd not only concerned him but hurt him. Although, I wasn't sure how…the situation revolving around Mak seemed to upset him the most.

I supposed if the tables were turned and he had a female Mak, I'd be sensitive about it. Fuck, I'd die of jealously if someone meant that much to him. Suddenly my heart ached to hold my best friend, to reassure the boy in him that he was still loved and wanted, regardless of what had happened between us…

Maybe it was time to address all of that. He had seemed open to it. In fact, he'd made it a part of our deal…so I decided I would ask, and that would be a start for us.

It was another hour before I finally heard his bedroom door creak open, his silent movements shifting around the room. The water barely turned on in the bathroom, along with the toilet flushing. I suddenly panicked that he might try to sleep on the couch, which was so insane I couldn't even wrap my brain around it—how fast I'd fallen into him, into wanting him close, wanting to hear him tell me about his day.

I stayed where I was, in the middle of the bed, pretending to be asleep while I waited to hear his footsteps. If he started for the door, I'd sit up and stop him. After a few minutes, the bathroom door opened, and no light escaped…then the mattress dipped, and he was sliding in next to me.

I turned over, curling into the crook of his arm, watching his features in the dark.

"You came back."

"I live here," he replied sleepily.

Oh right…it would make sense for him to return to the place he lived.

His finger traced the shape of my lips, making my skin pebble.

"I guess what I meant is…I'm glad you came back."

"Why?" he whispered.

The limited light from the moon came through his curtains, along with the small lights from his electronics.

I wet my lips, scooting closer. "Because…" I wanted to say so much, but I wasn't ready, so I settled for, "I worry about you."

He grunted in response, but I felt his body inch closer too. Our chests were practically aligned, our noses nearly touching.

"When are we going to discuss the past three years?"

He let out a small huff of breath. "When I'm in bed with you… my mind empties, Ry. I can't think of what I did five minutes ago, much less three years ago."

An exhilarated feeling took off in my chest.

Whispering, I asked, "What are you thinking about then?"

I knew the question was fire tossed into a keg of kerosine, carelessly flung into the night. But he'd lit me on fire the night prior, and I hadn't stopped burning.

"You don't want to know." He made a sound of irritation, or pain.

I inched closer. "I want to know…I'll tell you what I've been thinking about if you tell me what you're thinking about."

He seemed to wait, but after a few seconds, he muttered, "What we did last night…I think about touching you again."

I swallowed a massive lump of anxiety.

"Your turn," he whispered, his lips barely a breath away.

"Same…I feel like you started a fire and walked away from it, so it just obliterated all this stuff that was combustible. It's been all fireworks and molten heat in my body…aching for you to come back and touch me aga—"

His lips slammed into mine, his hand on my hip pulling me closer until our bodies were melded together. I was wearing a tank top, no bra, and just a cotton thong. His roaming hands seemed to realize this as a groan erupted from his throat.

"We have so much fucked-up history between us." Kyle's voice was raspy as he broke our kiss to move our bodies.

"Yeah." My chest heaved. "Think of it like a cluttered garage… eventually we'll get to it, but we can still live in the house, enjoy the perks of the property even if the garage isn't accessible."

He laughed, dipping his head into my cleavage. Gently, he tugged down the fabric of my tank and sucked my nipple into his mouth.

"So, you're saying we should enjoy each other even though we're a work in progress?"

I toyed with his hair, pulling on the strands. "I love renovation shows. Unfinished projects make the world go round."

He growled into my skin, and seconds later, I heard a rip accompanied by my breasts being freed. His tongue lapped at my nipples in rough strokes. It made my hips buck wildly as my mind conjured up what else he might think of doing tonight.

"Do you trust me?" he suddenly whispered in my ear, his lips pressing in close. He pushed my hair off my face then his hands lowered, continuing to rip the rest of the tank top.

"Yes," I replied breathily.

"First mistake, baby," he joked, pulling me up and fully removing the tank top.

I sat up, naked save for the thong I had on.

He was behind me, moving, and then the sound of fabric shredding filled the air, along with my heavy breathing. My hands were pulled behind my back, once again tied together…except he looped the fabric through the top of my thong so my hands were stuck behind my back and my underwear couldn't be removed due to the knot.

But he wasn't done. He walked into the bathroom and returned with something.

"Open your mouth and bite down, Rylie," he ordered, and I complied because he made me so hot I could explode.

He crumpled a dry washcloth and shoved it in my mouth. I bit down on the fabric and adjusted to breathing through my nose.

"I'm going to ask that you trust me, okay?"

I nodded as goosebumps erupted along my arms.

I heard him moving around behind me. The bed shifted and then he was standing, his feet pressing into the soft mattress next to me. He was hanging something above my head.

"You ever use resistance bands, Ry?"

I breathed through my nose, imagining what the fuck he'd come up with regarding those, and also feeling a little excited. I liked doing this with him, learning about each other's likes and what turned the other on.

"Well, you're going to feel the rubber against your skin here in a second, and then your ass is going to rise, forcing your face down into the bed. I'll be sure to turn you so you can breathe."

I didn't have time to process what he'd said. The rubber was slipping in between the thong and the restraint at my wrist, and my ass was being lifted as he tied the rest of the band off at the top of the wooden slat above his bed.

"Feel good, baby?"

I felt awkward, but the sensations of being exposed to him and vulnerable with him were intoxicating. He moved behind me, making some sort of groaning sound as his hands skimmed up and down the expanse of my ass.

"So round, and so fucking perfect," he murmured in between kisses and pinches against my flesh.

The band forced my thong to press into my ass crack, creating the world's worst wedgie. My natural instinct was to move and adjust it, but his fingers just pulled on the band, increasing the tightness.

"I like having you like this, Rylie. Lifted, your ass in my face so I can suck your pretty cunt into my mouth and slap this"—he smacked my left butt cheek—"as hard as I want."

God, the sensation of him slapping me there and then moving his lips against the spot, each time moving closer to my crack, was making my hips buck against thin air.

Finally, after a few smacks, his tongue separated my cheeks, swirling around the tight bundle of nerves at the center while his hands spread me wide.

"Fuck, Rylie." He hissed behind me. "Spread your legs apart," he commanded.

I did as he said. It was awkward because the band holding me up lifted me off the bed, but only just a little bit. Still, the resistance was there, making every movement a heavy sensation that I felt thrum against my core.

"That's it...just like that." His tongue swept along my crack until he was pulling me back against his face, and he began fucking me with his tongue, pushing it in and out of my center. He moved through my folds, licking and sucking while holding me to his face. Mine was still shoved into the mattress as I groaned into the gag in my mouth.

I breathed through my nose as my nerves rattled and pain jolted up through my center. The pleasure was overwhelming as a weightless feeling came over me.

"That's it," he murmured as he feasted on me.

His hands cupped my ass, pushing my pussy down against his face, and my hips began rocking as much as I possibly could to catch the friction of his mouth. He pulled against the resistance band, tugging my ass down. My cheeks were spread over his face and his tongue speared the tight bundle of nerves in my ass while he tilted his head and licked along my crack.

He groaned, his fingers moving to my clit while his tongue stayed busy with the most sensitive spot on my body. He spread the hole with a press of his tongue and then his finger, pushing in and then replacing his finger with his tongue.

The movement of our bodies forced the bed to rock and the wood to creak. I bucked my hips, chasing friction as he sucked and fucked my pussy with his mouth. It was filthy and erotic, and I couldn't see him, but the way he gripped me and manhandled me was getting me so hot I was about to come.

I was so worked up I hadn't even realized the bands had come loose and I'd slumped into the mattress.

"Get that ass up in the air, right the fuck now." He slapped me there hard, creating a loud echo through the room, and I moaned in response.

He had his way with me, moving his fingers and tongue over my sex and the tight hole that was considerably less tight after his ministrations. Then he was pulling me up until I was sitting taller on my knees, facing him.

This time, he removed my gag and kissed me, forcing me to taste myself.

Our kiss was hungry and messy, full of tongue and filthy promises of what we both needed from each other. Then his thumb held my bottom lip down while he sat on his knees and gripped his cock, guiding it into my mouth while he pushed my head down against his shaft.

Not having my hands seemed to heighten all my senses and made my own arousal so much hotter. I moaned around his girth. I tasted him, salty and perfect, swirling my tongue around the tip of his cock like he was my personal stash of candy.

I sucked on his length as he gripped my hair, pulling me closer and fucking my mouth with his engorged erection.

"Rylie." He increased his movements, and I lowered my head over his cock until I couldn't anymore. He held my head there while fucking the back of my throat. I choked, but he didn't let up, just went harder. The pain was minuscule compared to the sounds he made and how it made me ache between my legs. It was over too fast as he let me go and began pumping his length while staring down at me.

I knew what he wanted, so I tilted my head back and smiled at him, inviting him to spill himself on my face. He groaned, gripping my hair once again while he held fast to the base of his cock with his other hand, and then I felt it, the warm stream of his orgasm being spent on my face. I opened my mouth so some of it would hit my tongue, because I honestly loved the taste of him, and I knew it would make him crazy.

"Fuck, baby." He grit his teeth while spreading the liquid around my lips. Then his mouth slammed into mine, and he angrily kissed me before taking the rag that had gagged me and wiping away the mess he'd made on my face.

"You're so much better than anything I dreamed up."

He moved to the restraints at my back and untied me, rubbing at my wrists. It was his silent way to ensure I was okay.

"I loved that." I exhaled, lying next to him.

He twisted my hips until I was on his lap, his erection still hard as granite.

"We aren't done."

Letting out a silent breath, I stood on the bed and shoved my soaked thong down my legs then straddled him, rubbing my cunt against the base of his cock. As good as it felt, I realized I wanted the real thing. Like a hole expanding in my chest, I needed him to fill me.

I sat up, and then, holding his erection in place, I lowered myself, bare and not giving a single fuck. I tossed my head back as his size invaded, spread, and stretched me.

"Fuck," Kyle snapped, gripping my hips in a vise.

I watched his eyes in the dark, the small light from outside barely enough to see that he wasn't wearing his contacts. It spurred me into action, forcing my hips forward and then back, rotating at a brisk pace.

I was breathless as he pushed my waist down and jutted his up at the same time. My breasts bounced as I let go of all my inhibitions and began moaning loudly as my orgasm slowly spun and twirled inside me like wildfire.

"More," I begged, and he moved even faster, burying himself inside me so deep that the muscle in his jaw jumped.

I moved my hips at a frantic pace until he was flipping us, slamming my back into the mattress, hovering over me and burying himself inside me. He gripped my ribs as he jutted forward, thrusting his cock into my core, forcing a cry of pleasure to spill from my lips, a scream echoing around the room with his name on every breath.

He was close behind as his hips thrust violently forward, filling me so intensely that we began falling off the edge of the bed, his cock still buried deep inside me while my mouth gaped and another orgasm ripped through me.

His guttural scream mirrored my own, and this time my name was a prayer on his lips while the blankets sank to the floor with us. Our chests heaved while we lay connected, until he finally pulled out then wrapped his arm around me, tugging me into his chest.

My head was cushioned by his bicep, and with the darkness around us, I drifted off to sleep, wishing for once that the sun wouldn't come and we wouldn't have to move.

"Do you know what he looks like? Can you describe him?" my dad asked, and the question reverberated around the room.

Holt, one of the guards who was in the house at all times, raised his eyebrows, spearing a look at Garrison, the other guard who hung around Kyle and Scotty. They snickered, talking quietly in another language. Scotty kicked one of them in the leg to silence them.

"Uh…glimpses here and there." I thought about the night prior, how Kyle and I had succumbed to our lust, and again this morning, showering together while he pinned me to the wall and buried himself inside me. Fucking, moaning into my skin things we weren't ready to discuss.

Kyle smirked, likely thinking about the same thing I was.

"Okay, so what were the glimpses of? Is he tall, short, white, black…what?" Dad continued, sounding irritated.

"Medium height…larger stomach, older…" I started rattling off random characteristics, unsure what to say. My face heated with the lie.

"Are you staying with his crew? Dating one of them? I need more —where are you? Put your SIM back into your phone so I can ping it."

I froze, looking at Kyle, whose teeth were snapping together. Rage emanated from him, especially as he brought his knuckles up and cracked them, twisting his neck to the side.

I shook my head. "Dad, I could get hurt if I share too much…I told you that."

He let out a grunt. "Then I don't think I can help Mak."

My stomach pitched forward, tipping. "Dad, wait…just…" I frantically searched the table for an answer, feeling Kyle gently tip my chin up. He wrote on a tablet, telling me what to say, and my heart wilted at how kind it was.

"There's talk that he's taking on a partner…they keep traveling back and forth from New York to Florida…so they're thinking the partner must be from there."

There was silence on his end then an appreciative sigh. "Okay, I can work with this. Same time tomorrow, honey." Then he hung up.

No warm sentiments about love, or even gratitude. It stung, punching me in the chest.

So much so that I flipped the phone shut and shot away from the table, heading toward the garage, not even sure what I was looking for.

I paced along the waxed floors, relaxing at how much cooler the vast space was than the house. The door to the main house opened, and Kyle walked out. My head snapped up, watching his movements carefully, the way his arms shifted, the tattoos looking vibrant against his skin. I swallowed the desire that began spiraling inside my chest, twirling down and tugging at my gut in hope that he'd be who he once was to me.

He stopped in between his Charger and a newer Mustang, popping his hip against the driver side door. "Wanna drive?"

My anger with him was dissipating. The mask he'd worn on campus was slipping more each day, and the more we were together, the easier it was to eliminate the shit that had kept us apart.

I walked toward him, just needing him. I hated myself for it, but I walked right into his space, knowing his arms would come around me.

In seconds, I was enveloped in a tight hug, his chin going over my head, tucking me in closer. We stood there for a long time, his arms a band of steel around me, warding off the fear and rage that had started bubbling in my gut.

"Come on, driving always made you feel better." He let me go and tugged me toward his car.

It was an older muscle car, like the one he'd had on my eighteenth birthday. Modified, with extra chrome and valves that likely made it better, faster, and consume way more gasoline. Suddenly it felt like we were back in high school again, me about to put him in his place for having a vehicle that was killing the planet, but instead I just smiled.

He handed me the keys, and we settled in, just like we had that New Year's. I reversed out of the garage, and he directed me toward a secluded road where I drove with my window down and felt the speed of the car carry me to nowhere. With Kyle next to me, it forced a stupid smile to erupt along my lips.

He looked over, beaming.

"Feels good, right?" he asked, inhaling a cigarette.

"It feels like home" was all I could say. It was a truth he hadn't earned, but I gave it to him anyway. He could take it however he wanted, but deep down it meant he was home…always had been, always would be.

CHAPTER TWENTY-EIGHT

Rylie

THE NEXT TWO WEEKS WERE A MYRIAD OF DAYS THAT BLENDED INTO
one big blur. Every other day at exactly nine in the morning, I would
place a call to my father and deliver details...miniscule and stupid
things that were meant to send him on a wild goose chase. That
hadn't been my original intention when I struck this deal with Kyle,
but his rules were clear, as were Scotty's.

I was to ensure that nothing could ever lead back to them. So, I
did as I was told, hoping each lie would work to save Mak. During the
rest of my time, I drove with Kyle, sometimes at night, other times
right as the day would begin. More often than not, I'd ask to just sit
while he drove around.

Something told me he had stopped doing it since moving back to
the States. I liked the familiar feeling it gave me to sit next to him
while he sped down the road at a breakneck speed.

Some days he'd train me in the gym, teach me how to hit properly,
then he'd fuck me slow in the shower while we cleaned the sweat off.

He'd take me with him while he practiced shooting. More than a
few times, his arms would come around me, teaching me how to hold
a handgun, how to aim and hit my target. Just like racing, I loved the

exhilaration that hit me when the bullet flew from my gun, lunging into its target.

At night, we'd fuck slow and hard, experimenting with filthy things we'd been robbed of for so many years. I woke each morning wrapped in his arms...but we hadn't talked about our pasts.

Not once.

We just kept brushing the fragmented pieces of our selves under the rug then essentially fucking on top of it, trying to let our physical connection smooth it all out. No matter how much of a lie it was, we just kept going, and I indulged in the imaginary perfection that had suddenly become my life. I'd gotten too used to his smell, the way his lips felt against my skin, and the way he tasted on my tongue. I was addicted to him, and while we both knew the time for our deal had likely expired, we just kept waking each day, repeating the same things over and over.

Until one day, everything finally shattered.

Kyle and I had gone into town to get groceries, which caused a massive argument with the two main men of the house. I ignored their shouting and screaming, petting Bronson and Baretta, loving the way their heads rested in my lap. From what I overheard, the biggest issue was that Kyle had gone without backup, but I honestly thought Scotty's issue was merely the fact that it was me who was with Kyle.

Things were made worse when Scotty crossed a line.

"Just be honest, Kyle—you're not thinking like the head of a family because you're too worried about the head of your cock getting sucked."

My face flushed, knowing the whole house had probably heard us on a regular basis, but with guards everywhere, there was no way for someone not to hear us. Didn't help matters that Kyle didn't really care if someone was watching us or near us before he started in on me. One time, he'd shoved my leggings down my thighs while we were in the gym. No one was in there at the time, but that didn't mean people couldn't just walk in. He kept his back to the room as he shoved his cock into me from behind, sinking into my core, fucking me against one of the mirrors. It should have mortified me...but it was so hot that I couldn't think about anything but chasing my orgasm.

There was a commotion from the kitchen, breaking me out of my lust-filled thoughts. It sounded like a slap or a punch. Bronson whined, lifting his tall ears and looking back toward the room where the men were arguing.

"You need to back the fuck off." That was Kyle.

Scotty didn't wait long to rebound. "You want me to back off, throw away everything we've worked for? Fine…reach out when you're ready to act like the man I raised you to be." He stomped away, heading in our direction from the sound of it.

My stomach sank as I realized that meant he'd be taking the dogs.

As he rounded the corner, his narrowed eyes held mirth and hatred in them as he walked past me, glaring with every step. I glared right back because fuck him and his weird attachment issues to his nephew.

He snapped his fingers once he was close to the front door, and both dogs darted up, running past me and following after him.

I brushed off the small disappointment.

Kyle walked in a second later, eating an Oreo, talking around the piece in his mouth. "You wanted these, but I'm gonna eat 'em all if you don't get in here."

I laughed, jumping up and running into the kitchen.

I sat on the counter, dipping my cookie into milk while he dipped his in peanut butter and our favorite music blared through one of the Bluetooth speakers.

Gretta had taken the afternoon off, and the rest of his men were on the other half of the mansion, so it felt like we were truly alone for the first time.

"So, you didn't go to Europe?" I finally broke our tentative existence, asking about his past.

His eyes snapped up. Green, beautiful…*him*.

"I did go to Europe, but not with a girl, and not to fucking hike. I told Scotty that excuse would never fly with you."

He shook his head as if he were remembering it. I felt my lips crack in a relieved smile as a burden I had carried for three long years began to lift.

"After Ivan died, the families were all out for blood, as you overheard that night at Taylor's Christmas party. Scotty bought me six months where they didn't look for me. But because I was a massive fuck-up, I kept street racing, and they kept their eye on me. Finally, they'd had enough and told Scotty to bring me in."

Suddenly, his uncle wasn't sounding quite so terrible.

"But he didn't," I guessed, grabbing for another cookie.

Kyle shook his head, his jaw tensing. "No...he knew they'd kill me or force me to soldier up for a new family. They'd likely have forced me to shoot someone I loved as a way of initiation...honestly they probably would have picked you, if they'd paid enough attention."

"So, you left..."

"I had to." He sounded so apologetic about it, and I understood... but the sting of losing him was still there.

I dropped the topic, and he seemed to as well as the afternoon passed. We worked on one of his cars while we remembered people we'd gone to high school with and gossiped about who was doing what. We made lunch, standing shoulder to shoulder while he handed me turkey and I cut slices of cheese and tomato. Then we snuggled on the couch and watched a movie, falling asleep in each other's arms, only to wake up to a dark purple sky.

By then my curiosity was too big to contain, so I dredged up our previous conversation.

"Where did you go?"

Kyle looked over at me curiously.

"After our night together...you left, but where did you go?"

"Everywhere. Russia, the UK, Hungary...Italy. I learned a few languages...trained."

"To fight?" We got up and I followed him toward the back of the house.

He opened the doors to the patio and headed toward the hot tub. The wind was picking up, lightly whipping at our faces.

"To fight, to shoot, to kill..." He slipped his shirt off and then his jeans until he was just in his boxers. "Come on." He smiled, gesturing to the hot tub.

I followed suit, getting into just my bra and underwear, and dipped my toes into the heated water.

"Then you moved back here?"

I wanted to know why…and selfishly I needed to know if any part of it had to do with me.

"Once Ivan died, Scotty and I essentially stole everything from him. His territory, his product, his money…even his homes."

"Wouldn't all of that have gone to his next of kin?" I asked, a little curious why everything wouldn't have gone to Taylor.

"Yes…however, she didn't want any of it. We asked and got her blessing."

"What about Juan?" I quirked a brow, curious how her husband had handled that request.

Kyle smirked, relaxing his frame into the stone pool, the heated water molding around him. "We didn't ask Juan."

Ah, there it was.

"So that's how you got your start…" I stated, moving my hands through the water and staring up at the darkening sky. The lights in the pool kicked on, along with the automatic timers for the lights strung up across the back yard. I knew there were men guarding the property, but they were far enough away that I didn't worry about them seeing us.

Kyle shifted closer, wrapping his hand around my hip. "Scotty and I needed a significant jump on the competition, especially since they all wanted what Ivan had and wanted the man who had killed him dead."

I considered what he was saying…they'd stolen their start and created their own family.

"So, no one knows you're Kyle James?"

His eyes lowered. "No…that's why I look different when I go out, why it's so important to keep my identity a secret. It keeps my family safe."

"Do *they* know about all this?"

I felt stupid for asking considering he'd driven us to Decker's house that night and they hadn't seemed that surprised to see us.

"I kept up with Decker, just barely though…just updating him on the country or city and saying I was alive. I didn't know he'd had a kid."

I hadn't expected his response to hurt as badly as it did, but it landed as effectively as a bomb inside my chest. He had kept up with his brother…because Decker was his family. What did that say about what role I had played in his life that he couldn't reach out for three years? Why reach out to me at all?

The thought rolled around in my head like a gentle wave, coming in and floating out. He had seen me, knowing it was me a month prior to showing up in the pub…even then he hadn't been kind when he'd realized it was me. He had been angry with me, bitter and cold when he first saw me…why?

I didn't want to ask because it would make me seem pathetic. I didn't want to risk wearing my heart on my sleeve when he'd likely just cut it off and use it to fuck me.

I blinked away the emotions that were suddenly clogging my throat. I needed to change the subject. "Will you run any deals while I'm staying with you? You've seemed to lie low these past few weeks."

Kyle stared off into the tree line for a few moments, letting the sound of the whirring jets and the music from inside the house surround us. Then finally he let out a sigh and moved to the edge.

"I'm not sure…"

I moved in close to him. "You can…if you want. I'll just stay back while you run your business."

He looked over at me, narrowing his eyes. "Why the sudden plan to distance yourself from me?"

My brows dipped as I processed his words. "What do you mean?"

"I mean, one second you seem so content with me, like you could stay here forever…the next second you've got walls up."

I moved away from him, folding my hands on the edge of the spa, wrangling my emotions, but it was no use. I wanted him to feel the pressure that had been pushing against my heart since he left me.

"You managed to stay in touch with Decker, but you gave up on me. Then when you finally found me, you waited an entire month before you came to me…and even then you were so harsh and cold. I'm just trying to figure out why."

A brazen look crossed his features as he considered what I said. His posture went rigid, his hands gripping the edge of the stone tub. "You don't underst—"

Movement from the patio doors and muted shouting from the house had us both swinging our heads to the left.

"Boss, Scotty's been shot." Holt burst through the door with five men spilling out behind him. Their guns were up and pointed at the tree line, creating a circle around us.

Everything was a blur within seconds. Kyle jumped out of the pool while his muscles shifted and flexed, his face grim and his eyes severe as he lifted me up by my arms.

I clambered toward my clothes, trying to keep up with Kyle as his grip lowered to my hand, tugging me behind him. Chaos was everywhere, men holding guns, laser focused on guarding the two men in the center of the room. Scotty lay on the couch, bleeding from his shoulder and stomach, groaning in pain.

Kyle moved to the space in front of the couch on a bended knee, his hand gripping the bloodied man before him.

"What the fuck happened?" His voice cracked as his eyes roved over his uncle's form.

No one responded, forcing Kyle to lift his eyes and look around. "Tell me!"

One of the men finally said, "He was out alone, sir…we aren't sure. He didn't take anyone with him."

"Fuck," Kyle snapped. "Secure the perimeter, call Jones now, and find out who the fuck attacked him. Keva and Giles, you both take lead on getting intel. I want to know where Scotty went and who was watching him."

Men began moving and darting around the room, a few pulling out cell phones. Gretta ran in, holding rags and muttering things in a different language, one Kyle responded to in a fluid accent. It brought realization of how serious this was, how he lived a different life—a dangerous one that I was wholly unprepared for.

I didn't want to be in the way, but I also wanted to help. So, I followed Gretta around like a lost puppy, helping her rinse rags, get fresh water, and whatever else Jones, their doctor, needed. Kyle ignored me, not in an obvious way, more like he was just focused on Scotty and unaware of anyone else in the vicinity.

His uncle had been shot in the torso, through the stomach and shoulder, and was unconscious for a while, but when he'd initially come in, they'd said he had driven himself. I personally thought that was insane, but I didn't really know Scotty. Kyle didn't seem surprised when he learned that his uncle had done this, and I guess knowing what he taught Kyle to do behind the wheel, it wasn't so far—fetched.

Kyle was on edge, still shirtless, with all that ink on display and his hair a wild mess. He carried a massive handgun while a cigarette rotated between his lips every twenty minutes or so. His focus was on the doctor stitching up his uncle and on his cell. Anger radiated from him, and a few times I heard him screaming at someone on the phone in what sounded like Russian, but honestly, I wasn't sure.

I wanted to help him, reach out and hold him…but I was worried he'd reject me. Eventually, I realized I wasn't going to be of any help and I was out of my depth, so I pulled myself upstairs and curled into a cold, empty bed, confused about why I'd let my body succumb so easily to a man who hadn't even asked for my heart.

CHAPTER TWENTY-NINE

THE DOC FINALLY GAVE US THE GREEN LIGHT TO MOVE SCOTTY TO HIS bed. We laid him down so his dogs could be near him. He hadn't been lucid enough to tell me shit, so I was worried and pissed as fuck that someone had attacked my family.

I wasn't taking any chances; I pulled my phone out and texted Juan.

Me: Shit went sideways, make sure Decker & fam is safe.

Seeing that it was well past midnight, I doubted he would answer right away, but a few minutes later his response came through.

Juan: What happened?

Me: Scotty was shot, we don't know who, but we do know it was an ordered hit.

Juan: Fuck. Get here and we'll figure it out. If you don't have Scotty, you're alone...and chances are they know it.

I pocketed my phone and ran upstairs. Fuck, I hadn't even checked on Rylie, part of me too worried to let my mind wander to what would happen if she were hurt because of this, the other part distancing myself from her question because if I were honest with her, she'd fucking leave me again like she had after Taylor's Christmas party.

Rylie was asleep when I opened the door, her dark lashes fanned out on the tops of her cheeks. She looked so perfect in my bed, so at home and peaceful that I almost didn't wake her, but I needed to go, and I wasn't leaving her here.

I leaned down, pushing her hair back and kissing her forehead.

"Rylie."

Her lashes fluttered, but she didn't wake.

"Rylie, baby, wake up." I kissed her lips, moving down her jaw to her neck.

"Mmm." She finally began to stir.

"We need to go. Come on, get dressed." I pressed my lips to her forehead before moving to the closet to grab a bag in case we were gone for more than a day.

She quickly sat up, wiping at her eyes. "What's wrong?"

"I need to go somewhere, and I need you to come with me."

She moved from the bed and shifted around, tugging on a pair of jeans she'd discarded by the foot of the bed. She pulled a shirt over her head then slipped on her boots without socks. She always wore socks so I knew she was nervous, or at least scared.

I threw a few things of mine and hers in the bag then grabbed our cell phone chargers and held out my hand for her. She hesitated just for a second, which was understandable considering what all had happened tonight. She wasn't used to this shit, or this life. She wouldn't get any time to acclimate either.

We headed down to the car, and as tempted as I was to explain where we were headed, I figured nothing would properly prepare her for what was coming next.

OUR CAR SLOWED AS I TURNED DOWN JUAN'S DRIVEWAY AND ENTERED the gate code. I had taken the usual route, which was a myriad of turns and bullshit roads so they wouldn't be able to tail us if we were being followed. The gate slid open, and a few men came into focus, warranting a small gasp from Rylie.

"Where are we?"

I pulled forward until the house came into view. "Somewhere safe."

The men came up to the car, opening Rylie's side first. If I hadn't trusted Juan implicitly, his men would have been fucked for opening her door without my permission. She looked to me for what to do, and I gave her a small nod.

Hector helped her out, gripping her hand in a gentle manner, and I wanted to rip his arm from his body just because I was mental where she was concerned.

"She can walk without your fucking help, Hector," I snapped, grabbing our bag and walking around the hood.

Rylie softly pulled her hand free, giving him a half-hearted smile.

I grabbed her waist and pulled her into my side as he headed up the stairs. "He knows we're coming," I barked at Juan's right-hand man.

He followed us up, and within seconds, Juan opened the door, standing in a pair of sweats and a tight-as-fuck t-shirt. I'd be giving him shit for that later.

Rylie stopped dead, becoming a statue as she registered whose house this was. Her grip on my hand intensified, and her breathing turned shallow.

Juan crossed his arms over his chest, yawning. "Come in, unless you'd rather stay outside." He raised his brow at Rylie, not trying at all to help with her transition. "If my boys wake up, I have to take the shift, and I'm tired as fuck."

I tugged Rylie inside, not surprised one bit that Juan knew I'd be bringing her. Juan always fucking knew what was going on before anyone else.

He secured the door. "Welcome to our home. Taylor is asleep, but she knows you're here. Kyle, we'll talk in the morning..." His eyes flicked to Rylie and then back to me in a knowing way. "I'll show you to your room."

We followed him upstairs. Even though I stayed in the same room every time I spent the night, I knew he was doing me a favor by not telling Rylie. We moved down the hall away from his bedroom and his kids, on the other side of the balcony where his office and guest rooms were. I knew he had two, but like fuck was I mentioning that to Rylie.

Juan opened the door, flicked on the light, and yawned again. "Kyle knows where everything is." His slip-up about me knowing where things were was covered by a small wince before he shook his head. "Make yourself at home…just don't fucking wake up my kids or my wife."

He waved his hand as if he was brushing us off and headed back toward his room, flicking lights off as he went.

I shut the door and locked it, slow and steady as I faced Rylie.

Her movements were jerky as she ripped back the covers and fluffed the pillows. She stayed in her clothes as she crawled into the bed, turning away from the center. I knew she was hurt…the last time we'd been around Juan together, he'd threatened me, and she had found out I had turned into a murderer and then lied about it.

Fucking hell.

I was doing it to her again, and I knew she'd never forgive me if she found out I was just using her and hadn't planned on going after her until Delgado spilled his secrets. It wasn't that I didn't want to, but my uncle had convinced me to let her go, and after three agonizing years, I'd finally persuaded my brain to ignore my fucking weak heart and leave her alone.

I wasn't going to go after her.

The shame in that truth swallowed me, fucking drowned me as I sank into the mattress. I clicked off the light and lay next to the only person who'd ever brought me meaning, who made my life brighter and better.

I exhaled slowly, reaching for Rylie's hand, tugging it into mine.

She pulled away, but I held firm.

"Let me go," she said quietly, sternly.

I turned toward her, lying on my side. I reached over, and with my hand on her stomach, I tugged her against my chest.

"I can't."

Her chest heaved up and down. "You've had no issues whatsoever letting me go these past few years. Even though everyone else got to stay…I was the only one who had to go."

Her voice was brittle, cracking with each word, drilling a hole in my chest with every single syllable.

Putting my lips to her ear, I gripped her tighter. "Is that what you think?"

"Yes." She seethed. "Decker, Juan…Scotty—they all got to stay. They all knew about you, and I was the only one who was ignorant to it all. I was the only one who lost you." She pulled away from me as roughly as she could, ripping my grip in the process.

I moved with her as she tried to get off the bed. I was right there, grabbing her hips and pulling her back into my body.

"Do you know what I gave up for you? Do you know what it took for me to leave you?" I rumbled in her ear, feeling emotion clog my throat and stretch along my chest, burning every inch as it went.

She sank into my hold, allowing me to continue.

"I cut out my soul and cauterized it because I didn't want to feel or experience anything with anyone in that way ever again. We may have taken each other's virginity, but you took more than that from me. You took everything, and I wasn't fucking satisfied with having you once, because I knew that was my last night with you, so I filled you, took and kept you. Then I didn't touch another person for three goddamn years. Because it's *always* been you…it'll only *ever* be you. Your safety was the most important thing to me. Every time I checked up on you, it ripped my heart out to know you'd moved on, but I was happy because it meant you were living."

I exhaled heavily, loosening my grip on her.

She twisted in my arms, her green eyes on mine, her lips slightly parted, releasing heavy breaths.

I slowly shifted, bringing my hands up to cup her jaw. Her eyes darted to my lips.

Quietly and softly, I pulled her closer and confessed, "I've loved you my whole life, Rylie, even when I knew I shouldn't have…even when I couldn't. It never changed how badly I wanted you. I'll always want you, even after we break…even after this is over and we're done. I'll never stop."

Her forehead pressed against mine, waiting, breathing. Then, slowly and gently, her lips connected with mine. It was a caress with the briefest pause, a shudder running through her as she wrapped her hands around my neck and sank her nails into my hair.

Slanting her head to the side, she slowly moved her mouth in a cadence that was all her own, releasing whatever had been locked inside. It pranced along the seam of her lips, on the edge of her tongue as she moved closer, taking everything as she went, and I let her.

I brought her down to the bed with me, and instead of harsh and depraved moves, ours were gentle, careful, and lax, as though this were something precious to us. She pushed her hands up under my shirt, gently pressing her nails into my skin as she removed the shirt from my body, moving her mouth in open, frenzied kisses on my neck and torso.

Within moments we were both naked, lying on the bed, staring at each other while our mouths connected over and over in a song, a dance we hadn't been able to move to, bound by the chains of our friendship.

This moment was a crack in the ice, a melting point as our constraints began to fall away.

She raised herself above me, her hair cascading over her shoulders as lights from outside filtered in through the thick sham over the window. Her hands gracefully gripped my erection, lining it up with her center, and with a hushed gasp, she sank down.

I flexed, trying to restrain myself from reacting how I usually did. Something about her taking control and holding me in her own way made my actions pliant and subservient. I'd do anything for her, as long as she forgave me.

Her hips moved forward, which removed the small space left between our bodies. She let out a small sound, likely being respectful to all the sleeping people in the house. Her limbs were already shuddering as she rocked forward and then moved back, creating a rhythm so erotic I had to bite back my own groans. I wanted to flip her, fuck her hard until her body was sliding off the bed again. I wanted her screams, her unbridled self…but this was perfect too. Slow and perfect, lazy and yet…

Fuck the sensations were almost more agonizing because I was able to see her climax slowly build, the beauty in how it forced her head to tip back and her breasts to jut out, how it made her breaths shudder and hold. Her hips rolled faster and faster as she took what she needed from me. I moved in sync with her, matching her thrust for thrust, jutting up as she pressed down. Her mouth dropped open, and a sound of ecstasy finally erupted from her lungs as she tightened around me, so much so that I immediately released right along with her, pulling her waist down and spilling inside her.

Our heavy breathing filled the air, and because I needed to seal this, I pulled her off me, rolled us until she was beneath me, and I kissed her.

When we finally conceded, needing air, I confessed something else to her.

"I was brash with you when I came to the school…you hadn't recognized me at the club, and you were trying to get that fighter's attention. It killed me…so when I finally saw you again and wanted to get your attention, I just wanted you to hurt how I hurt. Then it became difficult not to try for a reaction from you because you wouldn't speak to me. So, I put on a show with the girls, the making out…but it didn't do any good because you never broke. I'm sorry, I shouldn't have done it…if I could take it back I would."

She seemed to consider it for a second, then bit her lip and asked, "Did you fuck any of them?"

I laughed, toying with the ends of her hair. "What you saw was the only time I ever touched them…if you weren't looking then I wasn't touching."

"Then why come after me a month after you saw me? I know you weren't really on a date with Stacey."

This was the moment to come clean with her…I knew it, knew I should just say we were using her as a way to leverage information and we wanted her in our pocket so if her dad turned, we could use her. I opened my mouth to say it, to spill the entire truth to her, to say I was using her more than she was me.

"One of our rivals confessed that he had eyes on your dad and planned to use you."

She brushed a stray strand of hair off my forehead, which made my breath get caught in my throat.

I knew I should tell her all of it. I needed to.

"Scotty and I…we wanted to be sure you were safe…felt like it was the right thing to do."

"So, your only role at the school was to watch over me?"

I silently nodded, praying to whoever listened to liars and killers that she'd accept it and, more than anything, that the rest of what I wasn't saying would never surface.

She seemed to accept it, settling into my chest and brushing her nails softly over my arms.

"I don't want to break…I don't want to leave. I want this for as long as you do." Then she pressed a kiss over my heart, and in the darkness of the room, sorrow pierced my heart, marking it. I didn't deserve her, and I knew eventually I would lose her.

When that time came, every crack and break in my soul that came from the fallout would be entirely warranted.

CHAPTER THIRTY

Rylie

THE FOLLOWING MORNING CAME WITH THE SOUND OF THUMPING FEET and then a small human body jumping on top of us, squealing about her uncle coming to visit again. The person's language was all soft Ls and zero Ss.

I blinked against the sunlight spreading along the opposite wall of the room and tried to make out who was on top of Kyle. Over the blankets, there was a small girl jumping up and down, her blonde curls bouncing with every pounce.

"Wake up! Mommy made pancakes…the kind you love!"

Sounded like *wuv*…so freaking cute.

"Alex…I love you, but give me a second okay?" Kyle grumbled from under the covers.

Suddenly she stopped, and her blue eyes clashed with mine. "Who's dat?"

Her tiny finger jutted in my direction, a look of confusion crumpling her cute little features. It took a second, then it hit me.

Alex.

As in baby Alex? A brief memory of a little bundle being passed around the room flitted through my mind.

"This is Rylie," Kyle answered, his hand finding my stomach under the covers.

"You wuv her?" Alex's tiny eyebrow rose.

He laughed. "I do."

Even though we'd essentially covered it the previous night, hearing his admission softened everything inside my chest, turning it to goo.

"Okay...I have to go tell Mommy. She needs to know there's another pancake plate." Alex tumbled off our bed and ran out into the hall.

"Didn't you lock the door last night?" I asked, snuggling into Kyle's neck.

He watched the empty doorway with a quizzical brow. "Yes...yes I did."

Once we dressed, we headed downstairs. I took in the house as we went, shocked that this was owned by the same people whose previous home had nearly blown me away all those years ago. This one was much smaller but enhanced by character and tiny little details that seemed so innately creative and tailored to them. Clearing the bottom of the stairs took us directly into the kitchen, where Taylor stood at the long island with a built-in gas stove. She cradled a cup of coffee while smiling down at two little baby loungers locked in place on the counter.

"You're awake!" She set down her cup and smiled broadly at us. "Rylie! Oh my goodness, come meet my boys."

She excitedly waved me over, and I eagerly complied. Her arms came around me before turning my shoulders toward the two babies. They wore the smallest little black onesies and had dark hair and olive skin. They looked just like their father.

"So cute, oh my gosh." I cooed, stroking one of their tiny feet. The baby smiled up at me and drooled all over his hand.

"Giovanni, or as we call him, Gio, and here is Kingston...or King."

"Gio and King...my gosh, Taylor, they're perfect."

I realized she was in a pair of baggy sweats and an equally baggy sweatshirt, one with a Hornets logo on it, her hair thrown up haphazardly in a bun. Still, to me she was gorgeous, but compared to the last time I saw her with a newborn, I was starting to feel like there *was* balance in the world.

"I haven't slept in weeks, but I'm happy." She smiled, moving back to the stove, and her eyes turned up toward Kyle. "Did you bring me coffee?"

He peeled a banana. "Why would I randomly have coffee for you?"

She flipped a small pancake, pursing her lips. "Because the last time you were here, keeping my husband up until midnight with that dumb video game, you swore you'd bring me coffee the next time you saw me."

My mind wandered to that night he'd disappeared, when he hadn't come home until nearly one in the morning, now connecting the dots that it was here he'd been. My heart pinched at the fact that they'd been friends this whole time…living a life together and creating cute little offenses like not bringing coffee.

"You have a cup of coffee right there." He gestured to the mug on the counter.

She shook her head. "Not the same and you know it. I told you not to get Juan started on that stupid game, now he's playing it with other people with that damn headset."

"It's not that bad…it's better than pretty much one hundred percent of the other games I could have gotten him addicted to."

She waved him off and turned toward the twins.

"Where did Alex go?" I glanced around the room, not seeing her or Juan.

"She's helping her daddy water the garden. It's her favorite chore." Taylor looked up, giving us a knowing grin.

Kyle and I settled on barstools, and Taylor caught me up on her life while Kyle shoveled pieces of pancake into his mouth. After a few minutes there was a barrage of sound as a door slid open from another room, and the high-pitched voice of a little girl filled the air.

"That's why the carrots no like the onions, Daddy. You have to seberpate dem," Alex explained while Juan walked in, hoisting the blonde-haired princess high in his arms. Juan's hair was disheveled in a way I had never seen…even that night he'd come in throwing punches in Kyle's face, his hair had been perfect and immaculate. Now, he had bags under his eyes and a suspicious stain on his t-shirt.

"Good, you guys are up." He set his daughter down, and she delicately put her fingers around a pancake, eating it like a cookie.

"Hi Juan…" I hedged, feeling awkward as hell.

Thankfully he smiled warmly at me before walking toward the sink to wash his hands, forcing everyone's eyes to the tiny dirt-caked fingers of the toddler who was shoving pancake into her mouth.

"Babe…" Taylor sighed, throwing a small glare at Juan, then picked up Alex, taking her to the sink.

"My bad." He laughed, reaching for a plate.

"How's Scotty doing? Not that I care, but Taylor told me it would be a nice thing to ask."

I hid a smirk because I was realizing I was team Juan if there were teams. It wasn't that I wanted Scotty to die…but the man did make me want to shoot him a time or two.

"Jones said he was recovering fine," Kyle answered. Walking up behind me, his hands went to the counter in front of us, boxing me in.

I toyed with the blueberry on my nearly empty plate, relishing the feeling of having him so close. The conversation from the night before had settled in my chest like gold. He'd finally confessed his truths, and we were finally together. It felt like having spring blooming in my veins, pumping me up with hope and happiness.

"No idea who it was that ordered the hit?" Juan asked, putting his hand to the small of Taylor's back.

Kyle toyed with the ends of my hair. "Not yet…I plan on asking around tonight, hitting up a few spots."

Juan crossed his arms, glancing at Taylor briefly before looking at us. "Which spots?"

Kyle's silence forced Juan and Taylor to both look at me, which meant he was headed to Deacon's.

"I want to go with you."

Kyle moved away from me. "Not happening."

I scuttled off the barstool, glancing back at Juan briefly before putting my attention back on Kyle.

"You'll be safer here, with them. I'll be back——"

"I know Mak's better than anyone, and they're going to be looking for you to pop back up, especially if it was an ordered hit. Mak will know something—let me go and talk to him."

"I can do that just as easily as you," Kyle argued, shoving his hands into the pockets of his sweats.

"Mak is terrified of you...he'll never talk to you, especially because he doesn't know what your connection is to me, but he knows you're to blame for the blackout and for losing me."

The words flew out of my mouth before I could even process how saying them would hit him. I knew my relationship with Mak was a sensitive subject with Kyle.

Kyle's expression hardened. "You're not going back there. The Delgado family knew about you..."

"They're in bed with the Russians," Juan quickly added, taking a bite of an apple before smiling down at his sons.

Like hearing that two different crime syndicates knew of my place of employment wasn't terrifying.

My nerves were rattled, but I wouldn't be talked out of this.

I glanced back over and saw Kyle smirk as he said, "See, not a good idea."

"You won't like this, but I actually agree with your girl...she should make contact with this Mak guy so there's no big scene. You don't need to be flashy, questioning people."

Kyle's lips slung to the side. "But I love being flashy, and I absolutely want a scene."

"Once you have a name, you can be as irresponsible as you want...but if you take her"—his gaze rose to mine—"you need to protect her."

"Do you honestly think I'd put her in danger?" Kyles's tone was solid ice, freezing the room over.

I looked over at Taylor and saw her expression mirroring mine. She hugged Alex to her chest and rubbed Juan's back before heading out of the kitchen.

"Let's get you dressed. You two have the boys." Taylor's blue eyes locked on mine, silently indicating I should follow her.

I trailed her up to Alex's bedroom. A mix of gold and pink exploded on her walls and her queen-sized bed, and stark pink curtains hung over her enormous window seat.

"Sorry…but you remember that party when Alex was just a baby. They can both get so intense," Taylor said apologetically, settling on the carpet next to me.

I settled on the floor next to a dollhouse that was taller than the almost four-year-old in question. "I'm still not caught up on how they went from nearly killing each other to Juan becoming his go-to person when the you-know-what hit the fan." I eyed Alex, trying to watch my language.

Taylor let out a sigh and waved her hand. "It was a deal that went bad. They tried to double-cross Juan and assumed Kyle would go with it…or whatever it is they're calling him." She shook her head like she couldn't keep up with it. "Anyway, Kyle eliminated the threat against my husband…saved his life, then came home and had dinner with us. He's been coming once a week for about a year now."

A flutter of hurt punched me in the chest. He had been so close, and yet he hadn't reached out to me…hadn't come and found me. He'd explained why, as far as keeping me safe…but I was in danger *now* according to them, so what made this time different from the times before?

"Hey." Taylor reached over and grabbed my hand, her eyes full of empathy. "I know it's hard to come to terms with everything. It killed him to be away from you. I don't think I had seen a grown man cry until I saw him break down on New Year's."

My emotions betrayed me, clogging up my throat and battering my eyes. "He has this whole world he's created, and I'm not a part of it…and I honestly don't even understand why he needs it. Why not just walk away?" A few tears slipped free.

Her brows furrowed while Alex talked about her dolls and their names. She'd somehow changed into a dress and tiara, and a long trail of flowers was tangled in with her hair.

"Has he talked to you about what they're working on together?"

I shook my head right as Kyle appeared in the doorway. Alex responded first, running into his arms. He hoisted her up, listening carefully to her talk animatedly about him making her fly faster than last time.

I quickly swiped at my face, offering him a smile, but I knew he'd already caught my meltdown. His furrowed brows proved as much, but he didn't allow it to stop his interacting with Alex. Taylor took the moment to pull my hand, walking with me out of the room.

"Come with me." She hauled me down a few doors until we were in her bedroom. I stood, feeling a little paralyzed, seeing the massive king-sized bed with mussed sheets and clothes strewn all over the floor.

"Sorry, we're a mess right now because of the boys, but come here." She walked to her closet and disappeared inside.

I was on her heels, padding along her cream carpet, taking in her racks of shoes and rows of hanging clothes. In the small area where her clothes began and Juan's ended was a space about as wide as Taylor's body. She pressed her palm against a panel, which produced a keypad. After she punched in a few numbers, the panel slid aside, and Taylor walked into what appeared to be a panic room.

"I want to give you something." She waved for me to follow her.

Hesitantly I followed after her, squeezing into the smaller area. Dark blue LED lights lit up the space, outlining a small hallway that opened into a room about as large as Taylor's walk-in closet. Instead of clothing littering the surfaces, there were rows and rows of guns and knives.

"Holy shit." I breathed out, my eyes raking over the different lengths of the knives, the different styles of guns, and how organized it all was.

"Everyone says this side of the law is gray, but…" She shrugged. "I've always felt that this side is more colorful and vibrant because it takes more work to find the beautiful." Taylor grabbed a handgun. It was black and smaller than most. "Whether you agree with it or not, this is Kyle's world right now. Until it's not, you need to be able to exist within it. I owe my life and my daughter's to Kyle…I have no doubt that if he hadn't shown up that day to kill my father, my father would have ended us both just to spite Juan."

She ducked her head, pressing a button on the handle of the gun. The bottom slid out, producing a clip, holding numerous golden bullets.

"If you decide you don't want this, no pressure…but Kyle needs people in his corner, loyal to the end. He slays giants, but deep down, he's just a little boy, wanting to be a part of the group and desperately in love with the girl he left behind. I hope you choose to love him back. I hope you choose to protect him." She slammed the clip back into place then handed it to me.

I'd done that a few times with Kyle's guns, but not enough to be super confident like her.

"This is a gift, yours—learn to hold it, to shoot it. Learn how to protect him, because everyone in this house would kill for that boy. We owe him our lives two times over, and we're very protective over who's choosing to stand beside him."

I gripped the gun, tightening my hand around it. "Thank you…" My voice was barely a whisper as emotions and gratitude overwhelmed me. I wanted Kyle to have people in his corner, and I felt honored that they were asking me to keep him safe.

We made our way downstairs nearly half an hour later, after Taylor ensured that I knew how to handle the weapon safely in her home and how not to accidentally shoot myself.

Kyle was ready to go as soon as I found him in the foyer. His hair was down, messy and in front of his eyes. His liner was on, colored contacts in. Black combat boots covered his feet, black jeans hugged his muscular legs, skinny and ripped at the knee, and black suspenders stretched over his black shirt. A silver ring was in his lip and eyebrow, and his dress shirt was rolled up to the elbows, showing his tattoos. My eyes trailed down to his hands where the name *JOKER* ran along the top of his knuckles.

The Joker stood in front of me, devastating and thrilling. I stepped into his space and tilted my head back, and his lips were on mine within seconds.

"You're with me," he stated, and I knew he was talking about this afternoon, but I felt his words wrap around the cords of our invisible link, securing them for much longer.

I nodded.

"Always."

CHAPTER THIRTY-ONE

Rylie

DEACON'S WAS PACKED, CARS BURSTING OUT OF THE DILAPIDATED LOT. Kyle directed the car to the rear and parked in the loading zone.

"You honestly think he didn't reinforce the back after what you did last time?"

Tugging the keys out of the ignition, he gave me a seductive smile. "I certainly hope not. I do love using the back entrance." His wink dripped with double meaning, and I felt my face flush.

I pushed open the door, joining him near the trunk. "Have you...I mean before...?" Because we hadn't, and I thought he'd said he hadn't touched anyone in three years.

"You...and maybe not with my cock, but my tongue and my fingers...why, you offering? Because this entire situation can wait— let's get back in the car." He thrust his thumb over his shoulder, still smiling down at me.

I pushed at his chest, holding back a laugh. "Let's go."

His hand was around my hip a moment later, pulling me along. We ascended the short steps up to the black door. The memory of being dragged down them by Scotty was still in my head as my boots stomped with every step.

Just when I thought Kyle would produce a tool of some kind to break in, the door swung open. A new security guard dressed in black greeted us with a grim expression.

"Boss."

Kyle nodded and pulled my hand so I was following behind him closely. I hadn't ever seen the guard before, which meant he was a new hire—that or he was a transplant from Kyle's crew, which also wouldn't have surprised me. I still had no idea how far his reach went.

I surveyed the back, hoping to catch sight of Mak and just be done with all of this. The sooner we left, the less likely it was that Kyle would be noticed. Unfortunately, the back was empty, including Mak's office, not that we even needed to go inside—the guard kept waving us forward, indicating that the person we sought was closer to the front. I clung to Kyle's hand as trepidation thrummed through me. I wasn't sure how Mak would respond to everything I had to tell him. Revealing Kyle's real identity wasn't an option, but Mak knew me and wouldn't just accept that I up and chose to be with some random, dangerous guy, especially after our first interaction.

There were two men punching and grappling with one another inside the cage as we came around the fringes of the bar. Trixie and Raven were mixing and serving drinks as a group of men and women huddled around the block top. There was too much going on, too much happening for me to notice who was here and who wasn't. I had been people-watching for years, picking up clues and serving them to my father on a platter; it really shouldn't have been that difficult to pick out a few players here and there, but they all seemed new.

"What's going on?" I breathed into Kyle's ear.

He'd settled along the back wall, toying with the ring in his lip while surveying the floor. The large flat screens broadcasting the fight to the rest of the patrons in the back showed Mak down on the floor, in the front row, sitting next to two similar-looking men in suits.

I didn't recognize them, but they seemed to drip just as much menace as any other big player did.

"Ivan's brothers have finally surfaced..." Kyle's lips skimmed my ear, but the words seemed to clatter around in my head, as if lead bullets had just been thrown in. Ivan was the man Kyle had killed...I took that fact and tried to tie it to what he'd just said. It obviously wasn't good that they'd finally turned up.

I kept my hand in Kyle's, remembering what Taylor had told me. "What do I do?"

The look in Kyle's eyes was murder and mayhem…he narrowed his focus on the men, not the screen, as if he could see them through the crowd. I suddenly desperately wanted Scotty here to tell me what to do. Kyle looked unhinged as he rolled the metal in his lip.

"Did I ever tell you anything about my training?" Kyle suddenly asked, slowly slipping out of his jacket, laying it over the high-backed chair behind us.

I swallowed thickly. "No."

"Well…there were these simulations my uncle would put me through. He'd put me in a situation where I'd have to fight for my life against trained killers, and all I had were my bare hands. Occasionally the simulation would change, and I would get a gun or a tire iron."

My heart ratcheted in my throat, twisting with fear.

"After I completed several simulations, in which I assumed the men were fake, like paid actors, as were their wounds…my uncle congratulated me and informed me I'd killed off three of the oldest and most deadly heads of European crime families." He smiled at me. "Guess who stepped in and took over their inventory and turf?"

Those blue eyes were deadly and created a tsunami of fear to billow inside me.

"One of the biggest lessons my uncle gave me was that if you're in a hen house and see that there are already a few foxes hunting…" He leaned in and pressed a kiss to my lips. "You remind them that you're a wolf."

I slowly connected all the metaphors and dots. He was going after the men…after Ivan's brothers.

I tugged on his arm as he began walking past me. "No." He turned, narrowing his gaze on the place I'd grabbed him. "It's a trap…I feel it in my gut. There's a reason the two men you want most are here together…and look." I glanced at the screen where Mak was. "He's nervous, uncomfortable. See how he's wringing his hands…and that thumb twitch. Something is going on…they knew you would come."

He hesitated, searching the faces of the men. His teeth clicked together, the muscles in his jaw jumping as fury swept over his features.

"Please don't do anything that will get you killed…we came here for information, and we got it—Ivan's brothers."

Realization seemed to finally dawn on him, his expression growing more and more severe. The question I had was how they'd known we'd come, and why the guard who seemed to be one of Kyle's guys hadn't warned him that the brothers were here. Something wasn't right.

Suddenly Kyle's hand was in front of me, putting his back to the crowd.

"Do you have anything from when you worked here…a locker or something?" His words were sharp, worry lacing each syllable.

I nodded deftly, swallowing the thick fear that clogged my throat. We moved deliberately; Kyle tucked his jacket under his arm as he kept his head down. We were in the back supply closet within seconds, in front of the small boxy locker that had my padlock attached to it.

I twisted in the combo with trembling fingers and ripped the door open, unsure what he needed. He sifted through the items, pulling out my pack of makeup remover wipes and another hoodie that was balled up in the back.

Plucking out his contacts, he quickly tossed them on the ground then began swiping at his eyes, removing all the liner. He turned down his suspenders then undid the dress shirt, swapping it for the hoodie, brushing the strands of his hair back and tugging the top over his scalp. Within seconds he transformed from a dangerous killer to a college student, here to watch a fight. Next, he plucked out his lip and eyebrow ring, pocketing them before slamming the locker door shut, and then we were heading back out with the bodies all crammed into the club.

His hands roved over my hips, keeping me close, touching me like a drunk date would. I kept my head lowered like he did, trying to blend into the shadows until I knew what he wanted to do.

We were blending, bodies swarming around us as we tucked into the wall, Kyle kissing my neck, marking me in a way that meant when my hair wasn't covering it, there would be a mark. I groaned into his ear, moving closer. His knee came between my thighs, resting right at my center. His hands were on my waist, pulling me over him, encouraging me to rub my aching center against him.

His eyes were hooded as I moved to the thrumming music overhead, the lights low and only chaotic colors of blue and pink lights breaking up the shadows. I watched as lust swept over Kyle's face, confirmed by the possessive way he held me, pushing me down against his leg. I rose up, wrapping my arms around his neck, rocking and moaning in his ear. I could feel his erection harden through his jeans, following his own groans of pleasure. I didn't know what we were doing, except that we'd slipped from the roles we had to play and were now existing under the cover of this new identity.

I slanted my head, deepening our kiss, then suddenly I heard a familiar voice, forcing me to break away from the cocoon of Kyle's arms.

My eyes darted to the bar, where Hazel had snuck and was pouring herself a drink, laughing with a regular.

My stomach tilted with excitement as I registered how much I had missed her. Her body shifted on a bout of laughter, forcing her head to the side, and her warm brown eyes collided with mine.

Her mouth mirrored mine, opening in shock, and then we were both moving—until Kyle gripped my elbow. "Careful…you'll make a scene. I don't want any attention on you."

I swallowed and waited there in his embrace for my friend to come to me. She gave me an odd look, like she wasn't sure why I hadn't moved, then she was pulling me away from Kyle and into her arms.

"Oh my god, girl. I was starting to worry about you. When I told your dad you had gone off with Kyle, I almost expected him to tell me he had no idea what I was talking about, but then he proved me wrong, saying he'd seen you both and you were safe—that was only after I forwarded him that picture you sent me though, so he was definitely as skeptical as I was in the beginning."

I felt Kyle tense behind me.

Fuck, her showing my dad wasn't something I had considered when I asked Kyle to take that picture with me.

"When did you send him the photo?" I asked hesitantly. It had been deleted from my phone, so I needed to match up the timeline. Maybe it wasn't Scotty who'd deleted the photo; maybe it was someone else.

Hazel waved me off, her eyes going to the tower of brooding energy behind me. "I showed him that very night. I couldn't believe Kyle had just shown up out of nowhere…you know…" She kept trying to look behind me, but Kyle's face was turned, making it difficult. "Well…" she said jokingly, "you going to pretend we didn't grow up together?"

Kyle's eyes slowly slid our direction, landing on Hazel as if she was one of the birds in the metaphorical henhouse he'd mentioned. I nearly pinched him to tell him to act normal, and thankfully he seemed to snap out of it. Within seconds he was hugging her, pulling her off the ground.

"Took me a second, Haze."

She hugged him back, giving me a look. "Holy shit, where have you been?"

"Here and there." He shrugged.

My eyes bulged as I saw Mak begin to make his way over, his eyes narrowing on the closeness of Kyle to Hazel. I doubted he'd even registered that I was standing next to her. Then it hit me.

"Hazel." I interrupted whatever she was saying to Kyle, gripping her wrist. "I need Mak…I need to talk to him in his office. It's really important."

She leaned in, narrowing her eyes. "Then just ask him."

I shook my head, realizing I only had seconds to get her on board. "He can't be seen walking back there with all of us. I need you to get him back there without raising suspicion."

She flicked her gaze to Kyle then back to me and nodded. I released her wrist and sank back into the shadows with Kyle.

Hazel walked toward Mak, stopping his trajectory toward us, and stood on her toes to whisper something in his ear. He gave a quick look back at the floor the other men were still on and then picked up his pace toward the back.

Kyle hauled me into him, pressing his lips to mine, moving his mouth in a rush of desire, sweeping his tongue against mine. Within a few seconds, Kyle's arms loosened as he watched Hazel and Mak's retreating forms. His lips came to my ear, saying, "Good thinking, babe."

He pushed off the wall, taking me with him, and we maneuvered the hallway while still holding hands. Right before we entered, he stopped us.

"I'm not going in with you. Being trapped in there without a way out is essentially turning my back to my enemy...I need to stay out here and keep an eye out. I'll be waiting." He kissed me then spun me toward the door and disappeared.

I twisted the knob on Mak's office door and came face to face with Hazel half naked in front of my old boss.

"Hazel, oh my god!"

She hissed, covering her bare tits with her palms. "Well, how else was I supposed to get him back here?"

Mak broke away from her, his eyes going wide as he registered what was going on.

"The fuck, Rylie?"

"Mak, I'm so sorry." I secured the door, taking a seat. "But I have to talk to you."

His eyes were daggers thrown at my best friend as he dismissed her with a gruff grunt. He adjusted himself before sitting down, facing me.

"What do you want?"

It hurt that he seemed so irritated by my presence. I hadn't asked Hazel to seduce him, just fucking get him back here, but maybe she knew better than I did how that would have played out. I wanted to tell him that, explain that I wasn't trying to hurt him, but with the way his eyes angrily narrowed on the girl beside me, I realized the point was moot.

"Well first of all, it's nice to see you...how have you been?"

"I've been fucking stressed, Ry. Shit hit the fan because of you.

Now I have guys showing up here because of your dad…let's just say I'm not exactly happy to see you."

My stomach flipped into a knot, making my voice breathless. "What do you mean because of my dad?"

Mak's gaze brooked no bullshit as he narrowed them on me. "He flipped—he's working for the Varga family now, and that's all shit too. I don't know who else they're working with, but the families have allied. They're all working together now to take down the Joker with the Vargas' at the helm."

"Why? I thought they were fighting over themselves to get to him." My pulse hammered in my throat, worried about Kyle outside.

Mak waved his hand, sitting back in his old office chair. "Something about a blood debt. The Varga brothers have reason to believe the Joker is the same one who killed their older brother Ivan, and now they're coming for him and his entire family."

I was going to throw up.

I needed one last piece of information before I darted out and ran to tell Kyle. "You're sure my dad is in their pocket?"

Mak leaned in, grabbing for a cigarette. "Your dad is the one who confirmed the connection…said he knew him, from a picture or something like that."

Hazel let out a small gasp of surprise next to me.

Mak seemed to slowly register his words, his gaze sliding up to meet mine. "You said Scotty Ventrelle threatened you because of his nephew…"

I didn't respond. Mak wouldn't hurt me, I knew this, but he could hurt the people close to me.

Mak's nose flared as he inspected my face and muttered.

"Scotty was shot a few days ago…the hit was ordered for the kid's uncle…"

"Mak…" My voice was raspy. "Dad said they were throwing you back in prison…he said he needed more information or else he'd put you away."

As if I'd slapped him, he reared back and then stood, sending the chair into the wall with a crack. "You didn't…Rylie, tell me you didn't."

A tear slipped free as I realized my own father had played me.

"Fucking hell." He ran his hand over his scalp, tugging on the ends. "My deal isn't even through your dad, it's through another agent. Your dad was a convenient place to load the intel, but it was always backed up with another source. They know your dad has turned...he's giving them doctored intel for a cut. You need to stay away from him."

I nodded, feeling Hazel's hand grip mine under the table. She likely was picking up what she could, slowly piecing it together with my past and what she knew of Kyle's.

Mak stopped pacing, his fingers dropping away from his head as his eyes slid over my face. He practically growled. "Is he here?"

I knew Mak was referring to Kyle, so I nodded.

"Get the fuck out!" he roared. "They were waiting for him...you need to go." Mak walked around the desk, hauling me up by the arm. Kyle was there in the doorway a second later, his eyes homing in on the gruff contact and the way Mak was touching me.

His jaw moved, that muscle jumping, and before all hell could ensue, I pulled away from Mak and threw myself into Kyle's arms to prevent Mak from getting murdered.

"We have to go—now. We need to warn everyone...they're coming for your family."

Kyle gave Mak one last scowl before turning us briskly. His hand grabbed mine, leading me through the clumps of people that had congregated toward the back. That wasn't good...it meant his VIPs were back there. We just kept going, pushing, moving. No one really looked at us, which was good.

The back door loomed ahead of us just as someone grabbed me by the hair, snapping me out of Kyle's arms.

I cried out as a hand came over my mouth. "Thought you looked familiar—I'd know that ass anywhere." It was the Finelli brother I had rebuffed that night in the bar.

"Close your eyes," Kyle ordered, and I knew it was for me, so I did as he said right as a loud thudding sound emanated and something wet hit my face. Then Kyle's hand was around mine again, pulling me away as gunshots and screaming broke out behind us.

My eyes opened in time to see the brother with a hole in his head, lying where he'd grabbed me. Kyle held a gun with a silencer attached in his left hand as he hauled me behind him with his right.

"We don't have time for the car—we're going to have to run."

I used my sleeve to swipe at my face, ignoring that it came away red, and ran as hard as I could, following Kyle.

We moved toward the front of the building, where the lot was full of cars and a line of waiting customers. We stayed low so we wouldn't be seen amongst the mass of cars.

"Start trying to open doors."

We split up, squatting low, hugging the metal of each car as we tried to find an open door. After a few, Kyle finally had luck with an old Honda. I hustled over, getting in while still hovering near the ground. Once I was inside, I laid my seat back and tried to catch my breath.

Within seconds, Kyle had tossed his unlocked cell into my lap and had begun working on hotwiring the car.

"Open the contact labeled H and text exactly what I tell you to."

I did as he said, prepping my fingers to move as the car reversed and Kyle gunned it.

"Punch in zero, three, three, nine."

I did as he said, and within seconds, there was a reply. "'Secondary' is all they texted back."

Kyle grunted, glancing in the rear-view mirror.

I sat up slightly to catch the passenger side mirror. "No one is following us."

"That's because they have checkpoints set up, waiting for our car…we need to ditch it as soon as possible."

I filled Kyle in on everything that had been said with Mak, which warranted a few more frustrated sounds but little else.

Once we pulled into a small space that looked similar to a storage garage and the door shut, we were thrust into darkness.

Kyle moved, suddenly hovering over me. "I never wanted you involved with this…I'm sorry." He pressed a kiss to my forehead.

"I put myself in this…it's not you." I stroked his hair.

"You're okay though?" He rubbed the back of my head.

I nodded. "He was just pissed that I didn't want to sit on his lap last time he came to the bar."

I felt Kyle's warm breath on my face as he sagged into me. "The next few hours are going to be a little crazy, but you'll be safe, and I love you."

That was all I really needed, I realized as we swapped cars for one that had been parked there for emergencies. As we drove to the secondary location, the night ebbed away, bringing dawn, and we just kept driving. I realized that as long as I had him, I could and would face anything.

CHAPTER THIRTY-TWO

I HAD THOUGHT WE'D HAVE MORE TIME.

Juan and I had been slowly working for years to end this, but we were supposed to have more time to put everything in place.

"Fuck it, you know as well as I do there would never be a good enough time to end it," Juan said, echoing my own thoughts. I watched the world outside his balcony window and mulled it over.

We were on the outskirts of New York, our secondary location for when shit went south with the family. My mother had been flown in, although she assumed it was for Thanksgiving. As far as I knew she hadn't questioned all the turns and the two different cars she transitioned out of to get here.

Decker, Mallory, and Carter were already in the city, living in their usual penthouse, still owned by Mallory's father. Decker had been working for him, so they kept it for any time the couple wanted to stay in the city. Thank fuck they hadn't gone back to Pinehurst after we left it, although they'd likely known trouble was brewing.

Taylor and Juan came with the kids and all of his men. Scotty was being transported, but the rest of my crew was being asked to lie low, go home, or find somewhere to disappear. I didn't know who I could trust at the moment after the guard I'd planted in Mak's led me into the den of the beast without a single fucking warning then left with his tail between his legs.

He'd pay, not for me, but because he put Rylie in danger—enough that someone had put hands on her.

"Have you spoken to Rylie about how she feels about all this?" Juan asked, sipping coffee. I knew he'd gotten shit sleep the night before, just like all of us, but more so because of the twins.

I turned away from the window, expecting Decker to come in any second. He was always less inclined to be a part of our shady conversations; I blamed his moral do-gooder wife, but really it was just him. To his bones, he was good.

"I haven't…" I slumped into the couch, unsure what the fuck options I even had. "He'll have to be put down, Juan…how do I tell her that?"

"You just do."

I shook my head, running my hands through my hair.

Juan quietly added, "It's better for her to hear it from you than find out once he hits the dirt."

"Yeah…" My words trailed off, going nowhere because that was how I fucking felt.

Eventually Juan and I broke away from our tower, three stories up in an older fixer-upper. I'd paid six months ago to have the place gutted and rebuilt with bulletproof windows, safe rooms, and built-in fire power. The place was fortified as fuck and would last us as long as we needed it; no one was allowed inside except the family. Our men patrolled and lived on the outside of the perimeter, and we cooked our own food, ordered our own groceries, and would clean our own goddamned toilets.

The kitchen was alive with noise and laughter. Mallory had her daughter in her arms, resting against Decker's chest while Taylor chopped fruit for Alex, and Rylie had my goddaughter in her lap, braiding pieces of her hair. I stood on the steps watching my best friend…or had we finally transitioned into boyfriend and girlfriend? Fuck if I knew…she'd always be my best friend either way, but she was more to me than just that. She smiled and laughed with everyone as if she had been here her whole life, made just for me. I knew as I watched her tuck a strand of hair behind her ear that from her, I would take, even though I didn't deserve her. I'd steal, I'd keep...I'd burn. Only for her. Always for her.

Feeling overwhelmed by the sensations swarming my chest, filling my lungs with panic and fear of losing her, I walked up behind her and kissed the top of her head, seeing Juan do the same with Taylor, and he pulled one of the twins into his arms as well.

"Hey you two," Mallory said, trying to break the ice. None of us had discussed why everyone was here, and while most had the loose idea that it was for safety, no one had the details.

I nodded at her and eyed my brother for confirmation that our mother wasn't downstairs yet. She was oblivious to what I'd been up to for the past three years, and I wanted to keep it that way.

"I'll cut to the chase." I played with Rylie's hair, relishing the soft feel of it in my hands. "Someone connected me to the death of Ivan, and now his two brothers are coming for our family...they already attacked Scotty. Rylie learned from her boss last night that the hit was put on everyone, so to be safe, we pulled you all in."

Taylor bit into a strawberry, but I didn't miss the way her face pinched when I mentioned her dad and her uncles.

"We're in this together...we stay safe."

Everyone nodded, but Taylor watched Juan, the two of them seeming to have a silent conversation. I'd been around them enough to know what she was thinking.

"Don't," I warned her, and those fiery blue eyes landed on me, daring me to try to stop her.

"Why?"

"Because it's not," Juan said plainly, burping Kingston against his chest.

"It is, and you know it." She sighed, struggling to fight off tears.

Rylie stood, forcing me to move out of the way. "I may not know everything you're talking about, but I know that look on your face."

Taylor turned to her, swiping at her face. "And what look is that?"

"The one where you feel like this is all your fault because of your fucked genetics."

Taylor glanced at me briefly then looked back at Rylie. "It's my fault, all of this."

Rylie shook her head. "It's actually mine...he was fine, off the radar, until a picture surfaced and my dad connected the dots. This is entirely on me."

"No," I argued, tugging her hand into mine. "It's on me...I chose to end Ivan, I chose not to own up to it. This is all on me."

"What kind of fucked game is this? If you want someone to blame, it's me." A raspy voice broke through the room, forcing all of our heads to shift to the entryway. Scotty hobbled in, leaning against the archway for support. His arm was in a sling, his face was gaunt, and dark circles decorated the space under his eyes.

"You made it," I said, trying to hide my relief that he was here.

Juan struggled to hide his disdain but recovered quick enough. "Glad you're safe."

That was it, and then Juan left with one twin in each arm, heading upstairs.

SCOTTY WIPED AT HIS FOREHEAD. "YOU AND JUAN...YOU'VE BEEN working together this entire time?"

I watched through the glass door as Rylie let Alex put makeup on her face. I was in one of the dens with my uncle while he got set up with meds and pillows. Since Jones wasn't allowed in, it was me who'd played nurse for the past hour.

"We wanted the same thing."

Scotty huffed, and in my peripheral, I saw him shake his head. "The dream I offered on a silver platter wasn't good enough?"

"Silver platter?" I eyed him, leaning forward in my chair. "I've worked my ass off to get here, murdered countless men."

"Bad men." Scotty narrowed his green gaze, hiding a wince.

"Who the fuck cares? I was killing people when I should have been in college…I lost Rylie for three years, to two other men because of that dream. What if she'd fallen in love? Wanted to settle down and pop out babies?"

Scotty rolled his eyes. "The second you showed up, she would have left the poor fucker, and probably the kids too."

"Fuck you. It took weeks for her to even say a word to me."

"That's because you were an asshole to her."

I stood, shaking my head. "Because I had lost her to two other men!"

"Are you finished yet?"

I breathed through my nose to try to calm down. Ever since Rylie had come back, he'd been so fucking difficult to deal with. I knew he was scared of his position, of losing it all…but did he really think this was forever for me?

"Scotty, what's the point of it?" I deflated into the chair again. "Why all this…why not cut our ties and go straight and narrow?"

Scotty shook his head like he was dealing with an infant. "Because once you're bent, broken, and molded by the crooked paths, it's impossible to walk anywhere else. We aren't meant for it. We operate in the gray…the cunning, the dark rooms and blood-soaked truths. That's our creed…we live by it, we kill by it, and if our aim is shitty, we die by it. Just look at your hero, Juan."

"What about him?" I narrowed my eyes, not arguing that he was my hero. He was…wasn't sure when that had happened, but it was true. Juan lived by a code shaped by a blade just as sharp as Scotty's, but Juan's was framed by love and left room for family and happiness, things that weren't a part of Scotty's. Those things had drawn me to Juan and were the sole reason I began working with him behind my uncle's back.

"He's not on the straight and narrow…he never will be. Even with his good intentions, the second his loved one is threatened, he turns into a fucking pit bull, foaming at the mouth, ready to tear out throats. For some of us, it's just in our DNA…it's who we are, and we can't turn our back on it."

"Doesn't change that I want to burn it all, be done with it."

My uncle shrugged, making him wince in pain. "Burn it—I handed you the matches years ago."

"What will we be when it's over?" I felt like a kid again, looking up to see if my uncle was watching and proud of me.

His gaze was heavy as it landed on me. "Hopefully we'll be us… just happier."

CHAPTER THIRTY-THREE

Rylie

It was late when Kyle finally crawled into bed. I was naked, lying on the clean white sheets, the window cracked to let in the cool breeze, a jasmine candle lit. Kyle inhaled my hair deeply and pulled me into his arms. I had learned that Kyle had bought this house and renovated it, making this room his own personal suite. The bedroom had an eighty-inch flat screen secured into the wall and a buttery soft couch that sat in front of an enormous fireplace. The room was triple the size of the one in his other house, and it had more of an old French farmhouse vibe with raw, exposed beams and creamy walls. I loved it.

"What did you decide tonight?" I whispered, running my fingers over his arms.

I watched the flame dance as bursts of air drifted to it from the window.

"We're …setting up a meeting. From what you told me, Mak won't say anything to anyone. He's not a fan of the fact that your dad turned, or that you've been implicated. So, we're going to risk a meeting, see if we can't straighten this mess out."

I continued running my finger up and down his arm, both our eyes fixated on the same wall as my back sank into his chest.

"What about my father?"

Kyle seemed to hesitate for a moment, and I had a feeling I knew why. I had been trying to prepare for this all day.

"We'll have to straighten that out too."

Fire bounced behind my eyes, daring me to cry.

I assumed the purpose of the meeting they were planning was to kill the brothers, and everyone else…which would mean the retribution would settle on my dad just like the other men. I didn't say anything in response…just kept stroking his skin, moving up and down in a cadence that nearly put me to sleep.

"I'm sorry," he finally whispered, kissing my neck.

I turned in his arms, pushing my fingers into his hair and sealing my lips to his.

Once we broke away, I let out a sad sigh. "It's a choice he made… although, I'd rather turn him over and have him in prison than die."

"I don't know if we'll have that luxury…you need to be ready for either one."

I nodded, fighting a swell of hurt that began bubbling in my chest. Hurt over my father, over what was happening to Kyle…over all of it. I knew he'd killed Ivan to save Taylor, a noble reason if there ever was one. I knew he hadn't asked for this life…but he had been in it prior to putting the knife in Ivan's back.

I was just angry at all of it.

"Tell me what's going on in your head," Kyle murmured into my skin.

I shook my head, feeling tears well up. "When you were with me in the bathroom that night, with the mirror…I need that again. I need to process and purge this anger…it hurts." My voice hitched, and Kyle was moving, pulling me roughly off the bed.

I blinked, so grateful I didn't have to push him, so glad I could count on him to understand me in a way no one had ever understood me.

Hauling me up against his chest, he kissed me fiercely, slowly walking us into the wall, where my back landed with a thud. His grip on my chin was firm and hard as he licked up the column of my throat and bit down on my ear.

"What do you need from me, Rylie?"

His cock was already hard and jutting against my skin as he pressed me into the wall.

"Pain, pleasure...I need you to make me feel something other than what's in my chest." I breathed out on a shudder.

I was ripped from the wall a second later and dropped to the ground.

He gripped my hair roughly, lust filling his gaze.

I got to my knees, realizing he was letting me take from him what I needed. I gripped his throbbing length in both hands, brought it to my mouth, and began sucking. What started as sweet turned rough moments later when Kyle began thrusting his hips forward, fucking the back of my throat, using my hair as a way to guide my mouth and hold me at the most useful angle.

"That's right, open that fucking mouth for me." His voice was gravelly with desire as he thrust his hips and I choked on his length. Spit came out of my mouth and dribbled down my chin as he let up and thrust back inside, hissing as I sucked and sucked. Just when I thought he'd finish in my mouth, filling my throat with his seed, he pulled out and lifted me by the hair. The pinch on my scalp hurt, but seconds later, his fingers were rubbing my clit. Then my hips were turned, and I was thrown over the arm of the couch with my ass up.

I didn't have time to prepare for him to enter me. His loud groan erupted around the room as he sank into my heat in one swift movement, pulling against my scalp as he went.

He waited there, fully seated inside me. Taking him in was always a process I had to do slowly, so him doing it all in one swift move came with a pinch of pain. "Tell me what you want." He gritted his teeth, tugging on my hair.

"Fuck me. Fuck me so hard I see stars."

On a growl, he moved. My neck was arched back as his nails dug into my scalp and his cock thrust into my core.

Over and over again, he pounded into me from behind. The sound of our skin slapping filled the room, his balls slamming against the backs of my thighs as he grunted and groaned. I wasn't quiet either, moaning with every thrust.

"Do I need to put something in that mouth to keep you quiet?" he asked, slapping my ass.

The hit was far louder than anything that had left my mouth, but to challenge him, I screamed his name.

"You just want the whole fucking house to hear you, don't you?" He pulled harder on my hair while pushing inside me impossibly deeper. "Fuck, Rylie." He groaned, increasing his speed.

"More," I begged.

He slapped my ass again, harder than before, and I hissed in pain.

Then we were moving again. I was pulled up and slammed into the wall once more. This time, Kyle coarsely fucked me against it, allowing the grooves and ridges of the door frame to dig into my spine. I cried out, moaning his name, and he chased his own release moments later, roaring while pumping in and out of me.

With heaving breaths, I slumped forward. Kyle caught me in his arms, slowly carrying me to the attached bathroom. Tenderly, he set me on the small bench and started the bath. While it filled, he brought in the candle from the bedroom and used it to light several more. Before long, the entire room was glowing in soft amber hues, casting his lean muscles in streaks of gold. I watched as he dipped his hand in to feel the temperature of the bath. The ink on his arms made him look like a dark prince from a fairy tale. My breathing finally slowed and calmed, allowing me to watch him in peace.

He poured a generous amount of bath salts and bubbles in then turned toward me with a smile. "Come on, babe."

I took his hand and lowered myself into the tub, hissing as the heat swirled around my legs and eventually my core as I sank lower. Pulling my knees to my chest, I watched the firelight cast shadows along the wall. Kyle crawled in behind me, carefully dragging me to his chest.

A few moments later, he twisted the knob, thrusting us into silence.

I closed my eyes, falling back into the crook of Kyle's neck, and his fingers began to stroke my stomach. We stayed that way long enough that my eyes started to drift shut, until Kyle's soft timbre stirred them back open.

"You haven't asked about them."

His tender voice soothed somewhere inside me, like a childhood lullaby. I knew what he was referring to, and deep down I knew if I asked him, it would make the fact that he had lived a life outside of me real.

"Do you want me to?" I pulled my hand out of the water and dipped it back in, pushing through the bubbles. The candlelight reflected off them, creating tiny rainbows locked inside each of the suds.

Kyle moved, just the slightest bit, bringing his arm around me more fully.

"I did them for you, so yeah…I guess one day I had hopes that you'd want to know about them."

I felt his chest rumble with a small laugh, and in turn I stroked the dark ink along the expanse of his arm.

"Then tell me."

He brought his left hand around, caging me completely in, pointing at his wrist. "This is the Danube River. I would look at it through my window when I lived in Budapest, and I'd think about how to describe it to you. Eventually I turned it into my first tattoo."

I followed the river with my finger, loving the bridge he'd had drawn along his upper arm. It was large and beautiful, covering a misty river with ornate brick buildings on the opposite bank.

"What was the second?"

His finger moved up to a gorgeous building with tall spires and arches tall enough for a giant to fit through.

"This is St. Stephens. The inside is so rich and full of color." His voice softened, plucking at the strings of my heart. "I remember standing there with my head tilted back, my neck aching as I tried to take in every detail, just so I could get it all right."

I stroked along the expanse of what looked like a constellation of stars that hitched up over his bicep, to his shoulder.

"What's this?"

His chin pinned my shoulder in place as he exhaled, taking a second before he replied.

"The stars that shone down on us that night we were together. I never wanted to forget."

His vulnerability was a solid lock of steel wrapping around my heart. I pushed the burning sensation aside and turned it into a joke, like he used to, like he'd trained me to do.

"Look at you having all this time to sightsee when you were training to become a stone-cold killer."

He chuckled softly, his lips landing against my ear. His words were silk and surrender as he said, "Remember those maps we'd leave each other when we'd go somewhere on a trip?"

My heart flipped in on itself. I did remember those maps; I had several tucked away in books to preserve them. I remembered riding in the back seat of our car, all alone, drawing my map for him of whatever trip we'd taken. My drawings were always horrible, but he never cared.

I'd draw him plans of our back yards, warning him of things to watch out for when he walked through that field. I drew him treasure maps; the prize was always something food related. He'd leave maps in my locker, some silly ones, some that didn't have much levity, and they always left a smile on my face. But the ones we made each other after we'd come home from a big trip…those were always the most important.

I nodded, unsure if I could even form words.

His arms flexed around me, hugging me tighter. "Each tattoo is a map for you, a way to find a path through my past, so you'd be caught up on every single piece of it." He pressed a kiss to the back of my head. "It made me feel like you were with me."

A burning sensation started behind my eyes, and after what had happened at Mak's and the knowledge of my father…I broke.

Tears poured, a sob escaped, and my body shook.

Kyle held me tighter, securing me to him. "You were always mine, Ry…always." He kissed my ear then my neck.

"Why did you wait so long to tell me?" I hiccuped, swiping at my face with wet hands, creating a mess.

He made some sort of sound, and the vibration in his chest told me it was regret or something close to it.

"I started racing for money, and you hated it…I was a dumb kid. I knew I had you, and deep down I knew I could never lose you…but…"

"You decided to gamble me?" My voice pitched higher than I intended.

He moved me, spinning me in his arms, his forehead kissing mine, my legs going wide over his waist. Water sloshed over the side of the tub, but he didn't seem to care.

"Never…I just didn't know how to do both. I loved you, Ry, but I knew you didn't really hate the racing because when I got you alone in the car, you came alive just like I did. You couldn't fake that, so I kept at it, thinking I could bring you with me. I just didn't want to ruin us."

I swallowed thickly, collapsing into him and relishing the firm grip he had around my back, holding me impossibly close. The weariness consumed me, taking every ounce of energy I had left.

"Let's go to bed." Kyle shifted us, helping me out and then himself.

He carried us to the mattress, soaking wet and all, then pulled the covers over us and tucked me under his chin, whispering things that blended with the sound of my pulse beating in tandem. My eyelids became heavy and sleep took over, but not before I heard him say, "Just keep me, Rylie. Promise you'll keep me."

CHAPTER THIRTY-FOUR

Rylie

THE WARMING SUN COVERED MY BARE BACK, STIRRING ME FROM SLEEP. Blinking, I looked around Kyle's room and realized he wasn't there. On the side of the bed, there was a small piece of paper with black permanent marker inked onto it.

As I picked it up, a smile erupted on my face.

It was a map with an X drawn on what was supposed to be the kitchen and a line moving up a set of poorly drawn stairs, and a heart was shaded in where the bed should be. I tossed the blankets off and ignored how sore my body was.

My throat felt like I'd shoved something against the back of it repeatedly, and well, yeah, the memory of the night before came back in full force. I fully embraced the wince with a hiss when I moved off the bed and headed for the shower, smiling with every step. I was happy, complete, and finally feeling like that missing piece had moved into place, like I was home.

With that thought in my mind, I dressed and jogged downstairs, listening for signs of life. I had no idea how long ago Kyle had left me the map, so there was no guarantee that I hadn't missed breakfast. Padding along the wooden floors to the massive kitchen, I saw that the bar and island were empty, and the microwave clock indicated it was almost noon.

I blew out a breath and decided to look around to see if I could find Kyle. Hearing a loud sound coming from the garage, I headed in that direction. I had no idea where Taylor or Mallory were, but with them being sisters, I felt a little awkward impeding on their time together, even if they were welcoming...there was just a bond they shared that I didn't want to get in the way of. So, I'd hang with Kyle, or maybe Alex.

Passing the laundry room that should have had its own zip code, I took the corner and tugged on the garage door, which led me into a small alcove, carpeted and more like an office than anything else. There were two fridges and three freezers standing upright on one wall, and a massive desk and three computer monitors sat along the other side. Through an open doorway was what looked like a modern garage with a raised ceiling, storage racks, and a sealed cement floor. There was what looked like a classic Mustang and Charger, and one of Kyle's racing cars was there too.

Walking forward, I was about to turn the corner to enter the heart of the garage when I heard metal clank loudly, as if thrown across the room, followed by yelling.

"Why are we even talking about this?" I recognized Scotty's voice immediately and cringed. Seemed he was back and operating as his usual asshole self. I eyed the cars and didn't see anyone, which meant they were on the other side of the space.

"Because I thought you had the right to know we'd changed the plan." That was Kyle, and he sounded defensive...not angry, but borderline apologetic. I decided not to interrupt them. It seemed like a tense conversation, but also Scotty was a prick, and I didn't want to deal with that on the cusp of such an amazing night.

Instead, I turned around, deciding I should just go eat until they were done...but then I heard Scotty say something that stopped me in my tracks.

"Does she even know why you suddenly came into her life?" His tone was mocking, almost sinister.

I paused by the door, fully invested in hearing Kyle's response.

Especially because as far as I knew, he'd already explained to me why he'd come back into my life.

"Pieces of it…" Kyle said, sounding a little defeated.

It made my heart dip into my stomach. Why did he sound like that? What more was there to tell me?

"So you told her you only showed up at the school to secure her as an asset…she knows she's only here because she's leverage to be used against her father?" Scotty's words were loud, as if he were standing right next to me, screaming in my ear.

Maybe that was just how it felt, but each syllable had me crumbling into a mess on the floor, pulling my knees to my chest as shallow breaths hit my lungs.

Kyle waited too long to respond.

"That's what I thought," Scotty said, sounding exasperated.

"Just drop it, Scotty…we're not—"

"No, I fucking won't drop it. This is exactly why we have her!" he screamed, throwing another metal object. "For leverage…to take her to her piece-of-shit father, and then we go into hiding again. It's how we survive. You know the plan—it's never changed. It's why you went after her to begin with, to secure leverage for when you needed it. Fuck, Kyle, why are you even considering anything else?"

Salty tears spilled down my cheeks as I processed what he was saying and all the words Kyle wasn't. There should have been an argument from him, something clarifying that Scotty was wrong, that he had the wrong idea about what was going on and why Kyle had come back for me. But there wasn't…he said nothing.

"Drop it, Uncle. We're not using her," Kyle said, followed by a shuffling sound.

"If you don't, you'll die…you know that."

There was more shuffling, and the echo of Kyle's next words hit me in the chest.

"Or jail…you always forget I could just end up in jail, Scotty. There's no harm in that."

"I won't let you do this." Scotty sounded determined, but Kyle laughed it off, saying something about how it was already done.

I moved, swiping at my face and moving behind one of the rolling tool chests. Kyle passed, his face looking stricken and pained. His hands were shoved deep into his pockets, and his green eyes were bright. His hair was combed back off his face, and he wore one of his old racing t-shirts. I wanted to curl into his chest and disappear away from all of this forever. This reality…this ugly truth that defined us…I didn't want it anymore.

I stood there for untold minutes, assuming Scotty had exited out the back or a different entrance, but as I rounded the chest, he came out from behind a locker off to the side.

His arm was still in a sling, his face still thin and pale. But I knew that look on his face now, the one that solved problems. He looked at me as if I were one.

"You heard?"

I stared him down, giving him a grim nod. Why try to lie about it? Wouldn't change anything.

"Then you know what's on the line, and what the original plan was. Can I count on you to do the right thing when the time comes?" He stepped closer, his eyes narrowing.

I felt empty, like a shell. More tears slipped free as I processed what he was asking of me. I was aware of the empty space at my back where the gun Taylor had given me should have been pressing…I hadn't grabbed it, and she'd given it to me to protect Kyle.

She owed her life to him…hers, Juan's, and Alex's. She said they'd do anything to protect him, and they needed someone in his life that would do the same.

I took the information I had and bundled it all in my chest, letting it fill me up and suffocate the dreams that had begun to breathe again. I nodded my head, knowing I'd do anything to protect him, because while he may not have loved me enough to come back just to be with me, I did love him that much. I loved him so much I'd give up my life for him. I'd even give up the life I dreamed of having with him…just to keep him safe.

Scotty didn't acknowledge me, just walked away as though I had never existed to begin with. What he didn't realize was—or maybe he just didn't care—if my father had turned, he wouldn't want me as leverage. He'd merely take me, and then his enemies would use me, or I'd be killed. But my father could no longer keep me safe, and the sinking feeling in my heart was that Kyle couldn't either.

CHAPTER THIRTY-FIVE

I HAD BUILT TWO DIFFERENT HOUSES WITH ALEX ON MINECRAFT...THE girl was disturbingly good at the game for only being a few months shy of four. Juan and Taylor both hated that I was the one who'd introduced her to it, but once the girl was hooked, there was no taking it away from her.

It was our thing. She loved building and showing me what she created, and normally I would give her my undivided attention, except now I was struggling to focus as I kept listening for Rylie.

It was getting closer and closer to one in the afternoon and our bed was empty. Rylie was gone, as was the map I'd left her, indicating she'd seen it...but where the hell was she? My uncle was brooding, going in and out of his room, likely ensuring he hadn't missed anything since our little yelling match in the garage. Juan had encouraged me not to share the new plan with my uncle, because he assumed Scotty would panic. Out of loyalty and pure habit, I spilled the entire thing to him, which of course sent him off the deep end.

I should have listened to Juan.

"We're ready," Juan said, sliding into the chair next to me. He pulled his daughter into his lap and watched her add flowers to every room in her house.

I kept my eyes on the screen, ignoring the nerves eating away at my stomach. "It's all set up?"

Juan didn't respond, just asked Alex questions about her house in a soothing tone. She loved getting asked questions about her creations. The fact that he wasn't answering meant he thought I was an idiot for inquiring about something he'd already answered.

"She's sure?" I turned toward my friend.

Juan's jaw tensed, his eyes unmoving from the screen as he focused. "She's sure…nothing I can do to change her mind."

"You don't, we just support her. Protect her."

Juan's gaze drifted over to mine, and for the first time since that night he burst into my mother's house and started beating me with brass knuckles, he looked afraid.

"If anything happens to her…" His voice was raspy, the smallest hitch affecting his tone.

I shook my head. "I'd die before anything could."

"But you have more to worry about now…you need to make sure Rylie isn't anywhere near that meeting. Lock her in a safe room for all I care, because if they find out who she is to you and that they can use her…we're fucked."

He would never risk Taylor, and I would never risk Rylie…so yeah, we would be fucked.

"She'll be here…Scotty and Decker will be here to watch over her." If I could fucking find her.

Juan stood, taking Alex with him, and then headed into the kitchen to feed her lunch. I took the moment to search the property again, looking for Rylie. Her burner was going straight to voicemail, and no one had seen her all day. Our meeting would be in just a few hours, so I needed to know where she was in order to be at peace. The situation with Scotty was still on my mind, reeling like a movie I'd seen play a million times. The edge in his voice, the way he handled the entire situation was proving that he was bordering on manic.

"I need to go in for a few pain meds and groceries." Scotty suddenly appeared, slowly making his way down the stairs in a pair of loose sweats and hoodie.

I gestured to the kitchen. "We have plenty of groceries, and I can send someone to get—"

"Do you honestly think I'd trust this to someone else?"

I swallowed the snappy retort I wanted to give him. I knew he was in pain, but he was being a complete dick lately. "Fine then, go…just try not to get shot this time."

He scoffed, shaking his head. "Fuck off."

I moved so he could leave and decided to ignore the strange tug in my stomach that told me he was hiding something.

Searching the house turned up nothing but another goddamned headache, to the point where I went outside to check in with the guard rotation to see if anyone had left.

But the answer was the same: "The only person who left was Scotty."

Worry began unfurling in my gut, and then as I was jogging to tell Juan the deal would have to wait and we had to figure this out first… she appeared.

Dressed in her ripped jeans, cropped shirt, and big boots, hair hanging down to the middle of her back. One word rolled through me so strongly it nearly took me to my knees.

Mine.

She was forever, and no one would fucking take her from me.

I didn't even wait as I walked into her space and viciously pulled her chin up, forcing her lips to mine. I slanted my head, deepening the kiss until she responded. Took longer than I was comfortable with, but it still seemed to calm the hurricane brewing in my chest.

"Where have you been?"

Our foreheads rested against each other as we breathed in the same air, and she closed her eyes.

"Just on a walk…everything okay?"

I brushed my hand down her hair and pressed a kiss to her mouth again. "I have to go…I just wanted to be sure you were safe before I left."

Giving me a small nod, she quietly asked, "Who all is going?"

"Juan, Taylor…me."

Her beautiful dark brows curved in while her green eyes popped up in surprise. "No Scotty?"

I shook my head. "Not this time."

She tugged her lip between her teeth as her eyes dropped. "Can I come?"

My heart thumped angrily behind my chest, thinking over what had been said earlier with Scotty…shame simmered under my words as I processed all our original plans, and how I had made them out of jealousy.

"It's too dangerous…I need you to stay here."

An expression like relief flicked across her face before she pushed against me, throwing her arms around my neck tightly. Burrowing her nose into my neck, she let out a small shudder.

"I love you, Kyle. No matter what…I love you."

I hugged her close, kissing her neck. "I love you too, and I'll keep loving you once I get back."

We broke apart as Juan came into the room. As we did, I saw Rylie wipe tears out of her eyes.

I tugged her wrist, lowering my head to catch her gaze. "I'll be back, okay?"

She nodded, giving me a smile.

I wanted to capture it, tuck into my heart, and carry it with me everywhere I went. I wanted to bottle up her magic and keep it buried in my veins.

I took the emotions filling me and prepared to leave. Even as I pulled on the pieces of the Joker that had now outlined my life, I kept her with me. I let her lead me, seeing her smile as I applied the dark smudges to my eyes and popped in my colored lenses. As I dressed for war, I realized no matter the outcome, I was already a captive.

Void and empty, completely surrendered to loving her, being here with her. I wanted what Juan and Decker had. I wanted a life, babies, a house, Rylie in my bed, at my table—I wanted forever with her. To get it, I'd risk the empire…I'd risk everything.

CHAPTER THIRTY-SIX

WE DROVE IN TWO SEPARATE CARS, TAYLOR AND JUAN IN ONE AND ME in another. The Varga family had picked the place, and everyone was to arrive at the same time, in varying rotations. Inside the mansion, each family member was taken to a secluded, private room. Of course, we were all searched and relieved of our weapons, so there would be no foul play.

This was supposed to be a safe space for the heads of families to meet. For once, we weren't counting on brute force or blood, but peace.

Within the hour, Juan, Taylor, and I were all being led into a large room with a table built for at least fifty to fit around comfortably. None of us were to bring guards of any kind, so it was just the extra servers who lived and served at the Mariano mansion.

Yeah, the meeting place was being held where it all began…where Ivan had been murdered. The brothers apparently thought it would be fitting. Markos agreed, saying he had no dog in the fight. Allied with no one, he was still shopping family alliances.

Seated somewhat together, we faced the heads of all the families that currently represented the east coast.

Within seconds of my ass hitting the chair, I realized most of the people in the room had at some point paid a ridiculous sum of money to have a chunk of my time and my product. Their anger and hatred were palpable, especially as their eyes raked over the two people to my left.

Juan sat without giving a single fuck in the world, and Taylor relaxed against him as though she was at some private event with friends. Easy, comfortable…they wanted to appear non threatening.

I tried a similar tactic, resting back in the chair, widening my legs…but based off the way everyone in the room looked at me with so much mirth that I thought they'd try killing me with their bare hands, I realized I was missing the mark.

My eyes slid across the table to where Ivan's brothers, Istvan and Andras, glared at me with murder shimmering in their eyes. I smiled, garnering some sort of growl from one of them, but I'd already shifted my gaze to the head of the table.

"Welcome to my home…I'm just going to go over a few rules," Markos started.

I kept the urge to roll my eyes at bay.

Taylor stiffened next to me as Markos' eyes stayed on her in a familiar way. I watched him, then her…then Juan. Her husband had definitely noticed how Markos' eyes kept dipping to Taylor's chest and moving back up to her tight eyes.

Fucking hell, this would be a bloodbath, and from the man who had told me not to react to anything anyone said in here.

Markos went on and on about respecting the families and using a marker, which was a flat, thin piece of marble, almost like a small paddle, raised in the air to show you wanted a turn to talk.

Before anyone could even begin, Taylor and Juan each raised their indicator.

Markos was halfway in his seat as he processed that they'd taken control of the room before anyone else had a chance to.

"I guess we're hearing from El Peligro first," Markos said in reference to the gang Juan and Taylor led together.

Taylor stood, pushing her chair back, narrowing her blue eyes on the two Varga men.

"Hello, uncles. I'm glad to see you healthy and well."

The men didn't nod or even blink toward Taylor. So far, not a great start.

She continued undeterred. "I understand there is a misunderstanding regarding the blood debt with my father."

That did warrant a reaction out of Istvan. His ice blue eyes swung to me. "Yes, we know who killed him."

"Do you know who originally planned it?" Juan asked, sounding as unfazed as ever.

Andras hissed, leaning forward, his longer hair shifting with him. "That doesn't matter...what's important is who actually did it."

"Fine, you've made your point, but the debt is not to be settled by you...the right goes to me," Taylor explained, sounding unbothered and bored. The other heads of family all seemed to have pinched expressions while watching as the conversation volleyed back and forth between the two parties.

The Varga brothers sat back in their chairs as if they'd been struck.

"Look up our family laws, the Varga creed—you'll see for generations what our family has lived by...if there is a blood debt to be paid, it's to be carried by the offspring, aided and supported by the siblings, or any parents who've survived their children...but fulfilled by the child."

"Bassza meg." Andras shook his head back and forth.

"Te csak egy gyerek vagy, nem tudsz semmit," Istvan replied angrily, staring at Taylor.

"English, we will only speak in English during this meeting," Markos boomed, interjecting from the head of the table.

Istvan slowly moved his head to Markos then allowed his death glare to sink back into Taylor.

"You are just a child. You know nothing."

Taylor laughed. "I stopped being a child when my father started forcing me to murder helpless creatures for fun. I know plenty, and you're angry because I'm right." She waved her hand.

One of the servers wearing a legit black and white maid's outfit moved from the corner, carrying a book. Gingerly she set it in front of Markos, as if he was the leader of this fucked-up little field trip.

"The highlighted section confirms that the blood debt goes to me," Taylor said, looking at Markos.

His eyes moved from the text up to hers, a warm smile gracing his lips as he dipped his head. "So it does."

Juan's teeth clicked together as Markos' pride was evident in the way he smiled at Juan's wife. He wanted to murder Markos, this much I knew, and if Markos didn't stop looking at Taylor like she was standing in front of us naked, Juan would sink something into the fucker's eyeball. He'd reminded me that we didn't play by their rules, didn't live by them, and sure as hell wouldn't die by them, so we were both carrying weapons that had gone undetected.

"Fine, then do your father the honor of putting a bullet between his eyes." Andras gestured to me.

Taylor turned to look at me, narrowing her focus as if she'd never seen me before.

"This man wasn't there the day my father died..."

Not a lie. I was a different man now.

"Bullshit!" Istvan exploded. "We confirmed it was him."

"Who confirmed this?" Juan tilted his head, bringing his hand to his chin.

Istvan looked back at Andras, the two speaking in muted whispers to each other, arguing over what to say.

"An informant...he saw the boy in a photo and confirmed it was the same one who killed Ivan."

"You never asked yourself if that cock-sucking, dirty fed was just looking to be cut into a family deal?" I asked, raising my eyebrow.

These fuckers were so gullible.

"We know it was you...just like it was you who took Ivan's territory, and all his money and product. That belongs to us!" Andras bellowed angrily.

Taylor made a chiding sound as if dealing with children. "Now, don't make me remind you who that all belonged to...it certainly wasn't you."

The brothers were turning purple with rage. Something was about to go down, I just wasn't sure which family would start it first. I checked the head of the Finelli family: he was staring at me with wrath, those bushy gray eyebrows caved in on his pasty forehead, likely angry about the fact that I had killed his son.

"We can prove it was him," Istvan barked.

"What good would that do? Taylor just proved the decision for punishment, and filling debts is up to her, not anyone else," I argued, putting my hands behind my head while I leaned back in the chair.

The new head of the Delgado family stood. "While that may be true…" Leo stared me down. "We have decided to take up our own blood debt with you."

The challenge landed in my chest like a grenade, except the explosion never came. It was a goddamn dud.

I stared at the heads of the family, realizing this was what they'd all waited for: me in one spot with no backup and no way out. Scotty wasn't here…Juan and I had tried to handle this peacefully.

A mistake. We should have just blown the fuckers up.

Juan swung his gaze over, meeting mine, and without even saying a word, I knew what he was saying. He wanted Taylor safe, no matter the cost.

I returned the look, reminding him he'd trained her to fight, to shoot…and more than that, we could hold our own.

"No." Taylor spoke up, silencing everyone. "You can't call a peaceful conclave then spring on us that you're actually here to get blood. That is not how it works—you all know this."

"Wasn't it the Joker who said he didn't care for our rules?" The head of the Irish family stood, taking a drag from his cigar. "Yes, I believe he said he didn't give a fuck about our rules or the codes that kept us each in our own lane. So, if he doesn't live by them, why should we?"

They'd do well to remember that if they wanted to live past this little gathering. Did they honestly think I wouldn't have a backup plan?

Oh well, we'd wanted to clean house anyway…I refused to glance over at Juan as I considered what sort of show I'd be giving the heads of families.

"By golly, sounds like y'all are angry." I smiled, standing slowly and putting distance between myself and Taylor. The less people realized we were connected, the better. "Do you want your product back?" I put my hands up. "Maybe a bit of your backbone?" I laughed, smiling in that unnerving way that had earned me a few nicknames.

"We want your fucking heart, torn from your chest, on this table." Gino, the man who'd caused all this shit to begin with by demanding me three years ago, seethed, pounding his fist against the table.

"No…" Andras stood, smiling at me. "We burn him."

"With fire?" My voice hitched as if I were shocked.

"Death is too good for you—we are handing you over to the feds. Ivan has members of his crew who are eagerly awaiting getting time with you…and just think about it: how many men are there, hating that you're out here, living and breathing free as a bird after you've stolen their family's money and product?"

The door closest to Markos opened, revealing several of his men, and in the center was a man wearing a blue jacket with white letters outlining his position in the federal government. Paul Jackson had just walked into a viper's den, and he probably thought he was here to arrest me. He was just a pawn—a poorly played one, but a game piece just the same.

Poor fucker had no clue he'd die before he had a chance to slap the cuffs on.

I smiled, realizing they'd stupidly shown their hand. Right as I was about to speak up and tell them both to fuck off, the back door burst open.

"What the fuck?" a few people yelled.

As I turned and saw who was barging in through those doors, my heart sped up then slowed down until it nearly stopped.

No.

"Hello Paul," Scotty said, staring past me toward the man surrounded by guards. My gaze stayed fixed on my uncle's hand; it was pushing cold steel into the side of Rylie's head.

My training slowly kicked in, but it didn't matter—I'd already betrayed my weakness by placing my murderous glare on Scotty, revealing my displeasure in his actions. *What the fuck has he done?*

"Dad." Rylie shuddered with fear, not looking at me…as if she were going along with it or truly believed we would hurt her. That nearly fucked me over more than anything else did.

What had Scotty told her?

"Rylie!" Paul screamed over the heads of the confused-looking family members. It was about as effective as calling out *Shark!* in murky waters when surrounded by great whites. *Useless.*

I knew Scotty needed me to get into character…I knew he needed me to act like we'd planned this, but I couldn't.

I just fucking couldn't.

"Why would you do this? She was your best friend…she loved you. You broke her heart," Paul barked, taking three steps closer.

My eyes moved back to the green ones I had planned on waking up to for the rest of my life, then over to Juan. His look was severe…it said what Scotty's did, and even Rylie's: to use her as a way out, a ticket to freedom. But Paul had just painted a red circle on his daughter's back by tying her to me, and my look of fear when Scotty burst through the doors had already confirmed that I was the boy in the photo, because the girl standing in front of them was in that picture too.

I curled my fists, pressing into my knuckles as painfully as I could, and began to physically shake. I couldn't take seeing the gun at her head, even for pretense.

I couldn't take the ruse anymore…I just couldn't. I had to protect her.

"Juan, take him down," I muttered, ensuring he knew I was talking about Scotty. Within seconds, something flew past my face and landed in my uncle's wrist.

Scotty didn't scream, just grunted as a few veins protruded from his forehead and neck, indicating he was in pain. He dropped the gun, cradling the injury with his free hand. Rylie stepped to the side, her eyes darting to Scotty and back to me, unsure of what to do.

The families were moving, standing and shouting about weapons, clamoring around the table, but my focus stayed on her. I opened my arms to get her to walk to me, but her eyes flicked over to her father first, which caused me to panic.

Is she leaving me?

"Forgive me." I moved, pulling her forcefully to me.

"Enough," Markos suddenly yelled at the top of his lungs, shattering his marble paddle against the table.

His hair was askew as his eyes surveyed the room. Andras, Istvan, and Gino had all upturned their chairs, ready to break them as a way to defend themselves. The other family members were on their phones, something that was also supposed to have been banned from coming into this room.

"No…" Rylie shook her head as tears welled up. She flicked her gaze back to Scotty, who was holding his wrist.

"We did not all agree on you taking him to the feds…you made that choice on your own, as a Varga family decision," Markos reprimanded the Varga brothers.

Was this guy actually going to defend me? It would help limit the number of casualties if he did, but he was definitely still going on my to-kill-later list.

"Now, will all of you take a seat please, so we can talk over a few of these terms?"

I shook my head, holding Rylie closer to my side. "We'll have to reconvene…there's been a misunderstanding in my family."

Markos smirked. "War is on the table—you can't walk away, not when you haven't heard what you're fighting for yet."

My gaze briefly lowered to Scotty; he'd fucked up, but if he had actually followed through on our protocol then it would be worth it. His nod, nearly imperceptible to anyone else, was all I needed to know we were good.

I stayed standing, and Juan hugged the space along the back wall, Taylor in his arms. We were ready to run, even if Markos thought he had us cornered.

"And what are we fighting for?" I lifted my chin, wishing Rylie weren't here. If she got hurt because of this, I'd never forgive myself.

"Well…the Varga family would like you to be handed over to the feds." He gestured to Paul. The guards stood at attention, but none of them had drawn their weapons yet. "The other members have requested your heart be torn from your chest…a little dramatic for my taste, but this *is* war." He shrugged, moving around the broken pieces of marble in front of him.

Something in my gut told me his request was going to be the thing that got me killed.

"And you, what do you want?" Juan was the one to ask it.

Markos' eyes never strayed from mine, until he licked his lips and tilted his head.

"I want a bride."

CHAPTER THIRTY-SEVEN

Rylie

This wasn't how things were supposed to go...

Scotty had explained it to me a thousand times. He knew the Varga family wanted to hand Kyle over to the feds; it was the only reason they'd be working with one, he told me, breaking down a bunch of crap that was still too complicated for my brain to grasp.

I was to walk in and be handed to my dad so Kyle could go free... they'd go into hiding again, but they'd be safe. It was a small price to pay to ensure the man I loved was protected. I'd survived his absence before, and I would do it again...maybe this time I'd really make something of myself, fall into happiness—maybe not love, but I could chase happy, and I knew I could find it.

None of what I had planned seemed to go as I hoped, especially not with the bomb that had just landed in the room with the leader's declaration, wanting a bride. The way his eyes seemed to seek out my every curve made me feel as though he was talking about me.

Kyle stiffened next to me, his breathing slowed, and those teeth seemed to click together in the way that made the muscle in his jaw tick. He was angry, but more than that, he seemed afraid.

His grip tightened around my waist as he stepped backward, toward Scotty.

"Sorry, Markos, can't help you there."

Markos, the man in front, started slowly departing from the table, his hands steepled in front of him. "Oh, I think you can…just open your arms and let that ravishing piece of ass walk over here." The man cleared the second chair, walking past my father and the group of men around him. "We'll strike a new deal…you know, sort of like the one I was supposed to have with Ari's father." His eyes swung over to where Juan and Taylor stood. "You see, I have my own blood debt with you, Kyle. If you hadn't stepped in that day with Ivan, I would have married Taylor."

Kyle's form strained next to mine as he burst out, "Bullshit! He planned to sell her, you fucking idiot."

"Ah, so the façade fades…" Markos stepped closer. His fingers came together, snapping, and the men around my father moved. "I'll let you walk out of here with your men and whoever else you want… as long as you agree that she stays put."

"She has no family connections…" Taylor stepped forward as Juan held her arm. She was seething, her eyes wide, liquid blue flames dancing underneath her thick lashes.

Markos turned toward her, his head tipped to the side. "Maybe not, but it would be enough that I took the Joker's plaything."

A few people started speaking, moving around the table and shouting in different languages. Suddenly the men around my father had multiplied with more and more flooding the room. Each person at the table had a long-barreled gun pressed to their temple, much like I had when I'd walked in with Scotty—except the gun he'd held wasn't loaded.

I tried to peer over my shoulder to see the man who'd brought me in and caught him messing with his gun. Juan was suddenly on the ground next to him, helping with whatever it was.

The man in the slate gray suit with dark hair and angry eyes stalked closer. "I want her. You'll give her to me, and I'll let you go free."

There was an electric current running through the room that made the muffled sounds of the people at the table fade. The blue eyes of the devil in front of us had frozen me from the inside out. I gripped Kyle's hand tight, even if I was shaking.

Kyle seemed to be shaking too, but it wasn't out of fear…it was pure rage radiating off of him.

"Fuck you. That's not the deal," a burly man yelled from the table in a thick European accent. The guard behind him hit him over the head with the gun, causing the man to falter forward.

Markos turned back toward the chaos. "This is my house. I will have order…or you'll die. I don't care who you are."

A man with graying hair and a protruding belly screamed, "So you're a renegade, just like him, shitting on all our rules?"

Markos ran his long fingers through his hair, smiling. "Not at all… I'm just securing a deal."

Kyle was suddenly shaking his head, dipping his chin to his chest as laughter emanated from him.

Everyone in the room stilled, including Markos. It was as if they all knew when the Joker laughed, it was a war cry, a declaration of death.

"What's so funny?" Markos narrowed his blue gaze on the man attached to me.

Even I knew better than to ask that.

"What's funny is you thinking you can claim something that's already mine."

My heart thumped behind my breast, silently claiming him right back. I tried to think of what Taylor would do right now; I had the gun she'd gifted me secured in the back of my jeans, right at the center of my back. Surely Kyle had felt it by now.

"She isn't yours. You may have had her…" Marko's head tilted toward Taylor again. "Like I had Taylor before him."

Juan moved forward, death and pain stamped across his brooding features as he stared the man down.

"So you had her." Markos shrugged, continuing with his rant. "I assume she's a decent fuck, but I'll find out for myself. All I'm really interested in is securing my family name, so be warned that I'll stick my cock so far within her, spilling inside her over and over again, that she'll be pregnant by sunrise."

Kyle's leash snapped.

In one move, Kyle shifted, and Scotty stood in the same stroke, both men moving fluidly, as if they knew what the other was thinking. Kyle had grabbed the gun from my waist and was pointing the weapon at the man who wanted me for his bride.

"You think I'd allow you to touch her? You honestly think I wouldn't burn this place to rubble and dust first? Fuck, I'm crazy enough to kill us both before I'd ever allow you to touch her."

The shot rang out, but the bullet landed in Markos's chest instead of between his eyes, where I had expected it to go. Markos's face dipped, inspecting the wound as he began faltering, seeking purchase. Chaos exploded as the guards turned their attention off the families, and in turn they began fighting back.

"Rylie!" Taylor called out as Kyle stepped forward and more shots rang out.

I fell to the floor, crawling on all fours toward her crouched form against the wall. Juan was throwing a long blade with his left hand, and in his right he had a gun, pointing and shooting with deadly accuracy. He and Scotty were suddenly behind Kyle, forming a V as they advanced on the room. Men began falling as blood spilled throughout the space. I ducked my head into Taylor as her arms came around me, holding on to me as we curled into the wall.

More men advanced into the room. Half were wearing bandanas around their heads and clothing that seemed to mirror the man who'd helped me at Juan's house, Hector. These men must have been his. The other half were in all black with long dark overcoats…and heavy artillery. Large slugs and loud explosions were now going off around the room as the stuffing in the chairs burst, along with the wood in the tables and surrounding windows. Glass shattered around us, forcing our hands to go over our heads.

"Hector!" Juan screamed out; his voice sounded somewhat close.

The next instant someone was pushing a small table over us, covering our heads. Their body was thrown over ours as more and more debris exploded around the room.

Everything was loud chaos, pounding against my ears, and then within seconds it went quiet.

I slowly lifted my head, blinking and trying to make out what I was seeing. The body over us was in fact Hector. He gave us a warm smile, helping to check us over for injuries before he stood to join the other men. Dust was everywhere, hanging thickly in the air as everything settled. Men moved, checking bodies. My father was gone; I had no idea where he'd gone...but he hadn't waited to see if I was actually safe. Although, I supposed hearing Kyle's declaration had told him enough.

Taylor wiped my hair out of my face. "You okay?"

I stiffly nodded, still trying to find my bearings. I peered over toward the man who had caused all this, Markos, but his body was being hauled up by Kyle.

"Aren't you glad I didn't kill you?" Kyle asked, smiling maniacally.

Markos groaned in pain. He had blood and rubble all over his suit as my best friend settled him against the wall, and before he could even slump over, there were blades flying to pin him in place.

"I wouldn't watch this if I were you," Taylor whispered into my ear.

I turned toward her, my brow furrowing. "Why?"

She looked back at where Juan and Kyle were. "He took me. When Kyle saved us...it was him who had taken me that night. He thought I was his to own. Since then, he's tried contacting me a few times. Juan has wanted this kill for a long time...and the way he talked about taking you, there's no way Kyle won't castrate him."

"Oh god." My stomach tilted. "Can we go?"

She smiled at me, wiping the dust from my face. "Yeah, let's go... Scotty will be waiting to watch for us, and besides, our men are here."

"Yours and Juan's?" I asked, rising to my feet with her, keeping my eyes away from the wall where the man pinned to it was screaming.

Taylor gripped my hand, tugging me out of the room. "Yours and ours...you're Kyle's, and as long as he wants these men, they'll be loyal to you too."

A flicker of pride surged in my chest as I looked around at the men in dark coats, watching for their leader, a few of them looking over at me.

We had nearly cleared the room when suddenly there was a tug on my hand, stalling me in place.

I turned to find Kyle staring down at me, covered in blood and debris. Before we could say anything to one another, he pulled me to his chest, and a relieved sob escaped me.

"It wasn't supposed to go like that," I whispered, clinging to him.

"Shh, baby no…" His voice broke.

"I'm so sorry," I wailed, hating that I had messed everything up. If we hadn't had weapons on us, we would have been in serious trouble.

He pulled away from me and stared down. His expression reflected his confusion, maybe shock…I didn't dare let myself believe it was awe.

I needed to explain what Scotty and I had done. "Let me expl—"

"Marry me," Kyle said abruptly, but his voice came out raspy as if it had been tugged from his soul on a rusty chain and thrown at my feet.

My lip trembled as I searched his face for the lie…the joke…whatever this was.

"What?"

He watched my lips and smiled. "Marry me, Rylie Jean. Be my wife. Don't spend any more time away from me. Be mine in every way."

I shook my head as happy tears slipped free; this couldn't be real. "Only you would propose to me covered in blood with fifty dead bodies around us."

He looked down and then around the room as his face flushed. "I'm a fuck-up, you know that…but I'm yours and I've never been anyone else's…so have me, take me, be mine."

I cupped his face in my hands and gently pressed my lips to his. "Yes, of course I will."

He pulled me closer, deepening the kiss as men milled about around us.

"Hate to break this up, but we need to get out of here," Juan finally said, standing off to the side with Taylor tucked under his arm.

We turned together and moved away from the house, going in

different directions. Our men created a wall around us as we walked to the courtyard and entered the dark SUVs I knew were bulletproof.

Scotty went in one with the men, leaving Kyle and me in one with Holt and Garrison. I sat in Kyle's lap, resting my head against his shoulder as the car took off and put distance between the mansion and our vehicle.

Trees flew by, but I couldn't help but look for a man in a blue coat, wondering if he was waiting to see if I'd made it out alive, or if he'd just stopped caring.

CHAPTER THIRTY-EIGHT

Rylie

THEY SAY WHEN YOU'RE ABOUT TO DIE, YOUR LIFE FLASHES BEFORE your eyes. I always assumed they meant the life you had lived, your past...but when I ducked against that wall, unsure of what would happen, it was my future that rushed through my mind.

Decker, Juan, and Kyle all in suits as I walked down the aisle to marry my best friend. Sunkissed mornings spent in bed with Kyle, his chestnut hair in my fingers as he lazily kissed my swollen stomach. Laughter from Carter and Alex as they played with our child. Taylor and Mallory posing for a selfie at Thanksgiving as we drank and laughed over prepping the food.

It all flashed in moments, and it filled me with so much joy that it helped to keep the fear at bay. Then I saw exactly why this small family unit lived on the wrong side of the law...because they fought for their own. They protected their own and lived to tell the tale.

I woke up in Kyle's bed...*our bed*. The exposed beams bathed in sunlight were a brilliant sight to see after the night we'd had. We had come home battered and a little bruised, hugged each other close, and then gone our separate ways for the remainder of the night. It seemed we all needed to hug each other a little tighter than usual.

I woke to an empty space, a bit apprehensive about where Kyle was, but as I reached over on the bed, there was another note like the previous morning.

I smiled, uncurling it and seeing there was a new map drawn out.

This time, it led me out to the back patio.

Tugging on a sweatshirt and sweats, I trudged downstairs, secretly hoping the X on the map would be leading me to coffee.

"Hello?" I asked out loud, realizing everything was far too quiet. The kitchen was empty, same with the dining room and living room.

Curious, I decided to stick to the plan and walked toward the patio. The curtains were drawn tight over the doors, preventing me from seeing outside. I pulled the door open as my nerves twisted, but within seconds, it was all liquid peace.

I gasped, putting my hand over my mouth.

Jasmine flowers were everywhere, dangling from the archway and somehow creating a curtain around the stone fire pit, where Kyle was standing in a black suit.

"What's going on?" I whispered, walking through the curtain of hanging jasmine and appreciating the little candles set up all over the ground, along the white rock of the patio.

"Hey, bestie." Kyle smiled down at me from his spot.

I looked around as elation filled me up. "Hi."

He leaned down and pressed a kiss to my lips. "Good morning."

I laughed, and he helped wipe away my tears. "Morning. What's going on?"

"I realized my proposal yesterday was horrific, and truly just unacceptable."

My heart galloped in my chest. "No…it was perfect."

"Perfect would be with your finger sporting a decent-sized rock."

I watched his green eyes, realizing he'd cut his hair…it was shaved on the sides, with longer strands on the top, curved upward in a handsome swoop. His green eyes danced as his hands came to my waist.

"I need to explain to you that I wasn't honest before…I found you in school because we heard another family was trying to pocket your dad. We thought if we had you…"

He trailed off, but I had already connected all the dots, and I knew what he'd done. I also knew his feelings for me weren't fake, and whether or not his intentions in the beginning weren't great, he was mine now, and I wasn't letting him go.

"I know." I waved him off.

He held me tighter. "I changed my mind though…I couldn't do it, and I—"

"I know…you mentioned I wasn't going, which told me enough. I overheard your fight with Scotty in the garage—it's why I disappeared for a bit."

He looked frozen as he slowly processed what I'd said. "So that's why he brought you…"

I nodded. "I wasn't forced, and the gun wasn't loaded."

"You did that…knowing we might be separated if I let you go with your dad?"

I nodded again. This time it was a little slower, heavier.

Kyle stepped closer. "And you thought I could do that again?"

"We did it once…"

He shook his head, that muscle in his jaw jumping. "Biggest mistake of my life…biggest risk of my life. I'm never letting you go, Ry…not ever. I need you to marry me and be my wife."

"That's not a question."

"You're right, it's not."

He lowered himself to one knee and produced a velvet box.

I covered my mouth in awe.

Inside was a massive diamond, white and dazzling.

"I've wanted to marry you since we were seven…so it would make me really happy if you said yes," he joked with a wobbly smile.

"You have not." I laughed, wanting to joke with him the way he always did with me, needing to stretch this moment so my heart could catch up.

"Fine, I'll prove it." He suddenly stood. "Hold this." He handed me the ring box, and I tossed my head back, laughing.

He pulled a piece of paper from his back pocket and unfolded it.

"I wrote this when I was seven, so be nice." His green eyes bounced to mine before landing on the paper. "*I don't really like my new neighbor…Mom said she's not new, but she's new to me. I see her at school, but she's annoying. Mom says I should be nicer, so I walked up to her today and told her my name is Kyle. She told me she already knew who I am…how stupid is that? I told her we'd probably get married someday and she pushed me off the slide."*

Tears blurred my eyes as I clutched the box.

Kyle held up a finger for me to wait as he dug for another folded letter. "This one is from when I was ten…much more lucid. *I saw Rylie today, and she told me she was going to marry Zack Martin. I was irritated…I don't know why. Maybe because out of all the girls, I think she's the prettiest…but she's my best friend, so I don't want to kiss her…but sometimes when I sleep, I dream that we're married. Don't tell her or she'll freak, but if Zach actually tries to marry her, I'm going to tell him she already said yes to me."*

I took the ring from the box and slid it on my finger. It fit perfectly.

He stared at me with a heated glare. "And this one…this is the last one. *She wore red today. It always looks good on her, but now…she looked fucking amazing. I walked, smoking just a few yards from her, and she had no clue I was there. She smiled at everyone who walked by and seemed to ignore all the guys who did a double take, checking out her ass after she walked past. Yeah, it definitely took willpower not to handle that situation…but I didn't want to miss her. It was the best part of my day when she left the science building and headed for her favorite bench. Sometimes I'll play out conversations I think we'd have. I pretend we're planning our wedding or going on a date somewhere. I talk for us both, knowing she won't hear…but every single time, I send up a prayer that one day she will."*

He left me breathless as tears burned the backs of my eyes. "I can't hear any more—my heart is going to burst." I threw myself at him.

"So you agree?" he asked, kissing along my neck.

"I already told you yes, you idiot." I kissed his neck, moving his shirt to access more skin. "Is everyone gone?" I asked between kisses.

"No, they're hiding over there until it's time to pop champagne and congratulate us." Kyle laughed into my mouth.

I pulled away from him, trying to adjust his suit.

"Don't let her undress you!" someone yelled from behind the flowers.

"We're still here, Kyle!" That was Mallory's voice.

I laughed, swiping at my tears as our family came from behind the flowers with champagne and warm hugs, embracing our exciting new journey.

Two weeks later

"WHEN DO YOU WANT TO GET MARRIED?"

Kyle tucked his hands into the pockets of his jacket and scooted back against the stone wall. "Are we for real not going to head inside?"

I rolled my eyes, pulling up my Pinterest finds on the tablet. "We can't plan a wedding in the library."

He looked around. "We shouldn't even be here, babe."

"Why not? I'm not dropping out." I held the tablet, peering over at my fiancé.

He wore a thick black wool coat and a black beanie on his head. His green eyes were bright under the cloudy skies. The temperatures had lowered significantly and it was pretty cold, but nothing we couldn't handle for a bit. Ever since hearing about that letter where he'd talked about planning a wedding with me outside the school, I could think of nothing else.

He leaned over, looking at the tablet. "Okay fine, let's talk wedding stuff."

I smiled at him, leaned over, and pressed a kiss to his mouth. Right as we pulled away, we heard a loud shriek.

"There you are, oh my god! It's freezing—why are we planning it out here?" Hazel sat down next to me, letting her bag thump to the ground.

I leaned over and pulled my best friend into a hug right as Kyle agreed with her.

"Thank you! She's crazy, right?"

Hazel rubbed her hands together. "Absolutely bonkers, especially because you have a freaking nice place now. This is so dumb."

Kyle had purchased an apartment right off campus for us to share after he found out I didn't plan on quitting school. We barely actually stayed in it since I still did mostly online school, so we let Hazel stay there as much as she wanted.

Things with Mak were still quiet…and tense. Kyle still had assumptions that Mak would rat him out given the chance, because his freedom was paramount to his friends, not that Kyle was considered one. Either way, Mak was off limits for a while.

Didn't stop me from sending him gift baskets and randomly mailing him cards, and secretly hoping he'd get together with my best friend.

I watched as Kyle and Hazel bent their heads closer together and let my heart catch up to the moment. I was going to marry my best friend.

Three years away from him, and still at night I would stare at how perfectly he fit with me, how maybe we'd needed to have this in order to appreciate it. Maybe if we'd had our time and broken it…or bent it somehow, then we'd never have this chance. What if it was over before it even started?

I shook my head, clearing it of the thoughts, and decided to be grateful for what I had and who it was that had me. The missing pieces were finally in place, and I was never letting them go.

EPILOGUE
SIX MONTHS LATER

Rylie

"Please welcome Rylie James to the stage. She graduates with the highest honors, and every single accomplishment you can think of."

Decker cupped his hands around his mouth, making his voice elevate over the back yard. "Boo, you suck!"

Kyle turned and adjusted his sunglasses. "Excuse me, do we have security here?" He acted as though he was searching the crowd, and the three guards currently eating cookies toward the back merely smiled at us in response. "As I was saying, she graduates with a doctorate in…" He hesitated, looking over at me.

"A bachelor's in criminology," I corrected him. "And I have no honors or accolades…I'm barely graduating."

He made a sound of disbelief. "But you *are* graduating, babe, and that's fuckin' huge."

I walked across the small stage my family had set up, wearing a cap and gown as the sole graduate, and I shook my husband's hand, but he didn't stop there. He pulled me to his chest, buried his nose into my neck, and handed me a rolled-up piece of paper.

"Open it later."

I smiled, pulling away while he tucked my curled hair behind my

322

ear. The look on his face still undid me. It was the same look I'd seen when I walked down the aisle toward him, surrounded by our small family.

Everyone cheered, jumping up and using air horns to act as though we had more of an audience than we did, and to fully embrace the effect, I looked out among them and tossed my hat in the air.

I ran down the three steps to the grass and was swallowed up by Taylor and Mal, who hugged me tight and told me how proud they were of me. They'd pulled me into their fold completely and treated me like their long-lost baby sister. Alex called me Aunt Rylie and constantly asked when we were giving her more baby cousins. She was insanely protective over baby Carter Marie, and even more so over baby Giovanni and Kingston.

"Good job, little one." Juan pulled me into a side hug.

That was his nickname for me, cemented for good when he bought me my own handgun with that name etched into the side. I practiced using it four times a week with Kyle.

Decker tugged me into his side, placing a kiss on the top of my head. "Knew you could do it."

I snickered, punching him in the side, remembering all the days I'd tried to stay locked away in my room, studying and doing course work online while he and Alex would play pranks on me and throw little snacks at my laptop every chance they got.

"Hey, you, can't believe we snagged an invite to this," Hazel joked, pulling me into a hug.

I turned to the man next to her and withheld the urge to cry. We'd talked some over the past few months, and Kyle had even gone with me to Deacon's to try to fix the relationship. Slowly, the two seemed to be working on being neutral.

"You made it," I said, smiling up at my old boss.

He handed me a small box wrapped in silver gift paper. "Your husband swore he'd burn down my club if I didn't."

I peered over my shoulder to see Kyle's eyes already on me. Of course he'd done that. I decided not to get hurt over it; I knew Hazel wanted him to be her date, just like she had for the wedding. Unfortunately at that point, he still hadn't come around, so she'd come solo.

"Well, either way, I'm glad you're here." I hugged him, and his arms carefully touched my back, like I had cooties. Kyle was probably glaring at him from across the yard. "Go inside and find some of Mallory's food—it's to die for," I encouraged, walking past them to see if I'd missed anyone.

Dad wasn't coming; he still wasn't allowed near where we lived, though I did meet him in public places, for coffee and dinner. We were slowly making our way back to each other, but a lot of trust had been lost and a lot of hurt had been dealt. It was up to him to want to fix it.

The sun was blinding. Even for May it was already too bright and too perfect, highlighting the expansive flowers Taylor had hung all around the enormous outdoor patio space. There was an acre of lush green grass with a myriad of toys for Alex to play with closer to the house.

We lived in our secondary home, slowly shifting our worlds so that any previous place we'd existed in was scrubbed clean. All except Mal and Decker, who still worked where they did previously, but their security measures were amped up by about a million percent. Her dad sold the penthouses they had in New York, moved offices, started them under a new name, and eliminated the trail leading back to Decker.

Mallory worked remotely for her job, only going in once or twice a week, and less so as Carter got older. Taylor continued her work, like Juan had. They hadn't given up their home but had stayed away for several months to ensure everything had cleared and no one knew where they lived. For the past few weeks, they'd slowly been going back and forth.

Things were normalizing, except for Kyle and me. The truth of the matter was that he couldn't operate in normal society. He had enough money to retire ten times over, so it wasn't an issue, but the question of him continuing to work was something we carefully discussed from time to time, with his final decision landing on opening a garage and helping Taylor with her nonprofit venture. He wanted to help low-income families have reliable, working cars. He'd provide mechanic services, tune-ups, and oil changes for free.

The Joker hadn't made an appearance since that day in Markos' mansion, but I wasn't so blind that I assumed he wouldn't ever come back out. There were still enemies, still people looking for revenge and likely wanting him to pay for it all.

I froze as a man in sunglasses stood like a tree near the back patio door. He wore a black suit, and his dark hair was smoothed back away from his face. Memories of our conversation from six months ago surfaced, reminding me that this man should be a part of our lives.

"You should know he wanted to come to you…that day in the bar, he did. I stopped him, told him things that were untrue about you, just to keep him back. I was worried about him…but I don't ever want you to think it wasn't his decision to come for you. It was mine. He was all in. He came for you that night, showing up to get the shots."

That conversation had shifted so much in my heart where Kyle was concerned, knowing he had come for me. He had wanted me. It healed everything.

I smiled, walking closer to the outcast in gray. "Hi Scotty."

He held out a wrapped gift, not saying a word. Bronson and Baretta stood next to him, their tongues out, eyes brown and big, looking up at me. I knelt down to pet their silky-smooth ears.

Standing, I glanced over my shoulder, seeing Kyle watch us carefully, like a wolf would a predator crowding his turf.

"Thank you."

I couldn't see Scotty's eyes, but I knew they were on his nephew.

"You going to try to talk to him today?" The soft spring wind blew over my face, and with it came the scent of Taylor's flowers. We'd kept a few hanging jasmine intertwined, just so I'd always remember that day Kyle asked me to be his wife…the proper way. I secretly loved the original way he had done it more.

Scotty dipped his head, the muscle in his jaw jumping up and down, which meant no.

After the big shootout, Scotty hadn't come back home for weeks. We had no idea where he had disappeared to, but it had been smart to allow Kyle to cool down. However, the fallout was a mess once he finally did surface. Kyle had tried to kill him, and ironically it was Juan who had stopped him. It didn't matter that I had told Kyle I'd chosen to go with Scotty, or that the gun he'd held to my head was empty, that we had both been so worried about him that we were willing to risk it.

Kyle said he'd warned Scotty not to endanger me.

Every now and then Scotty would surface, and every now and then he'd look at his nephew as if he was watching his own son, always out of arm's reach. It broke my heart.

I decided enough was enough. I tugged on Scotty's hand, pulling it into my own and walking toward my husband. Kyle became alert. His sunglasses hid his eyes, but I knew what he was thinking.

He wanted Scotty back in his life just as much as Scotty wanted him, and it was time they had it.

Kyle moved, meeting us halfway.

"It's time to move past this," I said quietly, still holding on to Scotty.

Kyle's eyes flicked behind me then down to my face. He didn't say anything, which was progress. Every other time, he'd shoved past his uncle as though he didn't exist.

"I need you to forgive and forget." I wet my lips, firming my resolve.

Hopeful, so hopeful.

Kyle finally shook his head back and forth like he was confused. "Why?"

I shifted on my feet until Kyle, Scotty, and I were in a tight circle. "Because I'm pregnant, and I need you both. Your enemies are still out there, Kyle…and now they're our enemies, and soon they'll be your child's. I need Scotty in our corner."

Scotty grunted. "I never left it."

Kyle was trembling, breaking the circle and spinning me toward him. "You fucking serious right now?" He kneeled before me, his face pressed against my stomach.

My fingers brushed through the short strands of his hair. "Yeah, I'm serious. I just found out last night after taking five or six tests."

"That's why you were in the bathroom forever…I thought Juan's dinner messed you up."

I tilted my head back and laughed as more of our family began forming a circle around us.

"Does he finally know?" Juan joked.

I stared at Taylor with my mouth open—she'd promised not to say anything.

She smacked his chest. "How did you know? I didn't tell you!"

Juan rubbed the spot. "She was puking this morning, plus she passed on tacos last week and this week…"

I stared, feeling a blush creep up…I hadn't even noticed that.

"I see everything, little one." His amber eyes danced with laughter as he tucked his wife under his chin.

Kyle stood, swiping at his eyes. Scotty was awkwardly surrounded, and it took a second, but Kyle took a step toward his uncle, then another.

Then, with a soft cry, Scotty pulled him to his chest and hugged him tightly. They murmured something to each other as they hugged, and I was an emotional wreck, crying and hiccupping as Kyle broke away and tugged me to his side by gripping my waist.

Once we all broke apart, I finally pulled the rolled paper out of the pocket of my robe. Straightening it out, I saw that it was a map, but before I could examine it, Kyle's hand was lowering the paper, catching my gaze.

"This was a ploy to get you to meet me somewhere so I could knock you up…looks like we don't need it."

I smiled, pulling him in for a kiss. "We'll always need this. Never stop making them for me. You never know when we'll need to find a way back to one another."

He pressed his lips against my forehead. "Only for fun. That's all our lives will be from here on out…"

I let him haul me away, toward the massive cake Mallory had made for me and all the delicious appetizers in the kitchen. I relaxed into the arms of the only boy I'd ever loved, the one I'd had to release, only to have him come back battered and bruised.

He had come to me as the Joker, but underneath was just a boy, missing his friend…desperate to find a way to her.

I looked around the room, feeling full and complete. I'd always love my father and wanted him here too, but I wouldn't apologize for the fact that I wanted this more. I wanted my husband, and for my baby to grow up with their cousins and surrounded by people who would kill for them in a heartbeat.

We had war in our veins, but only to defend…only to protect.

I'd found my missing piece, and I'd fight like hell to keep it in place forever, even if it meant I'd be separated from my father to do so.

Something told me it was only for a season. He'd tasted the other side of the law like I had, and now things weren't as black and white. Now it was all color and shades of gold and gray. Something told me he'd make his way back to me.

Just like Kyle had.

Thank you so much for taking the time to read this series, if you enjoyed it or even if you didn't, I would love it if you took a quick second to hop on Amazon and leave a review. Thank you for your support.

Want exclusive news and updates before it's posted anywhere else? Join my Reader Group
(Book Beauties)

You can also check out my website
www.ashleymunozbooks.com

ALSO BY ASHLEY

Finding Home Series

Glimmer

Single father, member of a local motorcycle club, bar owner...and currently looking for an accountant.

In another life, he was someone I'd stay away from.

Not because of his tattoos, his past, or even the messy single-parent drama.

It was his looks that would have kept me away.

Dark blonde hair, mussed and unfairly perfect, lake green eyes, and that strong jaw that could easily cut glass. Don't even get me started on those dark jeans that were always straddling his chrome bike and the white t-shirt he wore that barely fit his sculpted arms.

He was too much.

It didn't help matters that he was also a massive jerk.

But in this life, the one where I was broke and unemployed...he was my best shot.

All I had to do was resist his adorable kids, deny their movie night invitations, and under no circumstances crawl onto their trampoline and stargaze with them and their dad.

I had a plan, a way to keep my distance but I had never been great at following my own advice.

Maybe if I had been, I wouldn't have found myself being used as a pawn between a notorious biker gang and the man who was slowly claiming my heart.

Grab it here in Kindle Unlimited

Fade

Jackson Tate broke my heart into a thousand pitiful pieces.

I'm not too proud to admit it, I am, however, too proud to ever be in the same room as him again.

I had successfully avoided him for three months until an old threat surfaced, forcing him back into my life.

The detective in charge ushered us out of town and tucked us away, where no one would look:

My family's farm in small-town Indiana.

Suddenly Jackson was invading my home, my family, and sharing my Jack and Jill bathroom; lighting all my nerve endings on fire.

I wasn't sure which threat was more deadly; the one forcing me from Chicago, or the one sleeping across the hall.

Grab Fade in Kindle Unlimited

Standalone's

The Rest of Me

I shouldn't have been out in that storm.

I knew it the second my feet hit the ground, and my flip-flops slid in the mud.

Unfortunately, I had no idea what in the world I was doing. Not with my kids, or the three horses in my barn...and definitely not in the small, country town we'd recently moved to.

Being told all these facts, while being reluctantly rescued by my brand-new neighbor didn't help matters either.

Arrogant, bossy, and rude—and okay, impossibly sexy— Reid was easily the most infuriating person I'd ever met. I had zero plans to ever speak to the recluse again after that night.

Unfortunately, he happened to be the only local horse instructor and the only hope I had at getting my kids in a saddle.

Desperation had me creating an alliance with him.

Envy had me craving the connection he built with them.

Distracted by his gentle touches, and his smooth smiles, I missed how close his demons danced to my ghosts.

While I was slowly letting him into my heart, I didn't even realize he'd already stolen it once before.

Grab it FREE with Kindle Unlimited

Tennessee Truths

I was a liar, she was a coward.
Now she was home, and she wasn't mine.

At age fourteen, I handed my heart over to the boy who wrote me secret notes.

I didn't have much choice in the matter, our connection went so deep l that I could never be free of it.

Or so I thought.

At eighteen he shocked me, by breaking my heart. I didn't know that kind of heartbreak existed, but I didn't want to stick around for anyone to witness it.

So I ran away.

Now I'm returning home, four years later as a married woman.

Not much has changed, including the fact that boy I once loved, still lives here.

He even owns a mechanic shop and seems to show up everywhere I don't want him to. Saying the rudest things imaginable. Every barb tears through me, like a whip and in turn, I say the most horrible things right back.

I hate it.

I hate him.

And while the gossip in our small town is running rampant, all I want is to lay low and lick my wounds in private.

But in small-town Tennessee, there isn't much that stays private.

Including the lie he's hung on to or the secret I'm harboring.

Grab it for FREE with Kindle Unlimited

Only Once

No, I hadn't heard that Ryan Prince was staying at the very resort I had just started working at.

If I had, maybe I would have called in sick.

On second thought, maybe I wouldn't have, because I really needed that paycheck. Being a single mother and having a lapse in child support had made me that desperate.

Still, I would have rather avoided the circus that rolled into Hawk Tail Resort and the man who sauntered in with it.

All these years later and he was still that same gorgeous football player I left behind in college.

Except now he wasn't gracing the gridiron unless it was for a movie role.

I assumed he wouldn't even recognize me, not with the actress on his arm and the crowd pressing in around him.

Ryan Prince didn't just recognize me; the angry tilt of those lips on that too perfect face told me he remembered exactly what I did when I left.

I thought maybe this was a gift, a way to put the past to rest...but the look on his face told me he had plans to dig up everything that was unfinished between us.

The summer was about to end, but it felt like my penance for the last decade was about to begin.

Grab it FREE on Amazon with Kindle Unlimited

What Are the Chances

It all started with a dead cat and an international flight to Ireland...

Charlotte:

A dead cat, a stolen seat, and a mouthy Irishman—that's how this whole thing started. I thought I'd leave the red-headed stranger with dark green eyes behind and good freaking riddance. Except he's not even close to being gone. Mason McConnell is everywhere, drawing me in, like an invisible thread. I just hope that string doesn't snap and break my heart.

Mason:

Two weeks was all I needed to go home, spread my cat's ashes, and visit my brother. But one foolish decision at the airport managed to throw all my plans off track. Somehow, I had unknowingly cast the line, and Charlotte Kelley took the bait.
The chatty, prying American somehow had a way of bringing me back to life. I didn't want her under my skin, and I certainly wasn't expecting her to make her way into my heart, yet once she did, I didn't want her to leave. But with one secret wedged between us, I'm not sure I have the right to ask her to stay.

Grab it FREE on Amazon with Kindle Unlimited

Vicious Vet

I never imagined that I'd be adding Manager of Operations for Park Street Animal Shelter to my resume. Not until my firm closed up, my boss moved away, and I was asked, nearly begged to step in and help. I'd do about anything for my old boss and friend, and since I wasn't offered a spot with the firm when they moved, I needed something to keep me surviving here in Temecula, California.

Once I found a decent allergy medication and adjusted to the smell that accompanied the shelter, I was oddly excited to start my new venture.

That is until I met our on-call Veterinarian.

Greyson Knox.

Local animal doctor, famously rich, unfathomably gorgeous and my worst nightmare.

I can put up a good fight, always have, but against Greyson; I've always been flustered, irritated…weak.

Especially after what happened.

Four years I've managed to avoid him. I've stayed on my side of town with my head down and now he's here…and I can't escape him.

Some men are cordial, kind, professional…but Greyson Knox is nothing but a vicious vet looking to score.

My first order of business was to strip him of his job, get him out of my clinic. But like everything between us, it turned into a war.

Except for this time, losing would strip me of something I never expected to have. Something I've been too afraid to want and when Greyson plays dirty by revealing a secret he's been harboring; my battle lines grow weak, leaving me vulnerable for attack.

Grab on Amazon Free with Kindle Unlimited

ACKNOWLEDGMENTS

It took a lot to get through this book. More than I thought I had to give, more than I even thought was in me. I emptied myself completely for this book, and while it might not sing with soul, it's drenched with my time.

Time that worked against me as our family walked out getting hit with Covid and then losing a loved one to the disease. We buried my mother-in-law in November, and then had to walk out the holidays without her, and it was an experience that I wasn't sure we'd survive.

We moved from one house to another, dealt with not one, but two massive pine trees falling and downing power lines in our back yard, taking out our power and heat during some of the coldest temperatures we've seen. It was a lot.

So, this book, while it might not have turned out perfect (I always feel like there's more to give to these books and it's the end of the series), I consider it an accomplishment to have finished it, and to have tied up the series for all these amazing characters, but I couldn't have done it without a few key people.

Tiffany Hernandez, you were a rock during a very unsteady time. Thank you for not only being my PA, but my friend.

Jennifer Mirabelli, you helped me get this series where I needed and wanted it to be, helping me navigate my first real series and rapid release. Thank you for your time, our conversations and helping me believe in myself.

Brittany Taylor, thank you for your friendship, and for always being there when I needed to vent, or just send you a million and one voice clips.

To my beta readers, Amy, Kelly and Gladys. I COULD not have done this without your prompt help, or your willingness to read and critique this book until it worked. Your dedication to this, and to me makes me weepy. Especially knowing one of you even contracted COVID during the read through and yet you pushed through. The other had sick kids, and read through the night. You guys have skin in this, and I appreciate you so much.

To my editor, Caitlin- thank you for being so dependable, and getting this book back and polished so perfectly when I gave you an impossible deadline.

To Amanda, my cover designer, thank you isn't big enough of a word. Your vision, your help with the tattoos and creating Kyle's cover was pure perfection and honestly, you just make me want to cry because you make it so easy. Thank you for bringing this series to life.

To my agent, Savannah, thank you for helping me not only with the getting this series translated into another language (coming soon) but also negotiating that this whole series gets put into audio. I can't wait for the world to hear this series narrated and come alive in a completely different way.

To all the bloggers who signed up to help with this release, Thank You so so much. You make me believe in myself more than I deserve to, I appreciate your time, and your effort to promote my books, and can't thank you enough.

To all my readers, and to my book beauties- thank you so much for reading and loving my work.

Last but not least, thank you to my family- I can't even write the words without falling apart. You know what you went through, you know what we sacrificed to get here. I love you always and can't thank you enough for loving me in ways I don't deserve.

ABOUT THE AUTHOR

Ashley resides in the Pacific Northwest, where she lives with her four children and her husband. She loves coffee, reading fantasy, and writing about people who kiss and cuss.

I'm on Tik Tok

Printed in Great Britain
by Amazon

26738607R00199